James W. Gar

Goverment in the United State

James W. Garner

Goverment in the United State

1st Edition | ISBN: 978-3-75233-050-2

Place of Publication: Frankfurt am Main, Germany

Year of Publication: 2020

Outlook Verlag GmbH, Germany.

GOVERNMENT

IN THE

UNITED STATES

BY

JAMES W. GARNER

PREFACE

My aim in the preparation of this book has been to present in an elementary way the leading facts concerning the organization and activities of national, state, and local government in the United States. I have given rather greater emphasis than is customarily done in textbooks of this character to what may be called the dynamics of government, that is, its actual workings, as contradistinguished from organization. Likewise, I have laid especial stress upon the activities and methods of political parties, party conventions, primaries, the conduct of political campaigns, the regulation of campaign methods, and the like. The increasing importance of citizenship has led me to devote a chapter to that subject. To encourage wider reading among students, I have added to each chapter a brief list of references to books which should be in every high school library. The great value of illustrative material as a means of acquainting students with the spirit and actual methods of government is now recognized. For the convenience of teachers, I have therefore added at the end of each chapter a list of documentary and other illustrative material, most of which can be procured without cost and all of which may be used to advantage in supplementing the descriptive matter in the textbook. To stimulate the spirit of research and to encourage independent thinking among students, I have also added at the end of each chapter a list of search questions bearing upon the various subjects treated in the chapter.

I am under obligations to a number of teachers for reading the proof sheets of this book and for giving me the benefit of their advice. Among those to whom I am especially indebted are Mr. Clarence O. Gardner, formerly assistant in political science in the University of Illinois, Mr. W. A. Beyer, of the Illinois State Normal University, Mr. C. H. Elliott, of the Southern Illinois State Normal University, Mr. E. T. Austin, of the Sterling Township (Ill.) High School, and Mr. William Wallis, Principal of the Bloomington (Ill.) High School.

J. W. GARNER

URBANA, ILLINOIS.

CHAPTER I

LOCAL GOVERNMENT: TOWNS, TOWNSHIPS, AND COUNTIES

Kinds of Local Government.—Most of us live under at least four different governmental organizations: the government of the United States, the government of a state, the government of a county, and the government of a minor division, usually called a town or township. In addition to (or sometimes instead of) the county or township government, many of us live under a special form of government provided for urban communities,—cities, villages, or boroughs,—where the population is comparatively dense and where, therefore, the somewhat simple form of government provided for rural communities is insufficient. If the people of the smaller communities are allowed to choose their own public officials and, within certain limits, to determine their own policies in public matters of a local character, they have a system of *local self-government*. If, on the contrary, they are governed by some distant central authority which determines their local policies and by which their local officials are appointed, they live under a system of *centralized government*.

Merits of Local Self-Government.—In the United States, the privilege of local self-government is regarded as one of the chief merits of our political system, and it is often declared to be one of the inalienable rights of the people. One great advantage of local self-government is that it brings government near the door of every citizen, and permits the people of each locality, who are most familiar with their own local conditions and who know best what are their local needs, to regulate their own affairs as they see fit. Also, such a system is well calculated to secure responsibility. So long as the local authorities are chosen by the community from its own inhabitants and are constantly under the eyes of the people, to whom they are responsible, they can be more effectively controlled by local public opinion than is possible where they are chosen by authorities distantly removed. Another important advantage of local self-government is that it serves as a training school for the political education of the citizens. Allow them the privilege of choosing their own local officials and of regulating their own local concerns, and their interest in public affairs will be stimulated and their political intelligence increased and broadened. This not only will tend to secure more responsible government (local, state, and national), but will produce a more active type of citizenship.

Importance of Local Government.—With the growth and congestion of population in centers, and the increasing complexity of our industrial and social life, the importance of local self-government has enormously increased. The local governments touch us at many more points to-day than does either the state or the national government; they regulate a far larger proportion of the concerns of our everyday life; and hence we feel the effects of corrupt or inefficient local government more keenly than we feel the effects of inefficient state or national government. We depend largely upon our local governments for the maintenance of the peace, order, and security of the community; for the protection of the public health; for the support of our schools; for the construction and maintenance of roads and bridges; for the care of the poor; and if we live in a city, for protection against fire, for our water supply, usually, and for many other services essential to our comfort and happiness. Finally, the larger proportion of the taxes we pay goes toward the support of local government—a fact which makes it very important that our local governments should be efficiently, honestly, and economically conducted.

Types of Local Government.—The form of local government existing in each state is such as the state itself provides, the national government having no authority whatever over the matter. Such differences as exist are more largely the result of historical conditions growing out of the early settlement of the states, than of any pronounced differences of opinion among the people in regard to forms of government. Since colonial times there have been three general types of local rural government in America: the *town system*, in New England; the *county system*, which originated in Virginia and spread to other colonies and states; and the *county-township type*—a combination of the first two forms—which developed in the middle colonies of New York and Pennsylvania and was carried to many Western states by settlers from the middle states, and is now the most common form to be found.

TOWN GOVERNMENT

Town and County in New England.—The characteristic feature of the town system of government is that the management of local affairs devolves mainly upon the town (or township, as it is usually called outside of New England), while the county is little more than an administrative district for judicial and election purposes. In some of the New England states, where the town system originated and where it exists in its purest form, the county is almost ignored as an area for local government. In Rhode Island it performs practically no duties of local government and is merely a judicial district; there no county officers are to be found except the sheriff and clerks of the courts. In the other New England states the county plays a more important part than it does in

4

Rhode Island, but in none of them does it share with the towns in anything like an equal measure the burden of local government.

The New England Town.—The towns of New England are the oldest political communities in America, some of them being older in fact than the counties and states of which they are a part. Generally they vary from twenty to forty square miles in area, and are irregular in shape, being in this respect unlike the townships of many Western states, which were laid out in squares, each with an area of thirty-six square miles. In population they vary from a few hundred persons to more than 130,000 as is the case with New Haven, which, though an incorporated city, maintains a separate town organization.

Powers of Town Government.—The functions performed by the town governments are varied and numerous. The most important, however, are the support and management of public schools, the laying out and maintenance of roads, the construction of bridges, the care of the poor, and in the more populous towns, fire protection, health protection, the maintenance of police, lighting, paving of streets, establishment of parks, public libraries, etc. The towns also have power to enact ordinances of a police character, relating to such matters as bicycle riding on sidewalks, the running of animals at large, etc.

In addition to the management of the purely local affairs of the community, the town acts as the agent of the state government for carrying out certain state laws and policies. Thus it assesses and collects the state taxes, keeps records of vital statistics, enforces the health laws of the state, and acts for the state in various other matters. Finally, except in Massachusetts, the town is a district for choosing members of at least one branch of the legislature, and everywhere in New England it is a district for state and national elections.[1]

The Town Meeting.—The central fact in the system of town government in New England is the town meeting, or assembly of the qualified voters of the town. The annual meeting is usually held in the early Spring (except in Connecticut, where it is generally held in October) and special meetings are called from time to time as necessity may require. All persons qualified as voters under the state laws are entitled to attend and take part in the proceedings of the meeting. Formerly non-attendance was punishable by a fine, but that is no longer resorted to; it being supposed that each voter's interest will be sufficient inducement to secure his presence. The attendance is larger in the towns of New England than in the states of the West where the town meeting exists, and it is larger in urban towns than in those of a rural character. Formal notice must be given of the time and place of the meeting, and this is done by a warrant issued by the selectmen, which specifies also the matters of business to be considered. This notice must be posted in conspicuous places a certain number of days before the meeting. No other matters than those mentioned in the warrant can be introduced or considered. The meetings are usually held in the town hall, though in the early history of New England they were frequently held in the church, which was thus a "meeting house" for civil as well as for church purposes.

The meeting is called to order by the town clerk, who reads the warrant, after which an organization is effected by the election of a presiding officer called a moderator, and business then proceeds in accordance with the customary rules of parliamentary law. The next order of business is the election of the town officers for the ensuing year. This done, appropriations are made for the payment of the public expenses of the town, and the other measures necessary for the government of the town are then discussed and adopted. The most interesting fact about the New England town meeting is the lively discussion which characterizes its proceedings. Any voter may introduce resolutions and express his opinion on any proposition before the assembly. One great advantage of this system of local government is its educative effect upon the citizens. It affords a means of keeping alive interest in public affairs and thus tends to develop a more intelligent citizenship. Important measures may be carefully discussed and criticized before the final vote is taken, and it is difficult to "railroad" or smuggle an objectionable measure through, as is sometimes done in the legislatures and city councils. Everything the officials and committees of the town have done is subject to be criticized, everything they are to do is subject to be regulated by the meeting. The final action of the meeting, therefore, is pretty apt to represent the real wishes of the people.

Conditions Unfavorable to Government by Town Meeting.—Various causes, however, are at work in some parts of New England to weaken the system of government by town meeting and to render it less suited to the modern conditions under which it must be operated. The growth of manufacturing industries in many of the towns has introduced a conflict of interests between factory owners and operators on the one hand, and farmers on the other. The result is occasional squabbles and controversies which are not favorable to government by mass meeting. The influx of foreigners who are unaccustomed to local self-government and who are therefore unfamiliar with the duties of citizens in self-governing communities has in recent years also introduced an unfavorable element. Finally, the caucus has gained a foothold in many towns so that the election of officers and the determination of important policies are often controlled by a small group of persons who get together prior to the town meeting and prepare a "slate" which is put through without adequate discussion. It is also to be noted that with the growth of population, many of the towns have become too populous to be governed effectively by mass meeting. Frequently the town hall is too small to accommodate all the voters who attend, and satisfactory debate under such conditions is impossible. Often when a town reaches this size it organizes itself into a municipal corporation, and a city council takes the place of the popular assembly, but there are many places of considerable size which still retain the town organization.

Town Officers.—*Selectmen.*—From the beginning of town government it was necessary to choose agents to look after the affairs of the community during the interval between town meetings. These persons were called *selectmen*, and they have retained the name until the present day.

Every town now has a body of selectmen chosen at the annual meeting, usually for one year (in Massachusetts for three years) to act as a general managing board for the community. The number for each town varies from three to nine according to the size of the town, three being the most usual number. Reëlections are frequent; one selectman in Brookline, Massachusetts, served nearly forty years. Their duties vary in the different towns. Generally they issue warrants for holding town meetings, lay out roads, impanel jurors, grant licenses, abate nuisances, arrange for elections, control the town property, hear complaints, sometimes assess taxes (especially in the small towns), and may appoint police officials, boards of health, overseers of the poor, and other local officers if they are not chosen by the voters assembled in the town meeting.

The Town Clerk.—Besides the selectmen, there are various other officers of the town, the number varying according to its size and importance. One of the most important of these is the *clerk*, who performs some duties discharged by the county clerk in states outside of New England. The town clerk is elected at the annual town meeting, and is frequently reëlected from year to year. His principal duties are to keep the records of the town meetings, and of the meetings of the selectmen, issue marriage licenses, and keep registers of births, marriages, and deaths.

Assessors and Treasurer.—In the large towns there are assessors of taxes, who prepare tax lists; in the smaller ones, as stated above, the selectmen act as assessors. In all of the towns there is a town treasurer who receives and takes care of all taxes collected from the citizens, turning over to the proper officers the portion which goes to the state and to the county. He also keeps an account of all receipts and disbursements and makes an annual report to the town meeting.

Overseers of the Poor.—To care for the pauper and dependent class there are usually one or more overseers of the poor elected by the town meeting, though in the smaller towns the selectmen perform this duty. Their principal function is to determine who shall receive public aid.

Constables.—In every town one or more constables are elected. Formerly this office, like that of sheriff, was one of dignity and influence, but it has lost much of its early importance. As the sheriff is the peace officer of the county, the constables are the peace officers of the town. They pursue and arrest criminals and execute warrants issued by the selectmen and by the justices of the peace. In addition they sometimes summon jurors and act as collectors of the taxes.

School Committee.—Generally there is also a school committee elected at the town meeting. It is charged with establishing and visiting schools, selecting teachers, prescribing the courses of instruction, and appointing truant officers.

Other Town Officials are justices of the peace; road surveyors or similar officers with other titles, charged with keeping public roads and bridges in repair; field drivers and poundkeepers, who take up and keep stray animals until claimed by their owners; fence viewers, who settle disputes among farmers in regard to partition fences and walls; sealers of weights and measures, who test the accuracy of scales and measures; surveyors of lumber; keepers of almshouses; park commissioners; fish wardens; inspectors of various kinds; and a host of other minor officials, some of whom bear queer titles, and many of whom serve without pay or receive only trifling fees for their services. In some of the small towns, officials are so numerous as to constitute a goodly proportion of the population. The town of Middlefield (Mass.), for example, with only eighty-two voters recently had a total of eighteen officials.[2]

Town Government in the West.—Town government is not confined to New England; it has been carried to many Western states where immigrants from New England have settled, though in none of them does it possess the vitality or play the important part in the management of public affairs that it does in the older communities where it originated. In the states of the South and the far West, there is no general system of town government. Counties, however, are usually divided into districts for a few unimportant purposes.

COUNTY GOVERNMENT

The County.—The county[3] is a civil division created by the state partly for purposes of state administration and partly for local government. New York city embraces within its boundaries five counties; other cities, like Chicago, Cleveland, Buffalo, and Cincinnati, contain within their limits the larger part of the population of the counties in which they are situated. The population of a large majority of the counties, however, is predominantly rural rather than urban in character, and where there is a large city within a county, most of the affairs of that portion of the county lying within the city limits are managed by the city government.

Population and Area.—The population of the counties, and their areas, vary widely. Several counties in Texas in 1910 had less than 400 inhabitants each, New York county, on the other hand, had more than 2,750,000. The most populous counties are in the Eastern states, and the least populous in the South and West. There are now about 3,000 counties in all the states, the number in each state ranging from three in Delaware and five in Rhode Island to 244 in Texas. In proportion to population Massachusetts has a smaller number (fourteen) than any other state in the Union. In many states the minimum size of counties is fixed by the constitution. The minimum limit where it is fixed by the constitution is usually 400 square miles, though in some states it is 600 or 700 and in Texas it is 900 square miles. Where no such restrictions have been prescribed, however, as in some of the old states, the area is sometimes very small. In Rhode Island, for example, there is one county with an area of only 25 square miles. New York has one county (New York) with an area of 21 square miles, and another (St. Lawrence) with an area of 2,880 square miles. On the other hand, Choteau county in Montana has an area of over 16,000 square miles, being considerably larger than the combined area of several of the smaller states.

To prevent the legislature from creating new counties or altering the boundaries of existing counties against the wishes of the inhabitants, and to secure to the people home rule in such matters, the constitutions of a number of states provide that new counties may be formed, or the area of existing counties altered, only with the consent of the inhabitants concerned, given by a direct popular vote on the question.

Functions of the County.—The county is a judicial and elective district, and the jails and courthouses and sometimes the almshouses are county rather than town institutions. Outside of New England the county is also often the unit of representation in the legislature; and it acts as an agent of the state in collecting taxes and executing many laws.

County Officers.—*The County Board.*—The principal county authority is usually a board of commissioners or supervisors (in Louisiana it is called the police jury), elected by the voters either from the county at large or from districts into which the county is divided. In most states it is a small board, usually three or five members; in some it is larger, being composed of one member from each township in the county. In a few Southern states (Kentucky, Tennessee, and Arkansas), the county court of justices of the peace still acts as the county board, as in Colonial days.

This board is both a legislative and an administrative body for the county, for the executive and legislative functions in local government are not always kept so separate and distinct as they are in the state and national governments. It levies taxes, appropriates money for meeting the public expenses, has general control of county finances, has charge of county buildings and other property, settles claims against the county, approves bonds of county officials, and in many states it establishes roads, lets contracts for the erection of bridges and other public works and for repairing them, licenses ferries and sometimes inns, saloons, peddlers, etc., cares for the poor and dependent classes, and performs numerous other services which vary in extent and character in the different states.

PUEBLO COUNTY COURT HOUSE, COLORADO

The Sheriff.—The most important executive officer of the county is the sheriff. This office is a very ancient one, though it has lost much of its former dignity and importance. The sheriff is elected by the people of the county, in all of the states except Rhode Island (where he is chosen by the state legislature), for a term ranging from one to four years, the most usual term being two years. The sheriff is usually assisted by a number of deputies, who are either regularly employed by him or especially summoned in case of emergencies. He is the general conservator of the peace of the county and is charged with attending the court as its executive officer and with carrying out its orders, whether it be to sell property for nonpayment of taxes, to seize and sell property in execution of a judgment, or to hang a convicted criminal. He has the power, and it is his duty, to arrest offenders and commit them to the jail, of which he is usually the custodian, and to this end he may summon to his aid the *posse comitatus*, which consists of the able-bodied male citizens of the county. In case of serious disturbance and riot he may call on the governor for the aid of the militia. He must exercise reasonable care for the safe-keeping of prisoners in his custody, and in some states he may be removed from office by the governor for negligence in protecting them against mob violence. In some of the Southern states he is *ex officio* tax collector and in some he is also *ex officio* public administrator. Other duties of a special nature are imposed upon sheriffs in different states.

The Coroner.—Next to the sheriff among county officers in point of origin is the coroner, whose principal duty is to hold inquests upon the bodies of persons who are supposed to have died from violence or other unlawful means. In such cases it is the duty of the coroner to impanel a jury, usually of six persons, who from the testimony of witnesses, if there are such, and with the aid of a physician or other expert, decide the facts as to how the deceased met his death. A coroner's inquest, however, is not a trial but merely an inquiry into the circumstances of the death. By an old common-law rule, the coroner usually succeeds to the office of sheriff in case the latter dies or for any other reason is disqualified from acting.

County Clerk.—Usually in every county there is an official called the county clerk, who in most states serves both as the clerk of the county board of commissioners, and as clerk of the county court and of the circuit court. In the former capacity he keeps a record of the proceedings of the meeting of the board. His books must contain a record of all bids for the erection of county buildings, of all contracts let, notices of elections ordered, licenses granted, roads laid out or changed, and indeed of all transactions of the board. As clerk of the court he must prepare and keep the docket of all cases for trial and of the judgments entered, issue processes and writs, certify to the accuracy of transcripts from the records of the court, and keep all papers and records of the court. In Pennsylvania and Delaware the clerk of the common pleas court is known as a "prothonotary"; in Massachusetts the clerks of the probate courts are styled "registers of probate."

In a few states these two sets of duties are intrusted to different officials, one of whom is styled the county clerk and the other the clerk of the court. Usually the county clerk is also an election officer, being charged with the giving of notices of elections, the preparation of ballots, and the keeping of election records. County clerks are usually elected by the people of the county for a period ranging from one to four years, and reëlection is much more frequent than is the case with other county officials, because of the greater need of experience and familiarity with the duties of the office.[4]

County Treasurer.—An important county officer is the treasurer, who receives and has custody of the state and county taxes, though in a few states having the county system of local government there are special tax collectors, and, as we have seen, in some of them these duties are performed by the sheriff.[5] Nearly everywhere the office is filled by popular election, though in a few states treasurers are chosen by the county board or appointed by the governor. On account of the large sums of money often intrusted to their keeping, they are usually placed under heavy bond to insure the state and county against loss in case of defalcation or other misapplication of the funds in their charge. County treasurers frequently deposit the public funds in local banks and retain for themselves the interest which they receive therefrom. Recently the treasurer of Cook county, Illinois, agreed before his election to turn over to the county all interest received by him on county funds deposited in banks, and in 1904 nearly half a million dollars was thus paid into the county treasury by him.

County Auditor.—In a number of states the office of county auditor has been provided. Generally he keeps the accounts of the county, so as to show the receipts and expenditures of the public moneys, and issues warrants upon the treasurer for the payment of bills authorized by the county board. In some states his duties are limited merely to an examination of the accounts of county officers to see that they have been properly kept and that there has been no misapplication of public funds.

Recorder of Deeds.—In all the states there are officials charged with keeping records of certain legal documents such as deeds, mortgages, and leases. They are designated by different names, the most usual being register of deeds or recorder of deeds. They make exact copies of the instruments to be recorded, enter them in large books, and keep indexes by which such instruments can be readily found. In some states these duties are performed by the county clerk. The importance of the office is evident because upon the careful preservation and accuracy of the records must depend in many cases our rights to property.

School Officers.—In the states outside New England there is usually a county superintendent or commissioner of schools and in most of the Southern states a county school board. In a large majority of the states the county superintendent is elected by the people, though in a few he is appointed by the governor, elected by the local school boards, or chosen in other ways. The principal duties of the superintendent of schools are to examine teachers, issue certificates to teach, visit the schools, organize teachers' institutes, give advice on educational matters to teachers and school trustees, make reports to the state superintendent of public education, sometimes decide questions appealed to him from the district trustees, and in general watch over and promote the educational interests of the county. County school boards in the South establish schools as do the town school committees and school district boards in other states.

Other County Officials are the surveyor, who makes surveys of land upon the application of private owners, prepares plats, and keeps records of the same; superintendent or overseers of the poor, who have charge of almshouses, hospitals, and poor farms where they belong to the county; health officers or boards of health, whose duties are indicated by their titles; and occasionally other minor officials with varying titles and duties.[6]

THE COUNTY-TOWNSHIP SYSTEM

In most states the general type of local government is that which we have designated as the county-township system. It is a system in which there is a more nearly equal division of local governmental functions between the county and township than is found either in New England or in the Southern states.

The Two Types.—Growing out of the fact that the county-township system has two sources it has developed into two different types: the New York or supervisor type and the Pennsylvania or commissioner type.

A. New York Type.—In New York the town with its annual meeting early made its appearance, though the town meeting there never exhibited the vigor and vitality that it did in New England. Early in the eighteenth century a law was enacted in New York providing that each township in the county should elect an officer called a *supervisor*, and that the supervisors of the several towns should form a county board and when assembled at the county seat should "supervise and examine the public and necessary charge of each county." In time the management of most of the affairs of the county was devolved upon the board of supervisors, and the system has continued to the present. This board is now composed of not only the supervisors of the townships but also the representatives of the various villages and wards of the cities within the county. The county board thus represents the minor civil divisions of the county rather than the county as a whole. It has charge of various matters that in New England are managed by the towns. The town meeting exists but it is not largely attended, and does not play the important rôle in local government that it does in New England. This system in time spread to those states, like Michigan, Illinois, and Wisconsin, which were largely settled by immigrants from New York.

B. The Pennsylvania Type.—As New York was the parent of the supervisor system, Pennsylvania became the parent of the commissioner system. Instead of a county board composed of representatives from the various townships in the county, provision was made for a board of commissioners elected from the county at large. The Pennsylvania system spread to Ohio and from there to Indiana and later to Iowa, Kansas, Missouri, Nebraska, North Dakota, and South Dakota. In some states the commissioners are elected by large districts into which the county is divided for that purpose.

Thus, first to New York, and second to Pennsylvania belongs the honor of predetermining the character of local government in the West. The county-township system is the most widely distributed system of local government in the United States, and seems destined to become the prevailing system for the country as a whole.[7] The principal difference between the two types consists in the presence of the town meeting in the northern tier of states where the New York type prevails, and its absence in the states where the Pennsylvania type was introduced; in the different manner in which the county boards are constituted; and in the relative importance of the county and township in the local governments of the two groups of states.

Conflict of Different Systems in the West.—An illustration of the attachment of the people of different parts of the country to the local institutions to which they were early accustomed, is found in the conflict which took place in Illinois between the settlers in the northern and southern parts of the state. The southern part of the state was settled largely by people from the South, who brought with them the Southern ideas of local government, and as they constituted the bulk of the population of the state at the time it was admitted to the Union, the system of county government was established by law throughout the state; but the county board was organized on the Pennsylvania plan and not according to the old Southern system. The northern part of the state, on the other hand, was settled mainly by people from New England, who were likewise strongly attached to the local government to which they had been accustomed. They succeeded, therefore, in securing the adoption of a clause in the constitution (1848), allowing the people of each county to adopt the township system whenever the majority of the legal voters of the county voting at any general election should so determine. Under the operation of this "home rule" provision, 85 of the 102 counties of the state have adopted the township system. A somewhat similar conflict occurred in Michigan, where the Pennsylvania commissioner system was first introduced, but with the influx of inhabitants from New York and New England dissatisfaction with that system increased until finally it was displaced by the New York or supervisor type.

References.—BEARD, American Government and Politics, ch. xxix. BRYCE, The American Commonwealth (abridged edition), chs. xlvii-xlviii. FAIRLIE, Local Government in Towns, Counties and Villages, chs. iv-v, viii-xi. FISKE, Civil Government in the U. S., chs. ii-iv. HART, Actual Government, ch. x. HINSDALE, American Government, ch. lv. WILSON, The State (revised edition), secs. 1035-1043. WILLOUGHBY, Rights and Duties of Citizenship, pp. 260-265.

Documentary and Illustrative Material.—1. A map of the state showing its division into counties. 2. A map of the county showing the towns, townships, supervisors' districts, or other civil subdivisions. 3. A copy of a town meeting warrant. 4. A copy of the proceedings of the county board or town meeting, as published in the local newspaper. 5. The legislative manual or blue book of the state in which lists of counties and their subdivisions, with their population, area, officers, and other information may be found. Usually this may be procured from the secretary of state. 6. Reports of county officers. 7. Copies of the state constitution, which may usually be obtained from the secretary of state; and, if possible, a copy of the revised statutes of the state. 8. Volume of the census report on population.

1. What is the distinction between local self-government and centralized government? What are the advantages of a system of local self-government?

2. Why should counties, towns, and cities be subject in some measure to the control of the state?

3. What are the provisions in the constitution of your state in regard to local government?

4. How many counties are there in your state? What is the area and population of the largest? of the smallest?

5. How may new counties be created in your state? How may old counties be divided? How are county seats located?

6. Enter in your notebook a list of the county officers in your county. For how long a term is each elected?

7. Which one of the three forms of local government described above does the system under which you live most nearly approach?

8. How many members are there on your county board? Are they called commissioners or supervisors? Are they elected from the county at large or from districts?

9. What are the political subdivisions of your county called, and how many are there?

10. If you live in a state where the town system of local government exists, make a list of the town officers and state their duties.

11. Is the town meeting a part of the system of local government where you live? If so, how often is it held?

12. Are the public roads in your community under county or town control? the poorhouse? the assessment and collection of taxes?

13. How many justices of the peace and constables are there in your town or district? Give their names.

CHAPTER II

LOCAL GOVERNMENT, CONTINUED: CITIES AND VILLAGES

Need of Municipal Government.—The systems of local government described in the preceding chapter are those which have been devised mainly for rural communities, that is, communities containing a scattered population engaged principally in agricultural pursuits. In a sparsely settled community the governmental needs of the people are comparatively few, and a simple governmental organization is sufficient for supplying those needs. In a densely populated community, however, a more complex and differently organized form of government must be provided. When, therefore, a community becomes so populous that it cannot be governed effectively by town meetings, small boards, and the other forms of political machinery described in the previous chapter, it is incorporated as a municipality, that is, the state gives it a charter which confers upon it special powers and privileges and provides it with a somewhat different type of local government for the exercise of those powers. The minimum population necessary to constitute a city varies in the different states. They all require, however, that there must be a considerable number of inhabitants occupying a comparatively small area of territory, before the community can be incorporated as a city. In Illinois, for example, any community having at least 1,000 inhabitants resident within an area not exceeding four square miles may become a city. In some other states, a population of not less than 5,000 is required, while in some a still larger number is required. The census bureau of the United States, for statistical purposes, has at different times taken 8,000 and 2,500 as the minimum population required to constitute a city.

Growth of Cities.—One of the most remarkable political and social facts of the past century was the growth of towns and cities. When the Constitution of the United States went into operation there were but thirteen cities in the whole country with populations exceeding 5,000 each. Only about four per cent of the people then lived under urban conditions: rural life was the rule, and city life the exception. Since the middle of the last century, however, there has been a remarkable change in the relative proportion of the total population living in the cities and in the country. According to the federal census of 1910 there were 1,232 cities in the United States with a population of more than 5,000 each, and in them lived 42 per cent of all the people. The number is now considerably larger. It is estimated that 90 per cent of the people of Massachusetts now live in cities of over 5,000 inhabitants, and in a few other states the urban population constitutes more than two thirds of the whole. More than half the population of New York state is now found in the city of New York alone. Even in several states of the West, as Illinois, more than half the population is now living under urban conditions. What is even more remarkable has been the rapidity with which many American cities have grown to their present size. Thus New York in a period of 100 years grew from a city of 50,000 inhabitants to a city of more than 4,000,000. The growth of Chicago was even more rapid. In 1907 there was still living in that city the first white person born within its present limits. This person saw Chicago grow from a petty prairie village to a city of more than 2,000,000 souls.

Causes of City Growth.—The causes that have led to the extraordinary growth of cities are partly economic and partly social. With the more general use of labor-saving machinery in agriculture the number of men necessary to cultivate the farms and supply the world with food has decreased relatively, leaving a larger number to engage in the manufacturing and other industries which are generally centered in the cities. One man with a machine can now do the work on the farm which formerly required several, so that fewer farmers in proportion to the total population are needed. On the other hand, the development of trade and commerce and the rise of the manufacturing industries have created an increasing demand for city workers. Many persons are also drawn away from the country by the social attractions and intellectual advantages which the cities offer. In the cities, good schools are abundant and convenient. There also are colleges, libraries, picture galleries, museums, theaters, and other institutions for amusement and education. There the daily newspaper may be left at one's door often for a cent a copy; there are to be found fine churches with pulpits occupied by able preachers; there one finds all the conveniences of life which modern science and skill can provide—everything to gratify the social instinct, and little or none of the dullness of country life. These are some of the attractions that lure the young and the old as well from the rural communities to swell the population of the cities. These are the forces that are converting us from a nation of country dwellers to a nation of city dwellers.

Consequences of City Growth.—The congestion of the population in the towns and cities has had far-reaching economic, social, and political effects.

Economic Results.—As the city population becomes more dense the number of those who are able to own their own homes becomes less, and thus the city tends more and more to become a community of tenants. According to the census of 1900, while more than 64 per cent of the families of the United States living on farms owned their own homes, less than 35 per cent of those living in cities were owners of the houses they occupied. In New York city the proportion was only about 12 per cent, and in the boroughs of Manhattan and the Bronx it was less than 6 per cent. Of these hardly more than 2 per cent owned homes that were clear of mortgages.

Social Results.—Another result of the movement of the people to the cities is the evil of overcrowding. Manifestly where the area of a city is limited, as is often the case, there must come a time when the population will be massed and crowded together under circumstances that are dangerous to the health, morals, and comfort of the people. In some of the large cities to-day the conditions resulting from overcrowding are truly shocking. According to the census of 1900, while the average number of persons to a dwelling throughout the country as a whole was about five, the number in New York city was nearly fifteen, and in the boroughs of Manhattan and the Bronx it was more than twenty. In several parts of the city there are blocks containing more than 1,000 persons to the acre. Under such circumstances the rate of mortality is necessarily high, and immorality and vice are encouraged. In the great cities one finds a large floating population with no local attachment or civic pride, and thousands of persons, foreigners and natives alike, with low standards of life. There also the individual is lost in a multitude, and the restraining influence of public opinion, which is so powerful in the country, is lacking. Thus the tendency to wrongdoing is greatly accentuated.

Political Results.—Finally, the growth of the cities has had important political consequences, in that it has given rise to conditions that have increased enormously the problems of local government. As long as the population of the nation was predominantly rural and the cities few in number and small in size, the difficulties of local government were not serious. But the presence of such conditions as those described above, together with the task which devolves upon the city of performing so many services for the people that are not required in sparsely settled communities, has made the problem of city government the most difficult of all governmental problems.

Movement to Check Immigration to the Cities.—The abandonment of the farms and the movement of the people to the cities is viewed by many persons with regret, not to say alarm. There are some who think that the cities are the plague spots of the country, that city life tends to produce an enfeebled race with low moral standards; that they are tending to make of us a nation of tenants, tramps, anarchists, and criminals; and that the economic welfare of the country is being endangered by the drift away from the farm. Such a view, of course, represents an exaggerated conception of the dangers, though it will be readily admitted that the change is not without serious evils.

Lately we have heard a great deal of discussion among thoughtful men as to the possibility of checking the movement of the young to the cities. And notwithstanding the movement from the country to the city it is evident that the conditions of rural life are much more favorable than formerly. The daily free delivery of mail at the doors of the farmers, the introduction of the telephone and the interurban railway, to say nothing of the use of labor-saving machinery, have done much to add to the attractiveness of country life and to diminish the hardships of farm life and other rural occupations. But these advantages have not checked the movement to the cities, and other remedies must be found.

The Position of the City in the State.—The city occupies a twofold position in the state of which it is a part. In the first place, it is an agent of the state for carrying out certain state laws and policies. Thus it acts for the state when it protects the public health, cares for the poor, maintains peace and order, supports education, and collects the taxes for the state. In the second place, the city undertakes to perform numerous services which are of interest to the people of the locality alone and which do not concern the people of the state as a whole. When acting in this latter capacity, the city is merely an organ of local government and not an agent of the state. Thus the city sometimes supplies the inhabitants with light and water, protects them against fire, maintains sewers, disposes of garbage and other refuse, builds wharves, docks, and bridges, and maintains public libraries, museums, bath houses, and other institutions.

State Control of Cities.—The organization, powers, and privileges of the city are determined for the most part by the state constitution and laws. In a few states the financial transactions of city officials are subject to state inspection and audit, and in practically all of them their power to levy taxes and borrow money is placed under restrictions. It is felt that if the cities were left entirely free from state control they could not always be relied upon by the state to carry out the laws which they are charged with enforcing, and that in other respects their action might not be in harmony with the general policy of the state. In those matters, however, which are of purely local interest, the state should interfere as little as possible. Interference in such cases is contrary to the ideas of local self-government which Americans cherish as one of their most valuable rights. However, the right of the people living in cities to regulate their own local affairs according to their own notions is not always recognized, and there are frequent complaints that state legislatures have interfered when the interests of the state did not justify it.

The City Charter.—The city, unlike the county, township, and other minor civil divisions described in the preceding chapter, has a charter granted to it by the state which gives the city more of the character of a public corporation.

The charter contains the name of the place incorporated, a description of its boundaries, its form of organization, and a detailed enumeration of the powers which it may exercise. It is granted by the state legislature, though, unlike the charter granted to a private corporation, such as a bank or a railway company, it is not a contract but simply a legislative act which may be repealed or altered at the will of the legislature. Thus, legally, the city is at the mercy of the legislature. Its charter, indeed, may be taken away from it and the city governed directly by the legislature in such manner as it may choose, and this has sometimes been done in the case of cities which grossly abused their powers or got themselves into such hopeless financial condition that they were unable to meet their obligations or properly discharge their duties.

Methods of Granting Charters.—Formerly it was the custom in most states for the legislature to frame a charter for each city as application was made. The result was that different cities received different kinds of charters, some more liberal than others. Besides, the time of the legislature was taken up with the consideration of applications for charters, and abundant opportunities were offered for favoritism and for the use of improper influences upon members of the legislature by cities that desired new charters or amendments to existing charters. To avoid these evils many states adopted the practice of passing a general law for the government of all cities in the state, under which any community which desired to be incorporated as a city might by fulfilling certain prescribed conditions be organized under this general act, which then became the charter of the city. Under this system all cities in the state would have practically the same organization and powers.

"Home Rule" Charters.—The feeling that the people concerned should be given some power in framing the charters under which they are to be governed has led in comparatively recent times to the adoption of "home rule" provisions in the constitutions of a number of states—that is, provisions allowing the people of each city, under certain restrictions, to frame their own charters. Thus the Missouri constitution, adopted in 1875, allows each city of more than 100,000 inhabitants to prepare its own charter, which, when approved by the voters, shall go into effect provided it is not inconsistent with the state law. Other states having "home rule" charter provisions in their constitutions are California, Oregon, Washington, Minnesota, Colorado, Oklahoma, Michigan, Wisconsin, Texas, Ohio, Nebraska, Arizona, and Connecticut.

CITY HALL AND MUNICIPAL BUILDING, NEW YORK
THE CITY HALL IS IN THE FOREGROUND; THE MUNICIPAL BUILDING, CONTAINING
ADDITIONAL OFFICE ROOM FOR CITY OFFICIALS, IS THE TALLEST BUILDING SHOWN.

Powers of Municipal Corporations.—With the exception of a few cities, of which Houston, Texas, is an example, the powers that may be exercised by a city are specifically enumerated with great detail in the charter, and where that is done no other powers may be exercised by the city except such as are clearly incidental to, or implied in, those enumerated. Thus when the city of New York wished to build an elevated railway, it had to secure express authority from the legislature, which body insisted that the work should be carried out under the supervision of a state commission. Likewise when the city of Chicago wanted power to prescribe the width of wagon tires to be used on its streets, recourse had to be made to the state legislature for permission, though in neither case was the matter involved one which concerned directly anybody except the people of the cities affected.

Legislative Interference in the Affairs of Cities.—The power of the state legislature over the cities has sometimes been employed to interfere in their local affairs and to force upon the cities measures or policies to which they were opposed. Thus the legislature of Pennsylvania passed an act requiring the city of Philadelphia to build an expensive city hall which cost the taxpayers of the city something like $20,000,000, though it was not a matter of direct interest to the people outside of the city. Likewise the legislature of Ohio required the city of Cleveland to erect a soldiers' monument at a cost of $300,000 against the wishes of the taxpayers who had to bear the expense.

Sometimes the legislature employs its power of control over the cities in the interest of the political party which happens to be in control of the legislature, and it frequently passes laws relating to the hours of opening and closing of saloons in the cities when local sentiment may be opposed to such laws. But as to the moral right of the legislature to enact such laws as the last mentioned, there is a difference of opinion. The disposition of the legislature to interfere in the affairs of the cities by means of special acts—that is, acts applying to a single city—has come to be a crying evil and has been a cause of complaint from the people of nearly every large city. The New York legislature during a period of ten years passed nearly four hundred laws applying to the city of New York.

Constitutional Protection Against Special Legislation.—To protect the cities against special legislation and at the same time to remove the opportunity which such a practice offers for bribery and the employment of other improper means to secure special legislation or to prevent it, when it is not desired, the constitutions of many states contain provisions absolutely prohibiting the legislature from enacting laws applying to particular cities except where general laws are inapplicable. Where such constitutional provisions have been adopted, the legislatures have frequently evaded them by a system of classification by which acts are passed applying to all cities within a class when in reality there may be but a single city in such a class. And the courts have generally held such acts to be constitutional where the classifications are not unreasonable.

The New York constitution recognizes that special legislation applying to larger cities may sometimes be desirable, and instead of forbidding such legislation absolutely it classifies the cities of the state into three classes according to population,—New York City, Buffalo, and Rochester constituting the first class,—and allows the legislature to enact laws affecting a single city within a class, subject to the condition that the proposed law must be submitted to the authorities of the city affected, for their approval, and if disapproved it is void unless repassed by the legislature. Likewise by recent amendment to the constitution of Illinois the legislature of the state is allowed to pass special laws affecting the city of Chicago alone, but such legislation cannot take effect until it has been approved by the voters of the city at a general or special election.

Functions of Municipal Government.—The functions and activities of city government are numerous and varied, much more so, of course, in large cities than in small ones. First of all, the problem of police protection, the punishment of crime, and the care of the public safety in a community where thousands of persons of all nationalities and with varying standards of respect for law are living in close proximity, is very difficult and requires a small army of officials which would be entirely unnecessary in a rural community. Likewise the duty of caring for the public health, of preventing the spread of disease, of securing a wholesome water supply, of protecting the people against impure and adulterated food, and of securing wholesome and sanitary conditions generally, is very much greater in cities than in sparsely settled rural districts or in villages and small towns. Then there are the problems of fire protection, gas and electric light, street railway transportation, the construction and maintenance of streets, education, building regulations, the care of the poor and dependent class, disposal of sewage and waste, the maintenance of hospitals, libraries, museums, and other institutions, the regulation of traffic on the streets, and many other activities too numerous to mention.

The City Council.—The legislative branch of most city governments is a council composed of members elected by the voters for a term ranging from one year in some of the cities of New England to four years in certain other parts of the country, the most usual term being two years. The number of members ranges from 9 in Boston to more than 130 in Philadelphia. The city of New York has a council of 67 members; Chicago, 70; and San Francisco, 18. In the large majority of cities this council, unlike the state legislatures, is a single-chambered body, though in a few important cities, notably Philadelphia, Baltimore, St. Louis, and Louisville, it is composed of two houses.

Mode of Election.—Generally, the members of the city council are chosen by districts or wards, usually one member from each, though in some cities several are elected from each district; in Illinois cities two members are elected from each ward into which the city is divided. Where the council is composed of two houses, the members of the upper house are sometimes chosen from the city at large on a general ticket, and the members of the lower house by wards. In San Francisco, where the council is composed of but one house, the eighteen members are elected from the city at large. The same is true of Boston, whose council under the new charter is composed of but nine members.

The method of election by wards is open to the objection that it tends to the election of inferior men and of men who are likely to consider themselves the special representatives of their wards rather than the representatives of the people of the city at large. On the other hand, election from the city at large, or election of several members from large districts on a general ticket, unless coupled with a system of minority representation, is likely to give the majority party an undue advantage. Perhaps the best plan would be to elect a certain number from the city at large and the rest by wards.

Moreover, in some cities, of which Chicago is a conspicuous example, the ward system has led to inequality of representation. Thus it has sometimes happened that certain wards which are largely inhabited by the worst elements of the population are over-represented as compared with wards in other parts of the city inhabited largely by the better class of citizens. Finally, where the ward system prevails, the ward becomes the seat of a local political organization whose methods are so often corrupt and dishonorable that they constitute a great hindrance to good city government.

Powers of City Councils.—Unlike the state legislature, which is an authority of general powers, the city council in America has only such powers as are conferred upon it by the charter of the city. These powers are numerous and varied and relate to such matters as the laying out and care of streets, the protection of the public health, the regulation of the sale of liquor, the control of places of public amusement, markets, bathing places, traffic on the streets, the suppression of vice and immorality, protection against fire, the disposal of waste, the lighting of the streets, and in general the preservation of the good order and peace of the community. Its powers are exercised usually through acts called ordinances, which are framed and enacted after the manner followed by the legislature in enacting laws for the government of the state. The power of the council is frequently limited by the state constitution or laws. Thus very frequently it is forbidden to incur debts beyond a certain limit, or to levy taxes above a certain amount, and frequently the purposes for which taxes may be levied and money appropriated are carefully specified.

Franchises.—One of the most important powers of a city council is the granting of franchises to street railway, gas, electric light, water, and other public service companies to maintain tracks, wires, pipe lines, etc., in the streets and other public places. As these franchises are often of great value to the companies receiving them, a temptation is thus created for the employment of bribery and other improper means for securing concessions of this character. In some cities aldermen have been paid large sums of money for their votes on franchise grants, and indeed the practice has been so often resorted to that there is a popular belief that most public utility franchises in the larger cities are secured in this way. Formerly franchises were frequently granted for long periods of years or for an indefinite period, and often without adequate compensation to the city. This abuse became so common that the people gradually came to adopt constitutional provisions or state laws limiting the periods for which public service franchises could be granted, and indeed a few, notably those which have adopted the commission form of government, have gone to the length of making all such grants subject to the approval of the voters of the city at an election held for the purpose.

The Mayor.—The chief executive officer of the city is the mayor. With a few unimportant exceptions he is elected by the qualified voters of the city and serves for a term varying from one to four years, the most usual term being two years. In Boston, Chicago, and New York city, however, the term is four years.

Powers and Duties.—It is the duty of the mayor to enforce the ordinances of the city and also such laws of the state as he may be charged with executing. Like the sheriff of the county, he is a peace officer and as such is charged with the maintenance of order and the suppression of riots, and if a disturbance becomes so great that it cannot be suppressed by the police he may, like the sheriff, call on the governor for the militia. In some cities he is the presiding officer of the city council, though not a member of it. Generally he is required to submit messages to the council concerning the condition of the city, and may recommend measures for its consideration. Practically everywhere he has the power to veto ordinances passed by the city council, and some mayors have made extensive use of this power. The council, however, may pass an ordinance over the mayor's veto.

One of the important powers of the mayor is the appointment of officials, though usually the assent of the council is necessary to the validity of most appointments. In recent years there has been a considerable extension of this power in a number of the large cities, where the mayor has been given the absolute power of appointing the heads of the administrative departments. Indeed, the tendency now seems to be in the direction of concentrating larger powers of appointment in his hands as a means of fixing responsibility more definitely. There is also a tendency in the direction of giving him a large power of removal, subject to the provision that the official shall be removed only for good cause and that he shall be given a hearing and an opportunity to answer the charges made against him.

Finally, the mayor usually has the power to grant pardons for violations of the ordinances of the city, and this power is sometimes extensively used. Thus during the year 1909 the mayor of Chicago released more than 1,100 offenders who had been committed to prison, or about 10 per cent of the whole number committed. In some cities also he may remit fines that have been paid for violations of city ordinances.

Administrative Departments.—*Single Commissioner System vs. the Board System.*—In every large city there are, in addition to the mayor, a number of departments each charged with the conduct of some particular branch of the city's affairs. They are organized on one of two principles: each is under the control either of a board or of a single commissioner. Each method of organization has its advantages and disadvantages, but experience has shown that the single-headed department is the one best calculated to secure efficiency and responsibility, and it is the one most generally employed. The board system is well adapted to secure deliberation, but not promptness and unity of action nor responsibility, because one member may easily shift the responsibility for an error or blunder upon his colleagues. But for certain branches of administration such as the civil service, park administration, school administration, assessments, and possibly others, the board system has important advantages.

Number of Departments.—The number of these administrative departments varies widely among the different cities of the country. In general we find the following departments: a finance department, a law department, a health department, a fire department, a police department, a department of charities, and a department of public works. In some cities, however, the number of departments is much larger than this. Thus in some we find a street cleaning department, a department of buildings, a sewer department, a department of parks, a department of docks, and so on.

Choice of Heads of Departments.—The heads of these departments are in most cases appointed by the mayor, to whom they are responsible, though nearly everywhere the approval of the council is necessary to his appointments. In recent years there has been more or less criticism of the practice of choosing administrative officials by popular election. In every large city there is a great mass of unintelligent voters who are easily controlled by corrupt and scheming politicians. Moreover, it is impossible for the voters in a large city, however intelligent they may be, to become acquainted with the merits of all the numerous candidates when there are a considerable number of offices to be filled. It is believed by many municipal reformers, therefore, that better results could be obtained by allowing the mayor to choose all the heads of important departments, except possibly the chief finance officer, who might properly be chosen by the people. For the selection of the large number of subordinate officials, the best method yet devised is that known as the civil service system, which has been introduced in most of the larger cities. Under this system appointments are made on the basis of merit and fitness, which qualities are ascertained by an examination by a board of civil service commissioners.

City Finances.—One of the most remarkable features of American municipal development has been the extraordinary growth of municipal expenditures. The functions and activities of modern city government are indeed so numerous and varied as to require a larger number of officials and a greater expenditure of money than is required for the conduct of any other of the various governments under which we live. By far the larger part of the taxes contributed by those who live in the cities go to meet the expenses of municipal government. In 1920 the budget of New York city was over $270,000,000, while that of Chicago was about $130,000,000, in each case the amount being about five times as great as the appropriations for the support of the government of the state in which the city is situated. The annual cost of operating our largest city exceeds what was required to maintain the national government in its early days, and is greater than the national budget of a number of European countries to-day. New York city in 1910 had a debt almost as large as the national debt, her annual interest account alone being in the neighborhood of $30,000,000. The proper raising and expenditure of such vast sums of money is one of the most difficult tasks of a city government. For this purpose there are assessors, collectors, treasurers, comptrollers or auditors, and various other officials. The levying of the taxes is everywhere a power of the city council, though in many states the amount of taxes which may be levied by it is limited—usually to a certain percentage of the value of the taxable property within the city, and in some states the limit is fixed so low that the cities are handicapped in raising sufficient revenue to meet their expenses. The purpose of such restrictions is to prevent extravagance and wastefulness, and the history of many of our cities proves that they have, in general, served a good purpose.

Sources of Municipal Taxation.—The principal source of income for city, as for state and county, purposes is the general property tax, though cities are usually allowed to levy a great variety of other taxes, such as taxes on certain trades and businesses. Street peddlers are in many cases required to pay license fees. Before the liquor traffic was prohibited, many cities derived a large portion of their income from license taxes on saloons. Some cities receive a considerable income from franchises granted to public corporations. Thus Chicago receives a large percentage of the earnings of some of the street railways, the amount aggregating more than $1,500,000 a year. In many cities the expense of public improvements, particularly street paving and the laying of sidewalks, is met by what are called "special assessments," that is, assessments laid upon the owners of the property benefited, in proportion to the benefits received from the improvement.

Municipal Expenditures.—Appropriations are in most cities made by the city council subject to certain rules and restrictions prescribed by state law. In

New York city, however, the budget is prepared by a board of estimate and apportionment composed of a few high city officers, and in a few other cities the preparation of the budget is intrusted to other authorities than the city council. To secure accuracy and honesty in the expenditure of city funds, provision is commonly made for auditing the accounts of financial officials, and in a few states like Ohio, Indiana, and Iowa, provision is made by law for state inspection and audit of municipal accounts by state examiners. This plan has proved very effective. In one state, these inspectors found that municipal officials had misappropriated more than $500,000, over half of which was recovered and turned into the proper treasuries. In a number of cities where the commission form of government has been adopted provision is made for monthly financial statements which must be published in the local newspapers, and for annual examinations of city accounts by expert accountants.

City Debts.—For the construction of permanent improvements, the erection of public buildings, and the establishment of commercial enterprises such as waterworks and gas works, cities must borrow money; and so one of the powers always given them is that of incurring debts. This power, however, was greatly abused in the early history of our municipal development—so much so that many cities found themselves on the verge of bankruptcy. In order to check this evil, many states have placed a limit upon the municipal borrowing power, and some have provided that whenever a debt is incurred, provision shall be made at the same time for payment of the interest and the principal within a certain period of years. The debt limit is usually a certain percentage of the assessed valuation of the taxable property within the city. It ranges from 2 per cent in Boston, to 10 per cent in New York. In some cases the limit is so low that cities have been handicapped in constructing needed permanent improvements. Thus in Chicago, where property has been assessed at only one fifth of its real value, the result of the debt limitation has been to render extensive improvements very difficult, and to compel the city to meet the expense of many absolutely necessary undertakings out of its current revenues when the cost should have been distributed over a period of years. Chicago, as a consequence, has the smallest debt of any of the large cities of the country.

Police Protection.—Where large numbers of people are living together in close proximity the problem of maintaining order and preventing some from violating the rights of others is very much greater than in sparsely settled rural communities. One of the principal tasks of the authorities in a city, therefore, is to provide police protection for the inhabitants. This is done through the agency of a body of men organized and uniformed somewhat after the manner of an army. The size of this force varies ordinarily in proportion to the population of the city. In New York city, for example, the entire police force numbers more than 10,000 men—a body as large as the army of the United States was in the early days of our history. In Chicago there are altogether some 8,000 men in the police service of the city.

Organization.—The management of the police force is usually under the direction of an official called a commissioner, superintendent, or chief, though in some cities it is controlled instead by a board. In a few cities this board is appointed by some state official, usually the governor, for it is believed by many persons that since the police are charged with enforcing state laws as well as municipal ordinances, they should be under state rather than local control. Where they are entirely under local control, it is sometimes difficult to secure the enforcement of such state laws as those requiring saloons to be closed at certain hours during the night and on Sundays, especially when local sentiment is opposed to such restrictions. Below the head of the police force are usually deputy chiefs, inspectors, captains, sergeants, roundsmen, and finally the patrolmen. The city is usually divided into precincts, in each of which there is a police station under the charge of a sergeant or some other official. A number of precincts are grouped together in districts with an inspector in charge of each, and so on. In the large cities there are also usually special detachments of the police force organized for special services. Such are the mounted police, the bicycle squad, the river and harbor police, the sanitary police, and the detective force.

Police Corruption.—The control of the police branch of the city service is very difficult because of the opportunities for corruption which are open to the members of the force. It has not infrequently happened that the police in the large cities have systematically sold the right to violate the law. Gambling houses, saloons, and other places of vice sometimes regularly pay members of the police force for the privilege of violating the law, and the heads of the force have frequently found it impossible to prevent the practice. A recent police commissioner in New York, for example, said that there was an organized system among the police of his city for selling the right to violate the law; that many of the captains and inspectors had grown rich out of the proceeds, and that the system was so thoroughly intrenched that he was powerless to break it up.

Health Protection.—In densely populated districts the danger from the spread of disease is much greater than in rural communities where the conditions which breed disease are less prevalent, and where the spread of epidemics may be more easily prevented. In the smaller cities the chief health authority is a board, but in the large cities there is usually a department of health at the head of which is a single commissioner. Other officials are inspectors of various kinds, analysts, collectors of statistics, superintendents of hospitals, etc.

Work of the Health Department.—Among the principal duties of the health authorities are the inspection and abatement of unsanitary places and the suppression of nuisances; the inspection of public buildings and sometimes of private dwellings with special reference to drainage; the removal of garbage and other refuse (in some cities); the inspection of the city water supply; the inspection of food, particularly milk; the control of certain establishments of an offensive character, such as slaughterhouses, soap factories, and fertilizer factories; the vaccination of school children and often of other persons, as a precaution against smallpox; the isolation and quarantine of persons suffering from contagious diseases; the maintenance of pesthouses and hospitals; and the collection of vital statistics.

One great source of disease in cities is impurity of the food supply, especially of milk, and much of the activity of the health department is directed toward the inspection of milk and other food. Crowded, ill-ventilated, and poorly constructed dwellings are another source of disease, and many cities have undertaken to prevent this evil as far as possible through tenement house laws and building regulations requiring dwellings to be constructed according to plans prescribed by law. The enforcement of these laws often devolves upon the health department, which carries out a rigid system of inspection.

In recent years much more attention than formerly has been given to the problems of health administration, and great improvement has been made. So efficient is the health administration of some of our large cities that the death rate in proportion to the population is actually lower than it is in many small country towns where little or no attention is paid to this important branch of administration.

Fire Protection.—The danger from fire, like that from disease, is obviously greater in crowded cities than in country districts. Therefore, every large city and most small ones maintain an organized fire department. In the days of small cities reliance upon voluntary unpaid fire companies was the rule, and this is true even to-day in many of the smaller towns and cities. In the larger cities, however, there are organized professional companies, the members of which give all their time to the service and are paid regular salaries. New York city has more than 5,000 men in its fire department, some 900 pieces of apparatus including more than a dozen fire boats, and hundreds of thousands of feet of hose. At the head of the department there is usually an official called a fire chief or fire marshal, appointed by the mayor. The rank and file of the department are under civil service rules, the employment is of a permanent character, and many cities have provided a system of pensions for members who have grown old or are disabled from injuries.

Great improvement has been made in the methods of fighting fires and in the character of the apparatus employed, so that the danger from loss by fire has greatly diminished. Furthermore, the more general use of brick and stone for building purposes in the larger cities has made the danger from fire much less than in the old days when most houses were built of wood. Many cities have what are called "fire limits," that is, districts in which it is forbidden to erect wooden buildings.

Municipal Public Utilities.—People crowded together in cities depend largely upon public service companies for their water supply, for electric light and gas, for telephone service, and for the means of transportation. The furnishing of each of these services, from the very nature of the case, tends to become a natural monopoly. Moreover, such companies must use the city streets in serving their patrons. It follows, therefore, that they must be subject to public control, otherwise the public might be charged exorbitant prices and the use of the streets by the citizens unnecessarily interfered with. Before engaging in a service of this kind, therefore, the street railway company must secure permission from the city to lay tracks on the streets and to operate cars thereon. Likewise a telephone or electric light company must have permission to erect its poles on the streets or alleys, and a gas or water company must have authority to tear up pavements and put its pipes and mains under the streets.

MUNICIPAL LIGHTING, DENVER, COLORADO

PART OF THE LOS ANGELES AQUEDUCT, CALIFORNIA
THIS AQUEDUCT IS 11 FEET IN DIAMETER AND CARRIES WATER FROM OWENS RIVER 246 MILES TO LOS ANGELES.

Franchises.—The permit thus granted is called a "franchise," and is in the nature of a contract between the city and the company. Public service franchises are often of great value to the companies which receive them, for the business of these companies in a large city is apt to be very profitable. Sometimes the dividends which they pay their stockholders are very large, and not infrequently, to deceive the public as to the real amount, the profits are concealed by "watering" the stock, that is, by increasing it beyond the amount of the capital actually invested. Experience has shown that in granting franchises certain restrictions or conditions should be placed on the companies to whom they are granted.

First of all, the duration of the franchise should be limited. Formerly, it was not uncommon to grant franchises for fifty or one hundred years, and indeed sometimes for an indefinite period. The objection to this practice is that with the growth of the city, the increased value of the franchise resulting from such growth goes entirely to the company, while the city is deprived of the opportunity of making a better bargain with the company. A franchise ought, however, to be for a period sufficiently long to enable the company to derive a reasonable return on its investment. Obviously, no company could afford to establish an electric light plant or gas plant if its franchise were limited to a period as short as five years. The better opinion now is that twenty or twenty-five years is a reasonable period, and the constitution or statutes of a number of states forbid the granting of franchises for a longer period.

Frequently the franchise contains provisions in regard to the rates to be charged and the quality of service to be performed. In many states there are state commissions which have power to supervise the operations of all public service corporations and in some cases even to fix the rates which they shall be allowed to charge. As long as such rates are reasonable, that is, high enough to allow the corporation a reasonable return on its investment, the courts will not interfere.

It is now the practice to require public service companies to pay a reasonable compensation for the franchises which they receive. This is usually a certain percentage of the gross receipts, or sometimes, in the case of street railway companies, a certain sum for each car operated. When the compensation is a certain percentage of the receipts, provision ought to be made for examination of the books of the company in order to prevent the public from being defrauded of its share of the earnings.

Municipal Ownership.—Sometimes, instead of relying upon private corporations to supply the people with water, gas, and electric light, the city itself undertakes to do this. Very many cities own their waterworks,[8] while some own their electric light plants, and a few own their gas plants. In Europe, municipal ownership and operation of such public utilities is very common, and even the telephone and street railway services are often supplied by the city.

The advantages claimed for municipal ownership are that better service will be furnished when the business is conducted by the city, because in that case it will be operated solely with the interest of the public in view; and, secondly, the cost of the service to the community will be less because the earning of large dividends will not be the main end in view. The principal objection urged against municipal ownership in the United States is that "spoils" politics still play such an important part in our city government that the management of such enterprises is likely to fall into the hands of incompetent politicians and party workers. Experience with municipal ownership has been satisfactory in a great many cases where it has been tried, although the principle upon which it rests is contrary to the notions of many people in regard to the proper functions of government.

Municipal Courts.—In every city there are certain inferior courts called by various names, police courts, magistrates' courts, or municipal courts, which have jurisdiction over offenses against the ordinances of the city. These courts constitute a very important part of our governmental machinery, and they have rarely received the consideration which their importance requires. They are practically courts of last resort for a large number of persons charged with minor offenses, and from them many ignorant persons in the large cities gain their impression of American institutions. In the city of New York, for example, more than 100,000 persons are brought before these courts every year.

The magistrates who hold municipal courts are often men of little or no legal training, and the experience of some cities has been that many of them are without integrity. Recently there has been much discussion of how to improve the character and usefulness of these courts, and in several cities notable reforms have already been introduced. The Chicago municipal court recently established is an excellent example of what can be accomplished in this direction. It consists of thirty-one judges, and the salary paid them is sufficiently large to attract well-trained lawyers of respectability. The procedure of the court is simple and it is so organized as to dispatch rapidly the cases brought before it, so that justice is administered more swiftly, perhaps, in this city than in any other in America.

The Commission Plan of Government.—The increasing dissatisfaction with the government of our cities by mayor and councils has recently led a number of cities to abandon the system for a new method known as the commission plan. The principal feature of this method is that all the powers of government heretofore exercised by the mayor and council are intrusted to a small commission usually chosen from the city at large. The plan was first put into operation in the city of Galveston after the great storm of 1900 which destroyed the lives of some 6,000 of its citizens and left the city in a condition of bankruptcy.

Under the new charter which was adopted, practically all the powers of government were vested in a mayor and four commissioners, each of these men being put in charge of one of the five departments into which the administrative service was divided.

Merits.—Several advantages are claimed for this plan of municipal government. In the first place, it does away with the evils of the ward system by providing that the commissioners shall be chosen from the city at large, and this tends to secure the election of men of larger ability. Again, it is argued that a small body of men is better fitted to govern a city than a large council composed of members who consider themselves the special representatives of the petty districts from which they are chosen. The affairs of a city are necessarily complex and often technical in nature and require for their special management skill and efficiency. City government is often compared to the management of a business enterprise like a bank or a manufacturing concern, which, as experience has shown, can be better conducted by a small board of directors than by the whole body of stockholders. Finally, the concentration of the powers of the city in a small body of men tends to secure a more effective responsibility than can be secured under a system in which the responsibility is divided between the mayor and council.

Objections.—The chief objections that have been urged against the commission plan are that, by intrusting both the legislative and the executive power to the same hands, it sacrifices the principle of the separation of powers—a principle long cherished in America. In the second place, by doing away with the council, it sacrifices to a certain extent the representative principle and places all the vast powers of the city in the hands of a few men.

Nevertheless, the system has much to commend it, and it has been adopted in about four hundred towns and cities.

The City Manager Plan.—A still more recent form of municipal government vests the management of the affairs of the city in a single person, called the city manager. He is paid a reasonably high salary and is chosen by the commission because of his expert knowledge. This plan has been introduced in Dayton, Springfield, and Sandusky, Ohio; Newburgh and Niagara Falls, New York; Sumter, South Carolina; Jackson, Grand Rapids, and Kalamazoo, Michigan; San Diego and Alameda, California; and some seventy other cities and towns.

Village Government.—Differing from cities chiefly in size and in the extent of governmental powers, are small municipal corporations variously called villages, boroughs, and incorporated towns. The procedure of incorporation is usually by petition from a certain number of the inhabitants, and a popular vote on the question. The law generally prescribes a minimum population, which is usually small—sometimes as low as one hundred inhabitants.

Village Officers.—The principal authority is usually a small board of trustees or a council, consisting of from three to seven members elected from the village at large, though in some instances the number is larger, and some villages have the ward system. The village board is empowered to adopt ordinances relating to police, health, and other matters affecting the good order and welfare of the community. They may levy taxes, borrow money, open and construct streets, construct drains, establish water and lighting plants and the like, and may license peddlers, hack drivers, and other persons who use the streets for the conduct of their business. The chief officer of the village is the mayor, president, or chairman of the trustees, elected either by the voters or by the trustees. There is also usually a clerk or recorder, a treasurer, a marshal or constable, and sometimes a street commissioner, a justice of the peace, and an attorney.

When the population reaches a certain number, which varies in the different states (pp. 25-26), the village organization is put aside, the community organizes itself into a city, takes on a more elaborate organization, receives larger powers, and undertakes a wider range of activities.

References.—BEARD, American Government and Politics, chs. xxvii-xxviii. BRYCE, The American Commonwealth (abridged edition), chs. xlix-li. GOODNOW, City Government in the United States, chs. vi-xiii. HART, Actual Government, ch. ix. HOWE, The City the Hope of Democracy, chs. i-iv. STRONG, The Challenge of the City, chs. ii-iii. WILCOX, The American City, chs. ii, iii, iv, v, vi, ix, x, xii, xiii.

Documentary and Illustrative Material.—1. A copy of the city charter or municipal code of the state. 2. A copy of the revised ordinances of the city. 3. The volume of the last census report dealing with the population of cities. 4. The latest census bulletin on statistics of cities. 5. A map of the city showing its division into wards, police and fire districts, sewer districts, etc., and the location of the city building, police stations, fire stations, the source of the water supply, parks, slum districts, etc. 6. A copy of the last city budget and tax ordinance. 7. A copy of a paving or other public improvement ordinance.

RESEARCH QUESTIONS

1. What is the population of the largest city in your state? its area? How many cities in your state have a population of 8,000 or over? What percentage of the total population is found in the cities? How much faster has the city population grown during the past decade than the rural population? What percentage of the population of your city is foreign-born?

2. Why do cities require a different form of government from that which is provided for rural communities?

3. What are the provisions in the constitution of your state, if any, in regard to the government of cities?

4. How many representatives does the largest city of your state have in the legislature? What proportion of the total membership is it? Are there any constitutional restrictions upon the number of members of the legislature which may be elected from any one city?

5. Are there any restrictions upon the power of the legislature of your state to enact special legislation applying to a single city? If so, what are they?

6. If you live in a city, when did it receive its present charter? What are the provisions in the charter relating to the organization and powers of the city?

7. Do you think the people of a city should be allowed to frame their own charter and govern themselves without interference on the part of the state legislature?

8. How many members are there in the city council of your city? Are they chosen by wards or from the city at large? What is their term and salary? In what ward do you live, and what is the name of the alderman or aldermen from that ward?

9. For what term is the mayor of your city or town elected? To what political party does he belong? Does he preside over the meetings of the city council? What officers, if any, does he appoint?

10. Name the administrative departments in your city. Are they organized according to the board system, or is each under the control of a single official?

11. Does your city have a civil service law under which appointments to the municipal service are made on the basis of merit? If so, what are its principal provisions?

12. Does the city own and operate its waterworks plant, or is the water supply furnished by a private company? Does the city own and operate any of its other public utilities, such as the electric light or gas plant? If not, what are the terms of the franchises under which they are operated by private companies? Do these companies pay the city anything for the privilege of using the streets?

13. What are the duties of the public utilities commissions in New York and Wisconsin? Do you think the policy of regulation preferable to municipal ownership and operation?

14. How is the cost of street and sidewalk paving met in your city,—by special assessment on the property benefited, or by appropriation out of the city treasury?

15. What is the method of garbage disposal in your city?

16. Describe the organization and activities of the health authority in your city. What does it do to secure a supply of clean and pure milk?

17. Are there any improvement leagues or civic organizations working for the uplift and good government of your city? What are their methods, and what are some of the specific services they have rendered?

18. What are the principal sources of revenue in your village or city? What is the rate of taxation on the taxable property?

CHAPTER III

THE STATE GOVERNMENTS

Place of the States in Our Federal System.—Proceeding upward from the county, township, and city, we come to the state, the authority to which the local governments described in the preceding chapters are all subject. The consideration of state government properly precedes the study of national government, not only because the states existed before the national government did, and in a sense furnished the models upon which it was constructed, but because their governments regulate the larger proportion of our public affairs and hence concern more vitally the interests of the mass of people than does the national government.

The states collectively make up our great republic, but they are not mere administrative districts of the union created for convenience in carrying on the affairs of national government. They do not, for example, bear the same relation to the union that a county does to the state, or a township to the county. A county is nothing more than a district carved out of the state for administrative convenience, and provided with such an organization and given such powers of local government as the state may choose to give it. The states, on the other hand, are not creations of the national government; their place as constituent members of the union is determined by the Federal Constitution, framed by the people of the United States, and their rights and obligations are fixed by the same authority. Each state, however, determines its own form of government and decides for itself what activities it will undertake.

Division of Powers.—The Federal Constitution has marked out a definite sphere of power for the states, on the one hand, and another sphere for the national government on the other, and each within its sphere is supreme. Upon the domain thus created for each the other may not encroach. Each is kept strictly within its own constitutional sphere by the federal Supreme Court, and the balance between the union and its members is harmoniously preserved.

The states were already in existence with organized governments in operation when the national government was created. The founders of the national government conferred upon it only such powers as experience and reason demonstrated could be more effectively regulated by a common government than by a number of separate governments; they left the states largely as they were, and limited their powers only so far as was necessary to establish a more effective union than the one then existing. Experience had taught them, for example, that commerce with foreign countries and among the states themselves should be regulated by a single authority acting for the entire country: only in this way could uniformity be secured, and uniformity in such matters was indispensable to the peace and perpetuity of the union. Accordingly, the national government was vested with power over this and other matters which clearly required uniformity of regulation, and the remaining powers of government were left with the states, where they had always been. Thus it came about that the national government was made an authority of enumerated or delegated powers, while the states have reserved powers.

Prohibitions.—It was thought wise, however, to prohibit both the national government and those of the states from doing certain things, and thus we find provisions in the Federal Constitution forbidding both governments from granting titles of nobility, from passing ex post facto laws, bills of attainder, etc. Likewise the states were prohibited from entering into treaties with foreign countries, from coining money, from impairing the obligation of contracts, and from passing laws on certain other subjects which it was clearly unwise to leave to state regulation.

Powers of the States.—The powers left to the states, unlike those conferred upon the national government, cannot be enumerated. They are so varied in character, and so extensive, that an attempt to enumerate them would involve cataloguing all the multitudinous business and social relationships of life. The powers of the national government seem much greater by comparison than those of the states, partly because they are set forth in the Constitution and partly because of their application throughout the entire country, but in reality they are not only far less numerous but affect less vitally the great mass of the people. The powers of the states include such matters as the regulation of the ownership, use, and disposition of property; the conduct of business and industry; the making and enforcing of contracts; the conduct of religious worship; education; marriage, divorce, and the domestic relations generally; suffrage and elections; and the making and enforcement of the criminal law. In the division of governmental powers between the nation and the state, says Bryce, the state gets the most and the nation the highest, and so the balance between the two is preserved.

> "An American," says Mr. Bryce, "may, through a long life, never be reminded of the federal government except when he votes at presidential and congressional elections, buys a package of tobacco bearing the government stamp, lodges a complaint against the post office, and opens his trunks for a customhouse officer on the pier at New York when he

returns from a tour in Europe. His direct taxes are paid to officials acting under state laws. The state or local authority constituted by state statutes registers his birth, appoints his guardian, pays for his schooling, gives him a share in the estate of his father deceased, licenses him when he enters a trade (if it be one needing a license), marries him, divorces him, entertains civil actions against him, declares him a bankrupt, hangs him for murder; the police that guard his house, the local boards which look after the poor, control highways, impose water rates, manage schools— all these derive their legal powers from his state alone."

Rights and Privileges of the States as Members of the Union.—The states have certain rights and privileges which are guaranteed them by the Federal Constitution, and of which they cannot be deprived by the national government without their consent.

Republican Government.—Thus it is made the duty of the United States to guarantee to every state in the union a republican form of government, that is, a government by the chosen representatives of the people of the state. In a few cases rival governments have been set up in a state, each claiming to be the legitimate government and entitled to the obedience of the people; the one recognized by the federal authorities has always prevailed.

Protection Against Invasion.—It is also made the duty of the national government to protect the states against invasion. This is right and proper, since the states are forbidden by the Constitution to keep ships of war or troops in times of peace.

Protection Against Domestic Violence.—Again, it is made the duty of the national government to protect the people of the states against domestic violence arising from insurrection or riots, *provided* that application has been made by the proper state authorities. The purpose of this proviso is to remove the temptation to federal interference in state affairs for political or other reasons against the wishes of the people of the state. The ordinary procedure for the suppression of a local disturbance is for the sheriff of the county, or the mayor of the city, to make use of the local police, and if necessary he may call upon the citizens to come to his aid. If this is not effective, the governor may be called upon to order out the state militia for the suppression of the riot. If, however, the riot should spread and assume such proportions that the power of the state and local authorities is insufficient, it becomes the right and duty of the governor, or the legislature if it be in session, to call on the President of the United States for the assistance of national troops. If in the President's judgment the situation is one which warrants federal intervention, he sends a detachment of troops from a near-by military post to restore order. Many times in our history federal troops have been used to put down riots where the state authorities had shown themselves incapable of maintaining order; two recent examples being in connection with strikes among the miners of Nevada in 1907, and of Colorado in 1914.

Ordinarily the President has no lawful right to interpose in the affairs of the state by the employment of troops until he has received an application from the governor or the legislature, but if the disturbance is one which interferes with the operations of the national government or with the movement of interstate commerce, the President may intervene whenever in his opinion the situation calls for federal action. Thus during the Chicago strike riots of 1894, President Cleveland ordered a detachment of federal troops to that city against the protests of the governor, upon being assured that the strikers were interfering with the movement of the mails and with the conduct of interstate commerce and were also disregarding the writs and processes of the United States courts. The interference of the President was criticized by some persons, but the great body of citizens approved his course, and the United States Supreme Court upheld the validity of his action.

Other Rights of the States.—Among the other rights of the states under the Federal Constitution may be mentioned the right of equal representation in the senate, a right of which no state can be deprived without its consent, and the right of territorial integrity: no new state may be created within the jurisdiction of another state, nor may any state be formed by the junction of two or more states or parts of states, without the consent of the states concerned.

Obligations and Duties of the States.—Rights and privileges usually imply obligations, and so we find that the states owe certain duties to one another and to the union of which they are a part, and the harmony and success of the federal system are dependent in a large measure upon the performance of these duties in good faith.

Full Faith and Credit.—First of all, each state must give full faith and credit to the acts, judicial proceedings, and records of the other states. This means, for example, that a properly authenticated copy of a will or deed duly executed in one state will be taken notice of and rights depending on it will be enforced in other states as though the instrument were made therein. Likewise, a marriage legally celebrated in one state will usually be treated as valid in another state, and the facts of a case at law will be recognized in other states without the necessity of retrial. The provision as to full faith and credit does *not* mean that one state must enforce within its borders the laws of other states, or that its courts in reaching their decisions are bound by the decisions of the courts of its sister states. As a matter of practice, however, courts in one state in deciding difficult questions of law will examine the decisions of the courts of other states on similar points for their own enlightenment, and will show respect for these decisions, the degree of deference depending on the standing of the judges rendering the decision and upon the similarity of the laws and policies of the states concerned.

Surrender of Fugitives from Justice.—In the next place, it is made the constitutional duty of the executive of each state to surrender criminals escaping from other states, in order that they may be returned for trial and punishment in the state from which they have fled. The demand for the surrender of such fugitives is made by the governor of the state from which the criminal has fled, and the governor upon whom the demand is made ought to comply with it unless for very substantial reasons. There is no way, however, by which this obligation may be enforced, and there have been many cases where governors have refused to deliver up criminals escaping from other states—usually for the reason that, in the governor's opinion, the fugitive would not receive a fair trial in the state from which he had fled.

Treatment of Citizens of Other States.—Still another obligation imposed by the Federal Constitution on the states is that of treating the citizens of other states as they treat their own citizens, i. e., without discrimination. But this obligation has reference rather to civil rights than to political privileges. It does not mean that an illiterate man who is allowed to vote in Illinois may go to Massachusetts and vote where an educational qualification for the suffrage is required; nor does it mean that a woman who is allowed to practice law in one state may therefore practice in another state which excludes women from engaging in that profession. What the provision does mean, is that whatever privileges and immunities a state allows to its own citizens, it must allow the citizens of other states on the same terms, and subject to the same conditions and no more. Thus a state cannot subject the citizens of other states to higher taxes than are imposed upon its own citizens.

Other Obligations.—Finally, it goes without saying that it is the duty of each state to treat its sister states in the spirit of comity and courtesy; to carry out the mandates of the Federal Constitution relating to the election of senators, representatives, and presidential electors so as to keep up the existence of the national government; and, in general, to perform in good faith all their other obligations as members of the union, without the performance of which the republic would be a mere makeshift. The existence of the states is essential to the union, and their preservation is as much within the care of the Constitution as is the union itself. Indeed, the Constitution in all its parts, said the Supreme Court of the United States in a famous case, looks to an indestructible union of indestructible states.

The State Constitution; how Framed.—The governmental organization of each of the states is set forth in a written instrument called a constitution. Unlike the constitutions of some of the European states, which were granted by kings, and unlike, also, those of the British self-governing colonies, which were enacted by Parliament, all the American constitutions now in existence were framed by constituent bodies representing the people, and in most cases they were approved by the people before they went into effect. As Mr. Bryce has remarked, the American state constitutions arc the oldest things in the political history of America. Before the Federal Constitution was framed each of the thirteen original states had a constitution of its own, most of them being framed by popular conventions chosen especially for the purpose.

Later, when a territory asked to be admitted to the union as a new state, Congress, through what is called an "enabling act," empowered the people of the territory to choose a convention to frame a constitution which, when submitted to the voters and approved by them, became the fundamental law of the new state. In a number of cases, however, the people of the territory went ahead on their own initiative, and without the authority of an enabling act framed their constitution and asked to be admitted, and sometimes they were admitted as though they had acted under the authority of Congress. Whenever an existing state wishes to frame a new constitution for itself, the usual mode of procedure is for the legislature either to pass a resolution calling a convention, or to submit to the voters the question of the desirability of a new constitution. A resolution calling a convention usually requires an extraordinary majority of both houses of the legislature, two thirds of the members being the most common rule.

Ratification of New Constitutions.—When the draft of the constitution has been completed by the convention, it is usually submitted to the voters of the state at a general or a special election, and if it is approved by a majority of those voting on the constitution, or (in some states) of those voting at the election, it supersedes the old constitution and goes into effect on a day prescribed. In some instances, however, new constitutions were not submitted to popular vote; instead, the convention assumed the right to put them into effect without popular approval. Of the twenty-five state constitutions adopted before the year 1801, only three were submitted to the voters for their approval, but as time passed the practice of giving the people an opportunity to approve or reject proposed constitutions became the rule. In the twenty years between 1890 and 1910 eight new constitutions were submitted to the people, and only five were put into force without popular ratification, namely, those of Mississippi (1890), South Carolina (1895), Delaware (1897), Louisiana (1898), and Virginia (1902).

Frequency of New Constitutions.—The frequency with which the states revise their constitutions varies in different sections of the country. In New England new constitutions are rare, while in the states of the West and the South new constitutions are framed, on an average, at least once in every generation and sometimes oftener. Since the Revolution more than two hundred constitutions have been made by the states, though some of them never went into operation. Several of the states within a period of less than one hundred years have had as many as six, and a few have had even more. The constitution of Massachusetts of 1780, with several subsequent amendments, is still in force; but outside of New England there are few constitutions that are more than thirty years old. Some of the states, indeed, have inserted provisions in their constitutions making it the duty of the legislature at stated intervals to submit to the voters the question of calling a convention to revise the existing constitution or to adopt an entirely new one. In this way the people are given an opportunity to determine whether the constitution under which they live shall be revised or superseded by a new one, independently of the will of the legislature.

Contents of State Constitutions.—The early state constitutions were brief documents and dealt only with important matters of a fundamental and permanent character. They were remarkably free from detail and rarely contained more than 5,000 words. As time passed, however, there was an increasing tendency to incorporate in them provisions in regard to many matters that had formerly been left to the legislature to be regulated by statute, so that some of the constitutions of the present day are bulky codes containing detailed provisions concerning many matters that might more properly be dealt with by statute. The constitution of Virginia, for example, has expanded from a document of a few pages to one of seventy-five, from an instrument of about 1,500 words to one of more than 30,000. The present constitution of Alabama contains about 33,000 words; that of Louisiana, about 45,000; and that of Oklahoma, about 50,000. The Virginia constitution contains a lengthy article on the organization of counties; one on the government of cities, constituting a code almost as elaborate as a municipal corporations act; one on agriculture and immigration; one on corporations, containing fourteen sections; one on taxation and finance, etc. The constitution of Oklahoma contains an article of seven sections on federal relations, one of which deals with the liquor traffic; elaborate provisions regarding the referendum and initiative; a section describing the seal of the state; a detailed enumeration of those who are permitted to accept railroad passes; an article on insurance; one on manufactures and commerce; and one on alien and corporate ownership of lands.

Parts of a Constitution.—A typical constitution consists of several parts: (1) a preamble; (2) a bill of rights; (3) a series of provisions relating to the organization of the government and the powers and duties of the several departments; (4) a number of miscellaneous articles dealing with such matters as finance, revenue and debts, suffrage and elections, public education, local government, railroads, banks, and other corporations generally; (5) an article describing the procedure by which amendments may be proposed and ratified; and (6) a schedule. Many constitutions contain an article defining the boundaries of the state, and most of them one on the distribution of the powers of government. Some of the newer constitutions also prescribe numerous limitations upon the legislature, so great is the popular mistrust of legislatures to-day; while others lay down various rules as to the procedure of the legislature. The schedule contains provisions for submitting the constitution to the voters and making necessary arrangements for putting the new constitution into effect.

The Bill of Rights, says Bryce, is historically the most interesting part of the state constitution, and if we may judge by the space devoted to these provisions and the attention paid to their framing, they constitute a very important part of the constitution. In a sense they are the lineal descendants of great English enactments like Magna Charta, the Bill of Rights, and the Act of Settlement, and of the various declarations of the Revolutionary Congresses in America. They consist of limitations upon the government and of statements of the fundamental rights of man.

Some Provisions of the Bills of Rights.—Examining these bills of rights, we find that they all contain declarations in favor of freedom of religious worship, freedom of assembly, freedom of speech and of the press, and most of them forbid the establishment of a state church or the appropriation of money for the establishment or support of any religious denomination. Most of them contain declarations providing for trial by jury in criminal cases, indictments by grand jury, the privilege of the writ of habeas corpus, the right of the accused to a speedy and public trial; a declaration of the right of citizens to bear arms; the prohibition of excessive bail, cruel and unusual punishments, general search warrants, and imprisonment for debt; the prohibition of titles of nobility, ex post facto laws, and bills of attainder[9]; and provisions forbidding the taking of private property except for public purposes and then only when just compensation is made.[10] Many of them contain philosophical enunciations of political doctrines such as the assertion that all governments originate with the people, and are instituted solely for their good; that all men are equal; that all power is inherent in the people; and that the people have at all times the right to alter, reform, or abolish their government. Some of the newer constitutions declare that monopolies and perpetuities are contrary to the principles of free government; that every citizen shall be free to obtain employment wherever possible; that a long lease of office is dangerous to the liberties of the people; that aliens shall have the same rights of property as citizens; and so on.

The real importance of the bills of rights, now that executive tyranny is a thing of the past, is not very great.

Amendment of State Constitutions.—The practice of inserting in the constitution many provisions which are temporary in character, makes frequent alteration a necessity if the constitution is to meet the rapidly changing needs and conditions of the state. Some of the early constitutions contained no express provision for their own amendment, but as time passed changes became manifestly necessary, and in time they were all amended or supplanted entirely by new ones, notwithstanding the absence of amending provisions. Ultimately the advantage of pointing out in the constitution a legal and orderly way of amendment came to be generally appreciated, and at the present time all of the constitutions contain amending provisions. These clauses provide that amendments may be proposed, either by a convention called by the legislature, or by the legislature itself, usually by an extraordinary majority; in either case the proposed amendment must be submitted to the voters for their approval, and it becomes a part of the constitution only if ratified by a majority of those voting on the proposed amendment or, in some states, by a majority of those voting at the election at which the proposed amendment is submitted. A new method of amendment by popular initiative was adopted in Oregon in 1902. According to this method a proposed amendment may be framed by the people by petition and submitted to a popular vote without the necessity of the intervention of the legislature in any form.

In spite of the restrictions imposed, most of the constitutions are frequently amended. During the two decades from 1900 to 1919, 1500 amendments were proposed by the legislatures of the several states, or by popular initiative, and of these about 900 were ratified. At the general election of 1918, no less than 130 amendments were voted on by the people of the different states, and a number of others were awaiting the action of the legislatures soon to meet. In five western states alone 270 amendments were submitted from 1914 to 1919.

References.—BEARD, American Government and Politics, chs. xxii-xxiii. BRYCE, The American Commonwealth (abridged edition), chs. xxxiv-xxxv. DEALEY, Our State Constitutions, chs. ii-iii. HART, Actual Government, ch. vi. HINSDALE, The American Government, chs. xl, xli, xlix, l. WILSON, The State, secs. 1087-1095. WILLOUGHBY, Rights and Duties of Citizenship, ch. x. WILLOUGHBY, The American Constitutional System, chs. ii-x.

Documentary and Illustrative Material.—1. THORPE's Constitutions and Organic Laws, or POORE's Charters and Constitutions, both published by the Government Printing Office. 2. Pamphlet copies of state constitutions can usually be obtained from the secretaries of state of the various states. 3. The legislative manual of the state, where usually a review of the constitutional history of the state may be found.

RESEARCH QUESTIONS

1. In what two senses is the word "state" used? In what sense is New York a state and in what sense is it not?

2. Were the states ever sovereign? What were the two views in this country prior to the Civil War in regard to the sovereignty of the states?

3. The constitution and laws of the United States are declared to be supreme over those of the states; what is the meaning of that provision? Does that mean that any law passed by Congress will override a conflicting law passed by a state, even though the law passed by the state is clearly within its powers?

4. Distinguish between *reserved* powers and *delegated* powers.

5. Do you believe the powers of the national government should be increased so as to include the regulation of such matters as marriage and divorce, the business of corporations, factory labor, and insurance?

6. What is the purpose of the commissions on uniform legislation in the different states, and what are they seeking to accomplish? Is there such a commission in your state?

7. Which of the following matters fall within the jurisdiction of the United States and which within the jurisdiction of the states? (1) the levying of tariff duties, (2) the transfer of land, (3) the building of lighthouses, (4) the protection of religious worship, (5) the granting of passports, (6) punishment of crime, (7) the granting of pensions, (8) the regulation of labor in mines and factories, (9) the protection of the public health, (10) the support of schools, (11) the regulation of navigation, (12) the erection of fortifications.

8. Name some powers that may be exercised by both Congress and the states; some that may be exercised by neither; some that may be exercised by the states only with the consent of Congress.

9. May the United States government coerce a state? Suppose a state should refuse or neglect to perform its constitutional duties as a member of the union, could it be punished or compelled to fulfill its obligations?

10. May a state be sued by a citizen of the state? by a citizen of another state?

by another state itself?

11. Suppose a state should refuse to pay a debt which it has incurred, has the person to whom the debt is due any remedy?

12. Will a divorce granted in Nevada to a citizen of Massachusetts be recognized as valid in Massachusetts?

13. Suppose a man, standing on the New Jersey side of the Delaware River, should fire a shot across the river and kill a man in Pennsylvania, would the governor of New Jersey be bound to surrender the criminal upon demand of the governor of Pennsylvania, in order that he might be tried in Pennsylvania?

14. What is the difference between a constitution, a statute, and a charter? Between a written and an unwritten constitution?

15. When was the present constitution of your state adopted? Was it submitted to the voters before being put into effect? How many constitutions has your state had since its admission to the union? Were they all adopted by popular ratification? Who was the delegate from your county to the last constitutional convention?

16. How may the constitution of your state be amended? Is a majority of those voting at the election necessary to ratify, or only a majority of those voting on the proposed amendment? How many times has the present constitution of your state been amended? Do you think the method of amendment is too rigid?

17. What is the purpose of a preamble to a constitution? Does the preamble of your constitution contain a recognition of God?

18. What are the provisions in the bill of rights to your constitution in regard to the rights of an accused person? in regard to freedom of the press? freedom of assembly? freedom of worship? right of the people to change their government?

CHAPTER IV

THE STATE LEGISLATURE

Powers of the State Legislatures.—The powers of the state legislature, unlike those of the city council and those of the Congress of the United States, are not set forth in the constitution. In general, a state legislature may exercise any powers which are not denied to it by the Constitution of the United States or by the constitution of the state. Its powers, in other words, are residuary in character, rather than delegated or granted.

Limitations.—In recent years, however, mainly on account of the popular distrust in which our legislatures have come to be held, numerous limitations upon their powers have been imposed by the constitutions of many states. Thus they are frequently forbidden absolutely to pass local or special laws where a general law is applicable, or they are allowed to enact such laws only under certain restrictions. In most states, also, the legislature cannot run the state into debt beyond a certain amount, and its power to impose taxes and appropriate money is generally restricted. Finally, its power of legislation has been limited by the present practice of regulating many important matters in the constitution itself. In the newer constitutions especially we find a large number of provisions relating to schools, cities, towns, railroads, corporations, taxation, and other matters. To that extent, therefore, the legislature is deprived of its power of legislation on these subjects.

Extent of the Legislative Power.—In spite of the numerous restrictions, however, the power of the legislature is very large. It enacts the whole body of criminal law of the state; makes laws concerning the ownership, use, and disposition of property, laws concerning contracts, trade, business, industry, the exercise of such professions as law, medicine, pharmacy, and others; laws relating to the government of counties, towns, cities, and other localities; laws concerning the public health, education, charity, marriage and divorce, and the conduct of elections; laws concerning railroads, canals, ferries, drainage, manufacturing, eminent domain, and a great variety of other matters. The subjects concerning which the legislatures may enact laws are indeed so numerous and varied that it would be impossible to enumerate them all. For that reason the legislature is by far the most important branch of the state government, and it is highly important that it should be composed of honest, intelligent, and efficient members. Unfortunately, however, in many states the legislature has declined in public esteem. In the early days of our history the legislative branch of the government was all-powerful. It was not only practically unlimited as to its power of legislation, but it was intrusted with the choice of many important officers of the state. Now, however, there is a disposition to cut down its powers and place restrictions on the exercise of those that are left to it. In many states the people have secured the power to legislate for themselves by means of the initiative and referendum (pp. 85-89); and, to diminish the power of the legislature to enact useless laws, many constitutions limit the length of the sessions to forty or sixty days in the hope of compelling it to devote its time to the consideration of important measures of general interest.

Structure of the Legislature.—Every state legislature to-day consists of two houses. At first several states followed the example of the Congress of the Confederation and tried the single-chamber system, but they soon found its disadvantages serious, and substituted legislatures with two houses. The principal advantage of a bicameral legislature is that each house serves as a check upon the haste of the other and thus insures more careful consideration of bills. Nevertheless, proposals have recently been made in several states to establish a single-chambered legislature, and the question was voted on by the electors of Oregon in 1912 and in 1914, and by those of Arizona in 1916.

The lawmaking body popularly known as the legislature is officially so designated in some states, but in others the formal name is the general assembly or the legislative assembly, and in two, Massachusetts and New Hampshire, the colonial title, "general court," is still retained. In all the states the upper house is styled the senate. In most of them the lower chamber is known as the house of representatives, though in a few it is styled the assembly and in three the house of delegates.

Both houses of the state legislature are chosen by the people. The principal differences in their make-up are, that the senate is a smaller body and therefore each senator represents a larger constituency, the senators in many states are chosen for a longer term, and usually the senate is vested with special functions such as the approval of executive appointments to office, and the trial of impeachment cases.

The State Senate.—The size of the senate varies from seventeen members in Delaware to sixty-seven in Minnesota, the average number being about thirty-five. In about two thirds of the states the term of senators is four years; in New Jersey their term is three years; in Massachusetts it is one year; in the remaining states it is two years. In about one third of the states the terms of the senators and the representatives are the same. In some states the senators are divided into classes, and only half of them retire at the same time.

The House of Representatives.—The house of representatives everywhere is a more numerous body than the senate, and in a few states the disproportion is very great. Thus the New Hampshire legislature with a senate of 24 members has a house of representatives of more than 400 members, the largest in any state, a body about as large as the national house of representatives. The Connecticut legislature is composed of a senate of 35 members and a house of representatives of 258 members; Vermont has a senate of 30 members and a house of representatives of 246; Massachusetts has a senate of 40 members and a house of 240. The smallest houses of representatives are those of Delaware and Arizona, each consisting of 35 members.

Apportionment of Senators and Representatives.—Senators and representatives are apportioned among districts, usually on the basis of population. Political units, however, are often taken into consideration, and in some states such units rather than the number of inhabitants are the determining element. Thus it is frequently provided that each county shall be entitled to one senator, though the population of some counties may be many times as great as that of other counties. In some of the New England states the inequalities of representation are so glaring as to constitute a great injustice to the more populous towns. In Connecticut, for example, the members of the lower house are distributed among the towns of the state, without regard to their population. As a result each of the small towns of Union, Hartland, Killingworth, and Colebrook, with an average population of less than 1,000 persons, has two representatives, while New Haven, with 133,000 inhabitants, has only two. Hartford, with about 99,000, has only two, and so has Bridgeport with a population of 102,000, and Waterbury with 73,000. These four cities comprise about one third the population of the state, but they have only one thirty-second part of the membership of the house of representatives. A similar system of representation exists in Vermont and in the senate of Rhode Island.

Moreover, as a result of "gerrymandering" by the political party in control of the legislature the legislative districts are frequently so constructed as to give the majority party more than its fair share of representatives. As a result there are in some states great inequalities of representation among the different counties or legislative districts.

In order to prevent large cities from controlling the legislature and thereby dominating the state, a few constitutions limit their representation in the legislature. Thus in New York it is provided that no county, however populous, shall have more than one third of all the representatives, and a somewhat similar provision is contained in the constitutions of Rhode Island and Pennsylvania.

Minority Representation in the Legislature.—Where there are two political parties in the state, it is worth considering whether some provision should not be made for allowing each party to choose a number of representatives in proportion to its numerical strength, or at least for allowing the weaker party some representation in the legislature. It not infrequently happens under the present system that the majority party in the state succeeds in electing nearly all the representatives, leaving the other party practically without representation, although it may be strong enough to cast hundreds of thousands of votes in the state as a whole. In the Oregon state election of 1906, for example, the Republican party, with only 55 per cent of the voting strength, elected eighty-eight members of the legislature, while the Democratic party, though casting 34 per cent of the total vote, elected only seven representatives.

The present constitution of Illinois contains a clause which makes it possible for the minority party in each of the fifty-one legislative districts into which the state is divided to elect at least one of the three representatives to which the district is entitled. Each voter is allowed three votes, and he may give one vote to each of three candidates, or he may give all three to one candidate, or two to one candidate and one to another. Usually the party having the majority in the district elects two candidates and the minority party one, the voters of the latter party concentrating all their votes on the one candidate.

Legislative Sessions.—In the great majority of states the legislatures hold regular sessions every two years. In New York, New Jersey, Massachusetts, Rhode Island, Georgia, and South Carolina the legislature meets every year in regular session. Alabama is contented with a session once in every four years. In California the session is divided into two parts, the first being devoted exclusively to the introduction of bills. The legislature then takes a recess of a month to enable the members to consult their constituents in regard to the bills introduced, after which it reassembles for the enactment of such legislation as seems to be demanded. In all the states the governor is empowered to call extraordinary sessions for the consideration of special matters of an urgent character.

There is a popular belief that legislatures waste much of their time in the consideration of petty matters, and in many states the constitution either limits the length of the session,—sometimes to forty, fifty, or sixty days,—or provides that where the session is prolonged beyond a certain number of days, the pay of members shall cease. The wisdom of limiting the sessions to such brief periods, however, is doubtful, and several states that once imposed such restrictions have since removed them.

Legislative Compensation.—In all the states, members of the legislature receive pay for their services. This is either in the form of a definite amount per year, term, or session, or so much per day. The largest legislative salaries are those of Illinois ($3,500 per biennial session), New York ($1,500 per year), Massachusetts and Ohio ($1,000 per year), and Pennsylvania ($1,500 per biennial session). In New Hampshire, on the other hand, the salary is only $200 per biennial session, in Connecticut $300, and in South Carolina $200 for each annual session. In thirty states the per diem method of compensation prevails, the amount ranging from three dollars per day, which is the salary paid in Kansas and Oregon, to ten dollars per day, in Kentucky, Montana, and Nebraska, the most usual sum being four or five dollars per day. In several states, however, the per diem compensation ceases, or is reduced to a nominal amount, after the legislature has been in session 60 days or 90 days. Mileage ranging in amount from ten cents per mile to twenty-five cents is usually allowed, and in a number of states there is a small allowance for postage, stationery, and newspapers. In some states the pay of the legislators is fixed by the constitution, and hence the matter is beyond control of the legislature. Indeed, in only a few states is the matter of legislative pay left entirely to the discretion of the legislature without restriction.

In a number of them the constitution either forbids members to accept free passes on the railroads, or makes it the duty of the legislature to pass laws prohibiting the acceptance of such passes.

Organization of the Legislature.—Each house is usually free to organize itself as it may see fit, though where the office of lieutenant governor exists, the constitution designates that official as the presiding officer of the senate.

The Speaker.—The presiding officer of the lower house is styled the speaker, and in all the states he is chosen by the house from its own membership. He calls the house to order, presides over its deliberations, enforces the rules governing debate, puts motions and states questions, makes rulings on points of order, recognizes members who desire to address the house, appoints the committees, signs the acts and resolutions passed by the house, and maintains order and decorum. He usually belongs to the political party which is in the majority in the house, and in making up the committees and recognizing members for the purpose of debate he usually favors those of his own party.

The Clerk.—Each house has a clerk or secretary who keeps the journal of the proceedings, has custody of all bills and resolutions before the house, keeps the calendar of bills, calls the roll, reads bills, and performs other duties of a like character. He is often assisted by other clerks such as a reading clerk, an engrossing clerk, sometimes an enrolling clerk, etc.

STATE CAPITOL, HARRISBURG, PENNSYLVANIA

STATE CAPITOL, SALEM, OREGON

Sergeant-at-arms.—To execute the orders of the house in preserving good order and enforcing the rules, there is an officer called a sergeant-at-arms. He usually has custody of the hall in which the meetings are held, makes arrests when the house orders an outsider to be taken into custody for contempt, compels absent members to attend when ordered by the house to do so, and sometimes keeps the accounts of the pay and mileage of members.

Other Officers and Employees.—Usually, also, there is a chaplain who opens the session with prayer, though he is not always a paid employee; a postmaster; and a number of miscellaneous employees such as doorkeepers, janitors, copying clerks, stenographers, pages, etc.[111]

Committees.—For convenience in legislation the members of each house are grouped into committees, the more important of which are those on agriculture, corporations, finance or appropriations, ways and means, judiciary, railroads, labor, education, manufactures, engrossment and enrollment, and insurance. In the Western states there are usually committees on immigration, mining, dairies, forestry, fish and game, drainage, swamp lands, irrigation, levees and river improvements, etc. The number and size of the committees vary in different states. In some of the states there are as many as fifty or sixty committees, and occasionally as many as forty members are placed on a single committee. In addition to the standing committees of each house there are frequently select committees appointed for special purposes, and there are usually a number of joint committees made up of members of both houses. In the New England states most of the committee work is done by joint committees, there being usually only four or five standing committees in each house.

How Bills are Passed.—Each house is empowered to frame its own rules of procedure, but in order to insure publicity and careful consideration of bills the state constitutions have placed restrictions upon the legislature in the consideration and passage of bills. Thus in all the states each house is required to keep a journal of its daily proceedings; in most states it is provided that no law shall be passed except by bill, that no bill shall embrace more than one subject, which shall be clearly expressed in the title of the bill, that no money shall be appropriated except by law, that every bill shall be read at least three times before being passed, that no existing law shall be amended by mere reference to its title but the amended portion must be set out in full, and that the yeas and nays shall be recorded upon demand of a certain number of members. Some states require that every bill shall be referred to a committee, that every bill shall be printed and placed on the desk of each member, that no bill shall be introduced after the legislature has been in session a certain number of days, and that bills of a local or private character shall be introduced only after public notice has been given in the locality affected and to be valid must be passed by a two-thirds majority of each house; and so on.

In general these constitutional restrictions represent an attempt to eliminate the evils of undue haste, lack of consideration, extravagance, and objectionable local and private bills, and to compel the legislature to do its work openly, carefully, and in the interest of the public good.

Order of Procedure.—A common order of the procedure in passing bills is the following: 1. Introduction and first reading. 2. Reference to a committee. 3. Report of the committee. 4. Second reading. 5. Third reading. 6. Vote on passage. 7. Enrollment. 8. Approval by the Governor. This order of procedure, however, is often departed from under a suspension of the rules or by unanimous consent.

Usually any member can introduce a bill on any subject and at any time[12] except where the constitution forbids the introduction of bills after a certain date, and some legislatures have even found a means of evading this restriction. In most states a bill can be introduced by filing it with the clerk. It is then usually read the first time, though only by title, and referred to the appropriate committee for consideration and report. The committee may "pigeonhole" it and never report, or it may make a report so late in the session that consideration of the bill is impossible. If the bill seems worthy of being reported, the committee reports it to the house with a recommendation that it be passed either with or without amendments, or that it be rejected. If reported favorably it is placed on the calendar for consideration in its turn. At this stage it is open for general discussion and for amendment by the house. If the bill meets the approval of the house, it is finally ordered to be engrossed and read a third time. It is then put in shape by the committee on engrossment, after which it is read a third time and finally passed. It then goes to the other house, where the procedure is substantially the same. If passed by the second house, it is ready for the signature of the governor. If amended by the second house, it comes back to the first house for concurrence in the amendments. If the first house refuses its concurrence, a conference committee is usually appointed by the two houses to consider and recommend a compromise. The bill is not ready to send to the governor until it has been passed by both houses in exactly the same form.

Lobbying and Bribery.—In all our states a large proportion of the legislation enacted affects directly or indirectly the interests of particular persons, classes, or localities. As a result, interested parties bring great pressure to bear upon the members to pass certain bills or to reject certain others.

Methods of the Lobbyist.—Usually when the legislature meets, the paid representatives of interested individuals, corporations, or local governments appear on the scene to urge legislation in their interests or to defeat bills introduced that are unfavorable to them. These persons are known as "lobbyists," and the means they employ to secure or prevent legislation are often improper and sometimes venal. Sometimes money is used to bribe members to vote for or against pending measures, and there are few states indeed where charges of this kind have not been made. In one state recently, money was contributed in large quantities by persons interested in preventing certain legislation, and the sum thus contributed was known as the "jack pot" fund, out of which members were handsomely paid for their votes. In a special message to the legislature of New York state, Governor Hughes declared that certain disclosures had "caused honest citizens to tingle with shame and indignation and made irresistible the demand that every proper means should be employed to purge and purify the legislature." The situation described by the governor as existing in New York, unfortunately, exists in other states as well.

"Strike" Bills.—Some of the great corporations maintain regularly paid lobbyists at the state capitals when the legislature is in session, not so much for the purpose of securing legislation in their interests as to prevent the enactment of laws to which they are opposed. Sometimes they are practically forced to have lobbyists on the ground to prevent the enactment of what are called "strike" bills, that is, bills introduced by unscrupulous members for the purpose of extorting money from the corporations to pay for defeating them.

Anti-lobbying Legislation.—The evils growing out of the practice of the special interests in maintaining paid lobbyists near the legislature have led to attempts in a number of states to restrict such abuses by legislation. This legislation, in general, makes it unlawful to attempt to influence improperly any legislator. In several states lobbyists are required to make known the purpose of their business and to register their names with the secretary of state, and after the adjournment of the legislature to file a sworn statement of their expenses.

Direct Legislation: the Initiative and the Referendum.—The legislature is not the only agency for enacting law and determining the public policies of the state. Laws on certain subjects may be made by the people themselves acting directly in their primary capacity as well as through the agency of representatives. This is done through what are called the initiative and the referendum. The initiative is a device by which the people themselves may propose laws and have them submitted to the voters for their approval or rejection. Through the referendum the people reserve the power to approve or reject by popular vote certain laws enacted by the legislature.

Varieties of Referendum.—The referendum may be obligatory or optional in character, that is, the approval of the electorate may be required by the constitution before certain laws shall go into effect, or the legislature in its discretion may refer a law to the people for their opinion. Thus the constitutions of many states declare that no law for increasing the debt of the state beyond a certain amount shall be valid until it has been submitted to the voters and approved by them. Again, the referendum may be mandatory or advisory in character. Under the mandatory form, the legislature is required to carry out the will of the electorate as pronounced on any subject referred to the voters, while the advisory referendum is nothing more than an expression of opinion which may or may not be followed by legislative action.

Again, the referendum may be state-wide in its scope, as where a general law or question of public policy is submitted to the voters of the whole state, or it may be of a local character, as where a law affecting a particular community is referred to the voters thereof.

The referendum as a device for adopting constitutions and constitutional amendments is as old as the republic itself, and is now the general practice (pp. 65, 70). In all the states except Delaware proposed amendments must be submitted to the voters at a general or special election, and must be adopted by them before going into effect. The use of the referendum for ordinary lawmaking is also an old practice, though it is much more generally resorted to now than formerly. Thus very early in our history it was employed for such purposes as the incorporation of towns, borrowing money, the location of county sites, division of counties, subscription to stock in railroads and other enterprises by states, counties, or towns, and the levying of special taxes for the support of schools. One of the important uses to which it was put was the determination of the question whether intoxicating liquor should be sold in a particular locality. In time what were called local option laws were passed in many states, giving the people of towns, cities, or other local divisions of the state the privilege of determining by popular vote whether liquor should be sold within their limits. Other matters that have frequently been made the subject of a referendum are: the granting of the suffrage to negroes, and sometimes the enfranchisement of women; the location of state capitals; the sale of school lands; the incorporation of state banks of issue; the granting of aid to railroads; the adoption of the township form of local government; the construction of canals; the erection of public libraries; and many other matters too numerous to mention. There is no state in which the referendum is not provided by the constitution for certain kinds of legislation, and there is hardly a general election held nowadays in which the voters are not called upon to pass judgment upon some proposed act of the legislature or some question of public policy.

In Illinois there has been enacted what is known as the "public opinion law," which provides that upon petition by 10 per cent of the registered voters of the state the legislature is required to submit to the voters any question of public policy for their opinion. The popular vote, however, is nothing more than an expression of opinion by the voters and is not binding upon the legislature.

The Oregon System.—The idea of the initiative and the referendum has been carried out most fully in Oregon, whose constitution provides that 8 per cent of the voters may by petition propose an amendment to the constitution, and when so proposed it must be submitted to the voters and if approved by a majority of them the amendment becomes a part of the constitution. Likewise the constitution of Oregon provides for the initiation and adoption of ordinary laws by the people. It further provides that upon the petition of 5 per cent of the voters any act of the legislature, with certain exceptions, before going into effect, must be submitted to the people for their approval, and if not approved by a majority of those voting, it shall not go into effect. From 1904 to 1914, 130 constitutional amendments and statutes were submitted to popular vote, of which 46 were adopted. For the information of the voters, "publicity pamphlets" are provided, containing an explanation of the measures upon which they are called to vote, together with arguments for and against each proposition. In 1912 these arguments (on 37 measures) made a book of 252 pages.

Initiative and Referendum in other States.—Various other states (South Dakota, Utah, Colorado, Montana, Idaho, Missouri, Maine, Arkansas, Oklahoma, Nebraska, Arizona, Nevada, California, Washington, Michigan, Ohio, North Dakota, Massachusetts, and Mississippi) have established both the initiative and the referendum in some form or other. The initiative and referendum are in use also in many cities, especially those under the commission plan of government. Usually the number who are empowered to initiate a proposed law or ordinance is 8 or 10 per cent of the registered vote. In Texas the referendum is applied to the formulation by political parties of their party policies, 10 per cent of the voters being allowed to propose policies which must be submitted to the party for their opinion.

Merits of the Referendum.—One of the chief merits of the referendum is that it serves as a check on the vices, follies, and errors of judgment of the legislature. Another merit claimed for the referendum is its educative effect upon the electorate. Where the voters are frequently called upon to pass judgment upon the acts of the legislature or upon questions of public policy, they must, if they discharge their duty properly, study the measures submitted to them and thus become trained in public affairs. The enjoyment of such a privilege also tends to stimulate their interest in political affairs and increase their feeling of responsibility for the good government of the state.

The advantage of the initiative is that it puts in the hands of the people the power to bring forward needed measures of legislation and secure a vote on them whenever the legislature refuses to act in obedience to the popular mind.

References.—BEARD, American Government and Politics, ch. xxv. BRYCE, The American Commonwealth (abridged edition), ch. xxxix. DEALEY, Our State Constitutions, ch. vii. HART, Actual Government, ch. vii. REINSCH, American Legislatures and Legislative Methods, chs. iv-x.

WILSON, The State, secs. 1128-1142.

Documentary and Illustrative Material.—1. The legislative manual or blue book of the state. 2. A map showing the division of the state into legislative districts. 3. Rules of procedure of the two houses of the legislature. 4. Specimen copies of bills and resolutions. 5. Messages of the governor to the legislature. 6. The last volume of the session laws of the state.

RESEARCH QUESTIONS

1. How many members are there in the senate of your state legislature? How many in the house of representatives? What is the term of the members of each house? What are the qualifications for membership? What is the salary?

2. What is the principle of apportionment of the members of each house? Are there any inequalities of representation among the districts or counties from which the members are chosen? What county has the largest number of representatives? What county the smallest number? Have any charges been made that the state is "gerrymandered" in the interest of the dominant party?

3. How many committees are there in each house? Of what committees are your representatives and your senator members? What is the average number of members on each committee? Name some of the most important committees. What are the principal officers and employees of each house?

4. How often does the legislature of your state meet in regular session? Are there any constitutional restrictions on the length of the sessions? Have any extraordinary sessions been held in recent years? If so, for what purpose? Are there any restrictions on the power of the legislature when in extraordinary session?

5. How many acts were passed at the last regular session? How many joint resolutions were adopted? What is the difference between an act and a joint resolution?

6. What are the provisions in the constitution of your state in regard to the procedure of the legislature in passing bills? Find out from the rules of each house how a bill is introduced, considered, and passed. How are special and local acts passed?

7. Is there a law in your state to regulate lobbying? What is the penalty for accepting a bribe?

8. Is there a legislative reference bureau or other agency in your state for collecting information for the benefit of members or for assisting them in the preparation of bills?

9. Are there any provisions in the constitution of your state in regard to the initiative or referendum? Do you know of any instance in recent years in which the people of the state were called upon to vote on a proposed legislative act or a question of public policy? Is there a local option liquor law in your state? If so, have the people of your county or city taken advantage of it?

10. Do you think members of the legislature when instructed by their constituents to vote for or against a certain measure, should obey the instructions, or vote according to their own judgment of what is best without regard to the expressed will of the people?

11. Is there any organization in your state for studying the records of members and for securing the election of honest and efficient legislators?

CHAPTER V

THE STATE EXECUTIVE

The Governor; Election and Qualifications.—Each state has a chief executive styled a governor, who is charged with the execution of the laws. In all he is elected by the people. In nearly all, a plurality of the popular vote is sufficient to elect, but in a few states a majority is required and if no candidate receives a majority of the popular vote, either the legislature makes the choice, or a second popular election is held.

To be eligible to the office of governor, a man must have attained a certain age, usually thirty years, and generally he must be a citizen of the United States; in many states he must have been a citizen for a period ranging from five to twenty years. He is also usually required to have been a resident of the state for a period ranging from one to ten years.

Term.—The term of the governor in twenty-five states is two years; in the others it is four years except in New Jersey, where it is three years. Formerly the term was one year in several states, but by 1920 all of them had changed it to two years. A one-year term seems to have little to recommend it, for experience is as necessary for the successful administration of public affairs as for the conduct of private business, and familiarity with the duties of an office of such importance cannot be acquired in so short a time. However, where the one-year term prevailed, it was customary to reëlect the governor to a second term. In a number of states, the governor is ineligible to two successive terms, the idea being that if reëligible he would make use of his official power to secure his reëlection. A few state constitutions wisely provide that he may hold office until his successor has qualified, and thus the danger of a vacancy is obviated.

Salary.—The salary of the governor is everywhere comparatively small, though in recent years the tendency has been to increase it. In three fourths of the states now the salary is $5,000 per year or more. In California, Massachusetts, New Jersey, New York, Ohio, and Pennsylvania, it is $10,000 per year, and in Illinois it is $12,000. The smallest salary is $2,500 per year, which is the amount allowed in Nebraska. Frequently the state provides the governor with a residence styled the "executive mansion." A contingent fund out of which to meet the expense of emergencies in the execution of laws is usually placed at his disposal, but this fund cannot be used for private purposes. Some governors, however, have not been very careful to distinguish between private and official purposes, and not infrequently the use made of this fund has been the subject of legislative investigation and of popular criticism.

Organization of the Executive Department.—The organization of the executive department of the state government is different in one important respect from that of the executive department of the United States. In the national government the responsibility for the administration of executive affairs is concentrated in the hands of the President, and the heads of the various departments are all his appointees; they are responsible directly to him for the discharge of their duties, are, within the limits of the law, subject to his direction, and may be removed by him for any reason which to him may seem expedient. The executive power of the state, on the contrary, instead of being concentrated in the hands of the governor, is really divided between him and a number of other state officers, who are generally elected by the people and over whom he has little or no control. They are, in short, his colleagues rather than his subordinates. This method of organizing the executive power has justly been criticized on the ground that it introduces a division of responsibility and lack of co-ordination in the state administration. Thus, although the governor is charged with the execution of the laws, he usually has no power to direct the attorney-general to institute proceedings against a person or corporation for violating the law, as the President of the United States might do in a similar case. Again, he may have reason to believe that the state treasurer is a defaulter, but in most of the states he has no power to examine into the affairs of the treasurer's office, or to remove him from office. And so with the other principal officers that collectively make up the executive department. The responsibility of these officials is usually to the people alone, and responsibility in such cases cannot always be enforced, for they are elected for specific terms and cannot be removed before the expiration of their terms, except by the cumbersome method of impeachment.

The Lieutenant Governor.—In about two thirds of the states there are lieutenant governors chosen for the same time and in the same manner as the governor. About the only duty of this official is to preside over the deliberations of the senate. In case of a vacancy in the office of governor on account of death, resignation, or removal, or in case of his absence from the state, the lieutenant governor performs the duties of the office for the time being.

Executive Councils.—Three of the New England states (Massachusetts, Maine, and New Hampshire) have executive councils—survivals of colonial days—which share the executive power with the governor to a considerable extent. Their consent is necessary to the validity of many of his acts, such as the making of appointments, the granting of pardons, and the like. A modified form of the executive council is found in a few other states.

Other Executive Officers.—Besides the governor, who is the chief executive, there are in every state a number of state officers each in charge of a particular branch of the administrative service.

Secretary of State.—The first of these in rank is the secretary of state, who is the custodian of the state archives and of the great seal of the state; has charge of the publication and preservation of the laws; countersigns the proclamations and commissions issued by the governor and keeps a record of them; issues certificates of incorporation to companies incorporated under the laws of the state; and discharges other miscellaneous duties which vary in the different states. He is elected by the people in all the states except a very few where he is either appointed by the governor or chosen by the legislature.

The Treasurer of the state, as the name indicates, is the keeper of the public moneys, such as taxes, trust funds, and the like, and upon warrants issued by the auditor or other proper authority, he pays out money appropriated by the legislature. Everywhere he is elected by the people, usually for a short term, and is required to give a heavy bond so as to insure the state against loss in case of his carelessness or dishonesty. He is generally paid a salary, which is increased in some cases by the practice of treasurers depositing the state's money in banks from which they receive interest. The treasurer of a certain Western state received thousands of dollars a year in this way, until the legislature passed a law requiring him to turn into the state treasury all moneys received in the form of interest on state deposits.

Auditor.—Another financial officer found in all the states is the auditor or comptroller, whose duties, in general, are to audit the accounts of the state and issue warrants upon the treasurer for the payment of moneys which have been appropriated by the legislature. A warrant issued by the auditor is the treasurer's authority for paying money out of the treasury, and without such an order he has no lawful right to make a disbursement. Other duties of a miscellaneous character are imposed upon auditors in the different states.

Superintendent of Education.—Another important official is the superintendent or commissioner of public education, who has charge of the larger educational interests of the state. He supervises the administration of the school laws, distributes the school fund among the local districts, makes rules and regulations in regard to the holding of teachers' institutes, makes reports to the legislature concerning the educational conditions and needs of the state, and is frequently a member of the state board of education and of the boards of trustees of the state educational institutions.

Other Officers.—Besides the officials mentioned above, there are a multitude of other officers and employees in the larger states, such as the commissioner of agriculture, the commissioner of immigration, the commissioner of labor, state engineer, railroad commissioners, superintendent of public works, state printer, factory inspectors, pure food and dairy commissioners, state architect, land commissioner, mine inspectors, superintendents of insurance, and many others too numerous to mention. Of course, not every state has all these, but some of the more populous ones such as New York and Massachusetts have most of them and others in addition.

The Governor's Powers.—The powers and duties of governor may be roughly grouped into four classes: (1) his share in the making of the laws; (2) his power to execute the laws and administer the affairs of government; (3) his military power; and (4) his power to grant pardons for violations of the laws.

Legislative Powers.—*Power to Call Extra Sessions.*—Everywhere he is empowered to call the legislature together in extraordinary session. He uses this power in case of emergencies, and also to secure the enactment of needed legislation which has been overlooked or neglected by the legislature at the regular session. In New York recently, when the legislature adjourned without enacting a promised law against race track gambling, the legislature was summoned in extraordinary session and executive pressure and public opinion were brought to bear upon it to compel the enactment of the law. Sometimes a great catastrophe occurs when the legislature is not in session; for example, the California earthquake, the Cherry mine disaster in Illinois, and the Galveston storm, each of which required the immediate attention of the legislature. In order to prevent the legislature when in extraordinary session from taking action for which there is really no need, the constitutions of most states forbid it to consider any subjects not submitted to it by the governor; and in some states the length of an extra session is limited to thirty or sixty days.

LABORATORY FOR TESTING FOODS

ROAD MAKING, VIRGINIA

The Executive Message.—The governor is generally required to give the legislature information concerning the affairs of the state and to recommend the enactment of such laws as in his judgment the public good requires, the idea being that he is more familiar than any one else with the defects of the existing laws and with the legislative needs of the state. This information, with the accompanying recommendations, is communicated to the legislature in a message at the beginning of the session,[113] and is often followed by special messages from time to time recommending consideration of particular matters that may arise in the course of the session. The weight which the recommendations of the governor have with the legislature depends, of course, upon his influence with the members and his standing with the people. If he belongs to the same political party which is in control of the legislature, and the party is not divided, or if he is especially aggressive and is backed by a strong public opinion throughout the state, his recommendations carry more weight than they would under opposite conditions.

The Veto Power.—Finally, in every state except North Carolina the governor has the power to veto bills passed by the legislature. Owing to fear of executive tyranny, the veto power was generally withheld from governors for a considerable time after the Revolution; in fact, in only two states (Massachusetts and New Hampshire) was this power granted to the governor before the close of the eighteenth century. The worst fears of executive tyranny, however, proved to be without foundation, and the advantage of vesting in the hands of the governor the power to correct the mistakes of the legislature by refusing to approve objectionable laws soon came to be generally appreciated. Under the interpretation of the veto power the governor may refuse to sign a bill either because, in his judgment, it is inconsistent with the constitution which he has sworn to support, or because he thinks it unwise or inexpedient, in either case his judgment being conclusive. But manifestly, an absolute veto is too great a power to intrust to a single person, however wise he may be. The constitutions of all the states, accordingly, empower the legislature to override the veto of the governor by repassing the vetoed bill, in which case it goes into effect notwithstanding the executive objection. To do this, however, a majority of two thirds or three fifths of the members of the legislature is usually necessary, the idea being that the judgment of so large a proportion of the legislature ought to be allowed to prevail over that of the governor in case of a difference of opinion. In the few remaining states a bare majority of the members of the legislature may override the executive veto, though not infrequently the statement of objections by the governor in his veto message serves to convince some of those who voted for the vetoed bill that it is unwise, and thus the veto will be sustained. When a bill is presented to the governor for his signature he is allowed a period ranging from three to ten days in which to consider it before taking action. A subject of criticism in some states is the practice of the legislature of delaying final action on many bills until the last days of the session and then sending them all at once to the governor so that the time allowed him for considering their merits is necessarily too short.

A wise provision found in the constitutions of about thirty states is one which allows the governor to veto particular items in appropriation bills. Thus if the legislature passes a bill carrying appropriations for a variety of objects, some worthy and others objectionable, the governor is not under the necessity of approving or rejecting the bill as a whole, but may approve the desirable portions and veto the others. In this way wasteful and objectionable appropriations of the public funds may be prevented without inconvenience.

In a few states the governor may also veto particular sections of other bills.

Executive and Administrative Powers of the Governor.—The governor is generally charged by the constitution with taking care that the laws are faithfully executed, though, as already stated, the executive power is really divided between him and a number of colleagues.

Power over State Officers.—He generally has a certain power of oversight over the other principal state officers, but little power of control over them. There is a tendency, however, to enlarge his power in this respect.[14] Several constitutions, for example, empower him to require reports from the principal officers, and in some states he is given the right to examine into the condition of the treasurer's and comptroller's offices and under certain conditions to remove the incumbent from office. In a very few states, also, the governor may remove sheriffs or mayors for negligence or abuse of power in the enforcement of the state laws.

Power of Appointment.—The governor's principal executive power consists of the right to appoint certain officers and boards, and sometimes to remove them, subject to certain restrictions. In the early days of our history, many of the state officers were chosen by the legislature, but with the growth of the democratic spirit the selection of these officials was taken from the legislature and they were made elective by the people. In a very few states the legislature still retains a considerable power of appointment. In most states, however, the governor appoints all officers not elected by the people. In a few states he appoints the judges; in half a dozen or more he appoints several of the principal state officers, such as the secretary of state and the attorney-general, and in most of them he appoints some of the important administrative officers and the members of various boards and commissions. In New York, for example, he appoints the superintendent of insurance and banking, the members of the two public service commissions, the superintendent of public works, the commissioner of agriculture, the commissioner of health, and other important officials. In some states he appoints the railroad commissioners, the trustees of public institutions, members of the state board of health, the members of various examining boards, pure food commissioners, factory inspectors, game commissioners, mining inspectors, and so on. As compared with the President of the United States, his power of appointment, however, is very small. Moreover, his power to appoint is usually limited by the condition that his nominations must be approved by the senate or the executive council where there is such a body.

Power of Removal.—The governor can usually remove the officials whom he appoints, but rarely any others. But the power of removal must exist somewhere, because it would be intolerable to have to retain in the public service men who are dishonest, incapable, or otherwise unfit. The other methods of removal provided are impeachment, removal by resolution of the legislature, and occasionally removal by the courts. Removal by impeachment takes place by the preferment of a charge by the lower house of the legislature and trial by the upper house. This method, however, is cumbersome and is rarely resorted to—never in the case of minor officials. Removal by resolution of the legislature is sometimes employed for getting rid of unfit or corrupt judges. In several states, the method of recall has been instituted, by which, on petition of 25 per cent of the voters, the officer must submit his case to the voters, and if a majority of them pronounce in favor of his recall, he must retire.

The Military Powers of the Governor.—In every state the governor is commander in chief of the military forces of the state and also of the naval forces where there are any—a power which means little in times of peace. Whenever there are riots or serious disturbances, however, this power becomes important. When the disturbance is too great to be suppressed by the local authorities, the governor may order out a portion of the militia and may, if he elects, take charge of it himself. There are few states where the governor has not at some time or another been compelled to make use of this power. Mobs sometimes break into jails and take out prisoners and lynch them; and sometimes strike riots occur in mining or manufacturing communities, in which cases the governor may be called upon to send troops to the scene of the disturbance and keep them there until quiet and order have been restored.

Power to Suspend the Writ of Habeas Corpus.—A usual part of the governor's military power is the right to suspend the writ of habeas corpus in communities where great disorders prevail, that is, to suspend the power of the courts to release prisoners charged with violations of the law, thus leaving unhampered the power of the military authorities to restrain persons they may imprison. This power, however, is one which might be grossly abused; therefore many state constitutions forbid the suspension of the writ except under extraordinary conditions, and a few, indeed, permit it to be suspended only by the legislature.

The Military Forces of the State consist usually of a number of regiments of citizen soldiers, who are organized, uniformed, and officered after the manner of the regular army of the United States, who attend an annual encampment for purposes of drill and practice, and who must always be ready to respond to the call of the governor. At the head of the state militia is an officer called the adjutant general, through whom the military orders of the government are issued and carried out. The governor also has a military staff which accompanies him on occasions of ceremony such as the inauguration of the

President of the United States, grand army reviews, and the like.

The Pardoning Power.—In every state the governor is vested with the power of pardoning offenders against the laws of the state, but in most states the exercise of the power is subject to restrictions. The purpose of vesting this power in the governor is to make it possible to correct the errors of courts and juries, as where subsequent to the conviction evidence is brought to light showing that the person convicted is innocent, and has been wrongfully convicted, or where it becomes evident before the full penalty has been paid that the offender has been sufficiently punished and should be released.

In many states boards of pardon have been provided for sharing with the governor the responsibility for the exercise of this important prerogative.[15] These boards are of two kinds: first, those whose powers are limited to the hearing of applications for pardons and the making of recommendations to the governor, who is not bound by their advice; and second, those whose approval is necessary for the validity of any pardon granted by him. Convictions for treason and in impeachment cases are frequently excepted from the list of cases in which the governor may grant pardons, though in the case of treason he is sometimes given the power to suspend the execution of the sentence to await the action of the legislature. In a number of states notice of an application for a pardon must be published in the community where the applicant was convicted, in order that the people of the community who have been injured by his crime may have an opportunity to protest against the granting of a pardon to him. Sometimes also the approval of the presiding judge of the court in which the criminal was convicted is necessary before a pardon may be granted. It is usual to require the governor to make a report to the legislature at each session of all pardons granted, and at the same time give the reason in each case why a pardon was issued.

Generally with the right of pardon is included the power to grant reprieves, that is, stays of execution; commutations, that is, the substitution of a lesser punishment in the place of the one imposed; and remission of fines and forfeitures. The right also usually includes the power of amnesty or the power of granting by proclamation pardons to large numbers of persons, as in the case of uprisings or insurrections against the laws and authority of the state. A pardon may be absolute or conditional; in the first case, it is granted without restriction; in the second case, it is valid only on certain conditions, as where the offender is required to lead an upright life or where he is required to leave the state. Generally the governor of the state, unlike the President of the United States, has no power to grant a pardon to an individual offender before he has been convicted.

State Boards and Commissions.—One of the remarkable political tendencies of recent years has been the multiplication of boards and commissions to aid in the government of the states. Every state now has a number of such boards, and in some of the populous commonwealths such as New York and Massachusetts there are upwards of a hundred of them. Hardly a legislative session passes that does not create one or two commissions for some purpose or other. These boards or commissions fall roughly into five classes, as follows:

First, many of these boards are of an industrial character, such as boards of agriculture, food and dairy commissions, live stock, fish, and mining commissions, and the like. In general their purpose is to promote the agricultural, mining, and industrial interests, generally, of the state, through the collection and dissemination of information concerning the best method of conducting those industries.

A second class of boards are of a more distinctly scientific and research character, such as boards of health, bureaus of labor and statistics, geological commissions, forestry boards, and the like. Although some of these, like the board of health, are charged with the execution of certain laws, the general purpose of all of them is scientific research and the collection of data.

A third class of boards are those charged primarily with the supervision of certain businesses or industries affecting the public interest, and with the enforcement of the laws relating to such businesses. Such are the railroad commissions, commissions of insurance, public utility commissions, commissions of inland fisheries, and the like. In some instances these commissions not only have power to prescribe rules for businesses affected with a public interest, but also to fix the rates which they may charge.

A fourth group of commissions or boards are those charged with examining applicants for admission to practice certain professions or trades such as medicine, dentistry, pharmacy, architecture, and plumbing. The purpose of requiring such examinations is to secure a standard of efficiency, and to protect society against quacks.

A fifth class includes those which have supervision over the public institutions of the state, educational, penal, reformatory, charitable, etc. In recent years there has been a marked tendency to consolidate boards of this class, by putting all the charitable and penal institutions under the control of a single board, or under two boards, one for charitable and the other for penal institutions. In a few states all the higher educational institutions are under one board.

Members of all these classes of boards are usually appointed by the governor, though occasionally a board is made up of members chosen by popular election.

State Administrative Reorganization.—In 1917 a more systematic organization of state administration was established in Illinois. Nine main departments were established, each under a director, in place of a large number of former offices, boards, and commissions. Similar reorganizations have since taken place in a number of other states.

The State Civil Service System.—The number of persons necessary to carry on the state government in its various branches is very large. In order to provide a method by which subordinate employees can be selected with regard to their fitness rather than with reference to their party services, New York, Massachusetts, Illinois, Wisconsin, and other states have enacted civil service laws establishing the merit system of appointment.

The recent civil service laws provide, in general, for the classification of all positions other than those filled by popular election, by executive appointment, or by legislative choice, and for appointment to these positions only after an examination of the candidates. Generally, those who pass the examination successfully are placed on an eligible list in the order of the grades which they receive, and when an office is to be filled, the appointing officer is required to make his choice from the three candidates highest on the list. For the filling of certain positions requiring technical skill, special non-competitive examinations are given and less consideration is given to academic qualifications. Certain positions are not placed under the civil service rules, and the appointing authority is allowed to make his choice without the necessity of examinations. Such are the positions of private secretary, chief clerk, and other employees who occupy a confidential relation to the heads of departments.

The chief advantage of the examination system of filling civil service positions is that it eliminates the evils of the spoils system and places the public service on a merit basis. It must be admitted, however, that the system is not perfect, because fitness for the performance of administrative duties cannot always be determined by examinations. Nevertheless, it is much better than the old method known as the "spoils system," under which appointments were made for party services; and it will in time, no doubt, be adopted in all the states.

References.—BEARD, American Government and Politics, ch. xxiv. BRADFORD, Lessons of Popular Government, vol. ii, ch. 32. BRYCE, The American Commonwealth (abridged edition), ch. xl. DEALEY, Our State Constitutions, ch. v. FINLEY and SANDERSON, The American Executive and Executive Methods, chs. iii, vi, vii, viii, ix. HART, Actual

Government, ch. viii.

Documentary and Illustrative Material.—1. The legislative manual of the state. 2. Copies of the governor's inaugural address, messages to the legislature, veto messages, public proclamations, etc. 3. Copy of the revised statutes (chapter on the executive department). 4. Reports of the state officers to the governor.

1. What is the term of the governor of your state? the salary? Do you think the salary is adequate? What are the governor's qualifications? Compare the provisions of the present constitution with those of previous constitutions in regard to these matters. Is the governor eligible to succeed himself? Is it customary to reëlect the governor in your state? What, in your opinion, are the relative merits of a one-year term and a four-year term for the governor?

2. Suppose a question should arise as to who was really elected governor, what authority would determine the matter? Are there any circumstances under which the legislature may elect the governor? Is the governor of your state required to vacate his office immediately at the expiration of his term, or is he allowed to hold over until his successor has qualified?

3. Make a list of the names of the men who have held the office of governor of your state, indicating the years they served and the political parties to which they belonged. (This information can be obtained from the blue book or legislative manual or from some history of the state.)

4. Does the constitution of your state provide for a lieutenant governor? In general, what has been the type of men elected to this office?

5. Make a list (from the blue book) of the offices in your state that are filled by appointment by the governor. Do you think the appointive power of the governor ought to be enlarged? Mention some offices now filled by popular election which, in your opinion, should be filled by executive appointment.

6. May the governor of your state remove officers appointed by him? If so, under what conditions? May he remove any officers elected by the people? If he finds that the treasurer of the state has misappropriated a large amount of state money, can he remove him? May the governor of the state remove any local officers? Thus if the sheriff should allow a prisoner in his custody to be lynched by a mob or the mayor of a city should refuse to execute a state prohibition law, may the governor suspend or remove such officers for neglect of duty? If not, are there any means of punishing the negligent officer?

7. What were the principal recommendations in the message of the governor to the legislature at its last session?

8. May the governor of your state veto particular items in appropriation bills? May he sign a bill after the adjournment of the legislature? May he veto a bill upon grounds of public policy as well as upon grounds of unconstitutionality? How many bills were vetoed by the governor at the last session?

9. Is there a civil service law in your state? If so, to what offices and employments does it apply? How are appointments made under the law?

10. For what purposes and under what circumstances may the governor use the military forces in your state? Have there been any instances recently in which the militia was ordered out? What is meant by the governor's "staff"? Find out from the blue book how many regiments of the national guard there are in your state.

11. Are there any restrictions on the power of the governor to grant pardons? May he also grant reprieves and commutations? May he remit fines and forfeitures? May he grant amnesties? Is there a pardon board in your state? If so, how is it constituted and what are its powers? How many pardons have been granted by the present governor?

12. May the courts control the governor by issuing writs to compel him to do his duty or to restrain him from doing certain things? May he be arrested for wrongdoing? May he be compelled to give testimony in the courts? If not, why not? Is there any way by which an unworthy governor may be put out of office before the expiration of his term? Describe the procedure by which this is done.

CHAPTER VI

THE STATE JUDICIARY

Function of the Courts.—The legislature enacts the laws, the executive officers enforce them, the courts interpret their meaning and apply them to particular cases. The courts are also the instrumentalities through which the rights guaranteed us by the constitution and the laws are enforced. If your neighbor owes you a debt and refuses to pay, if you make a contract with some one and he refuses to perform the stipulations, if some one injures you in your person or property, in these and countless other instances you must look to the courts for protection or redress. They are the agencies for settling disputes among men, for enforcing contracts, for trying and punishing violations of the law, and for determining what our rights are when they are drawn in dispute.

Grades of Courts.—(1) *Justice of the Peace.*—At the bottom of the judicial system stand the courts of the justices of the peace, which have jurisdiction of civil cases involving small amounts, usually less than $150, and of petty offenses against the laws. On a level with these courts are certain municipal courts in the cities. The justice of the peace is a magistrate of ancient origin, and in reality his court is important since it is to this court that large numbers of persons resort for the settlement of their disputes. Too little attention is given to the choice of the men who fill this important office, and the result is that the court of the justice of the peace has long been and still is the weakest part of our judicial system. Generally there are several justices in every town or township. Usually they are elected by the people, though sometimes they are appointed. One of the sources of the evils connected with the system is that they are paid fees rather than salaries. This system of compensation often leads them to solicit business and sometimes to divide their fees with lawyers who bring cases to them for trial. They not only try petty civil and criminal cases, but they have the power to conduct preliminary examinations into more serious offenses in order to determine whether there is ground for holding the accused for trial. In case the justice thinks the evidence warrants the trial of the offender, he "binds" him over to await the action of the grand jury.

(2) *County Courts.*—Next above the court of the justice of the peace is, in some states, the county court, so called because its territorial jurisdiction embraces the entire county. This court has jurisdiction of civil cases involving large amounts and of more serious criminal cases. It also has the right to hear appeals from the justices of the peace.

(3) *Circuit Courts.*—Still higher in the judicial organization, in most states, are the courts whose territorial jurisdiction embraces a larger area of the state —usually a group of counties—and which are empowered to try any civil or criminal case without reference to the amount in controversy or the character of the offense. They are generally styled circuit courts, because the judge usually travels from county to county holding court in each county in the district or circuit. Sometimes, however, they are called district or superior courts, and in a few states "supreme" courts.

(4) *The Supreme Court.*—Finally, at the top of the judicial hierarchy is the supreme court, or court of appeals, as it is sometimes called. Unlike the other courts below, its jurisdiction embraces the whole state, and the judges are elected or appointed usually from the state at large. Unlike the other courts, moreover, instead of being held by a single judge, it is held by a bench of judges, the number ranging from three to nine in the different states. It has original jurisdiction in certain cases, but its most important function is that of hearing appeals from the decisions of the lower courts, and of deciding upon the constitutionality of the laws. In cases appealed to it from the lower courts, it has the final word of authority except where a federal question is involved, in which case an appeal may be taken to the United States Supreme Court.

Courts of a Special Character.—The justice's, circuit, and supreme courts are found in all the states, though sometimes designated by different names. In addition to these, however, we sometimes find other courts of a more or less special character.

Probate Courts.—Thus in many states there are separate probate courts for the settlement of the estates of deceased persons, for dealing with matters relating to wills and inheritances, and sometimes with matters affecting orphans and minors. They are occasionally called surrogate's or orphans' courts. In many states, however, there are no separate probate courts, the probate business being taken care of by the county court. In certain other states probate courts are separately provided only for the more populous counties.

Juvenile Courts.—Frequently in the more populous cities there are also juvenile courts for the trial of youthful offenders.

Equity Courts.—In a few states the distinction between law and equity is still maintained, and equity jurisdiction is intrusted to a distinct class of courts. Equity had its origin in the practice of the King of England in early times in granting relief to suitors who, owing to the deficiencies of the common law, could not obtain relief through the courts of law. In time all such petitions came to be addressed to an officer who stood very close to the king and who was called the chancellor. Out of this office there were ultimately evolved the chancery courts which administered justice, not according to the law, but according to a less technical body of rules called equity. Thus there came to be two bodies of rules according to which justice was administered, and two classes of courts through which it was done. The jurisdiction of equity courts included such matters as trusts, accounts, fraud, mistake or accident, and the like. Equity could also prevent wrongs, while law could only punish them.[16] Thus a court of equity could command a person to do something for the benefit of an injured person, or restrain him from committing an injury, while a court of law could only award him damages after the injury had been done —a remedy often worthless or inadequate. The English system of equity, like the common law, was transplanted to America, and both are still in force here except in so far as they have been modified by legislative acts. England, however, abolished the separate system of equity courts in 1873, and left the law courts to administer equity wherever it was applicable. Likewise, in the United States, separate equity courts have been done away with in all except five states, leaving the same courts to administer both law and equity.

The Judges of Courts.—*Qualifications.*—Generally no qualifications for the judicial office are prescribed by law, except in a few states where it is required that judges shall be lawyers or be "learned in the law." As a matter of fact, however, judges are nearly always lawyers, except in the case of justices of the peace and police magistrates, where extensive knowledge of the law is not essential.

Terms of Office.—The terms of the judges vary widely among the different states. In the early days of our history, the judges generally held their offices during good behavior or until the attainment of a certain age, usually sixty or seventy years. With the growth of democracy, however, most of the states came to adopt short terms for judicial as well as for other public officials. Only in Massachusetts and Rhode Island do the judges of the highest court now serve practically for life. In New Hampshire they serve until they are 70 years of age. Elsewhere the tenure varies from two years, in Vermont, to twenty-one years, in Pennsylvania. In Maryland, the tenure is fifteen years; in New York, fourteen; in several, it is twelve, in some nine, in many six. The advantage of a long term is that it enables the judges to acquire experience and renders them less affected by political influence and popular clamor.

Methods of Choosing the Judges.—In early times the judges were chosen either by the legislature or by the governor. Choice by the legislature was objectionable because it often resulted in selection by political caucuses and in a parceling of the judgeships among the different counties or sections of the state. Appointment by the governor was objectionable to many because it often resulted in the choice of political favorites. Most of the states, therefore, abandoned these methods of choice for popular election, Mississippi in 1832 being the first state to adopt this method. Only in Delaware, Connecticut, New Jersey, Massachusetts, New Hampshire, and Maine, are the higher judges now appointed by the governor,—subject to the confirmation of the state senate or the legislature,—and only in Rhode Island, Vermont, South Carolina, and Virginia are they elected by the legislature. In all the other states they are elected by the people.

The arguments in favor of popular election are that it is more in harmony with the principles of popular government, and, it is claimed by some, tends to secure a higher class of judges, thus doing away with the evils of executive appointment and of legislative choice described above. The objection to this method, however, is that it compels judicial candidates to engage in political contests, and by making their tenures dependent upon popular favor subjects them to the temptation of shaping their decisions to meet the approval of the people, who, obviously, are not always qualified to judge of the soundness of judicial decisions involving intricate questions of law. Such a method, it is claimed by some, tends to secure the election of able politicians rather than of able judges.

Compensation of the Judges.—The pay of the judges, like their terms of service, varies widely among the different states. The salary paid the judges of the highest court is not much more or less than the governor's salary. The highest salary paid in any state to the judges of the highest court is $13,700 per year, in the state of New York,[17] a salary about as large as that of the justices of the United States Supreme Court. In Illinois and a few other states, the justices of the supreme court receive $10,000 a year. Many states pay less than $5,000 a year. This scale of salaries is very low as compared with those in England, where the highest judges receive $25,000, and the lowest, the county judges, $7,500 a year. A few states have provided a system of pensions for their higher judges who have served a certain number of years or who have reached a certain age, after which they are allowed or compelled to retire, but this provision has not yet become general.

Trial of Civil Cases.—The cases brought before the courts for trial are of two general classes: (1) civil actions and (2) criminal actions. A civil action is a suit brought for the enforcement of a private right or to secure compensation for damages on account of injuries sustained through the violation of one's rights. Thus a creditor sues a debtor for refusing to pay a debt; an owner sues to recover property which has been wrongfully taken from him; a householder brings an action against his neighbor for trespassing upon his premises; and so on. The person who brings the action is called the *plaintiff*; the one against whom it is brought, the *defendant*; and the two together are known as the *parties* to the action.

Beginning of a Civil Case.—A civil suit is usually started by the filing of a complaint containing a statement of the facts, with the court, which then issues a summons directing the sheriff or constable to notify the defendant to appear and make answer. If the plaintiff is a creditor and has reason to believe that the defendant is preparing to dispose of his property with the intention of defrauding him, he may ask the court to issue a *writ of attachment* authorizing the sheriff to take possession of the property. Or if the defendant is in wrongful possession of property belonging to the plaintiff the latter may ask the court to issue a *writ of replevin* requiring the officers to seize the property and turn it over to the plaintiff. In both cases, however, the plaintiff is required to give a bond for the costs of the suit and for the return of the property in case the court should decide that it does not properly belong to him. The defendant now makes an answer or plea in which he denies the charges of the plaintiff as a whole or in part, or admits their truth but denies the right of action, or maintains that the court has no jurisdiction, or pleads something else in bar of the action. The complaint of the plaintiff and the answer of the defendant are known as the *pleadings*.

The Trial.—The issue is now joined and the case is ready for trial. If it is a suit in equity, it is tried by the judge alone without a jury. If it is a suit at law, either party may demand a jury, but if both parties agree to waive a jury trial, the case is tried by the judge alone. Frequently civil cases are tried without juries, the parties preferring to leave the decision to the judge. If, however, a jury trial is preferred, a list of qualified persons is prepared and from this list twelve persons, or six, as the parties may agree upon, are selected to try the case. After the jury is sworn the attorney for the plaintiff generally makes a statement of the facts upon which he rests his case. He then calls his witnesses, who testify to their knowledge of the facts as they are questioned by counsel. When the attorney for the plaintiff has completed the examination of each witness, the attorney for the defendant is allowed to cross-examine him. Witnesses are required to confine their testimony to what they know to be the truth, and are not permitted to tell what they believe to be true or what they have learned from mere hearsay.

After the plaintiff has introduced all his evidence, the defendant's case is presented in a like manner, the counsel for the plaintiff this time conducting the cross-examination. When the evidence for the defendant is all in, the plaintiff may introduce evidence in rebuttal, after which the defendant may do likewise. The next step is the argument of counsel. The attorney for each side addresses the jury and endeavors to convince it that the evidence sustains the facts which he has undertaken to prove. The burden of proof in civil cases is usually on the plaintiff, and his attorney generally has the privilege of closing the argument. If the plaintiff has failed to make out a case the judge may dismiss the suit without giving the case to the jury, or if the evidence is such as to admit of but one conclusion, the judge may direct the jury to return a verdict in accordance therewith. But if the evidence leaves the question as to the facts in doubt, the case is given to the jury and it alone can make the decision. Before sending the jury to their room the judge instructs them as to the law applicable to the case, but generally in this country he cannot comment on the weight of the evidence or express any opinion as to the facts. The jury, after receiving its instructions, retires from the court room and deliberates in secret. If, after a reasonable time, the jurymen cannot agree upon a verdict they so report to the judge and are discharged, and the trial must be gone through with again.

Judgment; Execution.—After the return of the verdict, the judge enters judgment in accordance therewith. In most civil cases the judgment, if for the plaintiff, requires the defendant to pay him a certain sum of money as a compensation for the damages he has sustained. If he refuses to pay, an "execution" is issued, that is, the sheriff is required to seize and sell a sufficient amount of the defendant's property to satisfy the judgment. If the suit is one in equity the "decree," as the decision is called, is not usually for the payment of damages but is a command to the defendant to do a specific thing, as, for example, to carry out a contract or to pay a debt; or to refrain from doing something, such as maintaining a nuisance to the injury of the defendant.

Appeal.—After the verdict has been rendered, the losing party may generally take an appeal to a higher court on the ground that errors were committed by the judge in the course of the trial, as, for example, the admission of improper evidence or the exclusion of proper evidence; or because the verdict was contrary to the law and the evidence. The higher court either affirms the judgment of the lower court or reverses it. If it affirms the judgment, it must then be carried out; if it reverses the judgment a new trial is granted and the whole procedure is gone through again.

Trial of Criminal Cases.—Criminal actions, unlike civil actions, are brought, not by the injured party, but by the state whose peace and dignity have been violated by the act complained of. The officer who brings the action in the name of the state is called the *prosecuting attorney*, the *district attorney*, or the *state's attorney*. He conducts preliminary investigations into crimes and presents cases to the grand jury for indictment. If the grand jury returns the indictment, that is, decides that the accused shall be held for trial, the prosecuting officer takes charge of the case and conducts it for the state.

The Arrest.—Usually the first step in the trial of a person charged with crime is to cause his arrest. The person injured, or any one else who may have knowledge of the crime, appears before a magistrate and makes a complaint setting forth the facts in regard to the crime. If the magistrate is satisfied as to the truth of the complaint, he issues a warrant commanding the sheriff or some other police officer to arrest the accused. The warrant must particularly describe the offense, the place where committed, and the circumstances under which it was committed, and must give the name of the person to be arrested. But in some cases an arrest may be made without a warrant, as when an offender is seen committing a crime or when an officer has good reason to believe that the person who is charged with committing a crime is the guilty person. In practice, policemen frequently arrest on mere suspicion, and if they do so in good faith they will rarely be held liable for damages. Any private individual, as well as an officer, may arrest without warrant a person whom he sees committing a crime. He may also arrest a person whom he suspects of having committed a capital crime, although without personal knowledge of his guilt.[18]

Commitment.—When arrested the accused is brought before a justice of the peace and examined. If the justice of the peace, after such examination, believes that the accused should be held for trial, he is committed to jail. If the offense is a minor one it can be tried by the justice of the peace. If it is a more serious crime the justice of the peace can hold the offender to await the action of the grand jury.

Habeas Corpus Proceedings.—If at any time it is alleged that a person is unlawfully deprived of his liberty, a judge may issue a writ of habeas corpus and inquire into the case. In this way an accused person may be set free if there is no sufficient reason for holding him.

Bail.—If the offense is not a capital one, the accused can secure his release from the jail while awaiting trial by giving bail. That is, he can get one or more persons to obligate themselves to pay to the state a certain sum of money should he fail to appear for the trial at the time set. Such persons are called sureties, and they have a certain power of control over the accused as a means of insuring his appearance for the trial. The constitutions of all the states allow the privilege of bail except in capital cases, and they all declare that the amount of bail required shall not be excessive, that is, shall not be more than is sufficient to insure the appearance of the accused for trial. What this amount is must be determined by the judge according to his own discretion, due regard being paid to the gravity of the offense, the nature of the punishment, and the wealth of the defendant or his friends. If the offender has been bound over to await the action of the grand jury, the next step in the proceedings is the indictment.

The Grand Jury is one of the ancient institutions of the common law. The number of persons constituting the grand jury was originally twenty-three, but many of the states have changed this, a common number being fifteen. The grand jury is chosen by lot from a carefully prepared list of persons in the county, qualified to serve. The members are sworn in on the first day of the term of court and are then "charged" by the judge to make a diligent inquiry into all cases of crime that have been committed in the county, and to return indictments against such persons as in their opinion should be held for trial. They then retire to their room and conduct their investigations in secret.

The Indictment.—It must be remembered that the procedure of a grand jury is not in the nature of a trial of the accused; it is only an inquiry to ascertain whether there is sufficient evidence of guilt to warrant his being put on trial. In conducting this investigation, the grand jury hears only one side of the case, that of the prosecution, neither the accused or his witnesses being heard. The prosecuting attorney attends the sessions of the grand jury and aids it in the conduct of its inquiries. He prepares the indictment and it is often upon his recommendation that the grand jury decides to indict or not to indict. In some states the procedure of indictment by grand jury for all offenses, or for all except the most serious ones, has been done away with, the accusation taking the form of an "information" filed by the prosecuting attorney. One of the reasons given for abolishing the grand jury is that it is often a source of delay since it can be called only when the court is in session, and in some communities the court is not in session for long periods in every year.

The Arraignment.—After the accused has been indicted the next step is to bring him before the court and arraign him. The charge is first read to him and he is directed to plead. If he pleads guilty, no further action is taken and the judge imposes the sentence. If he pleads not guilty, the trial proceeds. If he has no counsel to defend him, the court appoints some member of the local bar to act as his attorney, and the lawyer so designated is under a professional obligation to undertake the defense and do all in his power to clear him. In this way the murderer of President McKinley was enabled to have the benefit of counsel. Many writers on criminal law, indeed, contend that the state ought to employ regular public defenders for accused persons just as it employs public prosecutors, since it should be equally interested in seeing an innocent man acquitted as in seeing a guilty one convicted.[19]

Selection of the Jury.—The next step is the impaneling of a jury of twelve persons to try the case. The law requires that the jury shall be selected from the community in which the offense was committed, in order that the accused may have the benefit of any good reputation which he may enjoy among his neighbors. The jury is chosen by lot from a list of persons qualified to perform jury service, and the jurymen are sworn to return a verdict according to the law and the evidence. Each side is allowed to "challenge," that is, ask the court to reject, any juror who has formed an opinion of the guilt or innocence of the accused or who is evidently prejudiced. In addition, each may reject a certain number of jurors "peremptorily," that is, without assigning a cause.

The Trial.—After the jury has been impaneled, the prosecuting attorney opens the trial by reciting the facts of the case and stating the evidence upon which he expects to establish the guilt of the accused, for the law presumes the prisoner to be innocent, and the burden of proof to show the contrary rests upon the state. The procedure of examining and cross-examining the witnesses is substantially the same as in the trial of civil cases. There are well-established rules in regard to the admissibility of evidence and the weight to be attached to it, and if the judge commits an error in admitting improper evidence or in excluding evidence that should have been admitted in the interests of the accused, the prisoner may, if convicted, have the verdict set aside by a higher court and a new trial granted him. One of the rules of procedure is that the jury must be satisfied beyond a reasonable doubt, from the evidence produced, that the accused is guilty.

Verdict; Sentence.—After being charged by the judge as to the law applicable to the case, the jury retire to a room where they are kept in close confinement until they reach a unanimous verdict. If they cannot reach an agreement, they notify the judge, who, if satisfied that there is no longer any possibility of an agreement, discharges them; then the accused may be tried again before another jury. If a verdict of not guilty is returned, the court orders the prisoner to be set free; if a conviction is found, sentence is imposed and the punishment must be carried out by the sheriff or some other officer. The usual punishment is fine, imprisonment in the county jail or state penitentiary, or death inflicted by hanging or electrocution. In a few states, notably Maine, Michigan, Wisconsin, Rhode Island, and Kansas, punishment by death has been abolished.

Probation; Reformation.—Imprisonment is generally for a specified period, though recently in a number of states the indeterminate sentence has been provided, that is, the judge is allowed to sentence the offender for an indefinite period, the length of which will depend upon the behavior of the prisoner and on the promise which he may show of leading a better life after being released. When thus released he may be placed on probation and required to report from time to time to a probation officer in order to show that his conduct is satisfactory. If unsatisfactory, he may be taken up and remanded to prison. The tendency now in all enlightened countries is to adopt a system of punishment that will not only serve as a deterrent to crime but at the same time help to reform the criminal and make a better citizen of him. The old idea that the purpose of punishment was revenge or retribution has nearly everywhere disappeared, and in place of the severities of the old criminal code we have introduced humane and modern methods which are probably just as effective in deterring others from wrongdoing, and besides conduce to the reformation of many unfortunate criminals.

References.—BALDWIN, The American Judiciary, chs. viii, xii, xiv, xv, xvii, xxii. BEARD, American Government and Politics, ch. xxvi. BRYCE, The American Commonwealth (abridged edition), ch. xli. HART, Actual Government, ch. ix. McCLEARY, Studies in Civics, chs. ii, vii. WILLOUGHBY, Rights and Duties of Citizenship, ch. vii.

Illustrative Material.—1. The legislative manual or blue book of the state. 2. A map showing the division of the state into judicial districts. 3. Copies of legal instruments, such as warrants of arrest, indictments, subpœnas, summonses, etc.

RESEARCH QUESTIONS

1. What are the several grades of courts in your state? In what judicial district or circuit do you live? Who is the judge for that district or circuit?

2. What are the terms of the supreme court justices? The circuit or district judges? The county judges? Do you think these terms are too short? Would a good behavior term be better?

3. What is the pay of judges in your state? Do you think these salaries are large enough to attract the best lawyers of the state? Are the salaries fixed by the constitution or by act of the legislature?

4. How are the judges chosen? Has the existing method given satisfaction? Do you think judges should engage in politics? Where they are chosen by popular election, should they canvass the district or state as other candidates do?

5. Are there separate chancery (equity) courts in your state? separate probate courts? separate juvenile courts? If not, what courts have jurisdiction of such matters as belong to such courts?

6. How are justices of the peace in your state chosen? What is the extent of their jurisdiction in civil cases? in criminal cases? What is the method of compensating justices of the peace?

7. How often is the circuit court held in your district? How often the county court?

8. How are juries selected in your state? How could a better class of jurors be selected? Do the good citizens show a disposition to shirk jury duty? What are the merits and demerits of the jury system? Do you think a unanimous verdict ought to be required in criminal cases?

9. Is the grand jury retained in your state for making indictments? If not, how are indictments prepared? What is the difference between an indictment and an information?

10. Why are citizens never justified in resorting to lynch law even when there is a flagrant miscarriage of justice? Has there ever been a case of lynching in your county?

11. What are some of the causes for the "delays of the law"? How could delays be shortened and the trial of cases made more prompt?

12. What are the qualities of a good judge? Upon whom are the rights of the people most dependent, the executive officers or the judges?

CHAPTER VII

SUFFRAGE AND ELECTIONS

Nature of the Elective Franchise.—The right of suffrage, that is, the right to take part in the choice of public officials, is sometimes said to be a natural and inherent right of the citizen, but in practice no state acts upon such a principle. The better opinion, as well as the almost universal practice, is that suffrage is not at all a matter of right, but a privilege bestowed by the state upon those of its citizens who are qualified to exercise it intelligently and for the public good. No state allows all its citizens to vote; all the states restrict the privilege to those who are at least twenty-one years of age; all confine the privilege to those who are *bona fide* residents of the community; and some require educational, property, and other qualifications of various kinds. On the other hand, eight states allow aliens who have formally declared their intention of becoming citizens, to vote equally with citizens in all elections.[20] The terms "voter" and "citizen," therefore, are not identical or synonymous.

Existing Qualifications for Voting.—In the early days of our history restrictions on the voting privilege were much more numerous and stringent than now. Most of the early constitutions limited the privilege to property owners, and some prescribed religious tests in addition. It is estimated that at the beginning of the nineteenth century not more than one person in twenty had the right to vote, whereas now probably the proportion is two in five.

Federal Restriction.—In the United States the power to prescribe the qualifications for voting in both national and state elections belongs to the individual states, subject only to two provisions: in fixing the suffrage they cannot abridge the privilege (1) on account of race, color, or previous condition of servitude, or (2) on account of sex. The first provision is found in the Fifteenth Amendment to the Federal Constitution, adopted in 1870, and its purpose was to prevent the states from denying the privilege of suffrage to negroes who by the Fourteenth Amendment, adopted in 1868, had been made citizens of the United States. The second provision is in the Nineteenth Amendment adopted in 1920. These provisions do not, however, prevent the states from limiting the privilege on other grounds, such as illiteracy, criminality, vagrancy, nonpayment of taxes, and the like.

The Residence Requirement.—In the first place, all the states require residence for a specified period in the state and in the election district in which the voter exercises his privilege of voting. The purpose of this requirement is to confine the franchise to those who have become identified with the interests of the community, and to exclude outsiders or newcomers who are unfamiliar with local conditions and unacquainted with the qualifications of the candidates. The required length of residence in the state ranges from three months in Maine to two years in most of the Southern states, the more usual requirement being one year. The period of residence required in the county or election district is shorter, the most common requirement being three months in the county and one month in the election district.

Educational Tests.—In addition to this requirement, nearly one third of the states insist upon some kind of educational test. Connecticut in 1855 was the first state to require ability to read and write. Massachusetts followed her example shortly thereafter, and the precedent set by these two states was soon followed, with modifications, by California, Maine, Wyoming, New Hampshire, Delaware, and Washington.

The adoption of the Fifteenth Amendment in 1870, which indirectly conferred the right to vote on the negro race, and the unfortunate results which followed the enfranchisement of the large mass of blacks in the South, led some of the Southern states to adopt educational and other restrictions to diminish the evils of an ignorant suffrage. Mississippi in 1890 took the initiative, and required ability either to read the constitution of the state or to understand it when read by an election officer. South Carolina followed her example in 1895, but with the modification that an illiterate person who was the owner of at least $300 worth of property should not be disfranchised. Louisiana, Alabama, North Carolina, Virginia, Oklahoma, and Georgia followed with restrictions based on similar principles. In several of these states, however, the educational qualification does not apply to those who were voters in 1867 (when the negro race was still unenfranchised), or to their descendants, or to those who served in the army or navy during the Civil War. But in 1915 the Supreme Court of the United States decided, in the case of Oklahoma, that these so-called "grandfather" provisions were unconstitutional.

Other Persons Excluded.—Most of the states deny the right to vote to convicted criminals, idiots, and insane persons; some, particularly those of the South, insist that the voter must have paid his taxes; some exclude vagrants, paupers, and inmates of public institutions.

Woman Suffrage.—For a long time women everywhere were denied the right to vote, even long after their civil disabilities had been removed. The principal arguments advanced by the opponents of woman suffrage were: that active participation of women in political affairs would tend to destroy their feminine qualities by forcing them into political campaigns, and thus causing them to neglect their children; that it would tend to introduce discord into family life by setting husband against wife on political issues; that since women are incapable of discharging all the obligations of citizenship, such as serving in the army, militia, or police, they ought not to have all the privileges of citizenship; that a majority of the women did not desire the privilege of voting; and that men could be trusted to care for the interests of the whole family.

VOTER CASTING A BALLOT

WOMAN SUFFRAGE PARADE, WASHINGTON, D.C., MARCH 3, 1913

Arguments in Favor of Woman Suffrage.—In favor of giving the ballot to women, it was argued that differences of sex do not constitute a logical or rational ground for granting or withholding the suffrage if the citizen is otherwise qualified; that women should be given the ballot for their own self-protection against unjust class legislation; that since millions of them had become wage earners and were competing with men in nearly every trade and occupation and in many of the learned professions, the argument that the wage earner should have the ballot as a means of defense applied equally to women as to men; that since the old civil disabilities to which they were formerly subject, such as the inability to own real estate, enter into contracts, and engage in learned professions had been removed, it followed logically that their political disabilities should be removed also; and that since many of them had become property owners and taxpayers it was unjust to permit the shiftless nontaxpaying male citizen to take part in choosing public officials and at the same time deny the right to women taxpayers. Moreover, it was argued that the admission of women to a share in the management of public affairs would elevate the tone of politics and conduce to better government. Women are vitally interested in such matters as taxation, education, sanitation, labor legislation, pure food laws, and better housing conditions in the cities, and it was maintained that in those states where they had been given the right to vote they had been instrumental in securing wise legislation on many of these subjects. Finally, it was argued, the fact that some women do not care for the privilege is no reason why it should be denied to those who do desire it.

The Enfranchisement of Women..—These arguments in favor of suffrage for women gradually made a strong appeal to the men and one state after another conferred a limited suffrage on women citizens. At first they were allowed to vote in school elections, or in municipal elections, or on proposed bond issues (if they were taxpayers). From this it was a short step to equal suffrage with men in all elections and by 1920 there were some sixteen states in which this right had been conferred upon women. In the meantime various foreign countries, including England and even Germany, had granted the full right of suffrage to women. After long agitation on the part of American women, Congress in 1919 submitted to the state legislatures an amendment to the Federal Constitution providing for full woman suffrage in all the states, and this nineteenth amendment was ratified in 1920.

The Duty to Vote.—The better opinion is that the exercise of the suffrage is not only a high privilege conferred by the state on a select class of its citizens, but is a duty as well. Among the great dangers of popular government are indifference and apathy of the voters. If popular government is to be a success, we must have not only an intelligent and honest electorate but also one which is wide-awake and vigilant. Under a democratic system of government like ours, the character of the government is largely what the voters make of it. If we are to have capable and honest officials to enact laws and enforce them, the voters must see to it that such men are nominated and elected and compelled by the pressure of a vigorous and alert public opinion to the faithful performance of their duties. Every voter should inform himself as to the qualifications of candidates for office and as to the merits of policies upon which he is called to express an opinion, and having done this, he ought to go to the polls and contribute his share to the election of good men and the adoption of wise public measures.

Compulsory Voting.—The question has sometimes been discussed as to whether one who possesses the privilege of voting ought not to be legally required to exercise it just as the citizen is compelled to serve on the jury or in the militia. Several European countries, notably Belgium and Spain, have adopted a system of compulsory suffrage under which failure to vote is punishable by disfranchisement, an increase of taxes, publication of the name of the negligent voter as a mark of censure, etc. But however reprehensible the conduct of the citizen who neglects his civic obligations and duties as a member of society, it is hardly the province of the state to punish the nonperformance of such a duty. Moreover, if required by law the duty might be exercised as a mere form and without regard to the public good. Better results are likely to be obtained by treating it as a moral duty and a privilege rather than a legal obligation. But public opinion ought to condemn the citizen who without good cause neglects his obligations to society, one of which is the duty to take part in the election of those who are responsible for the government of the country.

The Registration Requirement.—Nearly all of the states now require as a preliminary condition to the exercise of the suffrage that the voter shall be "registered," that is, that he shall have his name entered on a list containing the names of all qualified voters in the election district who are entitled to take part in the election. The purpose of this requirement is to prevent double voting and other abuses of the electoral privilege. In densely populated districts it is impossible for the election judges to know personally all the voters, and hence without some means of identifying them it would be difficult to prevent persons outside the district from taking part in the election or to prevent those properly qualified from voting more than once. In a few communities, however, the old prejudice against such a requirement still prevails; for example, the constitution of Arkansas declares that registration shall not be required as a condition to the exercise of the elective franchise.

Methods of Registration.—Two general types of registration requirements are now in existence. One is the requirement that the voter shall present himself in person before the board of registration prior to each election and get his name on the list. The chief objection to this requirement is that it constitutes something of a burden to the voter and often disfranchises him on account of his negligence or inability to register on the day prescribed.

The other type of registration requirement is in force in Massachusetts, Pennsylvania, and many other states. Where this system prevails, when the voter's name is placed on the registration list, it is kept there so long as he remains in the district, and it is unnecessary for him to register each year. The principal criticism of this plan is that the registration list is less likely to be correct, because the names of persons who have died or moved away are likely to be kept on the list; whereas under the other method they would be stricken off.

Time of Holding Elections.—National elections for the choice of President and Vice President are held on the Tuesday after the first Monday in November every four years. Elections for representatives in Congress are held on the same date, in most states, every second year. Elections for state officers are generally held on the same day as national elections, though where state officers are chosen annually, state elections of course come oftener. A few states, however, prefer to hold their elections at a different date from that on which national elections are held. Four states, Kentucky, Maryland, Massachusetts, and Virginia, hold theirs in the odd years, while national elections always occur in the even-numbered years. A few others which have their elections in the even-numbered years hold them at a different time of the year from that at which national elections are held. Thus Arkansas and Maine hold their state elections in September, Georgia holds her election in October, and Louisiana holds hers in April.

In many of the states an attempt is made to separate national and state elections from municipal elections in order to encourage the voters to select municipal officers without reference to state or national issues. Thus in New York, where national and state elections occur biennially in the even-numbered years, city elections are held in the odd-numbered years. Likewise, in Illinois, city elections are held in April, while state and national elections are held in November. So, too, in some states judicial elections are held at a different date from other elections, in order to minimize the influence of party politics in the selection of judges.

Other local elections—township, county, and village—are held in some cases at the same time as the state election, and in other cases such elections, or some of them, are held on different days.

Manner of Holding Elections.—Before an election can be held, due notice must be given of the time and place at which it is to be held and the offices to be filled or the questions of public policy to be submitted to the voters. For the convenience of the voters the county or city is divided into districts or precincts each containing a comparatively small number of voters, and for each district there is provided a polling place with the necessary number of booths, ballot boxes, and other election paraphernalia. The responsibility for preparing the ballots, giving notice of the election, and providing the necessary supplies is intrusted to certain designated officials. Sometimes the county clerk, sometimes the city clerk, and sometimes, as in the large cities, a board of election commissioners, performs these duties.

Election Officers.—At each polling place, on election day, there is a corps of election judges or inspectors, poll clerks, ballot clerks, and the like. Each party is allowed to have one or more watchers, and frequently there is a police official to maintain order at the polls. While the polls are open, electioneering within a certain number of feet of the election place is forbidden, and usually no person except the election officers, the watchers, and the person who is casting his ballot are allowed in the polling room. Every polling place is equipped with one or more voting booths which must be so constructed as to insure secrecy on the part of the voter while he is marking his ballot. The polls are opened at a designated hour, and before the balloting begins the ballot boxes must be opened and exhibited to show that they are empty, after which they are locked and the casting of the ballots begins.

Evolution of the Ballot.—In the early days of our history, voting was by *viva voce*, that is, by living voice. Each voter as he appeared at the polling place was asked to state the names of the candidates for whom he desired to vote, and this he did in a distinct voice that could be heard by the bystanders as well as the election officials. The obvious objection to such a method was that it did not secure secrecy, and moreover it stimulated bribery because it was easy for a person who purchased a vote to see that the vote was delivered as paid for. The states soon began to experiment with the method of voting by ballot, and the advantages were so evident that in time this method was adopted in all of them, the last state to abandon the old method being Kentucky in 1891.

At first written ballots were generally used; then it became the practice for each candidate to print his own ballots; and later each party would put on the same ballot the names of all the party candidates and have them printed at the expense of the party. Each of these methods had its disadvantages. When the last method prevailed, for example, the ballots of the different parties were printed on different colored paper, so that it was easy to ascertain a voter's intentions by the color of the ballot in his possession. These ballots were distributed days before the election and were frequently marked by the voter before going to the polls. Such a system not only made secret voting difficult, but it afforded abundant opportunities for using undue influence over certain classes of persons to compel them to vote for particular candidates. To remove these and other evils which increased as time passed, the Australian ballot system, with modifications, was introduced into this country, first by the state of Massachusetts in 1888, and in one form or another it is now found in practically all the states.

The Australian Ballot.—The distinguishing features of the Australian system are the following: The names of all the candidates of every political party are placed on a single ballot; this ballot is printed at public expense and not by the candidates or parties; no ballots are distributed before the election, and none are obtainable anywhere except at the polls on election day, and then only when the voter presents himself to vote; and the ballot can be marked only in voting booths provided for the purpose, and in absolute secrecy.

The Australian system has been more or less modified in all the states where it has been introduced, so that it really does not exist in its pure form anywhere in this country, the nearest approach to it being the Massachusetts system. The prevailing forms may be reduced to two general types: the "office column" type, of which the Massachusetts ballot is a good example; and the "party column" type found in Indiana and many other states.

The "Office Column" Ballot has the names of the candidates for each office arranged in alphabetical order under the title of the office, and to vote such a ballot it is necessary for the voter to look through each column, pick out the candidate he favors, and mark a cross in a blank space opposite each name for which he votes. To do this requires not only considerable time, but a certain amount of intelligence and discrimination.

OFFICE COLUMN BALLOT
PART OF MASSACHUSETTS BALLOT OF NOVEMBER, 1908

PARTY COLUMN BALLOT
PART OF INDIANA BALLOT OF NOVEMBER, 1908

The "Party Column" Ballot arranges the candidates, not under the offices which they are seeking, but in parallel columns according to political parties, there being a column for each party. Opposite each candidate's name on the "party column" ballot is a blank space, and at the head of each column is a circle and usually a device or emblem to indicate the party. By making a mark in this circle the voter may cast a ballot for all the candidates of the party. This is called "straight" voting. He may if he wishes, however, vote a "split" ticket by putting a cross in the blank spaces opposite the names of candidates of his choice in the different columns. The chief objection that has been urged against this type of ballot is that by making it so easy to vote a "straight" ticket, it encourages strict party voting, whereas independent voting, especially in city elections, should be encouraged by every possible means.

The "office column" ballot, on the other hand, encourages independent voting by making it just as difficult to vote a "straight" ticket as a "split" one. In Massachusetts there has been a remarkable amount of independent voting, due partly to the form of ballot used. The "office column" type of ballot is now used for all elections in about one fourth of the states, and in a number of others for municipal elections.

Ballot Reform.—In recent years there has been considerable discussion of the subject of ballot reform, and not a little experimenting with different schemes. Political reformers generally demand the abolition of the "party column" form, or at least the abolition of the party circle, as a means of discouraging straight party voting, but the professional politicians insist upon its retention. Whatever may be the form ultimately adopted, one reform is desirable, namely, greater simplification, to the end that the electoral franchise may be exercised more intelligently and easily. In some of our states the number of elective offices has increased to such proportions, and the ballot to such size, that it has become a real burden to vote it.

A ballot used in Chicago in 1906 contained the names of over 330 candidates and was over two feet in length and nearly two feet in width. From this bewildering array of names the voter was compelled to pick out his choice for the following offices: state treasurer, state superintendent of public education, trustees of the University of Illinois, representative in Congress, state senator, representative in the state assembly, sheriff, county treasurer, county clerk, clerk of the circuit court, county superintendent of schools, judge of the county court, judge of the probate court, members of the board of assessors, judges of the municipal court for the two-year term (nine to be elected), members of the board of review, president of the board of county commissioners, county commissioners (ten to be elected on general ticket), trustees of the sanitary district of Chicago (three to be elected), clerk of the municipal court, chief justice of the municipal court, judges of the municipal court (nine to be elected), judges of the municipal court for the four-year term (nine to be elected). In Oregon in the election of 1912 the ballot contained the names of 177 candidates and 37 laws and amendments.

To vote ballots containing many names requires a good deal of care, if not experience, to avoid error which will result in having it thrown out, for the regulations governing the marking of the ballot are very strict and must be observed if the vote is to be counted. Accordingly, elaborate instructions covering large sheets are posted throughout the election district and at the polls for the guidance of the voters, and these have to be carefully studied by inexperienced voters who desire to avoid mistakes. Sample ballots also may be provided for practice. One result of the increasing complexity of the ballot is to give an undesirable advantage to the professional politicians who understand how to vote such ballots, and to discourage those who are not politicians.

Voting Machines.—A few states have adopted voting machines, especially for their large cities. These are so arranged that the voter may, by going into a booth and pulling a number of knobs, register his vote quickly and without the danger of spoiling his ballot. When the polls are closed the results are already recorded on a dial, and the long delay in counting the returns is eliminated. The chief objection to the voting machine, however, is the expense, and this has prevented its more general adoption.

Formalities of Voting.—When the voter presents himself at the polls[21] he must announce his name and address to the election officials. If his name is found on the registration list, he is given a ballot and his name entered on the poll book. He then enters a booth, where he marks his ballot, for which purpose he is allowed to remain therein not exceeding a certain length of time. He must not mark his ballot in such a way that it can be identified after it has been placed in the ballot box, and no erasures are allowed. If he spoils his ballot he will be given another, and if he is physically unable to mark it, or if, in some states, he is illiterate, he will be allowed the assistance of two persons representing different political parties. His right to vote may be challenged, in which case he will be required to identify himself or "swear in" his ballot, a record of which must be duly kept. When he has marked his ballot he must fold it in such a manner as to conceal its face, and hand it to one of the election judges, who announces the name of the voter; the fact of his voting is recorded, and the ballot placed in the box.

At a certain hour prescribed by law the polls are closed, after which the votes are counted; and when this task is complete the returns are announced. Generally the ballots must be preserved for several months in order that an opportunity may be offered for a recount in case the election is contested. Usually the ballots cannot be reopened and recounted except by order of a court or of the committee on elections of the legislature.

Legislation Against Fraudulent Voting; Corrupt Practices Acts.—For a long time in this country there was little legislation designed to regulate the conduct of elections and to protect the exercise of the electoral privilege against fraud. The principal evils of the old system were: lack of secrecy in voting; the use of separate ballots printed by the candidates or their party organizations; the distribution of these ballots before election day; lack of means for identifying the voters; bribery, intimidation, treating, and the use of other objectionable means for influencing voters; "repeating"; ballot box "stuffing"; and the like. To eliminate or diminish these and other evils, practically all the states have passed laws of one kind or another. They are generally known as corrupt practices acts and are, for the most part, based on the English law of 1883. Much of this legislation is detailed and complex, and some of it is still in the experimental stage.

The corrupt use of money in elections has come to be one of the greatest political evils of our time. The buying of votes is a very common practice in some communities, and unfortunately is not as strongly condemned by public opinion as it should be. Some 50 per cent of the voters in one county of Ohio were disfranchised by the court for selling their votes in the general election of 1910. The growth of great corporations, many of which desire legislation in their interest, or immunity from unfavorable laws, has introduced a more or less corrupting element in our political life. Some states have enacted laws forbidding corporations, under heavy penalties, from making contributions to the campaign funds of political parties. Others have forbidden the practice of political committees of assessing office holders for campaign purposes. Some have gone to the length of forbidding "treating" and other similar means of influencing voters. Some limit the amount of money that may be spent by a candidate or his friends in the conduct of his campaign, usually specifying the purposes for which expenditures may be made. Thus the Connecticut and New York laws allow expenditures only for such matters as the rent of halls, compensation of speakers and musicians, fireworks, printing, lithographs, advertisements, traveling expenses, postage, telegrams, hiring of carriages to take voters to the polls, and the like. A few, however, prohibit the hiring of carriages, and some forbid the giving away of liquor at elections. Some states require candidates to make sworn itemized statements of the expenditures incurred by them on account of the election, and some fix the maximum amount that may be expended. Thus in New York a candidate for governor may expend only $10,000 on account of his candidacy; candidates for other state officers are permitted to spend $6,000. The need of limitations was illustrated by the fact that the Democratic candidate for governor of New York in 1906 spent over $256,000 in the prosecution of his candidacy, and a candidate for state senator spent $30,000 to secure an election.[22] A recent candidate for the United States senate in a Western state admitted that his aggregate expenses were $107,000, and another testified that he spent

$115,000 in the effort to secure an election.

State Contributions to Party Campaign Funds.—In the belief that the state ought to bear a part of the candidate's expenses, to the end that the poor office seeker may be more nearly on an equal footing with the candidate of means, Colorado recently passed a law providing that the state should contribute to the campaign fund of each political party a sum of money equal in amount to twenty-five cents for every vote cast by the party for governor at the preceding election. The law allowed the candidates themselves to spend their own money to aid in their election, but prohibited other persons or corporations from making contributions. In short, the expense was to be borne by the state and the candidate alone. This Colorado law, however, was declared unconstitutional by the state courts.

Other Restrictions.—In some states also the expenditures of party committees are limited, and such committees are required to make sworn statements of their expenditures and the purposes for which they were made. Several states prohibit the payment by other persons of a voter's poll tax where the payment of such a tax is a condition to the voting privilege.

Everywhere there are laws against bribery, intimidation, fraudulent voting, and most of the other election offenses. More and more, public sentiment demands that elections shall be free from the taint of corruption, to the end that the results shall represent the real choice of the people and thus popular government made to be what its founders intended that it should be.

References.—BEARD, American Government and Politics, pp. 453-457; also ch. xxiii. FULLER, Government by the People, chs. ii-vi, viii-xi. GARNER, Introduction to Political Science, ch. xv. HART, Actual Government, ch. iv.

Documentary and Illustrative Material.—1. Legislative manual or blue book of the state. 2. The election laws of the state. 3. Copy of instructions to voters. 4. Specimen ballots.

RESEARCH QUESTIONS

1. What are the qualifications for voting in your state?

2. When were women first allowed to vote in your state?

3. Are there any offices in your state held by women?

4. How many voters are there in your state?

5. Is there a registration requirement?

6. Do you think the right to vote should be restricted to persons who are able

to read and write?

7. Give the date on which state elections are held in your state; city elections; judicial elections. Why should national, state, and city elections be held on different dates?

8. Name some offices in your state now filled by popular election which in your opinion should be filled by appointment.

9. Who are the election officers in your county?

10. What is the usual location of the polling place in your ward or precinct?

11. Explain the difference between a "party column" and an "office column" ballot. Which type of ballot is used in your state? In case the former is used does it contain a party circle and a party symbol at the head of each column?

12. Procure a specimen ballot used at the last election and explain how to mark and cast it.

13. Are voting machines used in your state? If so, where?

14. Is there a law in your state against the improper use of money in elections? Does it specify the purposes for which campaign expenditures may be made? Are candidates required to make sworn statements of their election expenses? Are there any limitations on the amount a candidate is allowed to spend?

15. Do you think corporations should be prohibited from making contributions to the campaign funds of political parties?

CHAPTER VIII

POLITICAL PARTIES AND NOMINATING METHODS

Nature and Functions of Political Parties.—Political parties are organized by groups of voters for the purpose of promoting the success of the policies in which they believe, and in order to secure the nomination and election of public officials who are in sympathy with those policies. Men differ in their opinions on matters of government as they do on matters of religion, and hence they come to constitute well differentiated groups. Whenever such a group becomes large enough to prosecute a concerted policy and organizes itself for the purpose of furthering its views in governmental matters, it becomes a political party. A political party is, therefore, composed of voters who hold substantially the same opinions in regard to certain public questions or certain principles of government. It is a purely voluntary organization, however, and any voter may decline to ally himself with any party, or, having done so, may change to another party whenever he wishes, or he may unite with others of a like mind and form a new party. While men can probably further the cause of good government best by means of organization and concert of action, no citizen should think more of his party than he does of his country, and whenever the purposes of a political party are prostituted for other ends than the public good no voter should feel morally bound to continue his support of such a party.

A National Nominating Convention

National Parties.—Under a system of popular government where public

103

policies are determined by the people and public officials are chosen by popular election, political parties are inevitable if not essential. Almost from the beginning, therefore, we have had political parties in this country, each believing in certain policies and each endeavoring to gain control of the government in order to carry out those policies. For the promotion of policies that are national in character, such as those relating to the tariff, the currency, or the foreign policy of the country, national parties have been formed with organizations extending throughout the entire country.

Local Parties.—For the most part the organization of the national parties extends downward through the states and their local subdivisions, and are made use of in local as well as in national elections. As the issues which divide the people in national elections, however, are not always the same as those which divide them in state and local elections, we sometimes have a realignment of parties in local contests, and sometimes new parties of a local character are organized. This, in fact, is to be desired for the reason that issues of a local character ought not to be determined with reference to the views of men on issues of a national character. It is wrong, for example, for Democrats and Republicans who agree upon the issues involved in a municipal election to oppose each other in such a contest merely because they do not agree on the expediency of a protective tariff or of a gold standard in money matters. In purely local elections national party lines should cut no figure; local issues should be judged wholly on their merits without reference to national questions.

Existing Political Parties in the United States.—At the present time there are two great political parties in the United States, the Democratic party and the Republican party, each with an organization extending to every part of the country, and together including the great majority of the voters.

The Democratic Party.—In a general way, we may say that the Democratic party is composed of men who believe that the sphere of the national government should not be extended beyond what a strict interpretation of the Federal Constitution warrants; that the rights of the states should be interfered with as little as possible; and that the activities of government, whether national, state, or local, should be kept down to a minimum so that the individual shall be allowed the largest measure of freedom consistent with the maintenance of order, peace, and security. This party has uniformly opposed a protective tariff, ship subsidies, imperialism, and the extension of the powers of the national government through "constructions" of the Constitution. On the money question the party has not always been united, though for the most part it has opposed the single gold standard and favored a bimetallic standard coupled with the free coinage of silver as well as of gold.

The Republican Party has contended for a liberal interpretation of the Federal Constitution, especially those parts relating to the powers of the national government, which it desires to see extended; it has shown less sympathy than the Democratic party for the rights of the states; it is the champion of the protective tariff, of internal improvements under federal auspices, of colonial expansion, liberal pensions for soldiers and sailors of the Civil War, of subventions for the merchant marine, negro suffrage, and of a gold monetary standard. From the accession of the Republican party to power in 1860 with the election of Abraham Lincoln as President, down to 1913, it controlled the executive department of the national government continually with the exception of eight years when Grover Cleveland was President (1885-1889; 1893-1897). During most of that period it controlled Congress, though several times the Democratic party had a majority in one or the other house and occasionally for a short time it was in the majority in both houses.

Some state governments are controlled by one party, and some by the other. Since 1875 the Democratic party has usually been in power in nearly all of the Southern states, and the Republican party in more than half of the other states; but in some states control often shifts from one party to the other.

The Progressive Party was organized in 1912 mainly but not wholly by those members of the Republican party who felt that this party was not sufficiently progressive in its policies and that it attached rather too much importance to the interests of special classes and too little to the rights of the masses of the people. First of all, it advocated a larger social and industrial justice for men and women, especially the working classes. It favored national jurisdiction over such matters as cannot be effectively regulated by the states; public ownership of forests, coal and oil lands, and water power; and suffrage for women. At the election of 1912 the new party polled a total vote of 4,100,000 for its presidential candidate, Theodore Roosevelt; but a few years later the party went out of existence.

The Prohibition Party.—Besides the Democratic, Republican, and Progressive parties, there are several minor parties with organizations of a national character. The oldest of these is the Prohibition party, organized in 1872 to promote the movement for the abolition of the manufacture and sale of intoxicating liquors. Since its organization, it has regularly nominated candidates for President and Vice President of the United States, and in many states it nominates candidates for state offices and for the legislature. Not infrequently it has succeeded in electing some of its candidates to the legislature, and it has been instrumental in securing the enactment of local option laws and even state-wide prohibition laws in several states.

The Socialist Labor Party, organized in 1892, advocates government ownership of land, railways, telegraph lines, and other means of production and transportation. *The Socialist Party*, organized in 1904 mainly from the Socialist Labor party, advocates essentially the same views. At the election of 1912 it cast about 900,000 votes throughout the country, and in 1916 about 600,000. In 1919 a large section of the party, composed of radicals who advocate the Bolshevist régime of government by the working class, split off and formed the *Communist Party*.

Party Organization.—Political parties, like other associations which have ends to promote, must have organization. For the conduct of national campaigns, each of the parties has a national organization; for state purposes there is a state organization; and usually there are a county and a district organization. The characteristic feature of party organization is the use which is made of committees. The organization everywhere consists of a committee, at the head of which is a chairman, and which has also a treasurer and usually a secretary. The chairman is usually an experienced political leader; sometimes he is at the same time an office holder.

The Convention.—The policies of the party are formulated by a convention which is a representative gathering composed of delegates chosen directly by the members of the party or by local conventions. The national convention, to be described hereafter, is composed of a certain number of delegates from each state, while the state convention is composed of delegates chosen from the counties, the legislative districts, or other units. The county convention is composed of delegates from the districts into which the county is divided, and the city convention of delegates from the wards or precincts. This is the usual rule, but here and there are variations. The state convention formulates the principles of the party and sets them forth in a document called the platform; it nominates the candidates of the party, except in those states where they are nominated by a direct primary; and it appoints the central committee, selects the chairman, and transacts such other business as may come before it. It is, in short, the supreme sovereign authority of the party in the state. It is usually a large body, sometimes comprising 1,000 or more delegates, and in Massachusetts as many as 2,000.

Committees.—The committee is a select body for carrying on the campaign and attending to such other matters as may be intrusted to it. The national committee is composed of one member from each state; the state committee, usually of delegates from the counties or legislative districts. The New York Republican state committee is composed of one delegate from each congressional district in the state, while the Democratic committee consists of one delegate from each of the fifty-one senatorial districts of the state. Similarly, the county committee is made up of delegates representing the political units into which the county is divided, towns, precincts, etc. Sometimes the county committee is a very large and representative body. The Republican committee of New York county is made up of about 700 delegates, each delegate representing 200 Republican voters in the county.

In the cities, there is not only the general city committee, but also a local committee for each ward or precinct. These ward committees come into close relation with the voters, and the success of the party depends to a large degree upon their activity.

Primaries.—As soon as political parties were definitely formed it became necessary to devise some sort of machinery for selecting the candidates which the party desired to put forward. In the beginning candidates for local offices were presented to the voters upon their own announcement or by a caucus (an informal meeting of the leading men of the party) or a primary (a mass meeting of the members of the party). In time the caucus, except as a means of selecting candidates for offices in legislative bodies, fell into disrepute, and the method of nomination by a convention composed of delegates representing the party became the accepted method. The delegates are chosen by the members of the party at an election called a primary, so called because it is the first or original meeting of the party voters in the process of choosing public officials.

Former Lack of State Control.—The calling of the primary, the manner of conducting it, and the fixing of the party test, that is, the determination of who may take part in the primary, are matters which for a long time were regulated by each party according to its own notions, without interference upon the part of the state. In short, it was assumed that the state had no interest in the manner in which political parties nominated their candidates, and it therefore kept its hands off. The control of the primaries, particularly in the more populous centers, fell into the hands of a small number of political leaders, or "bosses," who virtually dictated the nominations. Sometimes the primaries were held at times or places unknown to the bulk of the members of the party, or at inaccessible places, or in rooms inadequate to accommodate the mass of the voters. They were sometimes packed with henchmen of certain candidates; sometimes large numbers of the voters were kept away by "sluggers" or were intimidated by domineering leaders; sometimes the qualifications for participating in the primary were fixed in such a manner as to exclude the great mass of the voters. Men of other parties were sometimes brought in to aid in effecting the nomination of particular candidates, ballot boxes were "stuffed" or other frauds committed, and often the votes were fraudulently counted. In short, the abuses became so intolerable as to create a widespread demand for the regulation of primaries by law so that the results might more truly represent the real opinions of the members of the party.

State Regulation of Primaries.—Accordingly, one state after another began to pass laws regulating the holding of primaries, on the ground that the state was as much interested in the nomination of candidates as it was in the election of those nominated, for it was obvious that unless nominations were fairly made and unless the candidates selected really represented the free choice of the people, popular government would be at an end, since in many communities a nomination was equivalent to an election. At first, the laws enacted by the states for the regulation of primary elections were simple, and were designed to prevent only a few of the worst abuses that had grown up. They usually applied only to the large cities, and in many cases they were optional in character, that is, they applied only to such communities as chose to conduct their primaries in accordance with the laws thus passed. Beginning about 1890, however, the legislatures here and there began to enact state-wide primary laws which were mandatory upon all localities and all parties, and applied to nominations for the great bulk of the offices filled by popular election.

Existing Primary Laws.—At present nearly every state has a law regulating in some way the holding of primary elections. In general, these laws apply to every organized political party that cast at least a certain number of votes at the preceding election; and they provide that the primaries of all such parties shall be held on the same day (in some states at the same polling places, and by the same officials that hold the regular elections), and in accordance with the rules and safeguards governing the regular elections. They fix the date on which the primaries shall be held and require that due notice shall be given thereof; they prescribe the manner of nominating delegates (and such candidates for public office as are chosen directly by the primaries); they provide for the use of official ballots printed at public expense; they contain provisions in regard to the organization and powers of the party committees, and in general they regulate everything relating to the conduct of the primaries that would be a subject of regulation if they were regular elections.

The Party Test.—One of the most difficult problems in the enactment of legislation concerning the primary election is how to prescribe fairly the qualifications that must be possessed by those who shall be allowed to participate in the primary. It is often embarrassing and disagreeable for a voter when he appears at the polls to cast his vote to be compelled to reveal his party affiliation, yet unless he is required to do so, the adherents of one party might easily participate in the primary of another with a view to bringing about the nomination of its weakest candidates. Thus in a Western city some years ago where the primary law did not require a declaration of party affiliation, a large number of the members of one party entered the primary of the opposite party and brought about the nomination of their weakest candidate for mayor, and thus at the regular election the party to which the "invaders" belonged was easily able to defeat him with its own candidate. An "open" primary is open to any and all voters. Most primary laws, however, insist upon a statement by the voter of his party affiliation as a condition to participation in the primary, which is therefore called a "closed" primary. Usually the test of membership is that the voter must have affiliated with the party at the last election, and sometimes he must pledge himself to support at the coming election the candidates nominated at the primary of the party in which he participates.

As a closed primary is an election by the members of a political party, independents, or those who are not adherents of any party, are not allowed to participate. This discourages reform movements by independent voters, but there seems to be no way to remedy the matter. Sometimes an exception is made in the primaries for the nomination of candidates for city offices, on the ground that party lines should not be strictly drawn in local contests and that independent movements should be encouraged.

Nominations by Conventions.—Before the introduction of the method of nominating candidates by the direct primary, to be described hereafter, the universal method of nomination was by convention, and this is still the prevailing method in many states.

Preliminary Organization of a Convention.—The convention, as previously stated, is composed of delegates chosen at a primary election. The date and place of holding the convention are announced by the party committee some weeks in advance. It is called to order by the chairman of the committee, after which a temporary chairman of the convention is elected, and not infrequently a spirited contest takes place over the election, especially when there is likely to be a struggle for the nomination of the principal officers which the convention has been called to nominate. The temporary chairman, upon taking the chair, usually delivers an address in which he extols the party for its achievements in the past, after which usually four committees are appointed: one on organization, one on rules, one on resolutions, and one on credentials.

Convention Committees.—Frequently rival delegations appear from some county or district, and the convention must decide which one is entitled to seats. Questions of this kind are referred to the committee on credentials, which, after hearing both sides, reports to the convention recommending which delegation shall be seated, and the recommendation of the committee usually, though not always, is approved. Sometimes, however, both contesting delegations are seated, each delegate being allowed half a vote.

The committee on rules frames the rules of procedure by which the business of the convention is to be transacted; its report is usually adopted without alteration.

The committee on permanent organization proposes the names of candidates for permanent chairman, secretary, and such other officers of the convention as may be needed. The officers suggested by this committee are usually elected, though sometimes the convention elects a different ticket.

The chairman of the committee on resolutions presents a draft of the platform, which is adopted by the convention, usually, though not always, without change.

The Nominations.—The convention is now ready for the chief business for which it was called, namely, the nomination of candidates which the party desires to put forward for the offices to be filled at the coming election. The names of the candidates are usually presented to the convention in highly eulogistic speeches, and the nominations are generally seconded by one or more delegates. The balloting then proceeds until the nominations are all made. Sometimes where more than two candidates are placed in nomination no one of them is able to secure a majority, and a "deadlock" ensues, lasting maybe for days or even weeks, and terminated by the nomination of a "dark horse."

Objections to the Convention Method.—When deadlocks occur, the "dark horse" chosen is likely to be an inferior candidate. Another objection to the method of nomination by convention is that the nominations are frequently determined by a small number of leaders or "bosses" who control the convention, and thus the nominations do not represent the choice of the party. How a convention may be thus controlled by a few politicians is thus stated by a careful writer who is fully conversant with party methods:[23]

"The program of the convention, in practice, is almost always decided upon down to the minutest detail, before the convention meets. The party leader, or 'boss,' and his lieutenants discuss the relative claims of candidates and decide who shall be nominated. The party platform is written and submitted to the 'boss' for his approval. The officers of the convention are agreed upon and their speeches revised. All this is outside the law, which ignores the existence of the party leader and assumes that the delegates are free to exercise their own judgment. The real interest in the convention is usually centered in the secret conferences of the leaders which precede it and in which the contests over the nominations are fought out, sometimes with much stubbornness. The 'slate' is finally made up by agreement between leaders who control a majority of the delegates in the convention. The leaders of the minority may either surrender or they may register their protest by presenting the names of other candidates in the convention with the certainty of defeat, for it is rare in state conventions that there is so equal a division of strength as to leave the result in doubt.

"While the leaders are settling what the convention is to do, the delegates are left to their own devices, ignorant of what is going on in the 'headquarters' where the leaders are assembled. They are not consulted and their advice is not asked. It often happens that they do not know whom they are to nominate until they hear for the first time in the convention hall the names of the candidates agreed upon by the leaders. Although the law gives them the right to bring forward the names of other candidates, they seldom exercise it, and the delegate bold enough to disobey orders is regarded with disapproval."

Nomination by the People: the Direct Primary.—About 1889, because of growing dissatisfaction with the convention system, some of the states began to experiment with the method of popular nomination, that is, direct nomination by the primary instead of by convention. Instead of calling on the voters to choose delegates to a convention to which the task of nomination was intrusted, they were now called upon to vote directly for the candidates themselves. It was said that if the voters were competent to choose delegates to a convention they were equally competent to select the candidates themselves. The movement for the direct primary, as it was called, spread rapidly particularly in the South and West. Thus the convention has been done away with in a large number of states except where it is still retained to frame platforms, appoint the central committee, and select delegates to the national convention, and in some states it has been abolished even for these purposes, other means having been provided for taking care of these matters.

Objections.—The direct primary has been criticized because under it candidates for state offices need to canvass the entire state in order to become acquainted with the voters—a task which requires much time and is very expensive. Such a system, it is argued, gives the candidate of leisure and wealth a decided advantage over the poor man who cannot afford the large expense involved.

The direct primary method, however, has given general satisfaction where it has been adopted.

Nomination by Petition.—While most candidates for public office are nominated by the recognized political parties, the laws of many states allow candidates to be nominated also by petition of independent voters. The procedure of nomination by petition is for the candidate or his friends to prepare a nomination paper or petition containing the title of the office to be filled, together with the name and residence of the candidate, get a certain number of voters to sign it, and then file it with the proper election officer. The number of signatures necessary to nominate varies according to the nature of the office to be filled and the population of the district or territory over which the jurisdiction of the office extends. Thus in New York a petition for the nomination of a candidate for a state office must contain the signatures of at least 12,000 legal voters (including at least 50 from each county), while in Massachusetts 1,000 is sufficient. For the nomination of candidates for local offices the number of petitioners required is smaller. Thus in New York candidates for the legislature may be nominated by 500 voters; in Massachusetts candidates for local offices may be nominated by petitions signed by one per cent of the number of voters.

References.—BEARD, American Government and Politics, chs. vii, xxx. BRYCE, The American Commonwealth (abridged edition), ch. xlv. FULLER, Government by the People, chs. iv, v, xi. HART, Actual Government, ch. v. MERRIAM, Primary Elections, chs. i, v.

Documentary and Illustrative Material.—1. Legislative manual or blue book of the state. 2. Copy of the primary election law of the state. 3. Democratic and Republican campaign textbooks. 4. Copies of party platforms. 5. Specimen ballots. 6. Copies of delegates' credentials, nomination certificates, petitions, etc.

RESEARCH QUESTIONS

1. Do you consider political parties essential under a system of popular government? Would it be better if there were in each state of the Union at least two strong political parties instead of one, as is virtually the case in some of the Southern states as well as in some of the North?

2. Do you think every voter ought to join some political party and support its candidates and policies? Suppose he does not approve the candidates which it has nominated and the policies which it has adopted, what should he do? Ought independent voting to be encouraged? If so, why?

3. How many votes were cast by the Democratic party in your state for governor at the last election? How many by the Republican party?

4. How is the state central committee of each party constituted in your state? Who are the members from your county or district?

5. At what places were the last state conventions of the Democratic and Republican parties held in your state? How many delegates were there in each?

6. How are municipal officers nominated in your state?

7. Is there a primary law in your state? If so, what are its provisions?

8. Has the method of nomination by direct primary been introduced into your state? If so, to what offices does it apply? How are members of party committees selected? What test does the primary law of your state provide for participation in the primary? Does it permit the people to express their choice for United States senator? In what order are candidates arranged on the primary ballot? Did a large proportion of the voters take part in the last primary election? What is the date fixed for holding the primary?

9. Are any officers nominated in your state by conventions?

10. If candidates are nominated by a direct primary in your state, what is the method devised for preparing the platform of the party?

CHAPTER IX

THE ESTABLISHMENT OF THE UNION

The Articles of Confederation.—The Continental Congress, which managed the common affairs of the Union during the early stages of the Revolution, was a body whose authority was not defined by any constitution or fundamental law. It assumed large powers in the belief that the people, relying upon its patriotism and wisdom, would acquiesce in its acts. As yet, however, the states were not closely united, and each was free to go its own way. As time passed, the advantages of union became more manifest, and the states began to recognize the desirability of creating a common government with larger powers and with definite authority. After a debate lasting off and on for more than a year, Congress adopted in November, 1777, an instrument called the Articles of Confederation, which was to go into effect when ratified by all the states.

Ratification of the Articles.—During the years 1778 and 1779, all the states except Maryland ratified the Articles. Maryland withheld her approval because she doubted the advantage of a union among states, some of which held vast territory in the West while some did not. The states claiming lands northwest of the Ohio River were Virginia, New York, Massachusetts, and Connecticut. As these lands had been wrested from Great Britain while that power was weakened by her war with all the states, Maryland insisted, as a condition to her adhesion, that the states claiming these lands should surrender them to the nation for the benefit of all the states. This argument appealed to the sense of patriotism and justice of the states claiming this northwestern territory, and in the course of the next few years they ceded most of their lands to the United States for the common benefit. When it became certain that this would be done, Maryland ratified the Articles, and the Confederation of the states was completed.

Government under the Articles.—The Confederation thus formed was styled a "firm league of friendship" under the name of "the United States of America," and its declared purpose was to provide for the common defense of the states, the security of their liberties, and their mutual and general welfare. To secure these ends the states bound themselves to assist each other against all attacks upon either or all of them, upon any pretense whatever.

For the management of certain affairs common to the states composing the Confederation, the Articles provided for an annual Congress of delegates to be chosen by the states, no state to be represented by less than two members or more than seven. Unlike the Continental Congress, the Congress of the Confederation was given express power to deal with certain affairs, and therefore it did not have to assume the powers it exercised. Among these were the power to declare war and make peace; to send and receive diplomatic representatives; to enter into treaties; to make rules regarding captures on the high seas; to grant letters of marque and reprisal; to settle disputes between the states, upon petition of the disputants; to regulate the alloy and value of coin, whether struck under the authority of Congress or by the states; to fix the standard of weights and measures throughout the United States; to regulate trade and intercourse with the Indians; to make rules for the government of the land and naval forces; to establish post offices; and a few other powers of a like character.

No provision, however, was made for an executive department or for a national judiciary, with the single exception of a court of appeal in cases involving captures on the high seas in time of war.

Prohibitions on the States.—In the interest of the general peace and security, the states were forbidden, except with the consent of Congress, to send diplomatic representatives to foreign countries, or enter into treaties or alliances, or levy any duties on articles imported from abroad, if such duties should conflict with the provisions of foreign treaties; or keep ships of war in times of peace; or engage in war; or grant letters of marque and reprisal.

Defects of the Articles of Confederation.—Although the Articles of Confederation proved of great value in securing concert of action among the states in certain matters, the weaknesses of the union which they created and the defects of the governmental machinery provided by them soon proved serious.

The States Retained too Much Power.—The union turned out to be the loosest sort of a league, in which the states for the most part did as they pleased. Each retained its own sovereignty and could not be compelled to perform its obligations as a member of the Confederation. Some of them deliberately violated the treaty of peace with Great Britain, and the Congress was unable to prevent such infractions. Congress being thus powerless to carry out the stipulations of the treaty, Great Britain refused to perform her obligations thereunder. Since no executive department and no courts were created to enforce and apply the laws passed by Congress, the nation had to depend upon the states to carry out its will.

The Congress was not well Organized.—In the organization and procedure of Congress there were serious defects. No member could serve for more than three years in six, and each state paid its own members and might recall them at pleasure. Thus the dependence of the representative upon his state was emphasized and his character as a national representative minimized. Worse than this was the provision that allowed each state, regardless of its population and size, but one vote in Congress. Thus Georgia with a population of only a few thousand souls enjoyed the same power in all matters of national legislation that Virginia did, although the population of Virginia was some sixteen times as great. Still another serious weakness was the rule which required the assent of nine states to pass any important bill, such as those for borrowing or appropriating money, issuing bills of credit, declaring war, entering into treaties, coining money, building war ships, raising military forces, selecting commanders, and the like. As it was frequently impossible to secure the concurrence of so large a proportion of the states, needed legislation was often prevented by the opposition of a few members or by the lack of a quorum. Thus in April, 1783, there were present only twenty-five members from eleven states, nine being represented by only two members each. It would have been possible, therefore, for three members to defeat any important measure.[24]

Congress had No Power of Taxation.—Not only were the defects in the organization and procedure of Congress of a serious character, but the powers conferred upon it by the Articles of Confederation were so meager that its authority was little more than a shadow and carried little weight. One of the essential powers of government is that of taxation, yet the Congress had no authority to impose a dollar of taxes on any individual in the land. Money was needed to pay the soldiers who were fighting the battles of the country, to pay the salaries and expenses of diplomatic representatives who had been sent to Europe to negotiate treaties and solicit the aid of foreign friends, to pay interest on loans incurred in France and Holland, to defray the cost of building war ships and equipping the army, and to meet the various other expenses which every government must needs incur, yet the government of the Confederation was powerless to raise the necessary funds by taxation. In the absence of all power to levy and collect taxes, Congress adopted the policy of apportioning the national expenses among the states. But no state could be compelled to contribute a dollar toward its quota; some of them in fact contributed little, and most of those which did respond to the appeal of Congress did so grudgingly and tardily. Of the $15,000,000 apportioned among the states between 1781 and 1786 less than $2,000,000 was actually paid in. Often there was not a dollar in the treasury of the Confederation to pay the obligations of the government.

Two attempts were made to amend the Articles of Confederation so as to give Congress power to levy a five per cent tariff duty on imported goods, but since it required the assent of each of the thirteen states to adopt an amendment, the scheme fell through, in both cases on account of the opposition of a single state.

Congress had No Power to Regulate Commerce, either with foreign countries or among the states themselves. This was a serious defect. Each state had its own tariff system and its own customhouses, and collected its own duties on goods brought into its ports from abroad. As each state was anxious to exploit this source of revenue for itself, it naturally framed its tariff regulations and tonnage laws in such a way as to attract foreign commerce to its own ports. And so it was with regard to commerce among the states themselves. Each framed its trade regulations with its neighbors according to its own selfish interests and without regard to the general good. The result was continual jealousies, dissensions, and sometimes reprisals and retaliations. New York levied an import duty on certain articles brought in from its less fortunate neighbors, Connecticut and New Jersey, and each in turn retaliated as best it could. For purposes of foreign and interstate commerce, each state was a nation itself, and the Confederation was a nonentity.

The Annapolis Convention.—The worst evils described above reached a climax in 1786, and the political leaders of America such as Hamilton and Washington were convinced that the government of the Confederation must either be revised or superseded entirely by a new system. In September, 1786, there assembled at Annapolis, Maryland, a convention of delegates from five states, namely, New York, New Jersey, Pennsylvania, Delaware, and Virginia, called at the instance of the legislature of Virginia to take into consideration the subject of uniform trade regulation among the states, the lack of which had come to be one of the chief evils of the Confederation. So few states were represented that the convention decided not to enter upon the business for which it had been called, but instead determined to put forth an effort to bring about the assembling of a convention representing all the states and empowered to take into consideration the question of a general revision of the Articles of Confederation so as to render them more adequate to the needs of the nation. Accordingly, a resolution prepared by Alexander Hamilton, one of the delegates from New York, was adopted, calling on the states to appoint delegates to a convention to be held at Philadelphia on the second Monday in May next, for the purpose of revising the Articles of Confederation.

The Constitutional Convention of 1787; Personnel.—In pursuance of this resolution, all the states except Rhode Island promptly appointed delegates, the failure of Rhode Island being due to her satisfaction with the Confederation, under which she enjoyed larger commercial advantages than she could hope to enjoy if the Articles were amended so as to take away from the states their control over commerce. Altogether fifty-five members sat in the convention at one time or another, though only thirty-nine signed the

Constitution. From Virginia came George Washington, Edmund Randolph, and James Madison; from Massachusetts, Rufus King and Elbridge Gerry; from Connecticut, William Samuel Johnson and Roger Sherman; from New Hampshire, John Langdon; from New York, Alexander Hamilton; from New Jersey, William Livingston and William Paterson; from Pennsylvania, Benjamin Franklin, Robert and Gouverneur Morris, Jared Ingersoll, and James Wilson; from Delaware, John Dickinson; and from South Carolina, John Rutledge, Charles Pinckney, and Charles Cotesworth Pinckney. Some of the delegates, as Benjamin Franklin, had been members of the Albany Congress as far back as 1754; some had been members of the Stamp Act Congress of 1765; most of them had served in the Continental or Confederation Congresses; and a number of them were signers of the Declaration of Independence. A great many of them had served in the legislatures of their states, and of the whole number there was not one who had not had some legislative experience.

The Work of the Convention of 1787.—When the convention had been duly organized, "plans" of a proposed constitution were submitted by the delegations of several states, and these became the bases of the discussion which followed.

The Virginia Plan.—The plan submitted by the Virginia delegation represented the views of delegates from the larger and more populous states, and the Constitution as finally adopted embodied more largely the features of this plan than those of any other. The most important resolution of this plan was that a national government ought to be established consisting of a supreme legislative, judiciary, and executive. This resolution, adopted in committee of the whole, went directly to the root of the chief evil of the existing system, which contained no provision for an executive or a judicial department. It recognized also what has come to be a fundamental doctrine of American political science, namely, the separation of the legislative, executive, and judicial functions.

The New Jersey Plan.—The views of delegates from the small states were embodied in the New Jersey plan, which was laid before the convention by William Paterson. In general, the New Jersey plan provided for the retention of the principal features of the existing system, except that it proposed to enlarge the powers of Congress so as to make its authority more effective. This was all, in the judgment of the small states, that was necessary to remove the existing evils.

The Problem of Representation in Congress.—The convention without much discussion decided that Congress should consist of two chambers or houses instead of one as was the case under the Articles of Confederation. This done, the next problem was to determine the basis of representation in each. This proved to be one of the most difficult tasks of the convention. The delegates from the large states insisted that representation in both houses should be based on population, so that a state such as Virginia with sixteen times the population of Georgia should have sixteen times as many representatives in Congress. But to this system of proportional representation, the delegates from the small states objected. They maintained that the importance of a state was not to be measured by its population; that the states were sovereign political entities, and when it came to participation in the government of the nation they were all equal, large and small alike. There was no more reason, said a delegate from one of the small states, why a large state should have more representation in Congress than that a large man should have more votes than a small man. For a time the differences seemed irreconcilable, and more than once it looked as if the convention would be disrupted on this question. The spirit of compromise triumphed, however, and it was finally agreed that the states should be represented equally in the senate but in proportion to their population in the house of representatives. As a result of this rule, Nevada to-day with a population of less than 100,000 sends the same number of senators to Washington as does New York with a population of some 10,000,000 souls. New York, on the other hand, sends forty-three representatives to Congress while Nevada sends but one. This was the first great compromise of the Constitution.

The Question of Counting the Slaves.—The next problem, which was almost equally difficult and which likewise had to be settled by compromise, was the question of whether the slaves should be counted in determining the population of the state for purposes of representation. The delegates from the Southern states argued that slaves were an important factor in contributing to the wealth and power of the country and should, therefore, be counted for purposes of representation. To this argument the delegates from the Northern states, where the slave population was inconsiderable, objected on the ground that the slaves at law were treated merely as property and were not allowed to vote in the states where they resided. The discussion over this question was long and at times exciting, but finally a compromise was reached by which it was agreed that in determining the population for purposes of representation, all the white population but only three fifths of the slaves should be counted. At the same time it was decided that direct taxes among the states should be apportioned on the same basis. This compromise was favorable to the slave states in that it gave them an increased number of representatives, but it was unfavorable in that it increased their proportion of direct taxes. This is known as the three-fifths compromise.

Federal Regulation of Commerce.—Another question which became the subject of heated discussion related to the national control of commerce. The Northern states wished Congress to be given the power to regulate commerce, but the Southern states, which at the time furnished the principal articles of export, feared that the power might be employed in such a manner as to injure their commerce, and might also be used to prohibit the slave trade and thus prevent the Southern planters from stocking their farms with laborers. They accordingly insisted that Congress should be expressly prohibited from interfering with the importation of slaves, and that it should be allowed to pass navigation acts only by a two-thirds majority of both houses. The whole matter was finally settled by a compromise which forbade Congress to interfere with the importation of slaves before the year 1808, but which allowed it to pass laws by a majority vote for the regulation of commerce. This was the last great compromise of the Constitution.

Other Compromises.—Many other questions were settled on the basis of compromise, though none of them occasioned so much discussion as the three mentioned above. Some have regretted that such compromises as that which allows the states equality of representation in the senate, as well as the one which allowed representation on the basis of the slave population, should have ever found their way into the Constitution; but it is certain that without these compromises the Constitution could never have been adopted.

After the settlement of the questions mentioned above, the work of framing the Constitution proceeded with less difficulty. Finally, on September 17, the completed draft was signed by thirty-nine delegates, after which the convention adjourned. A few were absent and did not sign for that reason; others, such as Gerry of Massachusetts and Mason of Virginia, disapproved of the Constitution and refused to attach their signatures.

Ratification of the Constitution.—Before adjourning, the convention resolved to send the draft of the Constitution to Congress with the request that it should transmit the instrument to the legislatures of the several states and that these in turn should submit it to conventions for ratification. It was agreed, moreover, that when it should have been ratified by conventions in nine states it should go into effect between the states so ratifying.

Opposition to the Constitution.—As soon as the text of the Constitution was made known to the people of the states, a flood of criticism was turned loose on it from almost every part of the country. Those who approved the Constitution and favored its ratification were called Federalists; those who opposed it were called Anti-Federalists. The principal grounds of opposition were that in providing for a national government with extensive powers the Constitution had sacrificed, to a large degree, the rights of the states; that such a government would prove dangerous to the liberties of the people; that the

President for which the Constitution provided might become a dictator and a tyrant; that the senate would be an oligarchy; and that the Federal Constitution, unlike those of the states, contained no bill of rights for the protection of the people against governmental encroachment upon their inherent rights such as freedom of speech, freedom of press, freedom of religious worship, freedom of assembly, and the like. The last mentioned objection was removed by the assurance on the part of the friends of the Constitution that in the event of ratification they would endeavor to have the Constitution amended at the earliest opportunity in such a way as to provide proper safeguards for the security of these rights, a promise which was carried out soon after the new government went into effect, by the adoption of the first ten amendments.

Ratification by the States.—The first state to ratify the Constitution was Delaware, one of the small states whose delegates in the Philadelphia convention had been strongly opposed to changing the existing system. This state ratified on December 6, 1787, without a dissenting vote. Its action was shortly followed by Pennsylvania, New Jersey, Georgia, and Connecticut, the last three of which were small states whose delegates in the Philadelphia convention had also been in the opposition. In Pennsylvania, however, the Constitution was ratified with less unanimity and only after a fierce struggle in which the Anti-Federalists attacked almost every part of it. Massachusetts was the next to ratify, although by a narrow majority, many of the leading citizens being opposed or indifferent. Maryland and South Carolina followed, and finally the favorable action of New Hampshire on June 21, 1788, insured its success, since nine states had now ratified and the Constitution could be put into effect between the states that had so ratified. Four days later, before news of the ratification of New Hampshire was received, Virginia fell in line and ratified, in spite of the powerful opposition of Patrick Henry, Mason, Lee, and others.

Attention was now turned to New York, where the opponents of the Constitution were believed to be in the majority. Geographically, New York was like a wedge which divided the Union into two parts, and hence its adhesion was especially desirable. Because of its favorable commercial position, the state enjoyed great advantages under the Articles of Confederation, since it could collect and turn into its own treasury the duties on all articles coming into its ports from abroad—a privilege of which it would be deprived under the Constitution. There was good reason, therefore, why it should hesitate to exchange its position for one less favorable. When the state convention assembled to take action on the Constitution, it was found that about two thirds of the members were at first opposed to ratification. Among the friends of the Constitution, however, was Alexander

Hamilton, whose powerful argument prevailed, and the Constitution was ratified by a majority of three votes.

Rhode Island, like New York, enjoyed a favorable position under the Articles of Confederation, and was not in sympathy with the Constitution. She refused to ratify and remained out of the Union until May, 1790, more than a year after the Constitution had gone into effect. North Carolina likewise refused to ratify until November, 1789.

The Constitution Goes into Effect.—When the ratification of the Constitution had been assured, the old Congress of the Confederation enacted that the new government should go into effect on March 4, 1789. In the meantime senators and representatives were elected as the first members of the new Congress, and George Washington was chosen President. Thus the old Confederation passed away and the new Republic entered upon its great career.

The System of Government Created.—The government created by the Constitution is federal in character; that is, it consists of a system of national and state government under a common sovereignty. It is a republic as contradistinguished from such a limited monarchy as the British; that is, it is a government having a popularly elected executive rather than a titular executive who holds his office for life by hereditary tenure, who is politically irresponsible, and who governs through ministers who are responsible to the Parliament for his acts. It is also distinguished from confederate government or that form in which the states are practically sovereign and in which the general government is nothing but the agent of the states for the care of a very few things of common concern, such as defense against foreign aggression. Finally, the American system is one of popular rather than of aristocratic government, that is, it is government by the masses of the people instead of government by the favored few.

References.—ANDREWS, Manual of the Constitution, ch. ii. BEARD, American Government and Politics, ch. iii. BRYCE, The American Commonwealth (abridged edition), ch. ii. FISKE, Critical Period of American History, chs. vi-vii. HINSDALE, American Government, chs. vii-xi.

Documentary Material.—1. The Articles of Confederation. 2. The Constitution.

1. Trace the steps leading up to the meeting of the convention which framed the Constitution.

2. How were the delegates to the convention chosen? What, in general, was the nature of their instructions? Who was the oldest delegate? the youngest? the most distinguished? Who of them were signers of the Declaration of Independence? Who acted as president of the convention?

3. Name the members of the convention who refused to sign the Constitution.

4. Why did Hamilton, the author of the resolution calling the convention, take so little part in the work of making the Constitution?

5. Why did not New York send its ablest men to the convention?

6. Did the convention organize itself into committees for the transaction of business?

7. What was the attitude of some of the delegates from the Eastern states toward the West?

8. In general, what part of the country was in favor of the Constitution and what part opposed?

9. What were some of the objections urged against its adoption?

10. Why was the Constitution not submitted to a direct vote of the people as is the custom with state constitutions?

11. When the draft of the completed Constitution was laid before the Congress of the Confederation, did that body make any changes in it before submitting it to the states?

12. Might North Carolina and Rhode Island have remained permanently out of the Union? If so, what would have been their status?

13. Do you think the time has come when the best interests of the country require a new Constitution? What is your opinion of the proposition that the country has outgrown the Constitution?

14. What, in the light of more than a century's experience, do you consider some of the defects of the Constitution?

CHAPTER X

THE TWO HOUSES OF CONGRESS

The House of Representatives.—The Constitution provides that the national house of representatives—the lower house of Congress—shall consist of members chosen every second year by popular election. Under the Articles of Confederation members of the old Congress were chosen annually, but that term was too short to enable them to acquire that familiarity with their duties which is essential to efficient legislation. The term of a representative begins on the 4th of March in the odd-numbered years, though Congress does not meet until the first Monday in December following, unless the President calls it together in extraordinary session earlier.

Sessions of Congress.—There are two regular sessions of every Congress; the long session which begins on the first Monday in December of the odd-numbered years and lasts until some time in the following spring or summer; and the short session which begins on the same date in the even-numbered years and lasts until the 4th of March following, when the terms of all representatives expire. Each Congress is numbered, beginning with the first, which began March 4th, 1789. The sixty-seventh Congress began March 4, 1921, and will end March 4, 1923. Extraordinary sessions are sometimes called by the President to consider matters of special importance which need to be acted upon before the meeting of the regular session. From 1789 to 1921 there were only nineteen such sessions, the last being that called by President Harding to meet in April, 1921, to consider tariff and revenue measures and readjustment of international relationships.

Number and Apportionment of Representatives.—The Constitution provided that the first house of representatives should consist of sixty-five members, but that as soon as a census of the inhabitants should be taken the number was to be apportioned among the several states on the basis of population, not exceeding one for every 30,000 of the inhabitants. After each decennial census is taken a new apportionment is made by Congress on the basis of the new population. The total number of representatives at present is 435,[25] being in the proportion of one member for every 211,877 inhabitants, which is known as the congressional ratio. The largest number from any one state is forty-three, the number from New York. Pennsylvania has thirty-six, Illinois twenty-seven, Ohio twenty-two, and so on down the list. Five states are entitled to but one member each, namely, Arizona, Delaware, Nevada, New Mexico, and Wyoming. As the population of several of these states is less than the congressional ratio, they might not be entitled to a single member but for the provision in the Constitution which declares that each state shall have at least one representative.

Election of Representatives.—The Constitution provides that representatives shall be chosen in each state by vote of such persons as are qualified to vote for members of the lower house of the legislature of that state. Thus it happens that the qualifications for participating in the choice of national representatives varies widely in the different states. But the choice must be made by the people, not by the legislature or by executive appointment, and, under the Fifteenth and Nineteenth Amendments to the Federal Constitution, the states cannot, in fixing the suffrage, discriminate against any class of persons because of their color, race, or sex. Subject to these restrictions the states are practically free to limit the right to vote for national representatives to such of their citizens as they may see fit. It is true that the Fourteenth Amendment declares that whenever a state shall limit the right of its adult male citizens to vote except for crime its representation in Congress shall be proportionately reduced, but this provision has never been enforced. Some statesmen hold that it was really superseded by the Fifteenth Amendment.

UNITED STATES SENATE CHAMBER

UNITED STATES HOUSE OF REPRESENTATIVES

Manner of Choosing Representatives.—As in fixing the qualifications of the electors of representatives, so in the choosing of them, the states are left a free hand, subject to the provision of the Constitution which gives Congress power to alter the regulations of the states in regard to the manner and time of choosing members. For a long time Congress did not exercise its power in this respect and each state chose its representatives when it wished and in such manner as it pleased. Some states chose their representatives on general ticket from the state at large, while others chose theirs by districts; some chose by secret ballot, while others did not. To secure uniformity in regard to the method of choice, Congress enacted in 1842 that representatives should be chosen by districts of contiguous territory containing populations as nearly equal to the congressional ratio as possible. In 1871 it enacted that they should be chosen by written or printed ballots (later choice by voting machine was also permitted). In 1872 it enacted that representatives should be chosen on the same day throughout the Union, namely, Tuesday after the first Monday in November.[26]

"Gerrymandering."—When the number of representatives to which each state shall be entitled has been determined, after the decennial census, it devolves upon the legislature to divide the state into as many districts as it is entitled to representatives.[27] In the exercise of this power the political party in control of the legislature may arrange the districts in an unfair manner so as to make it possible for the party to elect a larger number of representatives than its voting strength entitles it to. This is done by putting counties in which the

opposite party is in a large majority in the same districts so that it may choose a few members by large majorities, while the other party carries the remaining districts by small majorities. Thus the voting strength of the party in power is economized while that of the other party is massed in a few districts and made to count as little as possible. This practice is known as "gerrymandering" and has often been resorted to by both the two great political parties, sometimes in such a manner as to result in flagrant injustice to the minority party.

The requirement that the districts shall contain as nearly equal population as possible, is sometimes flagrantly violated. Thus one of the Republican districts in New York recently contained 165,701 inhabitants while one of the Democratic districts had a population of 450,000. In 1910 one of the Illinois districts contained 167,000 while another contained 349,000.

Sometimes districts are so constructed as to have fantastic shapes. Thus a district in Mississippi some years ago was dubbed the "shoe string" district from its long irregular shape. It followed the Mississippi River for the whole length of the state though in one place it was less than thirty miles wide.

Qualifications of Representatives.—To be eligible to the house of representatives, a person must have been a citizen of the United States for at least seven years, must have attained the age of twenty-five years, and must be an inhabitant of the state from which he is chosen. Residence in the particular district which the member represents is not required by the Constitution or laws of the United States, but is nearly always required by public opinion. A nonresident, however able and distinguished he might be as a statesman, would have little chance of election.

Objections to the Residence Requirement.—This custom of insisting upon residence in the district has frequently been criticized, especially by foreign writers, as being a serious defect in our system of representation. It contrasts widely with the practice in Great Britain, where members of Parliament are very often chosen from other districts than those in which they reside. London barristers of promise are not infrequently chosen to represent country districts in which they are practically strangers. The late William E. Gladstone, a resident of Wales, represented for a long time a Scotch district. When an important leader of any party in the House of Commons happens to be defeated in his home district, it is a common practice for him to be made a candidate in some district in which his party has a safe majority. In the United States, in such a case, the man's service in Congress would probably be ended.

Finally, one of the worst evils of the district system is that it tends to make the member feel that he is the representative, not of the United States as a whole, but of the locality which chooses him. Instead of entertaining broad views upon purely national questions his views tend to become narrow and he votes and acts with reference to the welfare of his own district rather than with reference to the good of the whole country. On the other hand, it may be said in favor of the district system that it is better adapted to secure local representation and makes responsibility to the member's constituency more effective.

The Senate.—*Purposes.*—Regarding the desirability of creating a national legislature of two houses there was little difference of opinion among the members of the convention. Experience with a single-chambered congress during the period of the Confederation had revealed certain defects in such an organization. Moreover, all the state legislatures except two were composed of two houses and these exceptions were destined soon to disappear. If a state legislature ought to consist of two houses, it was all the more important that the national congress should be bicameral in organization, because, the union being composed of states, it was desirable to provide a separate house in which they could be represented as constituent political units just as the other house was to be a body representing the people without regard to political divisions. Aside from considerations growing out of the character of the federal system, there were the usual advantages which we associate with the bicameral system, such as protection against hasty and ill-considered legislation, insurance against the possible despotism of a single chamber, and the like. Having decided that Congress should consist of two houses, the convention felt that if the upper house was to exert an effective restraining influence on the lower house it ought not to be a mere duplication of the latter but should be differently composed. It should to a certain extent be a more conservative body than the lower house, which, being elected by the people, would incline toward radicalism; it should, therefore, be smaller in size, its members should be chosen for a longer term and by a different method, higher age and residence qualifications should be required, and it should be given certain powers which were not conferred on the lower house, such as a share in the appointing, treaty making, and judicial powers.

Term.—As already stated, the Constitution provides that the states shall be represented equally in the senate. It also provides that each state shall elect two senators and that each senator shall have one vote. Under the Articles of Confederation, each state had one vote in Congress, and the vote of the state could not be divided; but under the Constitution the two senators from a state frequently vote on opposite sides of a question, especially if they belong to different political parties. On the question of the term of senators there was much difference of opinion among the members of the convention. Some favored a two-year tenure, some four years, some six, some nine, while Alexander Hamilton favored a life tenure. The term finally agreed upon was six years, which seemed to be long enough to give the senate an element of permanence and independence, and yet short enough to secure responsibility to the people.

Classification of Senators.—The Constitution provided that immediately upon the assembling of the senators after the first election they should be divided into three classes and that the seats of those in the first class should be vacated at the end of the second year, those of the second class at the expiration of the fourth year, and those of the third class at the expiration of the sixth year, so that thereafter one third might be chosen every second year. The purpose of this provision is to avoid having the entire senate renewed at the same time. As a result, not more than one third are new and inexperienced members at any particular time. When a new state is admitted to the Union, its first two senators draw lots to see which class each shall fall in. In 1921 there were thirty-two senators in the first class, and their terms expire March 4, 1923; thirty-two in the second class, and their terms expire March 4, 1925; and thirty-two in the third class, and their terms expire March 4, 1927. The three classes are kept as nearly equal as possible.

Reëlection of Senators.—While the term of a senator is six years, he may be reëlected as often as his state may see fit to honor him, and in practice reëlections have been frequent. Justin S. Morrill of Vermont, John Sherman of Ohio, and William B. Allison of Iowa, each served continuously for a period of thirty-two years. Nearly one third of the senators in 1911 had served twenty years or more. Thus the senate is an assembly of elder statesmen and is a more conservative and stable body than the house of representatives.

Mode of Election of Senators.—In regard to the mode of election of senators there was a wide difference of opinion among the members of the convention. Some favored choice by the people; others favored election by the lower house of Congress; some proposed appointment by the President from persons nominated by the state legislatures; while others proposed election by the state legislatures, which was the method finally agreed upon. Choice by the legislature, it was felt, would be the means of forming a connecting link between the state governments and the national government and would thereby tend to attach the former to the latter—an important consideration then, in view of the prevailing jealousy of the state governments toward the national government. Finally, it was believed that choice by the legislature would tend to secure the election of senators of greater ability since the members of the legislature would be more familiar with the qualifications of candidates than the masses of the people could hope to be.

Objections to the Method of Choice by the Legislature.—One of the practical objections to the original method of choosing senators was that it frequently led to long and stubborn contests which sometimes ended in deadlocks. Not infrequently the legislature failed to elect a senator and the state was left with a vacancy in the senate. In such cases the governor could not fill the vacancy by appointment as he did when a senator died or resigned; the seat remained vacant until a senator was chosen by the legislature. From 1890 to 1912 not less than eleven states at one time or another were represented in the senate by one member only, and in 1901 Delaware, on account of repeated deadlocks, had no senator at all at Washington to speak for the state. Not infrequently such contests were broken through the selection of a second-rate man or by an alliance between the members of the minority party and certain members of the majority.

Bribery.—The breaking of deadlocks was sometimes accomplished by bribery or other improper influences. Indeed charges of bribery and corruption in connection with the election of senators came to be very common, and there is little doubt that between 1895 and 1910 a number of wealthy men found their way into the senate through the votes of legislators who were liberally paid for their support. Under these circumstances it was frequently said that the senate was no longer truly representative of the interests of the people.

Interference with Legislative Business.—A prolonged senatorial contest also interfered too much with the regular business of the state legislature. Where the session is limited to two or three months, as it frequently is, the inroads upon the time at the disposal of the legislature for looking after the needs of the state were considerable.[28] Members were badgered by candidates, passions and animosities were engendered, a party coloring was given non-partisan measures, and the votes of members on legislative measures were sometimes determined by the senatorial contest, rather than by the merits of the measure on which they were called to vote.

Popular Election of Senators.—The dissatisfaction with the old method of choosing senators led to a movement to secure an amendment to the Constitution providing for the election of senators by the people. But the senate itself for a long time blocked every attempt of this kind. Five different times between 1893 and 1911 the national house of representatives by a large majority proposed an amendment for this purpose, but each time the senate refused its concurrence. In one form or another the legislatures of thirty-one states approved of the method of popular election and wherever a referendum was taken on the proposition, as was done in California, Nevada, and Illinois, the popular indorsement was overwhelming. Finally, in 1912, the senate yielded, and both houses of Congress adopted a resolution proposing an amendment providing for the popular election of senators, which was ratified by the necessary number of states during the following year. Under this seventeenth amendment the senators of each state are elected by vote of such persons as are entitled to vote for members of the lower house of the legislature.

The seventeenth amendment provides that whenever a vacancy occurs in the senate the governor of the state in which the vacancy occurs shall issue a writ of election for the filling of such vacancy, but that the legislature may authorize the governor to fill the vacancy by a temporary appointment, the appointee to hold until a senator may be chosen by popular election. In practice special elections are rarely called for filling vacancies. In most states the governor makes a temporary appointment, the appointee holding until the next regular election when the people elect his successor.

Qualifications of Senators.—The qualifications prescribed for eligibility to the senate are the same in principle as those required of representatives, though a little different in degree. Thus a senator must be at least thirty years of age, must have been a citizen of the United States for nine years and must be a resident of the state at the time of his election. It was thought that the longer term and higher qualifications would tend to give greater dignity and strength to the upper chamber than would be found in the lower house, and at the same time a higher average of ability.

There is no provision of the Constitution which requires a senator to be a resident of a particular part of the state, but in some states there is a custom that the two senators shall be taken from different sections. Thus in Vermont custom requires that one senator shall come from the section of the state east of the Green Mountains and the other from the west side. Sometimes when there is a large city in the state it is the custom to choose one of the senators from the city and the other from the country. For a long time Maryland did not trust this matter to custom but by law enacted that one of the senators should be an inhabitant of the eastern shore and the other of the western shore.

Character of the Senate.—In the early days when the states were generally regarded as sovereign communities, senators were looked upon somewhat as ambassadors to the national government, and the right to instruct them as to how they should vote on important questions was sometimes claimed and asserted by the legislatures. Sometimes the senators obeyed the instructions, sometimes they refused; and in the latter case there were no means of enforcing obedience. Not infrequently senators are "requested" by the legislature of the state which they represent to vote for or against a particular bill.

The Senate undoubtedly possesses elements of strength and efficiency which are not to be found in the lower house. As it is a much smaller body, debate there can be carried on with more effectiveness, and the individual member has greater opportunity to make his influence felt upon legislation. The efficiency of the Senate is further increased by the fact that its members are generally men of more mature age and larger legislative experience, many of them having already served their apprenticeship in the lower house. Moreover, owing to the longer term, they are more independent of the popular opinion of the moment and, therefore, under less temptation to yield to popular clamor and vote for measures which their better judgment condemns. These facts, it may be added, have tended to increase the attractiveness of the Senate as a legislative body and to draw into it statesmen of larger ability than the lower house has been able to attract.

At the same time, these elements of strength have to some extent been sources of weakness. The attractions of the Senate have stimulated the ambitions of rich men who have few other qualifications than the possession of great wealth, and so it came to pass that a considerable proportion of the members of the upper house were representatives of great corporations and of other forms of wealth. This was not necessarily an evil, but it was often said that the senators were irresponsive to public opinion. Moreover, the Senate has been criticized for usurping to a considerable extent the powers of the executive department in regard to appointments and the conduct of foreign affairs, and has encroached upon the powers of the lower house in respect to the initiation of revenue bills. Finally, the tradition of senatorial courtesy, which makes it possible for a single senator to deadlock indefinitely the proceedings of the Senate, has been criticized as being quite out of harmony with reasonable notions of legislative procedure. All these charges, however, have been vigorously denied by many defenders of the Senate. Some of them are well founded, but all in all, the Senate compares favorably with the best upper chambers of other countries.

Decisions as to Congressional Elections and Membership.—Each house of Congress is the judge of the election, qualifications, and returns of its own members, that is, it is empowered to determine whether a member who claims to have been elected has been legally chosen and whether he really possesses the qualifications prescribed by the Constitution for membership in the house. It seems to be admitted that either house may also refuse to admit a member for other reasons than those prescribed by the Constitution, as, for example, for having been convicted of a crime or because he is insane or suffering with a dangerous contagious disease. Thus in 1900 the house of representatives refused to allow a member from Utah to take his seat because he was living in violation of the anti-polygamy laws, and in 1919 it excluded a Socialist member from Wisconsin for disloyalty during the war.

Contested Elections.—Frequently there is a contested election from a state or district, that is, two men claim to have been elected to the same seat, in which case the house must decide which one is entitled to the seat. In such a case the claims of the contestant and the contestee are heard by the committee on privileges and elections, which makes a report to the house with a recommendation as to which shall be given the seat. Unfortunately, contested election cases are not always settled on their merits, the seat being usually given to the claimant who belongs to the party which has a majority in the house. In England this source of party favoritism is removed by vesting the settlement of cases of contested elections in the courts, which are more apt to decide such contests on their merits.

Power of Expulsion.—When a member has once been admitted to his seat, he can be deprived of it only by expulsion, and to prevent the employment of this power for party purposes, the Constitution provides that the concurrence of two thirds of the members shall be necessary to expel a member. Several instances of expulsion have occurred in the past. Senator Blount of Tennessee was expelled from the senate in 1797, and a number of other cases occurred in each house during the Civil War.

Compensation of Members of Congress.—The Constitution declares that senators and representatives shall receive a compensation for their services, the same to be paid out of the treasury of the United States. Under the Articles of Confederation, each state paid its own members of Congress, and there was no uniformity in respect to the scale of compensation. Some states paid much smaller salaries than others and in order to reduce the burden of maintaining their representatives, the states generally sent to Congress the fewest number of representatives required, and as each state had only one vote, nothing was lost by having a minimum number present. One other objection to the method of state payment was that it tended to make the representative dependent upon his state and caused him to feel that he was the representative of a state rather than of the country as a whole.

In fixing the amount of the compensation of its members, Congress is subject to no restrictions. It may fix the salary at any amount it pleases, may make it retroactive in effect or may increase the amount at any time during the term for which the members are chosen. The present salary of senators and representatives is $7,500 per year, but the Speaker of the house receives $12,000 per year. In addition, each member receives an allowance for a secretary, a small sum for stationery, and mileage of twenty cents per mile going and coming by the nearest route between his home and the national capital. This mileage is intended to cover the traveling expenses of the member and his family.

In some of the countries of Europe until recently members of Parliament did not receive any compensation from the public treasury unless they happened to be members of the cabinet; this was the rule in Great Britain prior to 1911. Sometimes, however, members who represented the socialist or labor party were paid by voluntary contributions by the members of their party. The advantage of paying members of Congress a reasonable compensation is that it enables competent men without private incomes to serve the state equally with the well-to-do, who are not dependent upon their public salaries for a livelihood.

The Franking Privilege.—Another privilege which Congress allows its members is to send their mail through the post office without the payment of postage. The spirit of the law restricts the privilege to the official correspondence of members, but the privilege is generally abused. Thus a senator from South Carolina was recently criticized by the post-office department for franking his typewriter through the mails. President Taft in his annual message to Congress in December, 1910, dwelt upon the abuses of this privilege by members of Congress and other government officials. The postmaster general in 1914 called attention to a recent instance in which more than 300,000 pamphlets were circulated under the frank of a member of Congress, the postage on which would have amounted to $57,000. They related not to public business but to the interest of a certain industry in which he was concerned.

Rights and Privileges of Members of Congress.—The Constitution provides that members shall not be arrested in any case except treason, felony, and breach of the peace, during their attendance at the sessions of their respective houses and in going to and from the same; and for any speech or debate in either house, they cannot be questioned in any other place. The purpose of the first provision is to prevent interference with members in the discharge of their high and responsible duties, through arrest for trivial offenses or trumped-up charges. If a member, however, commits an offense amounting to a breach of the peace, his immunity from arrest ceases and he may be dealt with by the courts as any other offender. The object of the second provision is to secure to members absolute freedom of speech on the floor of Congress by relieving them from the liability to prosecution for slander for anything they may say in the course of debate.

Disqualifications.—On the other hand, the Constitution provides that no person holding any office under the United States shall be a member of either house of Congress during his continuance in office. This provision was adopted in pursuance of the view that the executive and legislative departments should, as far as practicable, be kept separate. Moreover, no senator or representative may, during the time for which he is elected, be appointed to any civil office which shall have been created or the emoluments of which shall have been increased during such time. The purpose of this provision is to prevent Congress from creating new offices or increasing the salaries of existing offices for the benefit of members who might desire to be appointed to them.

Special Functions of the Senate.—The senate is not only a coequal branch of the national legislature but it possesses in addition certain powers not enjoyed by the lower house.

Share in the Appointing Power.—First of all, it shares with the President the power of appointment to federal offices. The Constitution makes its approval necessary to the validity of all appointments made by the executive, the idea being that the participation of the senate would serve as a restraint upon the errors or abuses of the President and thus insure the appointment of honest and capable men to office. But it was never intended to give the senate anything more than the negative power of rejecting the nominations of the President. It is his power to nominate and that of the senate to approve or disapprove the nomination. Nevertheless, there has grown up in the senate a practice by which the senators from a particular state in which an appointment to a federal office is to be made, claim the right to select the appointee themselves and when they have agreed upon him to present his name to the President for appointment; provided, of course, that they are of the same party as the President. If the President refuses to comply with the request of the senators from a particular state, and nominates an official who is unacceptable to them, the custom of "senatorial courtesy," which has become one of the traditions of the senate, requires that the senators from the other states shall stand by their associates in question and reject the nomination of the President. In this way the senate has, in effect, assumed the power of dictating to the President appointments to many federal offices in the states, such as those of postmaster, federal judge, attorney, revenue collector, and the like. If the two senators from a state belong to different political parties, the one with whom the President is in political sympathy controls the federal patronage in the state.

Share in the Treaty-Making Power.—The senate also shares with the President the power of making treaties with foreign countries. The ordinary procedure is for the President, through the Department of State, to negotiate the treaty, after which it is laid before the senate for its approval. Approval by a two-thirds vote of the senators is necessary to the validity of the treaty. The purpose of giving the senate a share in the treaty-making power was to provide a check or restraint upon the possible abuses or errors of the executive. The extraordinary majority required for the approval of the treaty, however, has frequently proved a handicap and led to the defeat of a number of valuable treaties. Thus a small political minority can prevent the ratification of a treaty and sometimes does so when it sees an opportunity to reap political advantage thereby.

The Constitution speaks of the "advice and consent" of the senate, but in practice all the senate does is to give its consent. In the early days, however, the President not infrequently requested the "advice" of the senate before starting the negotiation of a treaty, and if the advice was unfavorable the proposed negotiations were abandoned. Even now if the President has doubts as to whether a proposed treaty would receive the approval of two thirds of the senate he will sometimes consult with the members of the senate committee on foreign relations and with other influential members, before beginning the negotiations.

The senate may reject a treaty *in toto*, and has done so in many instances, or it may amend a treaty laid before it, in which case it must be sent back to the government of the other country which is a party thereto for concurrence in the amendments. After the senate has consented to the ratification of a treaty, the President may ratify it or not as he likes.

LIBRARY OF CONGRESS, WASHINGTON, D.C.

THE WHITE HOUSE,—THE PRESIDENT'S HOME AND OFFICE

The Senate as a Court of Impeachment.—Another special function of the senate is that of acting as a court for the trial of impeachment cases. The Constitution declares that the President, Vice President, and all civil officers of the United States shall be removed from office on impeachment for and conviction of treason, bribery, or other high crimes and misdemeanors. Military and naval officers are tried by court-martial and are not therefore liable to impeachment.[29] To impeach an officer is to bring charges against him. So far as federal officers are concerned this power belongs exclusively to the house of representatives, which acts somewhat as a grand jury does in finding indictments against ordinary criminals. When sitting as a court of impeachment the senators are under a special oath, and when the President is on trial the chief justice of the Supreme Court is the presiding officer instead of the Vice President, who, in such a case, would be directly interested in the outcome of the trial, since in the event of the conviction and removal of the President he would succeed to the office. Managers appointed by the house of representatives appear at the bar of the senate to prosecute the charges preferred by the house, witnesses are examined, evidence presented, and the accused is defended by counsel of his own choosing. In order to prevent the employment of the impeachment power for party purposes, the Constitution provides that the concurrence of two thirds of the senators shall be necessary to convict.

The punishment which the senate may inflict in case of conviction is limited to removal from office and disqualification from holding office in the future. The Constitution makes it mandatory upon the senate to remove the convicted official, but whether he shall forever be disqualified from holding office in the future is left to the discretion of the senate. In England the House of Lords, which tries impeachment cases, is not limited in the extent of punishment which it may inflict, but may, at its discretion, sentence the convicted official to imprisonment or the payment of a fine. While the senate of the United States cannot do this, the person convicted and removed may, nevertheless, be indicted and tried by the courts as any other criminal may.

The procedure of removing an officer by impeachment is so cumbersome and unwieldy that it has rarely been resorted to. During our entire history there have been only eight impeachment trials of federal officers, and of these there were convictions in but three cases.[30] If this were the only method of removal it would be difficult to get rid of corrupt and incompetent officials, but it must be remembered that any federal official except the judges may be removed from office by the President for any reason that to him seems fit and proper; and the power is frequently exercised.

References.—ANDREWS, Manual of the Constitution, pp. 47-68. BEARD, American Government and Politics, chs. xii-xiii. BRYCE, The American Commonwealth (abridged edition), chs. ix-xii. HARRISON, This Country of Ours, ch. ii. HART, Actual Government, ch. xiii. HINSDALE, American Government, chs. xvii-xxiii. WILSON, Congressional Government, secs. 1273-1293.

Documentary and Illustrative Material.—1. Copy of the Congressional Directory. 2. Copies of the Congressional Record. 3. A map showing the Congressional districts of the state.

RESEARCH QUESTIONS

1. How many representatives in Congress has your state?

2. Is there any evidence that your state is "gerrymandered"?

3. In what congressional district do you live? How many counties are there in the district? What is its population? How much does the population vary from the congressional ratio? Who is your representative? How many terms has he served? What is his party? By how large a majority was he elected?

4. Who is the senior senator from your state? The junior senator? How many terms has each served? To which of the three classes does each belong?

5. If the first congressional ratio of one member for 30,000 inhabitants were now in force, what would be the number of representatives in the house? Give arguments for and against the proposition that a house of 435 members is too large.

6. Is the present salary of members of Congress sufficiently large to attract the best men? Do you think the European custom of not paying salaries to members of Parliament a wise one?

7. Do you think members of Congress are morally entitled to "constructive" mileage, that is, for mileage not actually traveled, as where one session merges into another?

8. Members of the British Parliament are elected for a term of five years, those of the German Reichstag for five years, those of the French Chamber of Deputies for four years. In view of these rather long terms, do you think a two-year term for American representatives is too short?

9. Do you think the practice of members of Congress of distributing large quantities of garden seed among their constituents at public expense a wise or a vicious one?

10. Do you think public documents printed by authority of Congress should be distributed free of cost to all who desire them?

11. What is your opinion of the practice of members of Congress of printing in the Congressional Record long speeches never delivered in Congress?

12. Would the nomination of members of Congress by direct primary be a better method than nomination by convention?

13. What would be the advantage in requiring a newly elected Congress to assemble shortly after the election instead of about thirteen months thereafter, as is the present rule?

14. Ought the qualifications for voting for representatives in Congress to be determined by national authority instead of by the states?

15. Ought a representative to be required to be a resident of the district from which he is elected?

16. Do you think the states should be equally represented in the senate?

CHAPTER XI

ORGANIZATION AND PROCEDURE OF CONGRESS

Organization of the Two Houses.—*Officers.*—Each house of Congress is free to organize itself in such a manner as it pleases, and to choose its own officers, except that the Vice President of the United States is, by the Constitution, made the presiding officer of the senate. The presiding officer of the house of representatives is called the speaker; that of the senate, the president. Each house has one or more clerks who keep the journals, call rolls, read bills, and have custody of all bills, resolutions, petitions, and memorials; a sergeant-at-arms who preserves order, has charge of the halls, pays members their salaries, and performs various other duties[31]; a postmaster; a doorkeeper; a chaplain; and other minor officials.

Opening of a New Congress.—When a new Congress assembles, the house of representatives is called to order by the clerk of the preceding house. He then calls the roll of the members whose credentials or certificates of election have been filed with him, and if a quorum is present the house proceeds to the election of a speaker. The members of each political party represented in the house have already in caucus agreed upon their candidates, and they are now put in nomination before the house by some member representing each party. Usually the action of the caucus of the majority party is equivalent to an election, and the house has only to ratify its choice. In several instances, however, the election of the speaker involved long and bitter contests. Thus in 1849, 63 ballots were taken, and again in 1855-1856, 133 ballots were necessary, and in each case a special rule was adopted permitting a plurality to elect.

The senate, on the other hand, is always an organized body. The presiding officer—the Vice President—at the opening of a new Congress calls the senate to order, and the other officers, who hold during the pleasure of the senate, resume their duties. The senate elects one of its own members as president *pro tempore* to preside over its deliberations during the absence of the Vice President or in case there is no Vice President, as has often happened.

The Oath of Office is usually administered to the speaker by the oldest member in point of service,—called "the Father of the House,"—after which the speaker calls the other members to the front—usually by state delegations —and administers the oath to them. Newly elected senators are escorted to the

Vice President's desk, usually each by his state colleague, and are sworn in individually.

Adoption of the Rules.—After the administering of the oaths of office, the house adopts the rules of the preceding Congress for regulating its procedure pending the adoption of new rules. Usually this is a perfunctory performance and is carried through without opposition. At the opening of the sixty-first Congress, however, strong opposition was manifested toward the old rules and they were not readopted until important amendments had been made in them.

After the adoption of the rules each house appoints a committee to notify the other of its readiness for business, and the two then appoint a joint committee to inform the President of the United States that Congress is ready to receive any communication that he may be pleased to make. The message of the President is then laid before each house and the business of Congress proceeds.

Quorum.—The Constitution provides that a majority of each house shall constitute a quorum for the transaction of business, but that a smaller number may compel the attendance of absent members in such manner and under such penalties as each house may prescribe.

Old Method of Counting a Quorum.—For a long time the method of ascertaining whether a quorum was present was by a roll call. If the roll call failed to show the presence of a majority, the speaker ruled that no quorum was present, even though every member of the house was actually in his seat. In the course of time this rule came to be frequently abused by the minority for the purpose of preventing consideration of measures to which it was opposed. Thus in January, 1890, when the Republicans had only a slight majority in the house of representatives, the Democrats were able, owing to the absence of a few Republican members, to break a quorum and prevent consideration of important measures, by refusing to answer to the roll call. On a notable occasion in January, 1890, the roll call showed 161 yeas, 2 nays, and not voting 165, the 165 who refused to vote being Democrats who were opposed to the taking up of a certain measure which the Republicans desired to pass. Under the rules the roll call did not show a quorum present, though more than two thirds of the members were actually in their seats.

The New Method.—The Republican majority therefore adopted a new rule, that members who were actually in their seats were to be counted by the speaker as present, no matter whether they voted or not. The action of Speaker Reed in enforcing this rule raised a storm of protest by the minority, but he courageously stood his ground. The new rule was readopted by the next Congress though the Democrats were then in the majority, and it has been continued ever since with the exception of one or two Congresses when the old rule was reverted to. Much of the business of Congress is really done, however, when there is no quorum present, this being permissible so long as the point of "no quorum" is not raised by any member.

Open Sessions.—The ordinary sessions of both houses are open to the public, though until 1794 the senate held its sessions in secret. When the senate goes into executive session, as it may do when it is considering nominations of the President to public office or is engaged in considering treaties, the galleries are cleared, the doors closed, and its deliberations are conducted in secret, though, the results of its transactions usually leak out in some way.

Seating of Members.—Until 1913 each member of each house was provided with a seat and a desk, but in that year the desks were removed from the house of representatives in order to bring the members nearer together. Prior to that date, seats were assigned to members by lot at the opening of Congress, but the leader of the minority party and one or two other members of long service were usually allowed to select their seats without resort to the lot. The Democrats are seated on the right of the speaker and the Republicans on the left. In the senate, each seat as it becomes vacant is assigned to the member who first makes application for it to the presiding officer. The house chamber is so large that members in the rear seats are at a disadvantage, and speech making is carried on with difficulty. In 1913, however, this inconvenience was diminished by a reduction in the size of the hall by about one third of the floor space.[32] The senate chamber is less spacious, and debate can be conducted with much greater satisfaction and effectiveness. It would be a great advantage if the number of representatives could be reduced to 250 or 300 so as to make the house less unwieldy, but there is little probability that such a reform will ever be effected. If smaller in size, the house could transact its business with more dispatch, give more careful consideration to bills, and allow members a greater opportunity for discussion.

Committees.—Obviously an assembly of more than 400 members cannot legislate effectively as a whole; its work must be done largely by committees. To some committee every measure and every petition is referred, as are also the various recommendations of the President. In the sixty-seventh Congress (1921-1923) there were thirty-four standing committees in the senate and sixty in the house. Usually there are also several select committees, and occasionally a few joint committees. In the senate, the committees vary in size from three to sixteen members; in the house from three to thirty-five.

The most important committees in the senate are those on appropriations, commerce, finance, foreign relations, interstate commerce, judiciary, military affairs, naval affairs, and public expenditures. The least important are those on disposition of useless papers, University of the United States, and Revolutionary claims, since there is little or no business referred to them. The most important committees in the house are those on ways and means, appropriations, banking and currency, public expenditures, foreign affairs, interstate and foreign commerce, judiciary, military affairs, naval affairs, public buildings and grounds, rivers and harbors, and rules (twelve members now, formerly five). The least important is that on the disposition of useless papers.[33]

Method of Choosing Committees.—In the senate committee assignments are nominally made by the senate itself, but in reality they are made by two committees on committees selected by a caucus of the members of each party, the recommendations of the two committees usually being accepted by the senate without debate. Both parties are represented on each committee, the dominant party, of course, being given a majority of the places. Thus on a committee of thirteen members, the majority party is usually represented by eight members and the minority by five; on a committee of seventeen, the numbers are eleven and six respectively, and so on.

In the house of representatives, from the beginning until very recently, all the committees were appointed by the speaker, a power which gave him great influence in shaping and determining the course of legislation, since he might constitute the committees with reference to their friendliness or unfriendliness toward legislative measures that were referred to them for investigation and report. In making committee assignments, however, the speaker was not entirely free to follow his own individual preferences. Thus the tradition of the house required that he must take into consideration the claims of members whose service had been long and distinguished, while political gratitude led him to reward with desirable committee assignments those to whom he was especially indebted for his election as speaker. Seniority of committee service was also taken into account when the chairmanship of an important committee became vacant, the next ranking member of the committee having a strong claim to be promoted to the vacancy. In 1911, however, the house, then controlled by the Democrats, adopted a rule providing for the election of all standing committees by the house; thus making the method of choosing committees the same as in the senate.

In the house, the chairmanship of every committee, whether important or unimportant, is given to a member of the dominant party, and of course also a majority of the other places on the committee, the proportion between the representation of the two parties being about the same as on the senate committees.

Introduction and Reference of Bills.—After the appointment of the committees the house is ready for the transaction of legislative business. Bills are introduced by sending them, indorsed with the name of the introducer, to the presiding officer's desk, where the fact of presentation is entered on the journal and the bill is given a number.[34] Thus the first bill introduced at the beginning of a new Congress is designated as "S. 1," if presented in the senate, and "H. R. 1," if presented in the house of representatives.

Reference to Committees.—The next step is to refer the bill to a committee for consideration, and in the meantime it is printed and placed on the desks of members. Reference to the appropriate committee is usually made by the presiding officer, though the house may direct that it shall be referred to a particular committee.

Some idea of the mass of legislative projects referred to the committees may be gained from the fact that in the sixtieth Congress 27,114 bills and resolutions were introduced into the two houses, and that of these, 7,839 were reported by the committees to which they were referred. We have here a good illustration of the necessity of the committee system, since it would have been a physical impossibility for either house as a whole to have considered even slightly so many bills. The committees sift out of the mass of proposed legislation such measures as they think worthy of enacting into law, and report their recommendations to the house as a whole.

Committee Hearings.—Committees charged with the consideration of important bills frequently hold public hearings at which interested parties may appear and present arguments for and against the measures under consideration. Thus the ways and means committee of the house in 1909 held public hearings at Washington for many weeks on the tariff bill, and scores of persons appeared to advocate lower or higher rates on various articles on which duties were to be imposed. Frequently members who introduce bills appear before committees and urge favorable action. The more important committees in each house have a regular day in each week for meeting, and a few of those in the house of representatives meet twice a week. Most of the committees, however, have no regular meeting day, being called together by their chairmen as occasion requires.

Forms of Committee Action.—The committee to which a bill is referred may pursue any one of the following courses: (1) It may report the bill back to the house with a recommendation that it be passed; (2) it may amend the bill and recommend that it be passed as amended; (3) it may throw the bill aside and report an entirely new one in its place; (4) it may report the bill unfavorably with a recommendation that it do not pass; (5) it may "pigeonhole" the bill, that is, take no action on it at all, or report it so late in the session that no opportunity is allowed for its consideration. The latter method of disposal, sometimes called "smothering," is the fate that awaits the great majority of bills introduced into Congress. The "smothering" of bills became the subject of so much complaint among members recently that the rules were amended so as to allow members to demand that their bills be reported to the house for consideration. The house, of course, may at any time instruct a committee to report a bill for its action, but this is rarely done.

The report to the house is usually made by the chairman of the committee, or some one designated by him. Not infrequently the minority members of the committee also make a report opposing the recommendation of the majority. The committee system of legislation is so thoroughly established in Congress that a bill favorably reported stands an excellent chance of being passed, while one adversely reported hardly ever passes.

Rules of Procedure.—The Constitution provides that each house may frame its own rules of procedure, though it requires certain things to be done in the interest of publicity and to insure a reasonable degree of careful deliberation. Thus each house is required to keep and publish a journal which must show how motions are disposed of and the vote for and against measures voted on. It also requires that on demand of one fifth of the members present the yeas and nays upon a measure shall be entered upon the journal. The purpose of this provision is to enable a small number of members to put the house on record so that the people may know how their representatives have voted on important measures.

Filibustering.—This requirement serves a useful purpose, but it is sometimes taken advantage of by the minority in "filibustering," that is, in obstructing and delaying legislative proceedings. Thus a member may move to adjourn or to take a recess and ask that the roll be called and the yeas and nays on the question be entered upon the journal. If one fifth of the members join in the demand, the roll must be called and the process may be repeated indefinitely. On one occasion in the fiftieth Congress the house remained in session eight days and nights, during which time there were over one hundred roll calls on motions of this kind.

The Rules of the House of Representatives have evolved gradually out of the experience of the house during its long existence, and have come to be so complex and elaborate that they are really understood by only a few of the members, principally those who have had long experience in administering them. They have been revised from time to time, but except in a few particulars they are essentially what they were in 1880. They prescribe a certain order of business for each day's work, which, however, may be departed from by unanimous consent of all the members or by the adoption of a "special order" reported by the committee on rules.

Committee of the Whole.—Revenue and appropriation bills are considered by the house of representatives in committee of the whole. When the house goes into committee of the whole, the speaker leaves the chair and calls some one else to preside in his place, and the presence of 100 members constitutes a quorum. Debate in committee of the whole is conducted rather informally, and greater freedom of discussion is allowed. It is when in committee of the whole that many of the lengthy speeches printed in the *Congressional Record* are supposed to be delivered. In reality, however, only a small portion of these speeches are actually delivered, for members after addressing the house a few minutes often secure leave to print the remainder of their remarks. Under this leave, members frequently print long speeches which have little or no relation to the subject under consideration but are intended for campaign purposes or for effect upon their constituents. They are then franked through the mails to the voters throughout the district which the member represents.

If the bill is a private bill, it is called up for consideration on Friday, which is private bill day. Most of the private bills are reported from the committees on claims and on pensions. Six or seven thousand such bills are passed by each Congress, and they constitute about nine tenths of the entire number enacted.

Suspension of the Rules.—The regular order of business may be departed from at any time on the demand of privileged committees like those on ways and means, appropriations, elections, rules, and a few others which have a sort of right of way in the house, because of the urgent character of the matters with which they deal. Furthermore, by unanimous consent, often granted, a particular member is allowed to bring up a bill for consideration outside the regular order. Finally, on two Mondays in every month and during the last six days of the session, the rules may be suspended by a two-thirds vote and measures to which there is little objection may be quickly passed and thus the business of the house expedited.

The Speaker and the Committee on Rules.—No discussion of the procedure of the house of representatives would be adequate without a consideration of the part played by the speaker and the committee on rules in determining the course and character of legislation.

The English Speaker.—The speakership is an ancient office inherited from England, where it originated in the fourteenth century, and is an outgrowth of the practical necessities of legislative procedure. The American speakership, however, differs widely from its English prototype. The speaker of the House of Commons has no such power in shaping legislation and controlling debate as does the American speaker. He is in fact little more than a moderator with power to put motions, state questions, and preserve order and decorum in debate. He is entirely impartial, with no party prejudices.

Powers of the American Speaker.—The American speaker, on the contrary, is not merely the presiding officer of the house, but he is an active party leader who seldom hesitates to give members of his own party every possible advantage in the course of debate. His right to appoint the committees of the house until 1911 gave him increased power over the shaping of legislation, because of the fact that the legislation of the house has come to be legislation largely by its committees. As has already been said, he gave the members of his own party all the chairmanships of committees, as well as a majority of the places on every committee, so that they easily controlled the work of the committees and hence of the house itself.

Recognition.—Moreover, his power of recognition, especially before 1910, that is, the power to grant or withhold the right of discussion, enabled him to a large degree to prevent consideration of measures to which he was opposed and to cut off debate by members of the minority party, joined with the Democrats and brought about several amendments to the rules, one of which is designed to do away with the chief source of complaint in regard to the power of recognition.

Committee on Rules.—Still another source of the speaker's power until 1910 was his control of the committee on rules. The committee consisted of five members, two from the majority, two from the minority, and the speaker, who was the fifth member. The speaker appointed his four associates on the committee and thereby controlled its decisions. If he wished at any time to have the house take up a bill at the bottom of the calendar instead of one at the top, or in any other respect depart from the established order of procedure, he could call the committee together (it was the one committee that had the right to meet when the house was in session) and have it report what was called a "special order," to that effect—an order which the house usually adopted. The opposition to the power of this committee and more especially to its domination by the speaker led in 1910 to the adoption of a rule depriving the speaker of membership on the committee, increasing its size from five to eleven, and taking the appointment of the committee out of his hands. Since then it has been elected by the house, and is, it is asserted, a more representative committee.

Caucus Methods.—It is a common practice for the representatives of each party to hold a caucus before the beginning of the debate upon an important measure, especially one of a political character, for the purpose of deciding what shall be the policy of the party toward the measure. Sometimes a rule is adopted by the caucus binding the members of the party to vote for or against the bill on the floor. Thus in 1913 caucuses of Democratic and representatives declared the tariff and currency bills to be party measures and pledged the members to vote for the bills without amendment. This practice has been criticized on the ground that where members have bound themselves to vote for a bill before it has been discussed on the floor, debate is useless since their minds are no longer open to argument. Perhaps a better procedure would be to hold the caucus after the discussion has terminated but before the final vote is taken.

Final Stages of Procedure.—The rules of the house of representatives restrict the time which may be occupied by any member in debating a measure to one hour, and this cannot be exceeded except by unanimous consent. If he chooses, he may yield a portion of his time to some other member. The chairman who reports the bill usually opens the discussion. He is followed by the ranking member of the minority on the committee, and these are followed by other members of the committee in their turn.

The Previous Question.—After the discussion has proceeded for a time, debate may be terminated and the house brought to a vote by means of the previous question, which is moved in the form, "Shall the main question now be put?" When ordered by the house it ends debate and brings the house directly to a vote. This is an effective method for putting an end to useless discussion of a measure and taking the sense of the house on its passage. It is a common form of procedure in legislative bodies, though the senate, until 1917, had no way of limiting debate.

Voting on Bills.—Questions on the passage of bills are put by the speaker as follows: "As many as are in favor say *aye*"; "As many as are opposed say *no*"; the speaker determining the result by the sound of the voices. If there is a doubt as to which side has prevailed, a "division" is called for, in which case those in favor rise and are counted after which those who are opposed rise and are counted. If there is still doubt as to the result, "tellers" may be appointed to determine the vote, in which case those in favor of the measure file between the two tellers, who make a careful count, after which those opposed pass between them and are similarly counted. If one fifth of the members demand that a yea and nay vote be taken, the clerk must call the roll and record each member's vote, and the result is published in the journal so that the way in which a member votes may be known to his constituents and all others who may be interested.

Passage by the Second House.—When a bill is passed by one house, it is signed by the presiding officer, after which it is transmitted to the other house, where it goes through practically the same stages of procedure as described above. If the bill is passed by the other house without amendment it is "enrolled," after which it is ready for the signature of the President. If, however, a bill as passed by one house is amended by the other, it is customary to appoint a conference committee, consisting usually of three members from each house, to discuss the differences and suggest a basis of compromise. The committee usually recommends that each house recede from its position on certain points, and the result is reported to each house, which usually accepts the agreement and the bill is passed. Many important bills are finally passed in this way, though occasionally the two houses fail to reach an agreement and the bill fails.

Approval of the President.—When the bill is presented to the President he is allowed ten days to make up his mind as to whether he will sign or disapprove it. If he refuses to sign it, he usually returns it to the house in which it originated, with a statement of his objections, after which the house must proceed to reconsider it, and if it is passed by a two-thirds vote it is sent to the other chamber and if repassed by it by a two-thirds vote it becomes a law notwithstanding the veto of the President. But in such cases the yeas and nays must be entered on the journal of each house so that the record may show that the bill was properly passed. In case the President does not approve the bill and neglects to return it within ten days to the house in which it originated, it becomes law in the same manner as if he had signed it, unless Congress should adjourn in the meantime so that it cannot be returned, in which case it does not become law. As a large number of bills are usually sent to the President during the last ten days of the session, an opportunity is thus afforded him for defeating bills by neither signing nor vetoing them. This method of defeating bills is popularly described by the term "pocket veto," a procedure sometimes resorted to where the President does not approve a bill and yet does not wish to take the responsibility for positively vetoing it.

Procedure in the Senate.—In the senate, partly by reason of its small size, partly by reason of its permanence, and partly by reason of the tradition of senatorial courtesy, the procedure is somewhat different from that of the house of representatives. For example, the senate rules are permanent, that is, they continue from one Congress to another and do not have to be adopted anew every two years.

The President of the Senate is little more than a moderator; indeed, he may belong to a different political party from that which is in control of the chamber—a situation that never happens in the house. He does not appoint the committees of the senate, and so has no power of predetermining the character of legislation. Moreover, he has no power to control debate through the power of recognition. The traditions of the senate require that he shall recognize the first senator who rises to speak, and that he shall treat the members of both parties impartially in according recognition for purposes of debate.

Unlimited Debate.—Until 1917 one of the usages of the senate was the right of unlimited debate. Owing to the small size of the senate, much greater freedom of discussion is possible than in the house of representatives, where there are more than four times as many members. Debate can also be conducted with much more ease and is much more effective, since the size of the hall is smaller and members are not under the necessity of speaking at the top of their voices. While a member of the house can rarely get an opportunity to deliver a speech and then only for a few minutes, a senator may usually speak as long as he pleases. Advantage of this privilege is frequently taken by senators to deliver long speeches, not so much to convince their colleagues, as to get their views before the country at large or to make an impression on their constituents at home. Under the rules as they were before 1917, there was no limit to a senator's right to debate. The privilege was made use of occasionally near the close of a session for "filibustering" purposes. Thus a few senators with strong lungs, large vocabularies, and a liberal supply of documents from which to read, might consume the time of the senate for weeks and prevent it from acting on measures to which they were opposed. Many times in our history a single senator has forced the senate to abandon the consideration of important measures, by threatening to consume the remaining time of the session by speech making. In the last days of one session of Congress, a senator from Wisconsin spoke continuously for more than seventeen hours in an effort to prevent action on a currency bill. Near the end of the 64th Congress (March, 1917) a small group of senators filibustered to prevent the senate from taking a vote on a bill to give the President authority to arm American merchant vessels for defensive purposes, notwithstanding the fact that nearly all the other senators desired to pass the bill. Shortly thereafter the senate adopted a new rule which makes it possible, by a two-thirds vote, to limit the debate on any measure to one hour for each senator. The rule was applied in November, 1919, to bring to an end protracted discussion of the treaty of peace with Germany.

References.—BEARD, American Government and Politics, ch. xiv.

BRYCE, The American Commonwealth (abridged edition), chs. xiii-xv. HART, Actual Government, ch. xiv. HARRISON, This Country of Ours, ch. iii. REINSCH, American Legislatures and Legislative Methods, ch. i.

Documentary and Illustrative Material.—1. The Congressional Directory. 2. The House and Senate Rules. 3. Precedents of the House of Representatives, published as a public document in 1909. 4. The Congressional Record. 5. Specimen copies of bills and resolutions. 6. The last annual message of the President. 7. Copies of committee reports. 8. Veto messages of the President. 9. Diagrams of the house and senate chambers.

RESEARCH QUESTIONS

1. Why are rules of procedure necessary in legislative bodies?

2. For what purpose does the Constitution require each house to keep a journal of its proceedings?

3. Which do you think the better practice, the American rule, by which each house of Congress settles election contests of its own members, or the English rule, which places that power in the hands of the courts?

4. What is the reason for allowing a small number of members of each house to compel the attendance of absent members?

5. Under what conditions may each house punish outsiders?

6. What is your opinion of the English rule which allows forty members out of a total of six hundred and seventy members to constitute a quorum?

7. Why should senators and representatives be privileged from arrest for any but serious offenses?

8. What are the principal differences between the rules of procedure of the senate and the house of representatives?

9. Do you think it would be a wise provision to permit the members of the cabinet to occupy seats in Congress without the right to vote?

10. Trace a bill through Congress, showing the various stages through which it must pass before becoming a law.

11. Of what committees is your representative a member? Is he chairman of any committee?

12. Do you think the minority party should be given a larger representation on the committees of Congress and larger privileges of debate?

13. Give the names of the five most distinguished speakers of the house of

representatives since 1789.

14. Why is debate more effective in the senate than in the house of representatives?

15. Which of the two houses exerts the greater influence in determining national legislation? Give your reasons.

16. What are some of the so-called "usurped" powers now exercised by the senate?

CHAPTER XII

FEDERAL FINANCE, TAXATION, AND MONEY

The National Taxing Power.—The lack of the power of Congress to levy taxes was, as we have seen, one of the chief weaknesses of the Articles of Confederation, voluntary contributions by the states being the chief source of revenue for the national government. When, therefore, the framers of the Constitution came to deal with this subject, they wisely provided that Congress should have power to levy and collect its own revenues. The power conferred is almost absolute, the only limitations being that no duties shall be levied upon exports; that excises and duties levied on imports shall be uniform throughout the United States, that is, they shall be the same in amount on a given article everywhere; and that where direct taxes are levied, they shall be apportioned among the states on the basis of population.

Forms of Federal Taxes.—The two general forms of taxes recognized by the Constitution are direct and indirect taxes. The only direct taxes, in the sense of the Constitution of the United States, are poll taxes, and taxes on real or personal property, all of which are required to be apportioned among the states on the basis of population, whenever they are levied.

On account of the obvious injustice of levying a tax on the states on the basis of population, inasmuch as there might easily be twice as much property in one state as in another having the same population, this method has fallen into general disuse. Indeed, it has been resorted to by Congress only five times in our history, and then only for very short periods in each case. It does not seem likely that this method of federal taxation will ever again be resorted to.

Until recently the two principal sources of federal revenue have been duties on imports, and internal revenue, or excise taxes, on certain articles produced in this country.

Customs Duties.—*Specific and Ad Valorem.*—Customs duties are taxes levied on articles imported into the United States from abroad. They are of two kinds, specific and *ad valorem*. Specific duties are those levied on the articles according to their weight or measurement without regard to their value. Thus a duty of one and a half cents a pound on imported tin plate, or five cents a pound on dyestuffs, or ten cents a yard on silk would be specific. An *ad valorem* tax is one levied with reference to the value of the article. Thus a duty of 50 per cent on the value of imported woolen goods is an example of an *ad valorem* duty. Sometimes both forms of duty are levied on the same article.

In favor of the specific duty is the ease of collection, since the article has only to be weighed or measured and then assessed. But it is often inadequate, since one yard of cloth or one pound of dye may be many times more valuable than another, and so with many other articles. One practical objection to the *ad valorem* method is the opportunity which is afforded for fraud in the matter of valuation, since in many cases it is difficult to ascertain the real value of the article taxed.

The Protective Tariff.—From the beginning of our existence as a nation, reliance upon customs duties as a chief source of revenue has been a part of our established policy. In 1921 the receipts from this source were $308,025,102; and in many earlier years they were nearly half of the entire ordinary income of the national government. Great diversity of opinion, however, has existed in regard to what articles should be taxed and the amount that should be imposed. The Republican party has always insisted upon a tariff not only for revenue but also for protection to American industries and American labor against the cheap labor of the Old World. The Democratic party, on the other hand, has generally opposed the protective feature and insisted upon a tariff primarily for revenue.[35]

The Preparation of a Tariff Bill devolves upon the ways and means committee of the house of representatives, where all revenue bills must originate.[36] In 1916 Congress provided for the creation of a bi-partisan Tariff Commission to investigate the operation of tariff laws and to make reports with a view to furnishing Congress with information for its guidance in the preparation of tariff bills.

The Maximum and Minimum Principle.—In 1909 Congress adopted for the first time the maximum and minimum principle of fixing tariff rates. The law provided for a maximum and a minimum rate on many articles and authorized the President to apply the minimum rate to goods imported from countries which extend the same concession to articles imported by their citizens from the United States and to apply the maximum rate to others.

Reciprocity Treaties.—At various times in the past reciprocity treaties have been negotiated with foreign countries by which it was provided that lower rates should be levied on articles imported from such countries in return for reciprocal concessions of a similar kind from them; or that there should be free admission of articles by one country from the other.

Collection of Customs Duties.—The collection of the customs duties is part of the work of the treasury department. The country is divided into collection districts, in each of which there are one or more ports of entry and customhouses at which all imported goods must be landed. In each district there are a collector and a corps of appraisers, weighers, gaugers, naval officers, surveyors, and the like.

By far the most important port of entry in the United States is the city of New York, where the aggregate receipts for the year 1910 were two thirds of the entire amount received from customs duties in the United States. Until recently a number of the collection districts, however, were unimportant, and in a few the expenses of administration exceeded the receipts. Thus the receipts of the Georgetown (S. C.) district in 1910 were only $49.38, while the expenses were $265; the receipts of the Rock Island (Ill.) district were $51.79 and the expenses $660; the receipts of the Saco (Me.) district were $9.08 and the expenses $753.92. In pursuance of an act of Congress passed in 1912, the President has recently abolished or consolidated many of these districts, so that the number is now only 49, whereas formerly it was 120. For a long time the secretary of the treasury had urged Congress to authorize this reform, mainly in the interest of economy, but it acted tardily.

When goods are purchased abroad to be imported into the United States, the importer files with the United States consul at the foreign port from which they are to be exported an invoice containing a list of the goods and a statement of their value at the place where manufactured or produced. The consul certifies to the correctness of the invoice and sends a copy to the collector of the port at which the goods are to be landed.

Appraisals.—Upon arrival in the United States, the cargo is examined by the customs officers to see that it corresponds with the description contained in the invoice. If it is found that the goods are undervalued the value will be raised by the appraiser. If there is evidence of fraud, the goods will be confiscated or a heavy fine imposed on the importer.[37]

There is a general board of appraisers to which appeals may be taken by the importer on questions of valuation, and recently there has been created a United States court of customs appeals for the determination of various questions arising in the administration of the tariff laws.

Internal Revenue Taxes.—The second important source of federal income is excise taxes, or what are popularly known as internal revenue duties, that is, taxes on commodities produced in the United States.

The Receipts from internal revenue taxes as compared with those from customs duties were inconsiderable before the Civil War. In 1862, however, Congress passed a comprehensive internal revenue law which increased the tax on liquors and levied a tax on tobacco, besides license taxes on various trades and occupations. So many articles were taxed that the revenue from this source in 1866 amounted to more than $309,000,000, the largest sum collected in one year from internal revenue taxes until 1915. In 1917, in consequence of the war, the rates of many taxes were increased and new taxes were levied on freight and passenger transportation, express charges, telegrams, insurance policies, theater tickets, automobiles and many other articles, and a great variety of business transactions, such as stock transfers, bond issues, etc. For some purposes the taxes on incomes, profits, and inheritances (page 224) are called internal revenue. The following are the principal items of internal revenue in the year ending June 30, 1921:

Income and profits tax	$3,228,137,673
Distilled spirits	82,623,428
Tobacco	255,219,385
Estate inheritance tax	154,043,260
Tax on sales	282,222,065
Tax on tickets of admission	95,890,650
Tax on corporations	81,525,652
Tax on bonds, stock issues and transfers, etc.	72,468,013
Tax on transportation, telegraph and telephone	301,512,413

Collection of Internal Revenue Taxes.—For convenience in collecting internal revenue taxes, the country is divided into some sixty districts, not by act of Congress as is the case with customs districts, but by the order of the President. Sometimes several states are grouped into one district; sometimes a state is divided into several districts. Thus there are four districts in Illinois, six in New York, and five in Kentucky. In each district there is a collector who acts under the supervision of the United States Internal Revenue Commissioner. The collection of internal revenue taxes is a much more simple task than the collection of customs duties, and is done for the most part by the sale of stamps to the manufacturer, who is required to affix them on the articles taxed. In assessing the tax on most articles their value is not taken into consideration, and hence there is less opportunity for arbitrary action on the part of the government officials and of course less likelihood of controversy, than is the case with the administration of the customs laws.

Other Sources of Federal Revenue.—Besides the receipts obtained from tariff duties and internal revenue taxes, there are a number of other sources of revenue such as those from the sale of public land, the tax on national banks, fines and penalties for violations of the laws of the United States, profits on coinage, naturalization, immigration, patent office and other fees, etc.

Income Taxes.—In very recent years (since 1918), the income tax, in its various forms, has become the greatest of all the sources of revenue for the federal government.

It was in 1862 that Congress levied for the first time a tax on incomes, the rate varying from five to ten per cent according to the amount of the income, all incomes below $600 being exempt from the tax. In 1872, the law was repealed; but a demand for reviving this method of taxation gradually increased, and it came to be a standing part of the national platform of the Democratic party. Accordingly when the Democrats got control of Congress in 1894, they enacted a law providing that all incomes in excess of $4,000 a year should be taxed at the rate of two per cent on the amount in excess of that figure. Shortly after the law went into effect, however, the Supreme Court, overruling its former decisions, decided, by a vote of five to four, that the law was unconstitutional, mainly on the ground that a tax on income from property was a direct tax in the sense of the Constitution, and not having been apportioned among the states according to their population was null and void. Sentiment in favor of such a tax, however, steadily grew, and in 1913 the constitutional impediment was removed by the sixteenth amendment.

Later in the year Congress levied an income tax, in connection with an act to reduce tariff duties. The income tax is one per cent on each individual's annual net income in excess of $3000 (or $4000 for husband and wife living together), plus an additional tax of one per cent on net income over $20,000 and not exceeding $50,000, two per cent on net income over $50,000 and not exceeding $75,000, and so on up to six per cent on net income over $500,000.

The Corporation Tax.—Congress in 1909 passed a law imposing a tax on corporations, joint-stock companies, and associations, to the extent of one per cent on the net income of each in excess of $5,000 a year. In the year 1912 the tax yielded $28,583,259. The next year the exemption of $5,000 was removed, thus making the entire net income of corporations liable to the tax.

Inheritance Taxes.—During the Civil War and the war with Spain, Congress levied a tax on inheritances, and the permanent adoption of this form of taxation was strongly recommended by President Roosevelt in his annual messages, but owing largely to the fact that many of the states have passed laws of this kind, the idea has never commended itself to Congress.

CUSTOMHOUSE, NEW YORK

IN THE MINT AT PHILADELPHIA

Deposit of United States Funds.—The taxes collected by the national government, together with its other funds, are kept partly in the treasury and partly in the nine subtreasuries located at Baltimore, Boston, Chicago, Cincinnati, New Orleans, New York, Philadelphia, St. Louis, and San Francisco. In addition the secretary of the treasury is authorized to designate national banks as depositories and to deposit certain of the funds therein. In times of financial stringency or threatened crises, this authority may be used by the secretary to relieve the money market, by distributing the public funds among the depositories.

Federal Appropriations and Expenditures.—Having studied the sources of federal revenues, we come now to the subject of expenditures. Revenue bills are prepared, as we have seen, by the ways and means committee of the house of representatives. At first the appropriations of Congress were embodied in a single bill prepared by the committee on appropriations, but as the operations of the government expanded, the appropriations came to be embodied in a number of bills, sixteen in 1920, prepared by nine different committees. The committee on appropriations was responsible only for the half dozen more general appropriation bills, while other committees prepared the the bills appropriating large amounts for the army, navy, diplomatic service, post office, Department of Agriculture, District of Columbia, Indian service, and improvement of rivers and harbors. In 1921, however, the committee on appropriations was enlarged and again entrusted with the preparation of all the various appropriation bills, the house thus returning to the earlier system of a single committee responsible for all expenditures.

The growth of national expenditures has been rapid. The appropriations for 1916 reached the unprecedented amount of $1,637,583,682; those for the period of the war (1917-1918), $32,427,000,000, including $9,000,000,000 loaned to European allies. In 1921, the appropriations were reduced to about $5,500,000,000.

The National Debt.—Whenever the revenues of the government are insufficient to pay its expenses recourse must be had to increased taxes or loans. In time of peace the ordinary revenues ought to be sufficient to meet expenses, but when extraordinary expenses must be incurred as is the case when war breaks out, or foreign territory is purchased, or some great public work is to be constructed such as the digging of the Panama Canal, the government must have recourse to the borrowing power. The Constitution of the United States expressly confers upon Congress the power to borrow money on the credit of the United States, and no limitations whatever are placed on the exercise of the power, such as are generally imposed on state legislatures by the state constitutions.

United States Bonds.—The usual mode by which the government borrows money is by the issue of its bonds, obligations similar in most respects to promissory notes made by individuals. A government bond is simply a promise to pay a certain sum at a particular time and with interest at a certain rate. The bonds issued by the United States government are of two kinds: "registered" and "coupon" bonds. A registered bond is made out to the person who purchases it; a record is kept of it at the treasury department, and when it is transferred to another person the record must be changed so as to show the new owner.

The advantage of such a bond is that if it is accidentally destroyed or lost the owner suffers no loss. The chief disadvantage is the difficulty in transferring it. A coupon bond is one which has interest coupons attached to it, which may be clipped off and presented to the treasury for payment as the interest becomes due. The government keeps no record of the owner and it may be transferred as any other personal property. If a coupon bond is lost or destroyed, however, the owner cannot collect the amount of the bond. United States bonds are issued in various denominations and for periods of time which vary widely. Usually bonds are sold to the highest bidder, but occasionally they are disposed of by negotiation with capitalists on the best terms that can be secured. During President Cleveland's administration $262,000,000 of bonds were sold to New York capitalists in this way.

Rate of Interest.—The rate of interest which United States bonds pay has varied from time to time. The Revolutionary War debt bore six per cent, and so did most of the civil war bonds. After the Civil War, however, the rate at which the government was able to borrow steadily declined, largely because of the desire of national banks to secure United States bonds (page 232). The rate of interest on bonds now outstanding ranges from two to five per cent.

Growth of the National Debt.—When the Constitution went into effect, the national debt, including the war debts of the states which were assumed by the national government, amounted to about $127,000,000; but by 1836 the debt was extinguished and there was a surplus in the treasury which was distributed among the states. The enormous expenses of the Civil War, however, had to be met largely by loans, and at the close of the conflict (1866) the interest-bearing debt was more than $2,000,000,000. During the next twenty years the debt was reduced to about $600,000,000, but this amount was increased between 1895 and 1899 to about $945,000,000 on account of bond issues to replenish the gold reserve and to meet a portion of the expenses of the war with Spain. On June 30, 1915, the interest-bearing debt stood at $969,759,090. In 1917-19 five bond issues aggregating more than $21,000,000,000 were made on account of the war with Germany.

In addition there is also a non-interest-bearing debt of $389,407,800, of which $346,681,016 consists of treasury notes issued during the Civil War, and popularly known as "greenbacks" from their color. The national interest-bearing debt of the United States on June 30, 1921, amounted to about $24,000,000,000. The total debt of England is now about $40,000,000,000, that of France about $46,000,000,000, and that of Germany over $30,000,000,000.

The Monetary System.—The coining of money is now regarded everywhere as a proper if not a necessary function of government. Under the Articles of Confederation, this power was possessed by the states as well as by Congress, though in fact it was exercised by neither. The framers of the Constitution decided that the most effective way of securing a uniform system of money would be to place the whole matter under the control of the national government, and so Congress alone was given the power of coinage. At the same time, remembering how the states had before 1789 flooded the country with paper money which in some instances had become worthless, the framers of the Constitution wisely decided to prohibit them from issuing bills of credit, that is, paper designed to circulate as money. Likewise they were forbidden to make anything but gold and silver coin a legal tender in the payment of debts.

The Acts of 1792 and 1834.—As soon as the new government under the Constitution had gone into operation, steps were taken to provide a system of metallic currency. In 1792, an act was passed providing for the establishment of a mint at Philadelphia and for the striking of both gold and silver coins.[38] The gold coins were to be the double eagle, the eagle, the half eagle, and the quarter eagle; the silver coins were to be the dollar, the half dollar, the quarter, the dime, and the half dime.[39] As the market value of a given quantity of gold bullion was then about fifteen times that of silver, the weight of the silver coins was made fifteen times that of the corresponding gold coins. But as the value of gold bullion presently began to increase in comparison with silver, it was necessary to readjust the ratio so as to keep both in circulation, and so in 1834 the weight of gold coins was reduced and the ratio made sixteen to one.

Demonetization of the Silver Dollar.—But soon the increase in the supply of gold again disturbed the ratio, making the silver coins worth more as metal than as money; and as the difficulty of keeping up the adjustment seemed insuperable, Congress decided to abandon the attempt and so in 1873 the silver dollar was practically "demonetized," that is, was dropped from the list of coins, and other silver coins were made subsidiary, that is, their weight was decreased so that the metal in them was worth less than their face value, and they were made legal tender for small sums only.[40]

Later Acts.—The opposition to the demonetization of the silver dollar, however, became so great that it was restored by the act of 1878 and made full legal tender. But the free coinage of silver was not restored; the act required the government to purchase and coin not less than $2,000,000 nor more than $4,000,000 worth of silver bullion per month. In the mean time the market value of silver had declined until the amount of silver in a silver dollar was worth less than eighty cents in gold, and it was believed that the act of 1878 by increasing the demand for silver would restore its market value. This, however, did not happen, and the market value of silver went on decreasing until at one time the amount of silver in a dollar was worth only about forty-six cents in gold. In 1890 Congress increased the use of silver by requiring the secretary of the treasury to purchase monthly four and one half million ounces of silver and pay for it with treasury notes which were redeemable in coin at the option of the secretary and which were to be canceled or destroyed when so redeemed. This act was repealed in 1893, since which date the government has purchased very little silver bullion for coinage purposes.

Free Coinage.—In determining its coinage policy, the government might follow either of two methods: (1) It might coin any and all bullion presented by its owners at the mints, or (2) it might purchase its own bullion and coin only so much as the necessities of trade or other considerations might require. The former policy is that of free coinage; it is also unlimited coinage since it involves the coinage of all bullion offered, without limit. From the very first, the practice of the government in regard to gold has been that of free and unlimited coinage; that is, any owner of gold bullion may take it to a mint and have it coined without charge except for the cost of the alloy. Prior to 1873, the same policy was followed in regard to silver, thus maintaining in theory at least a bimetallic or double standard. In 1873, however, Congress abandoned the policy of free coinage of silver and adopted the single gold standard. From then until now the government has coined no silver bullion for private owners.

Paper Currency.—In addition to the metallic money described above there is a vast amount of paper currency in the United States. This currency may be classified under five different heads.

Greenbacks.—First, there are the $346,681,016 of old United States notes or "greenbacks," already described. They were issued during the Civil War, they bear no interest, and are redeemable in coin upon the demand of the holder. Since 1878 the practice of the government has been not to retire them as they are redeemed but to reissue them and keep them in circulation.

Gold and Silver Certificates.—Second, there is a large amount of currency in the form of gold and silver certificates. The law under which such currency is issued provides that any owner of gold or silver coin may deposit it in the treasury and receive in exchange an equivalent amount of certificates. They are more convenient to handle than coin, and are equally valuable for paying debts and purchasing commodities. On the 1st of July, 1921, the amount of gold certificates in circulation was $452,174,709; the amount of silver certificates, $201,534,213. These two forms of currency constitute one eighth of our entire stock of money in circulation.

Sherman Treasury Notes.—A third form of paper money is the so-called Sherman treasury notes issued in pursuance of the act of 1890 already described. On July 1, 1921, there were $1,576,184 of them in circulation. The law declares that they shall be redeemed in *coin*, that is, either gold or silver, at the option of the government. To prevent the threatened depletion of the gold reserve[41] and provide the necessary gold with which to redeem the increasing issues of Sherman treasury notes, bond issues aggregating $262,000,000 were issued during the years 1894 and 1895. By the act of 1900 the policy of maintaining a single gold standard was definitely adopted by Congress, and it was provided that greenback notes, Sherman treasury notes, and other securities of the government should be redeemable in gold.

National Bank Notes.—The fourth class of paper money is national bank currency. A national bank, unlike other banks, not only receives deposits and makes loans and performs the other functions of banks, but also issues notes which circulate as money. There are about 8,200 national banks in the United States, with an aggregate capital of more than $1,000,000,000 and with a total circulation of $729,550,513 of notes outstanding (July 1, 1921).

Federal Reserve Notes.—The federal reserve banks, established under the act of 1913, not only receive deposits and make loans to other banks, but also have power to issue federal reserve notes which circulate as money. The amount in circulation July 1, 1921, was $2,680,494,274. This constitutes by far the largest amount of paper money in existence.

The total amount of money of all kinds in circulation on July 1, 1921, amounted to $5,776,437,473, or a per capita circulation of about $53.40.

The National Bank System.—Any number of persons, not less than five, may organize a national bank, the amount of capital required depending upon the population of the town or city where the bank is located. Prior to 1914 the organizers were obliged to purchase and deposit with the government, bonds of the United States equal to one fourth of the capital of the bank; now they may do so if they wish. The comptroller of the currency then delivers to the bank notes equal in amount to the par value of the bonds deposited. These notes when properly signed by the president and cashier of the bank may then be loaned by the bank or otherwise issued as currency, for though not a legal tender they are commonly used as money. It must also be remembered that the United States bonds deposited with the government remain the property of the bank and it receives the interest on them just as any other owner would.

Advantages of National Bank Currency.—If a national bank fails, depositors may lose their money just as depositors of money in other banks may, but the holder of a national bank note does not, for whenever a bank is unable to redeem its notes, the comptroller of the currency may sell the bonds which it has on deposit with him, and with the proceeds redeem its notes. Hence a bank note is as safe as any other form of currency. Moreover, national banks are subject to frequent and careful examination by government examiners, and failures among them occur with less frequency than among other banks.

Federal Reserve Banks.—By an important act passed in 1913 Congress provided for the creation of a series of federal reserve banks to be located in different parts of the country. The committee intrusted with the matter divided the United States into twelve districts, each of which is to have one federal reserve bank, located respectively in the following cities: Boston, New York, Philadelphia, Cleveland, Richmond, Atlanta, Chicago, St. Louis, Minneapolis, Kansas City, Dallas, and San Francisco. In each district the national banks are required to become members of the federal reserve association, and to subscribe for its stock. Other banks may do so, by conforming to certain requirements.

Federal reserve banks are under the supervision and control of a federal reserve board consisting of the secretary of the treasury, the comptroller of the currency, and five other members appointed by the President. The federal reserve notes which they issue are guaranteed by the United States government, and are secured by commercial paper—notes and drafts—deposited in the treasury. It is expected that these banks will provide a more adequate supply of money and credit when the need is greatest, as during the crop-moving season, and at the same time give greater stability to the business of banking.

Federal Land Banks.—In 1916 Congress passed the so-called rural credits law, which provides for the organization of a series of banks for lending money to farmers at low rates of interest and for long periods of time. Such banks are under the supervision of the federal farm loan board consisting of the secretary of the treasury and four other members.

References.—ANDREWS, Manual of the Constitution, pp. 81-89, 104-118. BEARD, American Government and Politics, ch. xviii. BRYCE, The American Commonwealth (abridged edition), ch. xvi. HARRISON, This Country of Ours, pp. 58-65. HART, Actual Government, chs. xxi-xxii.

HINSDALE, American Government, secs. 341-373. LAUGHLIN, Elements of Political Economy, chs. xxv-xxvii.

Illustrative Material.—1. Copy of the present tariff law. 2. Specimens of various kinds of money in circulation. 3. Copy of the last annual report of the Secretary of the Treasury.

RESEARCH QUESTIONS

1. What were the sources of national revenue during the period of the Confederation?

2. Why has the imposition of direct taxes on the states not been resorted to with more frequency?

3. What is your opinion of the law levying taxes on incomes?

4. What is the amount paid by your state in internal revenue taxes? How many internal revenue districts are in your state?

5. Are there any ports of "entry" or "delivery" in your state? Any customhouses? If so, what is the amount collected by each? (See report of the secretary of the treasury.)

6. Can you give the names of some articles now on the "free list"? Mention some articles on which, in your judgment, the tariff rate is too high. Mention some articles on which the tariff is levied according to the *ad valorem* method; the *specific* method; both methods combined. (See copy of the tariff law.)

7. With what countries do we have reciprocity commercial treaties? In brief, what are the provisions of those treaties?

8. Why is an internal revenue tax imposed on such articles as oleomargarine, filled cheese, and mixed flour?

9. What is the present rate on tobacco, cigars, distilled spirits, and fermented spirits?

10. What was the total amount of the appropriations of Congress at the last session? What were the largest items of expenditure?

11. What is the present mint ratio between gold and silver? the market ratio? What is the actual weight of a silver dollar? What is Gresham's law of coinage?

12. Which countries have a bimetallic monetary system? Which a single silver standard? Which a single gold standard? What are the arguments for and against free coinage of silver?

13. What would be the result of opening the mints to the free and unlimited coinage of silver?

14. Name the different kinds of paper money.

15. What was the amount of the interest-bearing debt according to the last report of the secretary of the treasury?

16. What do you understand by the terms "legal tender"? "fiat money"? "seigniorage"? "suspension of specie payments"?

17. What is the penalty for counterfeiting the currency of the United States?

[Answers to many of these questions may be found in the report of the secretary of the treasury which may be obtained gratis from the secretary.]

CHAPTER XIII

THE REGULATION OF COMMERCE

The Power to Regulate Commerce.—Under the Articles of Confederation, as we have seen, Congress possessed no power to regulate commerce among the states or with foreign nations. That power remained entirely with the states. Each state accordingly made such regulations as it saw fit, without regard to the general welfare. It was this want of commercial power on the part of Congress that contributed as much as anything else perhaps to the downfall of the Confederation. The Constitution as finally adopted gave Congress the exclusive power to regulate commerce among the states, with foreign countries, and with the Indian tribes, which were then treated somewhat as foreign nations for certain purposes. The only limitations placed on the power of Congress in this respect were that no duty should be levied on goods exported from any state; that no preference should be given by any regulation of commerce or revenue to the ports of one state over those of another; and that no vessels bound to or from one state should be obliged to enter, clear, or pay duties in another.

Regulation of Foreign Commerce. In pursuance of the power to regulate commerce with foreign nations Congress has enacted a large amount of legislation relating to tonnage duties, duties on imports, quarantine, immigration, the importation of adulterated foods, wines, teas, and other food products, the conduct of navigation, the construction and inspection of ships carrying passengers, pilotage, clearances, the protection of shipping, the rights of seamen, the registration and insurance of vessels, life-saving appliances, the use of wireless telegraph apparatus, and the like. It was also in pursuance of this power that the Embargo Act was passed in 1807 and the Nonintercourse Act in 1809—both of which were in effect prohibitions rather than regulations of commerce.

The Navigation Laws prescribe with great detail how vessels registered under the American flag shall be constructed and equipped for the comfort and safety of their crews and passengers; how they shall be inspected; rules that shall be observed to avoid collisions, how signals shall be displayed, etc.; the forms of papers vessels must carry; how the wages of seamen shall be paid, the nature of their contracts, etc.

The Tonnage Laws prescribe the rate of tonnage duties that shall be levied on vessels entering American ports. Tonnage duties, as the name indicates, are a form of taxation calculated on the basis of the tonnage admeasurement of the vessel; they are levied on American as well as foreign ships, though the rate is higher on the latter than on the former. Sometimes they have been higher on the vessels of some foreign countries than on those of others, in which case they are known as discriminating tonnage duties. Such discriminating duties are employed for the purpose of favoring the commerce of those nations which extend us commercial privileges and for shutting out or restricting that of nations which discriminate against our trade. In pursuance of the power to regulate foreign commerce, Congress prohibits foreign vessels from engaging in the coasting trade, and permits only citizens of the United States to serve as masters on vessels registered under the American flag. Formerly only American-built vessels could be registered, but in 1914, after the outbreak of the great war in Europe, Congress passed an act allowing ships built in foreign yards, when owned by American citizens, to be registered under the American flag; and more than 100 such vessels have been so registered.

Immigration.—By virtue of the commerce power Congress has enacted a series of immigration laws imposing restrictions on the coming of immigrants to our shores. For a long time immigration from Europe was encouraged rather than restricted, but within recent years so many undesirable persons have found their way to America that Congress has been led to pass various laws designed to shut out the worst of them and admit only the desirable ones.
|42|

First of all, the immigration laws exclude convicts, insane persons, paupers and those likely to become paupers, persons suffering with dangerous, loathsome, and contagious diseases; epileptics, persons afflicted with tuberculosis, idiots, feeble-minded persons, polygamists, anarchists, immoral persons, and others of this character.

In the second place, what are known as alien contract laborers are prohibited from entering the United States, that is, persons who come under contract already entered into, to perform labor, whether skilled or unskilled. The law excluding this class was enacted in obedience to the demands of the union laborers of the United States, who did not wish to be subjected to competition with foreign laborers specially imported for the purpose. Actors, teachers, lecturers, and members of other professions are exempted from the law, and so are skilled laborers if domestic laborers of like kind are not available in the United States.

A third group of excluded classes are Chinese laborers, the immigration of whom was first prohibited in 1882.

A law of 1916 provides, with certain exceptions, that no alien shall be admitted unless he can read English or some other language or dialect. A law passed in 1921 limits the number of immigrants who may enter annually from

168

each country, to 3 per cent of the number already in the United States, or a total of about 356,000.

There is now a head tax of eight dollars levied upon every immigrant who is admitted. Persons whose steamship passage has been paid by others or who have been otherwise assisted to come are not allowed to enter. When an immigrant has been denied admission by the commissioner of immigration at the port at which he has landed, he may take an appeal to a special board of inquiry. If the decision of this board is against him he may appeal to the United States commissioner-general of immigration, and finally to the secretary of the department of labor. If the final decision is against him, the steamship on which he sailed is required at its own expense to transport him to the port from which he sailed.

Quarantine.—In pursuance of the power to regulate foreign commerce, Congress has enacted a volume of legislation in regard to quarantine and medical inspection of ships and their passengers coming from foreign ports. In most instances inspections are made by the United States consul at the port from which the vessel sails, and a bill of health is furnished the master of the vessel, but in some Asiatic and South American ports regular medical inspectors are stationed. At various ports along the coast, national quarantine stations have been established at which inspections of incoming vessels are made and at which they may be detained if found to have on board persons suffering from dangerous contagious diseases.

Pure Food.—Congress has also provided for the inspection of foods imported from abroad. Whenever a vessel is found to have on board impure or adulterated foods or teas, it is forbidden to land the cargo or is allowed to land it only after certain conditions are complied with such as the change of labels to correspond with the actual contents of packages. In this way an attempt is made to protect the American consumer against impure and unwholesome food products shipped here from foreign ports.

Interstate Commerce has been interpreted to include the carriage of passengers from one state to another; the transportation of commodities of whatsoever character, including lottery tickets, obscene literature, and any other objects which may be the subject of transportation; and the transmission of ideas or information by telegraph or telephone from a point in one state to a point in another. In short, interstate commerce means not only transportation and traffic in articles but intercourse and communication by the modern devices for transmitting thought; and the power to prescribe the conditions under which such intercourse may be carried on across state lines belongs to Congress.[43] Congress controls also the coasting trade between parts of the same state and the traffic on all rivers which flow into the ocean or the Great

Lakes and thus constitute highways of interstate or foreign commerce.

IMMIGRATION STATION, ELLIS ISLAND, NEW YORK HARBOR

IMMIGRANTS READY TO START WEST

Power Retained by the States.—Nevertheless it is often difficult in a particular case to draw the line between acts which regulate interstate commerce and acts which merely affect it without regulating it. The Supreme Court in a long line of decisions has held that the states not only have complete power of control over all commerce originating and ending within their limits but that they may also enact legislation for the protection of the public health, safety, good order, and morals of their people even when such legislation affects commerce among the states, the only restriction being that such legislation must be reasonable and must not amount to a direct interference with interstate traffic. The right of the states in this respect is known as the *police power*—a power which is very extensive and of which they cannot be deprived by Congress. Thus they may enact reasonable quarantine laws forbidding the entrance into their territory of diseased persons from other states or the importation of diseased live stock. Likewise they may limit the speed of interstate trains running through their towns, may require railroads to provide gates at crossings, safety appliances for cars, and the like.

The Original Package Doctrine.—A state, however, prior to 1920, could not without the consent of Congress prohibit the importation of liquor in original packages into its territory from other states, although it might be a prohibition state.[44] But Congress itself, by an act passed in 1913, prohibited the transportation of intoxicating liquors into states having prohibition laws.

Likewise, the states cannot impose taxes on passengers passing through their territory bound for points in other states, or require interstate trains to stop at county seats, or impose taxes on telegraph messages sent to points in other states, or on bills of lading of freight destined to points in other states, or on goods intended for exportation, and so on.

Regulation of Interstate Railway Traffic.—For a long time Congress took no action toward regulating railway traffic among the states, thus leaving the railroads free to carry on their business as they pleased, regardless of the interest of the public whom they served. But with the enormous development of the railway system of the country gross evils began to creep in, in the form of excessive rates, discriminations, combinations for the suppression of competition, inadequate provision for the safety of passengers, etc., in consequence of which a widespread demand grew up for legislation bringing the railroads under governmental control. The outcome of this agitation was the interstate commerce act of 1887, the provisions of which have been amended and extended by several subsequent acts, notably the Elkins act of 1903, the railway rate law of 1906, and the interstate commerce law of 1910.

Interstate Commerce Commission.—The law of 1887 created an interstate commerce commission which now consists of eleven members appointed by the President and paid a salary of $12,000 a year each, which commission has general supervision of the execution of the several acts mentioned above. It hears complaints against the railroads, makes investigations upon petition, and to this end may summon witnesses and compel the production of papers and records, and conduct hearings. If, after an investigation, it finds that the law is being violated by a railroad company, it may request the proper federal authorities to institute a prosecution of the offending company, and the law requires that such a prosecution shall be made. For a long time the commission had no power to fix rates, but only the negative right to say that a given rate was unjust and unreasonable. But by the act of 1906 it was given the power, after a full hearing, to determine and prescribe just and reasonable maximum rates and charges, as well as to prescribe regulations for the conduct of railway traffic.

The Laws Now in Force prescribe that all railway rates and charges for carrying freight and passengers must be just and reasonable; that no rebates, drawbacks, or special rates shall be granted to particular shippers; that no discriminations shall be made as to rates or service to certain persons or places; that no free passes, with certain specified exceptions, shall be granted; that no greater charges shall be made for a "short haul" than for a "long haul"; that no railroads shall be allowed to transport commodities which they are engaged in producing, with certain exceptions; that competing railways shall not be allowed to pool their freight or earnings; that schedules showing rates, fares, and charges shall be published and kept open for inspection and cannot be changed except after thirty days' notice to the commission; that all railroads shall keep their accounts according to a uniform system prescribed by the commission; and that they shall make annually to the commission a full and complete report of their business and earnings.

An important extension of the interstate commerce act was made in 1906, when express and sleeping car companies, pipe lines used for transporting oil from one state to another, and telegraph, telephone, and cable companies engaged in sending messages from one state to another or to foreign countries, were brought under the operation of the law and their business subjected to the same conditions and restrictions as those applying to railroads. By an act of 1912 railroads were prohibited from owning, controlling, or having any interest in competing water carriers, and by an act of 1913 provision was made for preparing a valuation of all railroads in the United States.

Congress has also enacted laws requiring interstate railroads to equip their cars with automatic couplers and other safety appliances, fixing the liability of railway employers for injuries sustained by railway employees, encouraging the arbitration of railway strikes, and establishing an eight-hour work day on railways (1916). An act excluding the products of child labor from interstate commerce (1916) was declared unconstitutional by the Supreme Court.

In pursuance of acts of Congress passed in 1916 and 1918, the President in 1918 took over the control of railroads, telegraphs, and telephones for the duration of the war.

Federal Anti-trust Legislation.—The commerce clause of the Constitution has also furnished the authority for some important congressional legislation against what are popularly known as "trusts," that is, combinations of corporations or business associations formed to avoid the wastes of competition and to secure economy of management. But the control of the supply of a commodity means the elimination of competition and usually the maintenance of high rates to the injury of consumers. For a long time the greater part of the business of the country was conducted by individuals, companies, or corporations, and the advantages of competition were preserved to the public, but in the course of the economic development of the country, corporations began to consolidate for the reasons stated, with the result that the supply of many commodities came to be controlled by single combinations. At first the states undertook to deal with the problem by passing anti-"trust" laws, but the business of so many of the more powerful organizations was interstate in character that state legislation was inadequate to deal with them.

The Sherman Anti-"trust" Law.—Finally, in obedience to a widespread popular demand, Congress took action in 1890 by passing what is popularly known as the Sherman anti-"trust" act to protect trade and commerce among the states against unlawful restraint and monopolies. This act declared that every contract, combination in the form of trust or otherwise, or conspiracy in restraint of trade or commerce among the states or with foreign nations was illegal, and it prescribed appropriate penalties for violations thereof. This law, however, applies only to "trusts" which are in restraint of trade among the states or with foreign nations. It has no application to those whose activities are confined entirely within the boundaries of a single state; with such "trusts" the states alone have the power to deal.

In pursuance of the act of 1890, prosecutions have been instituted in the federal courts against a large number of "trusts," and some of them have been broken up, but the larger number have escaped. In 1911, for example, the Supreme Court decided that the Standard Oil and tobacco "trusts" were illegal, and their dissolution was decreed.

The Clayton Anti-"trust" Act.—In 1914 Congress passed another important act directed against combinations in restraint of trade. In brief, it prohibits price discriminations among purchasers, exclusive trade agreements between manufacturers and retailers, the holding of the stock of one corporation by another, and interlocking directorates. Like the other anti-"trust" acts it applies, of course, only to persons or corporations engaged in interstate commerce or trade. To enforce the act a *federal trade commission* was created. It consists of five members appointed by the President, at a salary of $10,000 each.

Federal Pure Food Legislation.—The commerce clause of the Constitution is also the source of some important legislation designed to protect the public against impure, unwholesome, and adulterated foods produced in the United States. We have already called attention to the legislation of Congress against the importation of impure foods, and teas from abroad. Still more recently Congress passed an interstate pure food law prohibiting the transportation among the states and territories of any food products which are adulterated or which contain foreign substances not indicated in the labels. The law also provides for the fixing of a standard of pure foods and other products transported from one state to another or intended for interstate transportation, and provides that they must come up to the standard prescribed.

The Meat Inspection Law.—To protect the public against unwholesome meat products, Congress enacted in 1891 a law which was strengthened in important particulars in 1906, providing for the inspection of slaughtering houses whose products are intended for interstate commerce. The law requires the registration of all establishments engaged in slaughtering animals the products of which are to be shipped into other states or are intended for export. Each is given a number, and federal inspectors are assigned to inspect the animals intended for slaughter, to inspect their carcasses in certain cases, and to see that the business of slaughtering is conducted under clean and wholesome conditions. Animals found suffering with certain diseases are not allowed to be slaughtered for food purposes, and meat discovered to be unwholesome must be rejected. Supervision is also exercised over the processes of packing and canning, and there are detailed regulations in regard to labeling.

References. ANDREWS, Manual of the Constitution, pp. 89-95. BEARD, American Government, ch. xix. COOLEY, Principles of Constitutional Law, pp. 66-88. HART, Actual Government, ch. xxiv. HINSDALE, American Government, secs. 374-380. JOHNSON, Railway Transportation, ch. xxvi.

Illustrative Material.—Annual reports of the Interstate Commerce Commission, of the Department of Agriculture, of the Attorney-General, of the Commissioner of Navigation, of the Commissioner of Immigration, and of the Public Health and Marine Hospital Service.

RESEARCH QUESTIONS

1. What were the reasons for giving Congress control over foreign and interstate commerce?

2. Why did the delegates from the Southern states oppose giving this power to Congress?

3. What is meant by the "original package" doctrine?

4. Why should a railroad company be prohibited from granting rebates? For charging more for a "short haul" than for a "long haul"? From transporting the products of its own mines and manufactories? From pooling its freight or earnings?

5. What are the arguments for and against granting government subsidies for the upbuilding of the merchant marine?

6. What have been the principal reasons for the decline of the American carrying trade?

7. What is the amount of money annually appropriated for improving the rivers and harbors of the country?

8. How has the commerce clause of the Constitution been the source of important extensions of the power of the national government? Mention some important recent acts of Congress that have been passed in pursuance of this clause.

9. Should Congress, in your judgment, impose greater restrictions upon immigration than it now imposes?

10. Do you think Congress should have power to regulate the business of life insurance? To regulate marriage and divorce?

11. Is the policy of governmental regulation of railroads preferable to governmental ownership? Give your reasons.

CHAPTER XIV

OTHER IMPORTANT POWERS OF CONGRESS

THE POST OFFICE, COPYRIGHTS, PATENTS, THE ARMY, THE NAVY, ETC.

The Postal Service.—The beginnings of the postal service in the United States date back to the action of the Continental Congress in creating a post office department in 1775, and appointing Benjamin Franklin as its head. Under Franklin's direction postal routes were established throughout the colonies and the mails were carried over them at intervals of one or two weeks. In 1776 there were twenty-eight post offices located in the more important towns. The Constitution gave Congress power to establish post offices and post roads, and when the new government was established, the postal service was reorganized and extended. In 1790, however, there were only seventy-five post offices in the thirteen states, and less than 2,000 miles of post roads. The total revenues were only $37,000, and the expenditures only $32,000. Now there are more than 60,000 offices and over 25,000 different routes, with an aggregate mileage of about 450,000 miles. A recent postmaster-general has well said: "The postal establishment of the United States is the greatest business concern in the world. It handles more pieces, employs more men, spends more money, brings more revenue, uses more agencies, reaches more homes, involves more details, and touches more interests than any other human organization, public or private, governmental or corporate." Some idea of the magnitude of the service may be gained from the fact that during the year 1919 about twenty billion pieces of mail were handled, more than $1,000,000,000 worth of domestic money orders were issued, and more than 120,000,000 articles were registered. The receipts for the year 1919 aggregated $364,847,126, and the expenditures $362,497,635.

The Postal Deficit.—For many years the postal service was operated at a loss, the principal causes of the deficit being due to the loss sustained by the government on the transportation of second-class matter and through the rural free delivery service. During the fiscal year 1917 the loss on the former account aggregated $72,000,000 and on the latter about half that amount. There is also a heavy loss on mail carried free under the Congressional frank. Thus in 1917 more than 60,000,000 pounds of such mail was carried, the postage on which would have cost more than $20,000,000. Nevertheless by rigorous economy the deficit was made to disappear in 1911 for the first time in thirty years. In 1917 there was a surplus of more than $9,000,000.

Mail Matter.—Congress has power to decide what matter shall be admitted to the mails and what shall be excluded. In addition to books and printed matter generally it allows parcels of merchandise weighing not more than seventy pounds to be carried through the mails; also seeds, bulbs, roots, samples of flour, dried fruits, cut flowers, geological and botanical specimens, soap, nuts, live queen bees, dried insects, etc. On the other hand, the following matter is denied admission to the mails: parcels weighing over seventy pounds; poisons, explosives, live animals, liquors and other objects unsuitable for transportation in the mails; obscene matter and articles adapted or designed for immoral purposes; all matter relating to lotteries and schemes for swindling the public, and, by acts of 1917, advertisements of intoxicating liquor intended for distribution in prohibition states and printed matter advocating treason, insurrection, resistance to the laws, disloyalty, etc.

"Fraud Orders."—The mails are so frequently used by dishonest concerns for circulating advertising matter designed to defraud the public, that a law has been passed authorizing the postmaster-general to withhold the privileges of the postal service from persons using it for such purposes. In pursuance of this authority, he frequently issues "fraud orders," instructing the local postmaster not to deliver mail to specified fraudulent concerns. It was reported in 1913 that in two years such concerns had swindled the people out of $129,000,000.

Classification of Mail Matter.—Mail is classified into four different classes: *first*, letters and postal cards; *second*, newspapers and other periodical publications; *third*, printed matter not admitted to the second class; and *fourth*, merchandise not comprehended in the other three classes.

The Rates of Postage on the different classes have varied in amount from time to time. In the early history of the post-office department the rates for transporting letters were regulated on the basis of the distance carried, and according to the number of sheets in the letter, the amount ranging from six to twenty-five cents. Since 1863, however, there has been a uniform rate on letters irrespective of distance. In 1883 the rate was fixed at two cents; in 1917, three cents; in 1919, two cents. Before 1847, when the adhesive postage stamps were introduced, payment of postage was made in cash and the amount indorsed on the envelope. Postal cards were introduced in 1872.

On the transportation of first-class mail the government realizes a profit estimated at $60,000,000 per year, notwithstanding the long distance much of it is carried. There is also a substantial profit derived from foreign mail.

Second-Class Matter mailed by the publishers is carried at the rate of 1½ cents a pound, with an added charge (depending on distance) for advertising matter;[45] but newspapers are carried free to any office within the county of publication except in cities having free delivery service. The government has sustained heavy losses in carrying second-class matter. In the year 1917 more than 1,200,000,000 pounds was transported at a loss of over six cents per pound. It constituted over 60 per cent of all domestic mail, but yielded less than five per cent of the postal revenues, the loss being greater than the profits realized on all other classes of mail combined.

Should the Second-Class Rate be Increased?—For some years there was considerable agitation in favor of increasing the rate paid by publishers, especially on magazines which are overloaded with advertising matter and on other publications which are devoted largely to advertising purposes. Successive postmasters-general urged a readjustment of the rates, but until 1917 Congress took no action further than to appoint a commission to investigate and report on the subject. The two suggestions most considered were, that a higher rate should be imposed on magazines than on newspapers in view of the fact that the average distance of transportation is greater in the case of magazines than in the case of newspapers, and that a higher rate be imposed on advertising matter than on purely reading matter.

Against these arguments it was contended that the educational benefits derived from the extensive circulation of second-class matter are very great, and that for this reason the government can well afford to contribute something toward the dissemination of advertising information among the masses of the people. Moreover, it was argued that the circulation of second-class matter is responsible for a large amount of first-class matter and thus the government makes up in the increased profits on first-class matter what it loses on second-class matter. Thus it was said that fifty pages of advertising matter in a popular magazine might lead to the writing of 50,000 letters. Consequently a reduction in the volume of second-class matter would inevitably be followed by a corresponding reduction in first-class matter.

Finally in 1917 Congress passed a law providing for a graduated increase in the rates on the advertising portions of newspapers and magazines, the amount depending on the distance carried.

Free Delivery Service.—The extension of *rural free delivery* service has been the most rapid and remarkable of all the undertakings of the post office department. It began as an experiment in 1897, when less than $15,000 was appropriated to test the advantage of free delivery in country districts, and it has been extended until it now constitutes one of the largest branches of the postal service, the annual expenditures on account of the service exceeding $50,000,000. This is the largest item of expenditure by the post office department on any of its services except the transportation of mail on the railroads, which foots up nearly $55,000,000. There are more than 40,000 rural free delivery routes in operation, and nearly three billion pieces of mail are annually delivered to 27,000,000 people along these routes. An investigation made in 1909 showed that the postage on the average amount of mail collected on a rural route was $14.92 per month, while the average cost of the service was $72.17. The average cost of the service on a rural route, therefore, exceeded the average revenue derived from postage by $687 per year. On that basis the total loss on the operation of the service was estimated to be about $28,000,000. But while the loss to the government in money has been great, the advantage to the country districts served has been notable. Besides the convenience to the country residents it has brought them into closer relation with the centers of population, made country life more attractive and less monotonous, increased farm values, and encouraged the improvement of country roads, since the department insists upon the maintenance of the highways in good condition as a prerequisite to the introduction and continuance of the service.

Free Delivery in Cities.—Free delivery of mail in the larger towns and cities was first introduced during the Civil War, and the service has been extended to include all places of not less than 10,000 inhabitants or where the postal receipts are not less than $10,000 per year. In 1885, provision was made by which immediate delivery ("special delivery") of a letter upon its arrival at a city post office could be secured by payment of ten cents.

Registry Service.—In 1855, Congress established the registry service, by which upon the payment of extra postage—the extra rate is now ten cents per letter or parcel—special care is taken of letters or parcels registered. Thus the safe delivery of a valuable letter or parcel is practically assured, and by a recent law the post office department has provided a system of insurance against the loss of parcels mail—the maximum amount allowed in case of loss being one hundred dollars.

Money-Order Service.—In 1864 the money-order service was established, by which upon the payment of a small fee, ranging from three to thirty cents according to the amount of the order, money may be sent through the mails without danger of loss. At all the larger post offices and at many of the smaller ones, international money orders may also be obtained at rates ranging from ten cents to one dollar, payable in almost any part of the world where the mails are carried. The primary object of the postal money-order service is to provide for the public a safe, convenient, and cheap method of making remittances by mail, and it is the declared policy of the department to extend the service to all post offices where its introduction is practicable.

Postal Savings Banks.—One of the most important extensions of the postal service is the establishment of a system of postal savings banks, authorized by an act of Congress passed in 1910.[46] This service has long been performed by the governments of many other countries, and its introduction into the United States had been strongly recommended by successive postmasters-general for a number of years. The proposition was also indorsed by both of the great political parties in their national platforms. In favor of the proposition it was pointed out that in many communities private savings banks are inaccessible, there being only one such bank to every 52,000 of the population of the country, as a whole; that on account of the popular distrust of private savings banks in many communities, savings were hoarded and hidden and thus kept out of circulation; that on account of the popular confidence in the government the establishment of savings banks under its auspices would cause the money now hidden to be brought out and put into circulation; that it would encourage thrift and economy as well as stimulate loyalty and patriotism among depositors; and that it would improve the conditions of farm life, thus supplementing the work of the rural free delivery service, the telephone, and the interurban trolley car.

The new law for the establishment of postal savings banks, as amended in 1918, provides that any person may deposit with the local postmaster of any office which has been made a depository (there were over 7000 such offices in 1918) any amount from one dollar up to $2500 and receive interest thereon at two per cent per annum, provided the amount has been on deposit at least six months. Detailed provisions are made for the investment by the government of the sums deposited in the post offices throughout the country. There were in 1919 over 565,000 depositors and the total deposits were $167,323,260,—an average of nearly $300 per depositor.

Parcel Post Service.—In many countries the post office department also performs, through the parcel post service, what amounts to an express business. Thus in a number of the European countries one may send boxes or parcels weighing as much as fifty or even one hundred pounds through the mails at very low rates of postage. In the United States books and packages of merchandise may be sent through the mails, but the weight of the package except in the case of books was until 1913 limited to four pounds.[47] The limitation as to weight and the comparatively high rate of postage—sixteen cents per pound—made resort to the express companies necessary much more than in Europe. For some years there was a widespread agitation for the establishment of a parcel post system in the United States, and in 1912 Congress provided for the installation of such a system on January 1, 1913. The maximum weight limit of parcels that might be transported through the mails was increased to eleven pounds (and later to fifty pounds; seventy pounds for short distances), and the list of mailable articles was enlarged so as to include butter, eggs, meats, fruits, and vegetables. In 1914 books were added to the list. The country is divided into zones according to the distance from each post office, and the rate of postage varies both with the weight and with the zone to which it is sent. About one billion parcels, weighing over two billion pounds, are handled annually. So popular is the service that in 1914 the postmaster-general recommended that the government take steps toward acquiring the telegraph and telephone service of the country.

Postal Subsidies.—In recent years there has been considerable agitation, principally by the postal authorities and the commercial organizations of the country, in favor of extending our postal facilities with certain foreign countries, notably South America and the Orient, where they are now very inadequate. While most of the European governments have quick and frequent postal communications with these countries, ours are slow and infrequent. Most foreign governments have adopted the policy of subsidizing private steamship lines to carry the mails to out-of-the-way places. In 1891, Congress passed a law for this purpose, but the amount appropriated is so small that the post office department has not been able to extend our mail facilities with foreign countries as rapidly as needed.

POST OFFICE, NEWARK, NEW JERSEY

POST OFFICE, DES MOINES, IOWA

Shipping Board.—With a view to building up the American merchant marine, which in recent years had greatly declined, Congress in 1916 provided for the appointment by the President of a federal shipping board composed of five commissioners with power to construct or purchase merchant vessels suitable as naval auxiliaries and for the carriage of American commerce. The board is also to supervise common carriers engaged in transportation by water. As a war measure, the extent of its building operations was greatly increased in 1917.

International Postal Union.—In this connection it may be noted that practically all the countries of the world have joined in forming what is known as the International Postal Union, for the reciprocal exchange of mails between the post offices of all countries belonging to the Union. The rates are fixed by a congress which represents the member states and which meets, in normal times, every five years. A letter may therefore be sent from one country to any other in the Union at a uniform rate, which, with some exceptions, is five cents. By special arrangement the rate on letters between the United States and the British Isles has been reduced to two cents. Likewise the rate between the United States and Canada or Mexico or most of the West Indies is by special arrangement two cents.

Classes of Post Offices.—Post offices are grouped in four classes on the basis of their gross annual receipts. First-class offices are those whose gross receipts exceed $40,000 a year.[48] They are usually located in buildings owned by the government, and in the larger cities there are branch offices or sub-stations in different parts of the city. Fourth-class offices are those whose annual receipts are below $1,000. Salaries of postmasters of the offices of the first three classes are determined mainly on the basis of the receipts of the office. Fourth-class postmasters receive no fixed salary, but instead are paid a percentage of the value of the stamps cancelled. In the larger post offices there are in addition to the postmaster one or more assistant postmasters and a force of clerks and carriers, the number depending on the amount of business and the size of the city. All postmasters are appointed after examinations under the civil service rules. Postmasters of the fourth class are appointed by the postmaster-general; those of the other three classes are appointed by the President.

Copyrights.—The Constitution gives Congress the power to promote the progress of science and useful arts by securing for limited times to authors and inventors the exclusive right to their respective writings and discoveries. The purpose of the copyright law is to protect authors from having their books and other writings republished without their permission, and hence to prevent the rewards of their talent and industry from being appropriated by others. In pursuance of this provision Congress has enacted legislation enumerating the productions for which copyrights may be granted, the conditions under which they may be secured, and the terms for which the protection shall last. The law provides that copyrights may be granted for books, musical compositions, maps, works of art, photographs, and even for unpublished works. In the case of published works two copies of the best edition must be deposited with the register of copyrights at Washington. The ordinary form of copyright notice is "Copyright, 19—, by A. B."

The term of the copyright is twenty-eight years, but it may be renewed for another period of twenty-eight years. During the period of the copyright the author has the exclusive right to print, publish, and sell the article copyrighted, and in case of infringement he may have recourse to the federal courts for damages on account of the loss sustained. A copyright may be sold or otherwise transferred, but the fact must be recorded by the register of copyrights.

International Copyright.—Formerly the writings of an American author might be republished in a foreign country without his consent, and thus he had no protection outside of his own country. Accordingly, to secure protection to American authors against the republication of their works in foreign countries without their consent, Congress enacted laws in 1891 and 1909, looking toward the reciprocal protection of American and foreign authors against infringement of the rights of each in the country of the other. In pursuance of these acts a copyright will be granted to a foreign author protecting him against the republication of his works in the United States, provided the government of which he is a subject will grant similar protection to American authors. But in the case of foreign books published in the English language the book must be printed and bound in the United States in order to secure the benefits of copyright. International copyright treaties designed to secure protection of this sort have been entered into between the United States and a number of foreign countries.

Patents.—A patent is a form of protection granted by the government to an inventor to secure to him for a limited period the exclusive enjoyment of the fruits of his skill and industry. Patents were granted by the state governments until the Constitution conferred this power on Congress. In 1790 Congress passed a law authorizing the granting of patents for new and useful inventions, and this law has been amended and its scope extended several times since.

The Patent Office.—In 1836, an office or bureau charged with receiving applications, conducting examinations, and granting patents was created in the department of state, but it was transferred to the department of the interior in 1849. This office has grown to be one of the largest and most important branches of the government service. It has a large number of examiners and experts arranged in groups, each of which examines the applications for patents for inventions of a particular class.

Conditions.—The applicant for a patent must declare upon oath that he believes himself to be the original inventor of the article for which he desires a patent, and he must submit with his application a full description or drawing of the invention, and if demanded, also a model of the same. The invention must be a useful one, for patents will not be granted for inventions which have no practical or scientific value. If the patent is refused by the commissioner of patents, the applicant can take an appeal to the court of appeals of the District of Columbia. A fee of fifteen dollars is charged for filing the application, and one of twenty dollars for issuing the patent.[49] The term for which a patent may be issued under the present law is seventeen years, which term may be extended only by act of Congress. When a patent is granted the word "patented" with the date on which it was issued must be placed on the article in order that the public may have notice of the fact that it is patented. During the term of the patent the inventor has the exclusive right to manufacture, use, or sell the article, and in case of infringement the law allows him to apply for an injunction to restrain the infringer, or to sue for damages. Patents, like copyrights, may be assigned or otherwise transferred, provided a record of the transfer is made in the patent office.[50]

Number of Patents Granted.—The inventive genius of the American people is shown by the large number of patents which have been issued since the first patent law was passed in 1790. The number granted during the year 1919 alone amounted to 37,259. The annual reports of the commissioner of patents, containing a list of the patents granted, together with specifications and drawings of the inventions for which patents have been issued, constitute a remarkable record of the growth of the country along industrial and scientific lines.

The Military Power of Congress.—The Constitution confers upon Congress the power to declare war, grant letters of marque and reprisal, and make rules concerning captures on land and water. In England and some continental European states the power of declaring war belongs to the crown, though the means of carrying it on must be provided by the legislative branch of the government. The framers of the Constitution, however, with their distrust of executive power, wisely left the whole matter to Congress. In the exercise of this power Congress has several times declared war against foreign nations.

A Letter of Marque and Reprisal is the technical term for a commission issued to an individual by a belligerent government authorizing him to prey upon the commerce of the enemy. The vessel commanded by a person holding such a commission is called a *privateer.* Privateering was long recognized as a legitimate mode of warfare, but the evils of the practice, due mainly to lack of control over the person bearing a commission of this sort, were so great that a congress of European nations held in Paris in 1856 declared privateering to be abolished. Although the United States has never formally adhered to this act, there is no likelihood that our government will ever again resort to privateering.

Captures.—In pursuance of the power to make rules concerning captures on land and sea, Congress has adopted a code of rules, though that matter is regulated for the most part by international law. Formerly it was the practice to allow the commander and crew a share of the proceeds of prizes captured on the sea in time of war, but in 1898 a law was passed abolishing prize money and providing that the proceeds from the sale of prizes should be turned into the treasury of the United States. In case of rebellion or insurrection the whole matter of the liability of the property of insurgents is within the control of Congress. Thus during the Civil War acts were passed for the confiscation of all property of the Confederates used in the prosecution of the war, as well as all abandoned property, that is, property belonging to persons who were away from their homes and in the Confederate service.

The Army.—The Constitution expressly authorizes Congress to raise and support armies, subject to the limitation that no appropriation for the support of the army shall be for a longer period than two years. This period corresponds to the term of Congress, and hence the limitation serves to keep the army under the control of the people. There was more or less jealousy of standing armies at the time of the adoption of the Constitution, and for a long time the regular army of the United States was very small; in 1898, for example, it was only 27,000 men.

Present Strength of the Army.—By an act passed in 1916 provision was made for increasing the peace strength of the regular army to 480,000 men; for establishing officers' reserve training corps at colleges and universities; for maintaining camps for giving military training to citizens who apply for it; and for creating a regular army reserve, the members of which are to receive at least fifteen days' training each year. Provision was also made for reorganizing the militia and for increasing its strength ultimately to about 425,000 men. The expense of the training camps and of equipping, training, and paying a small salary to the officers and men of the organized militia and of the regular army reserve is to be borne by the national government. After the beginning of the war with Germany (1917), provision was made for raising a large army by conscription of able-bodied young men between the ages of 21 and 31 years—later on between 18 and 45.[51] By the act of June 4, 1920, the strength of the regular army was reduced to 150,000 men on October 1, 1921.

The General Staff.—In 1903 the office of "commanding general" was abolished and in its place a general staff was created, to prepare plans for the conduct of military operations. By the acts of 1916 and 1920 the general staff was reorganized. At its head is a chief of staff with the rank of major general, who in time of peace is the actual head of the army. Among his assistants are: a chief of cavalry, a chief of field artillery, a chief of coast artillery, a chief of infantry, and a chief of chaplains.

Military and Naval Expenditures.—The expenditures on account of the military and naval establishments have increased enormously in recent years. Before the war with Spain the appropriations for the maintenance of the army did not exceed $50,000,000 per annum. The budget of expenditures for the year 1922 as submitted to Congress by the President aggregated nearly $4,000,000,000. It contained the following items: war department, $390,000,000; navy, $478,000,000; pensions, $258,000,000; veterans bureau, $438,000,000; interest on the national debt, $976,000,000; total, $2,539,000,000, or more than 60 per cent of the total, leaving less than 40 per cent for civil purposes. In the hope of bringing about an agreement among the nations for a reduction of their military and naval expenditures, a conference of the Powers, called by President Harding, assembled at Washington in November, 1921. Here an agreement was reached to reduce naval expenditures.

Volunteers.—Except during the Civil War and the war with Germany, resort has never been made to conscription for recruiting the army—a practice almost universal in Europe. In most of our wars the chief reliance has been on volunteers and the militia. Thus at the outbreak of the Civil War the President was authorized to accept the services of 500,000 volunteers, and at the outbreak of the war with Spain in 1898, the President called for 200,000 volunteers. It takes much training to convert an inexperienced volunteer into an efficient soldier; but many of our great battles have been fought chiefly by the volunteer forces.

The Militia.—The Constitution also authorizes Congress to provide for calling forth the militia to execute the laws of the Union, suppress insurrections, and repel invasions; and to provide for organizing, arming, and disciplining the militia, and for governing such part of them as may be employed in the service of the United States. The militia as defined by act of Congress consists of all able-bodied male citizens of the United States between the ages of eighteen and forty-five. That portion of the militia regularly organized, uniformed, and occasionally drilled and taught military tactics constitutes the national guard.[52]

Each state organizes and controls its own militia, and the national government has no control over it until it has been called into the service of the United States, when it becomes subject to the rules and discipline prescribed for the government of the regular army. In 1795, Congress passed an act prescribing the conditions under which the militia might be called into the service of the United States. This act conferred on the President of the United States the power to call out the militia whenever, in his judgment, it was necessary or expedient. Such calls are addressed to the governors of the states, who are the commanders of their several portions of the militia. When, however, the militia has been mustered into the service of the United States the President becomes their commander in chief. In pursuance of this authority the President has called out the militia on two different occasions; during the War of 1812 to repel invasion; and during the Civil War to suppress insurrection. In 1898 when the war with Spain was declared, the call was issued not for the militia but for volunteers.[53] Nevertheless many of the volunteers who responded were as a matter of fact members of the organized militia of their respective states. In pursuance of authority conferred by Congress in 1916, the President drafted the organized militia into the federal service in that year for service on the Mexican border, and again in 1917 on account of the war with Germany.

The Naval Militia.—In a number of the seaboard states and some of those bordering on the Great Lakes, there are organized bodies of naval militia, with training ships loaned by the United States for the purpose of drill and instruction. Like the land militia, the naval militia of each state is under the control of the state and until called into the federal service is under the command of the governor.[54]

The Navy.—Congress is also authorized by the Constitution to provide and maintain a navy. In pursuance of this authority, Congress created a small naval establishment in 1794, but it amounted to little until the War of 1812, when it was strengthened by the improvisation of a number of war vessels which won brilliant victories over the ships of Great Britain. Thereafter the navy was neglected until the necessities of the Civil War required its rehabilitation. At the close of the war the vessels in the service numbered 683, but they were sold or otherwise disposed of, and what was once the most powerful navy in existence was allowed to go to pieces. In 1881 a board of naval officers prepared a somewhat elaborate naval program and recommended the construction during the next eight years of some 120 naval vessels. The work was begun in 1883—a date which may properly be fixed as the beginning of our present navy. The first important appropriation, that of 1883, was less than $15,000,000. Each year the amount was increased until in 1917 it had reached $535,000,000.

Present Strength of the Navy.—The number of officers and enlisted men in the navy in August, 1919, was 241,357, besides about 19,000 men in the marine corps. The total number of vessels of all kinds for fighting, built or in process of construction, was about 1070. These included 50 battleships, 18 armored cruisers of various types, 7 monitors, some 30 unarmored cruisers of different types, about 360 destroyers and torpedo boats, about 160 submarines, 336 submarine chasers, and about 100 gunboats and patrol vessels.

According to the report of the Secretary of the Navy in 1919, the naval standing of the great powers was as follows:

	NUMBER OF SHIPS	TOTAL TONNAGE
Great Britain	812	2,691,211
United States	339	1,070,576
France	222	552,755
Japan	129	540,426
Italy	237	287,923
Russia	101	254,148
Germany	36	116,886

For administrative purposes the ships of the navy are grouped into fleets, and these are again subdivided into squadrons. Thus the North Atlantic fleet is divided into a coast squadron and a Caribbean squadron. Within each squadron there are usually a number of divisions. There are navy yards where ships are either built or repaired at a number of places on the Atlantic and Pacific coasts,[55] and there are several training schools for recruits, and a naval academy at Annapolis (founded in 1845), where young men are educated for service in the navy.[56] There is also a naval war college at Newport, Rhode Island, for advanced study of naval problems and questions of international law.

Ranks.—Until 1862, the highest official rank in the navy was that of captain, although the title commodore was popularly applied to officers in command of a squadron. The following table is a list of the officers of the navy, beginning with the highest, together with the corresponding ranks in the army:

Navy	*Army*
Admiral.	General.
Vice Admiral.	Lieutenant General.
Rear Admiral.	Major General.
Commodore.[57]	Brigadier General.
Captain.	Colonel.
Commander.	Lieutenant Colonel.
Lieutenant Commander.	Major.
Lieutenant.	Captain.
Lieutenant, junior grade.	First Lieutenant.
Ensign.	Second Lieutenant.

Marine Corps.—Officers in the Marine Corps have the same ranks as in the army. While serving generally under the direction of the secretary of the navy, the corps may serve with the army by order of the President.

Bankruptcy Legislation.—The Constitution confers upon Congress the power to pass uniform laws on the subject of bankruptcies throughout the United States. Bankruptcy is the condition of a person whose liabilities exceed his assets, and a bankruptcy law is one which provides for the distribution of the assets of such a person among his creditors and for his discharge from further legal obligation to pay his debts, thus enabling him to make a new beginning in business. The discharge is only from the *legal* obligation; the *moral* obligation remains, and should be fulfilled in case of ability to do so in the future.

State Insolvency Laws.—Before the adoption of the Constitution the states passed insolvency laws discharging debtors from their legal obligations, and it has been held by the Supreme Court that they may still pass such laws, subject to the condition that they can affect only citizens of the state in which the law is passed, and apply only to such contracts as may be entered into subsequent to the enactment of the law. If there is a federal bankruptcy law in force it supersedes all conflicting provisions in the state laws on the subject.

Federal Acts.—Since the Constitution went into effect Congress has enacted four different bankruptcy laws, namely, in 1802, 1840, 1867, and 1898, the first three of which were in operation only fifteen years altogether. The present law—that of 1898—provides for both "voluntary" and "involuntary" bankruptcy. Any debtor, except a corporation, may voluntarily have himself adjudged a bankrupt by filing a petition in a United States district court, showing that his liabilities are in excess of his assets. Any debtor except a corporation, a wage earner, or a farmer, may, against his will, upon petition of his creditors, be declared a bankrupt under certain conditions.

Bankruptcy petitions are referred to "referees" for examination and report. After hearing the testimony on the petition the referee reports his findings to the court, which makes its decision largely on the basis of such findings.

Implied Powers.—After expressly enumerating in succession the various powers of Congress, the more important of which have been described above, the Constitution concludes with a sort of general grant, empowering Congress to make all laws which shall be necessary and proper for carrying into execution those enumerated above. This is sometimes called "the elastic clause," since it is capable of being stretched by interpretation to cover many matters that Congress might not otherwise feel authorized to deal with. It is doubtful, however, whether it really adds anything to the power of Congress, since that body would unquestionably have authority to do whatever is necessary and proper to carry into effect the powers expressly conferred upon it. It is a maxim of constitutional construction that wherever power to do a particular thing is conferred, the means for doing it are implied. Manifestly it would have been impossible to set forth in detail all the incidental powers necessary to be exercised in carrying into effect the mandates of the Constitution relating to taxes, coinage, post offices, making war, etc.

Liberal vs. Strict Construction.—The question of the interpretation of the scope and meaning of this grant of powers arose very early in the history of the national government, in connection with the proposition of Hamilton to establish a United States bank. Hamilton contended that the authority to establish such an institution was clearly implied in the power to borrow money and pay the debts of the United States. A federal bank, he urged, was a proper if not a necessary means for carrying into effect these important powers of Congress, just as the establishment of a mint was necessary to carry out the power relating to the coinage of money. Jefferson and his school of political thinkers, however, held to a strict interpretation of the Constitution and maintained that Congress had no right to exercise any power which was not expressly conferred. The view of the "loose" or "liberal" constructionists, however, prevailed, and from the beginning Congress has relied upon the doctrine of implied powers for its authority to legislate on many important questions.

Examples of Implied Powers.—It was upon this authority that foreign territory has been purchased and governed; that a protective tariff has been levied; that a national bank was established; that legal tender paper money has been issued; that the construction of the Panama Canal has been undertaken; that ship subsidies have been granted; that postal savings banks have been established; that education has been fostered; and many other activities undertaken. The policy of liberal interpretation was first adopted by Chief Justice Marshall of the Supreme Court and his associates, and with rare exceptions has been followed by the court throughout its entire history. The effect has been to strengthen the national government and render it capable of fulfilling the great purposes for which it was created. The whole course of our political and constitutional history is different from what it would have been had the view of the strict constructionists prevailed.

References.—ANDREWS, Manual of the Constitution, pp. 120-148. BEARD, American Government and Politics, ch. xix. COOLEY, Principles of Constitutional Law, pp. 94-111. FAIRLIE, National Administration, chs. ix, x, xii. HART, Actual Government, ch. xxiv.

Documentary and Illustrative Material.—Copies of the annual reports of the Postmaster-General, the Librarian of Congress, the Commissioner of Patents, the Secretary of War, and the Secretary of the Navy, all of which may be obtained gratis from the officials mentioned.

RESEARCH QUESTIONS

1. Why should the postal service be conducted by the government? Should the transportation of the mail be a government monopoly?

2. Should the rates of postage on second-class matter, in your opinion, be increased? Why?

3. What are the advantages of a postal savings bank system?

4. Ought the government to establish a parcels post system? To what extent do we already have a parcels post service?

5. Do you think our postal facilities with South America and the Orient should be improved by means of ship subsidies?

6. What would be the advantage of making the tenure of postmasters permanent?

7. Why should the granting of copyrights and patents be placed under the jurisdiction of the national government rather than under that of the state governments?

8. Why should the term of a copyright or patent be limited?

9. Socialists argue that since the granting of a patent to an inventor secures to him a monopoly of the manufacture and sale of his invention, the government ought not to grant patents for such purposes. What is your opinion of this argument? Would it be better for the government to compensate the inventor and remove the restrictions upon the manufacture and sale of his invention?

10. Why are the appropriations for the maintenance of the army limited to two years?

11. Should the expenditures on account of the army and navy, in your opinion, be reduced?

12. What do you understand by the movement among the nations for disarmament? Do you think disarmament desirable or practicable?

13. Tell something of the objects and results of The Hague Peace Conferences. Give examples of some disputes between the United States and other countries that have been settled by arbitration.

14. What is the purpose of a bankruptcy law, and why should the power to enact bankruptcy legislation be conferred upon Congress rather than left to the states?

15. What is the distinction between "implied" and "inherent" powers under the Constitution? Give some examples of each.

16. Which in your judgment is the safer policy, that of strict construction of the Constitution or liberal construction?

STATE, WAR, AND NAVY BUILDING, WASHINGTON, D.C.

MIDSHIPMEN OF THE NAVAL ACADEMY, ANNAPOLIS, MARYLAND, ON THEIR WAY TO A DRILL SHIP

CHAPTER XV

THE PRESIDENCY: ORGANIZATION AND MODE OF ELECTION

The Presidential Office.—One of the weaknesses in the organization of the government under the Articles of Confederation was, as we have seen, the lack of an executive to carry into effect the resolutions of Congress and the treaties of the United States. There was no doubt, therefore, in the minds of the framers of the Constitution in regard to the desirability of providing for an executive department coördinate with the legislative department. It was accordingly declared that the executive power should be vested in an officer called the President of the United States.

Proposed Executive Council.—While the convention was practically unanimous in the view that the supreme executive power should be vested in a single person, a good many members looked with favor on a proposition to associate with the President an executive council which should share with him the exercise of the executive power in certain important fields. Most of the state constitutions then in force had provided such councils, and now that a national executive with far larger powers was being created there was all the more reason why it should be placed to some extent under the guardianship of a council. But the proposition was rejected, and in its place the Senate was charged with acting as an executive council to the President in negotiating treaties and the making of appointments, but in no other respects.

Qualifications of the President.—The Constitution requires that the President shall be a natural born citizen of the United States,[58] that he must have attained the age of thirty-five years, and must have been fourteen years a resident of the United States. The same qualifications are required of the Vice President.

The Presidential Term.—There was considerable discussion in the convention regarding the term of the President. It was first decided that the term should be seven years and the President made ineligible to a second term, but upon further consideration the convention decided to fix the term at four years and nothing was said in regard to reëligibility. The result is, the President may serve as many terms as the people may see fit to elect him. The following Presidents have been elected to two terms: Washington, Jefferson, Madison, Monroe, Jackson, Lincoln, Grant, Cleveland, McKinley, and Wilson.[59] Cleveland, after serving one term, was renominated by his party but was defeated by the Republican candidate. He was then nominated for the third time by his party and was elected. Washington declined a third term and his example has been followed by his successors. The precedent thus established, that the President shall serve only two terms, has become part of our unwritten constitution, and but two attempts have ever been made to break the custom.[60]

Mode of Election.—No question consumed so much of the time of the convention as that relating to the method of choosing the President. Various schemes were proposed. A few members favored election by the people; others urged election by Congress. Against the method of popular choice it was argued that the people were not competent to choose a chief magistrate for the entire country, and besides, under such a system, they would be influenced by demagogues and scheming politicians. Again, the tumults and disorders, the "heats and ferments" of a popular election would convulse the community to the breaking point. Against the method of election by Congress, it was urged that the President would be a mere creature or tool of that assembly and would be under the temptation of making promises or entering into bargains with influential members in order to secure an election. Moreover, such a method was contrary to the great principle upon which all the members were agreed, namely, that the three departments of the national government should be kept separate and independent of one another.

The clause as finally adopted provides that the President shall be chosen, not directly by the voters, but by electors to be appointed in each state in such manner as the legislature thereof may direct, each state to have as many electors as it has senators and representatives in Congress.

Breakdown of the Electoral Plan.—It was at first expected that the electors of the different states, composed of leading citizens presumably well acquainted with the qualifications of the candidates for the chief magistracy, would meet at the state capitals, discuss among themselves the strength and weaknesses of the several candidates, and then exercising their full judgment, cast their votes for the fittest. But the scheme quickly broke down in practice, and instead of a real choice by small bodies of men, we have a system which amounts to direct election by the masses of the voters, though the form of indirect election is still followed. As soon as political parties were thoroughly organized, the electors, who were intended to be men "capable of analyzing the qualities adapted to the Presidential office," were reduced to the position of party puppets who no longer exercised their own judgment in choosing the President but merely registered, like automata, the will of their party. As Ex-President Harrison once remarked, an elector who should fail to vote for the nominee of his party would be the object of execration and in times of very high excitement might be the subject of a lynching.[61] So closely do the electors obey the will of their party that we always know at the close of election day, on Tuesday after the first Monday in November, when the electors themselves are chosen, who will be the next President, though in fact the electors do not meet in their respective states until the following January, formally to register the choice of the people.

Choosing Presidential Electors.—In the beginning the presidential electors of each state were chosen by the legislature, either by joint ballot of the two houses sitting together, or by concurrent vote. In the course of time, however, popular election of electors was introduced, South Carolina (1868) being the last state to choose its electors by the legislature.

Choice by General Ticket.—When the system of popular choice of electors was adopted, two different methods were followed: choice by districts, and choice on general ticket from the state at large; but by 1832 all the states except Maryland had adopted the general ticket method, and now there is no state which follows the district method.

Representatives in Congress, as we have seen, are elected by districts, and hence the delegation in Congress from a particular state is often divided between Democrats and Republicans. But not so with Presidential electors; usually the party in the majority in the state, however small the majority, chooses all the electors. Thus when the Democratic party carried New York by a majority of hardly more than 1,000 votes in 1884, the entire electoral vote was counted for Cleveland.[62]

Among the results of the rule which gives the entire electoral vote of the state to one of the candidates, notwithstanding the size of the vote polled by the other candidate, is that each party concentrates its efforts in the large "pivotal" states whose votes are decisive, and thereby bribery and fraud in such states are powerfully stimulated.

Candidates for the office of elector are nominated usually by the state conventions of each party. No senator or representative or any person holding an office of honor, trust, or profit under the United States is eligible to the office of elector. Congress, under the Constitution, has power to fix the day on which the electors shall be chosen, and it has fixed the day as Tuesday after the first Monday in November.

Electoral and Popular Vote.—Generally the candidate for President whose electors receive the largest popular vote will also receive the largest electoral vote; but this has not always happened, and usually there is only a rough correspondence between the popular vote and the electoral vote. Thus in 1860 Lincoln received only about forty per cent of the popular vote, though he received a substantial majority (about fifty-nine per cent) of the electoral vote. Again, in 1864 he received only about fifty-five per cent of the popular vote, but ninety-one per cent of the electoral vote. In 1912 Wilson received forty-two per cent of the popular vote, and eighty-two per cent of the electoral vote. Such discrepancies are due to the fact that the entire electoral vote of a state is usually cast for the candidate who receives a plurality of the popular vote of the state, however small it may be. A party, therefore, may carry enough states by small margins to secure a majority of the electors and yet be in a minority so far as the popular vote of the entire country is concerned.

Choice of the President by the Electors.—The electors, on the second Monday of January following their election, assemble in their respective state capitals for the purpose of choosing the President.[63] The Constitution as it now stands requires the electors to vote by ballot for President and by a distinct ballot vote for Vice President, and make separate lists of all persons voted for as President and of all persons voted for as Vice President.

The Original Method.—The Constitution as originally adopted did not require the electors in casting their ballots to indicate the person for whom they were voting as President and whom for Vice President, or to prepare distinct lists. The one who received the highest vote (if a majority) was to be President, and the one receiving the next highest number (whether a majority or not) was to be Vice President. The result of this method of choosing the President was that as soon as political parties were formed and the electors came to vote strictly on the basis of party there would be a tie between the two persons highest on the list, and as there was nothing to show on the record which was intended for President and which for Vice President there would be no election. This happened in 1801, when Jefferson and Burr each received seventy-three electoral votes, and the choice between them had to be made by the house of representatives as the Constitution provides.

Twelfth Amendment.—To remove the difficulty, the Twelfth Amendment was adopted in 1804, requiring the electors in preparing their ballots to indicate their choice for President and their choice for Vice President so that the person intended for the latter office could not be confused with the person intended for President. The amendment also requires a majority of the electoral vote to elect the Vice President as well as the President.

Restrictions on the Electors.—In casting their votes the electors are prohibited from voting for candidates for both offices from the same state as themselves. The purpose of this provision is to prevent the electors from one state—if any state should ever become powerful enough—from choosing both the President and the Vice President from that state. This does not mean, however, that both the President and the Vice President could not be elected from the same state, since the electors of the other states are not prohibited from voting for two candidates from the same state.

Formalities and Precautions.—The Constitution requires the electors of each state to sign, certify, seal, and transmit to the president of the United States senate, a list of the votes cast for President and Vice President. The statutes also require two additional lists to be prepared, one to be sent to the president of the senate by special messenger, and the other to be deposited with the nearest United States district judge. These extra precautions are taken to prevent the loss of the state's votes through accident or otherwise. This done, the office of the Presidential elector expires and the electoral colleges cannot be again summoned to correct errors or to make a new choice in case the President elect should die before inauguration.

Counting the Electoral Vote.—The Constitution directs that the votes transmitted to the president of the senate shall be opened in the presence of both houses of Congress and that the votes shall then be counted. The Constitution does not say who shall count the votes. Apparently the framers believed that the process of counting would never involve anything more than a simple act of addition. But in the course of time disputed returns began to be sent in, and then the process of counting came to involve the more difficult task of determining what should be counted. Thereupon the question was raised, who shall count? Was the president of the senate to count and the two houses act merely as spectators, or was the president of the senate to open the votes and the two houses do the counting? For a long time, when the disputes were not serious enough to affect the result, the president of the senate was allowed to count the vote and proclaim the result.[64] In 1865 by a joint rule Congress assumed the right to count the electoral vote, thus taking the power away from the president of the senate.

The Disputed Election of 1876.—In 1876 a serious election dispute arose, involving the presidency. Both Hayes and Tilden claimed to have been elected, and the result depended upon which of two conflicting lists of votes from Florida, Oregon, South Carolina, and Louisiana should be counted. Under the joint rule mentioned above, either house could reject a questionable vote. One of the houses was Democratic and the other Republican, and because of the great excitement over the matter, it was feared that the votes of many states might be rejected for trivial reasons. After much discussion, in the course of which many ugly threats were made, Congress agreed to the creation of an electoral commission, to decide the disputed votes. The commission was to consist of five senators, five representatives, and five justices of the Supreme Court. As finally constituted it was composed of eight Republicans and seven Democrats, and by a strict party vote the commission decided in favor of Hayes in every case, thus insuring his election. The minority accepted the result, but not without protest and criticism.

The Act of 1887.—After this decision, Congress took up the task of devising permanent rules for counting the electoral vote, and finally in 1887 it passed an elaborate act which now regulates the electoral count. In brief, it places the responsibility so far as possible on the state authorities, and provides that the determination of each state as to how its electoral vote was cast shall, under certain conditions, be final. If, however, a state neglects to settle its own election contests, and double returns are transmitted to the president of the senate, the two houses of Congress sitting separately must determine how the votes shall be counted. But if the two houses fail to agree, as they did in counting the vote of 1876, then the vote of the state is lost. The day fixed by Congress for opening and counting the vote is the second Wednesday in February.

Election by the House.—In case no candidate receives a majority of the electoral votes, the choice devolves upon the house of representatives. But in that case the house votes by states, each state having one vote, irrespective of its number of representatives, and the choice is made from the three candidates standing highest on the list.[65] A quorum for the election of a President by the house consists of a member or members from two thirds of the states, and the vote of a majority of all the states is necessary to a choice.

Objections to Election by the House.—The objections to this method of choice are obvious. It is undemocratic, because the house on which the choice would devolve in any case would be, not the new house chosen at the recent election, but the old house, which might indeed, as has often happened, be in the hands of the political party defeated at the late election. In the second place, under such a scheme, New York with a population over 100 times as great as that of Nevada would have no larger share in choosing the executive. In 1873, for example, had the choice devolved upon the house, it would have been possible for 45 members (being a majority of the representatives of nineteen states) to determine the choice in spite of the wishes of the other 247 members. Finally, the state delegations in the house might be equally divided politically, and hence fail to elect.[66]

Instances of Choice by the House.—Twice has the electoral college failed to make a choice, thus giving the election to the house of representatives.

In 1801, there was a tie between Jefferson and Burr, each having the vote of a majority of the electors. There were then sixteen states, of which eight voted for Jefferson, six for Burr, and two were evenly divided. On the thirty-sixth ballot the two divided states voted for Jefferson and he was elected, as the electors had originally intended.

The second instance occurred in 1825, when the electoral vote stood as follows: for Jackson 99; for Adams 84; for Crawford 41; and for Clay 37, no one having a majority. Under the Twelfth Amendment Clay was dropped from the list and the choice was confined to the three highest candidates. There were then twenty-four states, and of these the representatives of thirteen voted for Adams, seven for Jackson, and four for Crawford.

Election of the Vice President by the Senate.—The Constitution also provides that if no candidate for Vice President receives a majority of the electoral vote the choice shall devolve upon the senate, in which case the election shall be made from the two highest on the list. Two thirds of the senate constitute a quorum for this purpose, and a majority of the whole number is necessary to a choice. Only once has the choice devolved upon the senate, namely, in 1836, when Richard M. Johnson, candidate for Vice President on the ticket with Mr. Van Buren, failed to receive a majority of the electoral vote. He was promptly elected by the senate.

Methods of Nomination.—Neither the Constitution nor the laws of the United States make any provision in regard to the nomination of the candidates for President and Vice President. That is left entirely to the regulation of the political parties themselves. In the early history of the republic, before political parties had risen, no nominating machinery was devised, for none was needed.

Early Methods.—With the rise of political parties, however, the method of nomination by congressional caucus was introduced; that is, the members of Congress belonging to each political party assumed the power of selecting its candidate in secret conclave. In this way Jefferson was nominated by the Republican members of Congress in 1800 and 1804, Madison in 1808 and 1812, and Monroe in 1816 and 1820. In the same way the Federalist members put forward their candidates. In some cases, however, presidential candidates were nominated by state legislatures. In the course of time, strong opposition grew up against the method of nomination by members of Congress, and after 1824 the caucus system was never again resorted to. The new nominating machinery which took its place was the national convention, which came into use between 1831 and 1840.

The National Convention.—A national convention to nominate candidates for President and Vice President is composed of delegates from each state and territory in the Union, the number to which each is entitled being usually twice its number of senators and representatives in Congress.[67] Altogether the national convention consists of about 1,000 delegates. For each delegate there is an alternate who attends the convention and in case of the absence of the delegate, takes his place.

Formerly the four delegates-at-large of each party were chosen by the state convention, and the other delegates by congressional district conventions. When direct primary laws were introduced, some states provided that the latter delegates should be selected by the voters of each party at the primary, leaving the delegates-at-large to be chosen as formerly by the state convention. In 1912 a number of states passed what are known as "presidential preference primary" laws under which delegates to the national conventions of that year were chosen. Some of these laws permit the voters to choose their delegates to the national convention but without allowing them to indicate their preference for any presidential candidate; others allow a direct expression of the popular preference for presidential candidates but make no provision for binding the delegates to nominate the candidate preferred by the majority of the voters; some, however, provide both for an expression of the popular preference and for binding the delegates to the national convention. More than one third of the states now have laws of one or another of these three types.

The Time and Place for holding the national convention are fixed by the national committee. The date usually falls in the latter part of June or early in July of the year the President is to be elected, and the place is usually some large city centrally located.

Procedure of a National Convention.—The convention is usually held in some spacious building especially erected for the purpose. Besides the delegations of the states, there are the alternates, hundreds of politicians who are not delegates, newspaper reporters, and thousands of spectators from all parts of the country, for all of whom accommodations are needed.

Organization of the Convention.—The convention is called to order by the chairman of the national committee, and the secretary of the committee reads the call for the convention. Next come the choice of a temporary chairman, and the appointment and report of committees on credentials, on permanent organization, on rules, and on resolutions much as in the state conventions described on pp. 153-155.

The Platform is a series of resolutions commending the national administration, or denouncing it, as the case may be, and setting forth the position of the party on the political issues of the day. Declarations are often made in the platform to attract or conciliate large masses of voters, sometimes when there is no real intention of carrying them out. The platform is usually adopted by the convention as reported by the committee on resolutions, but sometimes important changes are made on the floor after a spirited contest.

The Nominations.—After the adoption of the platform, the nomination of candidates for President is in order. The clerk calls the roll of the states in alphabetical order so that each is given an opportunity to present the name of its choice. The vote is then taken by a roll call of the states, the chairman of each state delegation usually announcing the vote of the state. Under the rules of the Republican party the delegates vote as individuals, so that the vote of a state is often divided between two or more candidates, unless the conventions which appointed the delegates have instructed them to cast the vote of the state for a particular candidate. According to the "unit rule" of the Democratic party, the state delegations vote as units and not as individuals, so that there is no division of a state's vote; the majority of each delegation determines how the votes of the state shall be cast.[68] The rules of the Democratic and Republican parties also differ in the majority necessary to nominate a candidate.

The Vote Necessary to Nominate.—According to the rules of the Republican party, a majority of the delegates is sufficient to nominate, but under the rules of the Democratic party the concurrence of two thirds of the delegates is required. Thus if there are 1,000 delegates in the convention, 501 may nominate under the Republican rule, while 667 would be required under the rules of the Democratic party. The large majority necessary to nominate in the Democratic convention has often resulted in the defeat of the leading candidate and the nomination of a "dark horse," that is, a candidate whose name has not been previously presented to the convention or which has not been prominently kept before it. Presidents Polk and Pierce were nominated in this way.

Nomination of Vice President.—Usually there is little contest over the nomination of the Vice President, the nomination usually being given to some one supported by a defeated faction or group of the party, or to a particular section of the country. Thus if the presidential nomination goes to an Eastern man, the vice presidential nomination is likely to be given to a Western man. In view of the comparatively large number of Presidents who have died in office it is to be regretted that so little consideration is given to the nomination of candidates for Vice President.

Notification of the Candidates.—The candidates are formally notified some weeks later by a committee specially appointed for the purpose. The nominee in a formal speech accepts the nomination and pledges himself to support the platform. Usually this is followed by a letter of acceptance in which the views of the nominee are elaborated more at length. This completes the formalities of nomination, and the next step is to inaugurate the campaign for the election of the nominees.

Conduct of a Presidential Campaign.—*The National Committee.*—The main task of managing the campaign falls on the chairman of the national committee. This committee is made up of one member from each state and territory, and is chosen by the national convention which nominates the candidates.[69] The chairman is usually an experienced political leader with a wide acquaintanceship, and is a trusted friend of the presidential candidate, by whom, in fact, he is usually selected.

Soon after the adjournment of the convention, the national committee meets and organizes. In addition to the national chairman a treasurer and a secretary are chosen. The treasurer raises and has custody of the enormous funds expended in the conduct of the campaign. As the national chairman may be compared to a general who commands the forces, the treasurer is the man who raises the sinews of the war.

Work of the National Committee.—The headquarters of the committee are usually established in New York city, with branch offices in Chicago or Washington, though during the campaign of 1908 the principal headquarters were located in Chicago. The work of the committee is usually divided among bureaus or divisions, one of which has charge of the mailing of campaign literature, another is engaged in the tabulation of reports, another looks after the employment and assignment of speakers, another has charge of the organization of voters' clubs throughout the country, etc.[70] Large quantities of campaign literature, consisting of a "Campaign textbook," speeches of the candidates or of members of Congress, pamphlets, leaflets, posters, lithographs, and in fact everything calculated to influence the voters, are sent broadcast throughout the country and particularly in the close or doubtful states where the principal efforts of the committee are concentrated.[71]

Activity of the Presidential Candidate.—Formerly it was not considered proper for the presidential candidates themselves to take an active part in the campaign by traveling about the country and making speeches, but in recent years there has been a change in this respect. Mr. Bryan in 1896 traveled about the country and delivered hundreds of speeches in behalf of his candidacy, and he pursued a similar course in 1900 and again in 1908 when he was the Democratic candidate. In the latter year, Mr. Taft, the Republican candidate, likewise entered actively into the campaign and delivered more than 400 speeches in thirty different states. In 1912 Mr. Wilson and Mr. Roosevelt made extensive campaign tours and delivered many speeches. Similar tours were made in later campaigns.

Raising and Expenditure of Campaign Funds.—The management of a national political campaign requires the expenditure of large sums of money for printing, postage, telegrams, express, rent of halls, music, expenses of speakers, organizing clubs, and the like. This money is spent solely under the direction of the national chairman, who until recently was not required to render an account of the moneys contributed for this purpose.

The Raising of Campaign Funds.—Prior to 1884 the expenditures on account of a national campaign were comparatively small and were raised by the party in power largely by assessments on federal office-holders; but the civil service law enacted in the year previous forbade assessments of this kind and thus cut off an important source of supply. More attention then began to be turned toward the great corporations, many of which desired to become the beneficiaries of special legislation or to secure immunity from government interference with the management of their business. In a recent campaign, one corporation, a life insurance company, contributed $200,000; one railroad company gave $100,000; and many others $50,000. Sometimes a corporation contributes equally to the campaign funds of both parties, on the principle that it is a wise policy to be on good terms with each.

Contributions of Corporations now Forbidden.—The raising and spending of so much money as a part of the process of electing a President has recently given rise to a demand that the sources of national campaign contributions should be made public. Moreover, it is coming to be regarded as an evil that the large corporations who desire beneficial legislation or immunity from prosecution should have become the chief contributors to campaign funds. This feeling led to the enactment by Congress in 1907 of a law forbidding national banks and other corporations which have charters granted by Congress, from making contributions to the campaign funds of any party at any election, national, state, or local. The law also prohibits any corporation, whether chartered under the authority of the national government or not, from making campaign contributions at any election at which the President of the United States or any member of Congress is to be chosen.

Publicity of Campaign Contributions.—In 1910 Congress passed a law requiring the treasurer of each national party committee to make and publish after the election a sworn statement showing every contribution of $100 or more received by him, every expenditure of $10 or more, and the totals of all other contributions and expenditures.

Finally, in 1911, Congress went still further and passed a law requiring the publication of such statements *before* the election. The elections affected by these acts are those of President and members of Congress. The act of 1911 forbids any candidate for representative to spend or promise more than $5,000, and any candidate for senator more than $10,000, in his campaign. And such candidates are required to file statements of all campaign receipts and expenditures.

The Succession to the Presidency.—The Constitution declares that in case of the removal of the President from office, or of his death, resignation, or inability to discharge the powers and duties of his office, the same shall devolve upon the Vice President. In case of the removal, death, resignation, or inability of both the President and the Vice President, Congress is authorized to provide for the succession. The only way in which the President may be removed is by impeachment and conviction. President Johnson was impeached, mainly for the violation of the tenure of office act, but the senate failed by one vote to convict him. Had he been convicted the office would have been declared vacant. There has been no instance of the resignation of a President.[72] Five Presidents have died in office: Harrison, Taylor, Lincoln, Garfield, and McKinley. In each case the dead President was succeeded by the Vice President. No case of inability to discharge the duties of the presidential office has ever been construed as existing, though in fact such a case existed from July 2, 1881, when President Garfield was shot, to September 19, when he died. A similar case existed during the period in which President McKinley lingered on his deathbed, from September 6 to September 14, 1901. In neither case did the Vice President assume the reins of office until death had made the office vacant. Likewise during President Wilson's serious illness in 1919-1920, the Vice President did not act.

Succession Law of 1792.—Congress provided by law in 1792 that in case of the removal, death, resignation, or inability of both the President and the Vice President, the president *pro tempore* of the senate should succeed, and after him the speaker of the house. There were several practical and political objections to this arrangement, however. In the first place, there might be considerable periods of time when there was no president *pro tempore* of the senate or speaker of the house, and consequently no one to succeed in case of a vacancy.[73] Another objection to the law—political in character—was illustrated by the situation that existed in 1886. The Democratic Vice President Hendricks had died, and in case the presidential office had become vacant it would have been filled by a Republican president of the senate. Thus the executive branch of the government would have passed from the hands of the party that had carried the country at the last election, to the other party, merely by the death of a public officer.

Succession Act of 1886.—In 1886 Congress changed the law so as to give the succession to the presidency to the members of the cabinet, in the order of the creation of their departments, in case of the death or removal of both the President and the Vice President. As the members of the cabinet usually belong to the same party as the President and Vice President, the office in such a contingency would remain in the control of the party which elected the President at the last election. No special provision has yet been made, however, in regard to the succession in case the President elect and Vice President elect should die after their election by the electoral college on the second Monday in January and before their inauguration on the 4th of March. The electoral college could not be reconvened because it becomes *functus officio* immediately after electing the President. As the law stands, the succession would probably go to some member of the old cabinet, who might be of the opposite party. In such a case, however, Congress might provide for a special presidential election.

References.—ANDREWS, Manual of the Constitution, pp. 166-177. BEARD, American Government and Politics, ch. ix. BRYCE, The American Commonwealth (abridged edition), chs. vi, vii, lii-liv. FULLER, Government by the People, ch. vii. HARRISON, This Country of Ours, chs. iv-v. HART, Actual Government, pp. 261-267. HINSDALE, American Government, chs. xxix-xxxi. STANWOOD, History of the Presidency. WOODBURN, The American Republic, pp. 116-136.

Documentary and Illustrative Material.—1. Congressional Directory. 2. Copy of the call for a national convention. 3. Addresses of the temporary and permanent chairmen of the last national convention. 4. The Democratic and Republican campaign textbooks. 5. Copy of the election returns. 6. Specimen ballots containing the names of candidates for presidential electors.

1. How many votes is your state entitled to in the electoral college? What proportion of the total electoral vote is that? Can you give the names of any of the presidential electors from your state at the last election?

2. What was the popular vote received by the Republican candidate for President in your state at the last election? By the Democratic candidate?

3. Name the Presidents who received only a minority of the popular vote.

4. Suppose a vacancy should occur in the electoral college of a state by the death of an elector, is there any way by which it could be filled?

5. Suppose the candidate for President should die after the popular election in November and before the meeting of the electors in January, for whom would the electors cast their vote? Have there been any actual instances of this kind?

6. Suppose the President elect should die before the votes are opened and counted by Congress, who would be declared President?

7. Have there been any instances since 1820 in which a presidential elector voted against the candidate of his own party?

8. What would be the principal advantage in extending the term of the President and making him ineligible to succeed himself?

9. Do you think the custom a wise one which prohibits the President from serving more than two terms?

10. What were the controversies at issue in the disputed election of 1876?

11. What were the objections to the method of nomination by congressional caucus? Who was the last candidate to be nominated by this method?

12. Tell something about the first national convention held in the United States for the nomination of candidates for President and Vice President.

13. How many parties nominated candidates for President and Vice President in the last presidential election? Give the popular vote received by each, in your state and in the country as a whole.

14. Read the platforms of each party and contrast their positions on the leading political issues.

15. How many delegates is your state entitled to in the national convention? Who were the delegates at large from your state in the last Democratic national convention? In the last Republican national convention?

16. Where did the Democratic and Republican parties hold their last national conventions? Who was the permanent chairman of each?

17. What is your opinion of the "unit rule" followed by the Democratic party? Of the "two-thirds" rule?

18. Do you think it would be a wise rule to apportion the delegates from each state to the national convention on the basis of the party strength rather than on the basis of population?

19. Since the people of the territories take no part in national elections, ought they to be allowed to send delegates to the national convention?

20. What is your opinion of the proposal to nominate candidates for President and Vice President by direct primary as state officials are nominated in many states?

21. What is meant by the doctrine of "availability" in choosing candidates for President? What presidential candidates has your state furnished?

22. Is Mr. Bryce's assertion that great men are rarely elected President true? If so, why?

23. Do you think presidential candidates should make campaign tours and deliver campaign speeches?

CHAPTER XVI

THE PRESIDENCY (CONTINUED): INAUGURATION; POWERS AND DUTIES

The Inauguration.—It is no longer the practice to notify the President officially of his election, and so without certificate of election or commission, he presents himself at the national capital on the 4th of March to take the oath of office required by the Constitution and to enter upon the discharge of his duties. Toward noon on that day he proceeds to the White House, as the official residence of the President is styled, where he joins the outgoing President and both are driven to the Capitol, followed by a procession. *The oath of office* is usually administered by the Chief Justice of the Supreme Court on a platform erected for the purpose at the east front of the Capitol, and in the presence of a vast throng of spectators from all parts of the country. [74] Following the custom set by the first Chief Executive, the President delivers a short *inaugural address* in which he foreshadows in a general way his policy as President, after which he returns with the Ex-President to the White House, where he reviews for several hours the procession of visitors.

Inaugural Pageantry.—The inauguration of the President is made the occasion of a great pageant, to which hundreds of thousands of visitors throng from every part of the Union. In the procession which escorts the President to the Capitol are militia companies, headed by governors of states, and civil organizations of every variety. Owing to the inclemency of the weather which often prevails at this season of the year, it has been proposed to change the date of the inauguration, but since this will involve an amendment to the Constitution if the inauguration is to take place at the beginning of the presidential term, the success of the movement is doubtful. [75]

Compensation of the President.—The Constitution declares that the President shall, at stated times, receive for his services a compensation which shall neither be increased nor diminished during the time for which he has been elected. He is also forbidden to receive any other emolument either from the United States or from any state.

The salary of the President was $25,000 a year until 1873, when it was raised to $50,000. In 1909 it was raised to $75,000. Besides this salary there is an allowance of $25,000 a year for traveling expenses, and allowances for clerks, automobiles, house furnishings, fuel, lighting, etc., making in the aggregate some $250,000 a year. In the White House the nation furnishes the President with both a private and an official residence.

Extent of the President's Powers.—The powers of the President are partly conferred by the Constitution, partly by acts of Congress and treaties, and are partly the result of usage and precedent. The power which has been wielded at any given time, however, has depended upon the initiative and force of the President and the extent to which he enjoyed the confidence of Congress and the people. Again, the power which may be rightfully exercised depends upon the state of affairs under which the office is administered. In time of war the power of the President may be so expanded as to be limited in effect only by the necessities of the national existence. The powers wielded by President Lincoln during the Civil War were so great as to cause him to be frequently referred to as a dictator. After the outbreak of the war with Germany in 1917 vast and unprecedented powers were conferred on President Wilson by a succession of far-reaching acts of Congress. Among the extraordinary powers thus conferred on him were: the control of the manufacture and distribution of commodities needful for war purposes, the requisition of ships and other war supplies, the fixing of prices of coal, wheat, sugar, steel, and various other commodities, the taking over and operation of private ship-building plants, the closing of liquor distilleries and the seizure of their stocks, the prohibition of exports to foreign countries, the seizure of German ships in American ports, the making of regulations in respect to the treatment of enemy aliens, and the taking over and operation of railroads, telegraphs, and telephones.

Classes of Powers.—The various powers and duties which have been conferred on the President by the Constitution and the laws may be grouped under the following heads:

1. The power and duty of executing the laws, including the power to appoint, direct, and remove public officers.

2. The management of the foreign affairs of the country.

3. The power to command the army and navy.

4. Legislative powers, including the sending of messages to Congress, the calling of extra sessions, and especially the power to veto acts of Congress.

5. The power to grant pardons for offenses against the laws of the United States.

Execution of the Laws.—The President is the head of the executive branch of the government, and it is his duty to see that the Constitution is preserved, protected, and defended, and that the laws enacted in pursuance thereof, the treaties made under its authority, and the decisions rendered by the federal courts are enforced throughout the United States. For these purposes the army, the navy, and the militia are at his disposal, and in case of resistance to the laws and authority of the United States, they may be employed by him in such manner as he may direct, to overcome such resistance. Moreover, nearly all the civil and military officers of the United States are appointed by him and are, to a large degree, subject to his direction.

The President's Responsibility.—Unlike the state governments, the national government is so organized as to concentrate the power and the responsibility for the enforcement of the laws in the hands of a single executive. Those who are charged with aiding him in carrying out the government are his own appointees, and their responsibility is primarily to him alone.

Power of Appointment.—The Constitution declares that the President shall, with the "advice and consent" of the senate, appoint all officers of the United States whose appointment is not otherwise provided for by the Constitution, except that Congress may vest the appointment of inferior officers in the President alone, in the courts of law, or in the heads of departments.[76] This is one of the most important powers devolving upon the President, and probably consumes more of his time than all his other duties together. In the early days of the Constitution, the number of appointments was small, but as the government service expanded, the number of offices to be filled steadily increased until there are now about 11,000 important presidential offices, that is, offices filled by the President and the senate. The tenure of office act of 1820 fixed the terms of the great bulk of federal offices at four years, and even where the term is not prescribed by statute, it is the custom for most appointees to be replaced at the expiration of four years, so that in practice the four-year tenure is universal, except for federal judges, and each President must during his term make appointments to nearly all the presidential offices. In making these appointments he is not limited by any constitutional or statutory requirements in regard to qualifications. He is the sole judge of the fitness of candidates for appointments. The only limitation upon his power is the necessity of securing the approval of the senate, a requirement already discussed in chapter x, pages 190-191.

Appointments to Minor Positions are often made upon the recommendations of the representative in Congress from the district in which the office is located, though many such appointments are now made on the basis of examinations, under civil service rules. Obviously the President or the head of the department could not fill the thousands of minor positions of this sort without reliance upon the advice of others. They cannot investigate personally every application for appointments of this kind. It is natural, therefore, that they should accept the recommendations of members of Congress, who are more apt to be acquainted with the qualifications of applicants in their districts, and who are familiar with local conditions.

Power of Removal.—While the Constitution expressly authorizes the President to appoint officers, with the consent of the senate, it is completely silent on the question of whether he may remove an officer, either with or without the consent of the senate. The only provision in the Constitution in regard to removal is that which relates to impeachment. It might, therefore, be contended that the only constitutional method of depriving an incumbent of an office to which he has been appointed is by impeachment. But this process of removal is so cumbersome and unwieldy that if it were the only means of getting rid of incompetent office-holders many unfit persons would remain in office indefinitely, and, besides, it would be impossible for the President, upon whom the responsibility for the enforcement of the laws rests, to surround himself with officials in whose integrity and fitness he has confidence. Moreover, to resort to the process of impeachment to remove a person from a petty inferior office would be very much like shooting birds with artillery intended for destroying battleships.

From the first, therefore, it was recognized that there was another process of removal than by impeachment. But there was a difference of opinion as to whether that power lay with the President alone, or whether he could remove only with the consent of the senate, as in the case of appointments; or whether the power lay with Congress to prescribe how removals might be made. The matter was threshed over in the first Congress after the Constitution went into effect, and it was decided that the President might remove alone, without the necessity of securing the consent of the senate. But there was considerable fear that he might abuse the power, and Madison is said to have declared that the wanton removal of a meritorious officer would subject him to impeachment.

Early Practice.—For a long time the power of removal was used sparingly. Several of the early Presidents, in fact, made no removals at all, and during the first forty years of our national existence the total number of officers removed probably did not exceed 100. With the incoming of President Jackson, however, what is known as the *spoils system* was introduced; that is, large numbers of office-holders were removed in order to make places for those who had rendered political services to the party in power. Henceforth appointments were made largely as rewards for party service, often without regard to merit and fitness. Nevertheless, the right of the President to make removals for any cause that seemed to him proper, or for any cause whatsoever, continued to be recognized and acquiesced in by all parties until the breach occurred between President Johnson and Congress in 1867.

Act of 1867.—The action of President Johnson in removing officials who were in sympathy with Congress greatly offended that body, and in 1867 a tenure of office act was passed forbidding the President to make removals except with the consent of the Senate.[77] Thus the custom which for seventy-eight years had recognized the unlimited right of the President to remove officers without the necessity of securing the consent of the senate was now reversed. The violation of this law by President Johnson was the chief cause of his impeachment in 1868. With the incoming of President Grant, however, the law was modified, and in 1887 it was repealed. Thus after a brief interval the original interpretation was reverted to, and it has been followed ever since.

The Present Rule.—The right of the President to remove any federal officer appointed by him, except the judges, for any cause whatsoever, is now recognized, and Congress cannot abridge that right by prescribing the conditions under which removals may be made. His power in this respect is absolute and unlimited and may be employed for rewarding his political friends and punishing his enemies as well as for getting rid of incompetent and unfit persons in the public service.

Power of Direction.—Resulting from the power of removal is the power of the President to direct the officers whom he appoints, in regard to the discharge of their duties. Through the threat of removal, he may compel obedience to his orders, though of course he cannot require an officer to do an act which would amount to a violation of the law. Many of the duties of federal officers are prescribed by law, and the President cannot change these duties or require an officer to do his duty differently from the way in which the law requires him to do it. But the law expressly recognizes that the President has the power to direct many officers as to their duties. Thus the secretary of state in the negotiation of treaties and the settlement of disputes with foreign countries is almost wholly under the control of the President. The President may instruct him to begin negotiations with a particular government or to cease negotiations, and the secretary must obey his orders. So the President may direct the secretary of war in regard to the disposition of the armed forces. In the same way he may order the attorney-general to prosecute a "trust" or institute proceedings against any violator of the federal laws, or may direct him to drop proceedings once begun. Some officers, however, such as the secretary of the treasury and the postmaster-general, are less under the direction of the President, their duties being prescribed with more or less detail by acts of Congress.[78]

The Civil Service System.—For a half century following the introduction of the spoils system by President Jackson, both parties acted on the principle that the offices of the federal government were the legitimate spoils of victory at the polls. Under such circumstances the public service was demoralized and enfeebled, and the time of the President and heads of the departments was taken up with considering applications for office when it should have been devoted to more important matters. After the Civil War, a movement was started which had for its purpose the establishment of the merit system in the public service and the elimination of the spoils system.

The Civil Service Law of 1883.—The assassination of President Garfield in 1881 by a disappointed office seeker aroused public opinion to some of the worst evils of the existing system, and in obedience to the demands of public sentiment, Congress in 1883 enacted the civil service law which forms the basis of the present civil service system. This law provided for the creation of a commission of three persons, not more than two of whom should belong to the same political party. The commission was charged with forming rules for making appointments to the public service, and with carrying out the provisions of the law.

The Classified Service.—The act provided for the classification of the positions in the departments at Washington and in the customhouses and post offices where at least fifty persons were employed, and for the holding, under the supervision of the commission, of competitive examinations to test the fitness of applicants for appointments to positions in the classified service. The classified service now includes the departmental service at Washington, the customs service, the post office service, the railway mail service, the Indian service, the internal revenue service, and the government printing service.

Extent of the Classified Service.—At first the law applied to only about 14,000 positions, but since then the number has been increased from time to time by the creation of new offices and by orders of Presidents extending the rules to other classes of positions. A large extension, for example, was made by President Cleveland in 1896. President Roosevelt also made large extensions, so that when he went out of office there were about twice as many positions under the rules as there were when he became President. In 1912 President Taft added over 36,000 fourth-class postmasters and 20,000 artisans employed in the navy yards; and in 1917 President Wilson placed 10,000 first-, second-, and third-class postmasters under the rules. Of 517,805 officers and employees in the executive civil service in 1917, 326,899 were subject to competitive examination.

Exempt Positions.—Among the positions not under the rules and for which competitive examinations are not required are the more important presidential offices such as cabinet officers, assistant secretaries, chiefs of bureaus, United States attorneys, marshals, judges, ambassadors and ministers, besides a large number of minor officials like private secretaries. The income tax and currency acts of 1913 exempted from the operation of the civil service laws employees who collect the income tax and employees of the Federal Reserve Board. By an act of the same year deputy collectors of internal revenue and deputy marshals were withdrawn from the operation of the laws. These acts have been criticized by civil service reformers.

Examinations.—Civil service examinations are held at least twice each year in every state and territory, and any citizen of the United States is eligible to take the examination for any position to be filled. The commission keeps a list of eligibles, that is, of persons who have passed an examination, and whenever an appointment is to be made, it certifies to the appointing authority a list of those who are qualified, and from the three standing highest on the list the appointment must be made. But in making the appointments preference must be given to persons honorably discharged from the military or naval service by reason of their disability resulting from wounds or sickness. The examinations are required to be practical in character and of such a nature as to test, as far as possible, the capacity and fitness of the applicants to discharge the duties of the position for which they desire an appointment.

No appointment is permanent until after six months of probationary service, during which time the appointee must have demonstrated his capacity for the office. The law also prohibits members of Congress from making recommendations for appointments to positions in the classified service except as to the character and residence of the applicant, and also forbids the levying of assessments on government employees for campaign purposes or the solicitation of contributions from employees.[79]

How Removals are Made.—When an appointment has been made in pursuance of the civil service rules, the appointee is protected from removal for political reasons. The rules now in force declare that removals from the competitive service can be made only for just cause and for reasons stated in writing, with an opportunity to the employee to be heard. "Just cause" is defined as being any cause not merely political or religious, which will promote the efficiency of the service.

The Effect of the competitive system has been to give the public service the character of permanency and increased efficiency. The administration may change at Washington, but the more than 200,000 officials under the civil service rules are not affected thereby. There is no longer a "clean sweep" at the beginning of every administration, no longer the demoralization that once characterized the government service when a new party came into power. Thus the whole tone of the public service has been improved, and the

President and heads of the departments have been partly relieved from the burden of listening to the appeals of the army of office seekers who used to descend upon Washington at the beginning of every new administration.

Management of Foreign Affairs.—The United States as a leading member of the family of nations has an extensive intercourse with other countries. There is no nation with which it has not entered into relations of some kind or another. With every civilized country and some that are not civilized, we have one or more treaties regulating certain of our relations with them.

How Treaties are Negotiated.—The President, by and with the advice and consent of the senate, two thirds of the members concurring, is charged with the negotiation of all treaties. The share of the senate in the negotiation of all treaties has already been discussed in chapter x.

The President usually does not conduct negotiations himself,[80] but acts through the secretary of state, who is a sort of minister of foreign affairs. The secretary is subject to his directions, however, and while conducting negotiations keeps the President fully informed of their progress, and secures his approval of all points which in his judgment should be submitted to him for an opinion. Foreign ministers at Washington who wish to discuss questions of foreign policy with the President are referred to the secretary, who is his responsible minister in such matters. Ambassadors, ministers, and consuls of the United States are appointed by the President, though the approval of the senate is essential to the validity of the appointment. Diplomatic representatives sent abroad bear letters of credence signed by the President, and from time to time they are given instructions as to the action they shall take in negotiations with foreign governments. These instructions are prepared by the secretary of state, though in important cases he consults the President and ascertains his wishes in the matter. The President may transfer a minister from one post to another, may recall him, or dismiss him whenever he likes.

Power to "Receive" Foreign Ministers.—The President is also the authority designated by the Constitution for receiving ambassadors and ministers accredited by foreign governments to the government of the United States. To receive a foreign minister is to recognize him as the official representative to the United States of the government which has appointed him. When a new minister arrives at Washington, he is escorted to the White House by the secretary of state on a day agreed upon, and is received by the President. The new minister presents his credentials and delivers a short ceremonial address, to which the President responds. He is then recognized as the official organ of communication between the United States government and the government which he represents. The President, however, may refuse to recognize a minister from a country whose independence is in doubt, or one who is personally objectionable to the United States government. He may also request a foreign government to recall a minister accredited to the United States, or may dismiss one for conduct highly offensive to the government.

The Military Powers of the President.—The Constitution declares that the President shall be commander in chief of the army and navy and also of the militia of the several states whenever it is called into the service of the United States. The power to declare war, however, belongs to Congress, though the President may through his management of the foreign affairs of the country bring about a situation which may make a declaration of war a virtual necessity. Congress also determines the strength of the army, the method of raising the forces, their terms of service, pay, subsistence, organization, equipment, location of forts, and indeed everything relating to its make-up.

Extent of the President's Power.—The President, as commander in chief, decides where the troops are to be located, and where the ships are to be stationed. It is upon his orders that the troops are mobilized, the fleets assembled, and the militia of the states called out. He may direct the campaigns and might, if he wished, take personal command of the army, the navy, or the militia, though in practice he never does, the army, in fact, being commanded by a military officer and the navy by a naval officer. He may do whatever, in his judgment, may conduce to the destruction of the power or the weakening of the strength of the enemy, so long as he acts within the accepted rules of international law. His power, in short, is limited only by the requirements of military necessity and the law of nations. Thus he may declare that any property used by the enemy for warlike purposes or which may in other respects be a source of strength to the enemy shall be subject to confiscation. It was in pursuance of this power that President Lincoln issued the emancipation proclamation freeing the slaves in certain of the Southern states during the Civil War.

Power to Govern Occupied Territory.—When an enemy's territory has once been occupied by the army, the President, as commander in chief, may assume control and govern it through such agencies and in such manner as he may see fit. He may displace the existing authorities or make use of them as he wishes. He may appoint military governors and set up special tribunals in the place of existing courts. He may suspend the writ of habeas corpus, institute martial law, and deprive the inhabitants of other safeguards established by the Constitution for their protection against the arbitrary encroachments of the government. By virtue of this authority President Lincoln governed for some time those parts of the South which came under the jurisdiction of the military forces of the United States during the Civil

War. In the same way President McKinley governed Porto Rico and the Philippines for many months during and after the war with Spain.

Conclusions.—From this summary it will readily be seen that the powers of the President as commander in chief during war are very great, in fact almost unlimited. He may become, as President Lincoln did, practically a dictator, and if he should choose to abuse his powers he might deprive the people of a large portion of their liberties.

In time of peace, the military powers of the President are far less than during war, though they are still considerable. His duty to protect the states against invasion and his power to order out the troops to suppress domestic violence upon the application of the state executive or legislature are discussed in chapter iii. Whenever the movement of interstate commerce or the instrumentalities of the national government are interfered with by rioters it is his right and duty to employ the army or the navy if necessary to suppress the disturbances.[81] By an act of Congress passed in 1795 and still in force, the President is authorized to call out the militia whenever the laws of the United States are opposed or their execution obstructed by combinations too powerful, in his judgment, to be suppressed by the ordinary course of judicial proceedings, or by the federal marshals. And the President is the sole judge of the existence of the state of facts thus described, and no court in the land can review his decision in regard thereto. It was in pursuance of this act that President Lincoln issued his first call for the militia in 1861.

The President's Share in Legislation.—While the chief duty of the President is to execute the laws, he is at the same time given a share in their making. This share is both positive and negative in character.

Presidential Messages.—The Constitution makes it his duty to give Congress from time to time information of the state of the Union and to recommend for its consideration such measures as he may judge necessary and proper. This requirement rests upon the obvious fact that he possesses more extensive sources of knowledge in regard to the state of public affairs than any one else, and is also familiar with the workings of the laws, and hence is in a position to recommend legislation for their improvement.

The information required to be furnished Congress is contained in an annual message communicated at the beginning of each session, and in special messages communicated from time to time during the session.

Early Practice.—It was the custom at the beginning of our national history for the President to deliver an address at the opening of Congress, in the presence of both houses assembled in the senate chamber, and for each house thereafter to draw up a suitable reply, in accordance with the English custom.

This plan was followed by both Washington and Adams, but Jefferson inaugurated the practice of communicating what he had to say in the form of a written message. From that time down till 1913 all the presidential messages to Congress were in written form only; but in the latter year President Wilson revived the practice of addressing Congress in person.

Character of the Annual Messages.—The annual message contains a review of the operations of the government during the preceding year, together with such recommendations for additional legislation as the President thinks the interests of the country require. It also usually contains a summary of the reports of the several heads of departments, and is accompanied by the full reports of the departments. Sometimes one or the other of the houses adopts resolutions calling on the President for information on particular subjects, and if in his judgment the communication of the information is not incompatible with the public interests, the request is complied with.

The message is printed in full in nearly all the daily newspapers of the country on the day on which it is communicated to Congress, and it is widely read by the people and commented on by editors. When the message has been received by the Congress, it is ordered to be printed, and the various recommendations which it contains are distributed among the appropriate committees of each house. The consideration which the recommendations receive at the hands of Congress depends upon the influence which the President wields with the two houses. If he belongs to a different political party from that which is in control of Congress, or if for other reasons Congress is out of sympathy with his policies, his recommendations count for little.

Power to Call Extraordinary Sessions.—The President has power to call extraordinary sessions of Congress for the consideration of special matters of an urgent character. Of course the President cannot compel Congress to adopt his recommendations at a special session any more than at a regular session, but he can sometimes hasten action and if he is backed by a strong public opinion he may be able to accomplish even more. The authority to call extraordinary sessions has been exercised by Presidents Adams, Jefferson, Madison, Van Buren, Harrison, Pierce, Lincoln, Hayes, Cleveland, McKinley, Roosevelt, Taft, and Wilson. In all these cases Congress was called together to deal with extraordinary situations such as foreign difficulties, financial panics, rebellion, the enactment of appropriation bills which had failed at the regular session, the enactment of tariff bills for which there was an urgent demand, the approval of reciprocity treaties, and the like. The senate has often been convened in extraordinary session at the beginning of a new administration for the purpose of approving the nominations of the President, but the house of representatives has never been called alone.

Power to Adjourn Congress.—The President is also authorized to adjourn the two houses in case of disagreement between them as to the time for adjourning the session. Only one such case of disagreement has ever occurred, namely, in the special session of November, 1903, when the senate proposed to adjourn and the house of representatives refused. President Roosevelt did not, however, exercise his power in this case, so the special session continued about two weeks longer, until it was ended by the beginning of the regular session.

Power to Issue Ordinances.—Under the legislative functions of the President may also be included what is known as the ordinance power, that is, the power to issue certain orders and regulations having the force of law. Such are the regulations for the government of the army and navy, and those relating to the postal service, patents, pensions, public lands, Indian affairs, the customs service, internal revenue service, marine hospital service, the consular service, the civil service, and many other branches of administration. Some of these regulations are issued by the President under express authority conferred upon him by acts of Congress; others are issued as a result of the necessity of prescribing means for carrying into effect the laws of Congress and sometimes of interpreting them;[82] while still others are issued in pursuance of the constitutional powers of the President. Such are the regulations issued for the government of the army and navy, in pursuance of the authority of the President as commander in chief.

The Veto Power.—Finally, the President is given an important share in legislation through the constitutional requirement which requires that all bills and resolutions passed by Congress shall be submitted for his approval.[83] The power to withhold his approval of the acts passed by Congress is popularly known as the veto power. It was called by the framers of the Constitution the President's "qualified negative." This prerogative constitutes an exception to the principle of the separation of governmental powers, and was conferred upon the executive as a means of enabling him to defend his constitutional powers and privileges against the encroachments of the legislative department, as well as to provide a check upon hasty and careless legislation by Congress. The conditions under which the right of veto may be exercised, the forms which it may take, and the procedure by which it may be overridden by Congress are discussed in chapter xi. The President may veto a bill because he believes it to be unconstitutional, or because he believes it is unwise or inexpedient, though in both cases a wise executive will be slow to set his judgment against the combined judgment of the members of Congress.

No Power to Veto Items in Appropriation Bills.—Unlike the governors of many of the states, he cannot veto particular items in appropriation bills, as a result of which he is sometimes confronted with the embarrassing duty of signing a bill carrying certain appropriations to which he objects, or of vetoing the entire bill. President Cleveland on one occasion vetoed the rivers and harbors bill carrying an appropriation of many millions of dollars rather than approve certain items in it which he considered wasteful and extravagant. If the President had the power to veto particular items in appropriation bills he could prevent useless and extravagant appropriations in many cases without being under the necessity of defeating at the same time those which are desirable and necessary.

Use of the Veto Power.—The early Presidents either did not make use of the veto power at all, or employed it sparingly. Neither John Adams, nor Thomas Jefferson, nor John Quincy Adams, while in the presidential chair, vetoed any bills; and Washington, Madison, and Monroe together vetoed only eight. Many of the later Presidents used the veto power more freely.

No bill was passed over the veto of a President until the administration of Tyler, when one was so passed. Four bills were passed over the vetoes of Pierce, fourteen over those of Johnson, three over those of Grant, one over a veto of Hayes, one over a veto of Arthur, two over the vetoes of Cleveland, one each over the vetoes of Harrison, Taft, and Wilson.

Joint Resolutions as well as bills are usually presented to the President for his signature, and must be approved before they have any validity, though it has not been the practice to submit to the President, for his approval, joint resolutions proposing amendments to the Constitution. Concurrent resolutions, which do not have the force of law, but are merely expressions of the sense of the legislative department on some question of interest to it alone, do not require the approval of the President.[84]

Importance of the Veto.—The threat of the President to employ the veto may be used to great effect. A strong President who has positive ideas in regard to the kind of legislation which the country needs and which public opinion demands, may compel the adoption in whole or in part of those ideas by the threatened use of the veto. The necessity of obtaining the approval of the President really gives him a powerful share in legislation. Roosevelt, for example, on a number of occasions threatened to veto bills about to be passed by Congress unless they were changed so as to embody the ideas which he advocated, and the threats were not without effect.

The Pardoning Power of the President.—The Constitution authorizes the President "to grant reprieves and pardons for offenses against the United States except in cases of impeachment."[85] The President cannot, of course, pardon offenses against state law. Offenses against the postal laws, the revenue laws, the laws against counterfeiting, and the national banking laws are those for which pardons are most frequently sought. Crimes committed in the territories are, however, offenses against the laws of the United States, and are frequently the object of applications for pardon.

With the exception of the limitation in regard to impeachment offenses, the President's power of pardon is absolute. His power is not restricted by a board of pardons as is that of the governors of some of the states, nor can Congress in any way abridge his power or restrict the effect of a pardon granted by him. Moreover, he may grant a pardon before as well as after conviction, though this is rarely done in the case of individual offenses. It is sometimes done, however, where large numbers of persons have become liable to criminal prosecution for participation in rebellion, resistance to the laws, and similar acts.

Amnesty.—In such cases the pardon is known as an "amnesty," and is granted by proclamation. Thus in December, 1863, President Lincoln issued an amnesty proclamation offering a full pardon to all persons in arms against the United States provided they would lay down their arms and return to their allegiance. In April, 1865, President Johnson issued a proclamation offering amnesty to all those who had borne arms against the United States, with certain exceptions and subject to certain conditions. The last instance of the kind was the proclamation issued by President Harrison, in 1893, granting amnesty to those Mormons who had violated the anti-polygamy laws of the United States.

Commutation.—The power to pardon is held also to include the power to commute a sentence from a heavier to a lighter penalty, and also to reduce a fine or remit it entirely.

Parole.—In 1910, Congress passed a law providing for the release on parole of federal prisoners sentenced to a term of more than one year, except life prisoners, provided their conduct has been satisfactory. At each of the three federal prisons there is a board of parole charged with hearing applications for release.

Immunity of the President from Judicial Control.—Being at the head of a coördinate department of the government, the President, unlike other public officers, is not subject to the control of the courts. They cannot issue processes against him, or restrain him or compel him to perform any act. During the trial of Aaron Burr for treason, Chief Justice Marshall issued a subpœna directed to President Jefferson requiring him to produce a certain paper relating to Burr's acts, but the President refused to obey the writ, declaring that if the chief executive could be compelled to obey the processes of the courts he might be prevented from the discharge of his duties. Even if the President were to commit an act of violence, he could not be arrested or in any way restrained of his liberty. The only remedy against acts of violence committed by him is impeachment by the house of representatives and trial by the Senate. If convicted, he must be deprived of his office, after which his immunity ends and he is liable to prosecution and trial in the ordinary courts as any other offender. The principle upon which the President is exempt from the control of the courts is not that he can do no wrong, but that if he were subject to judicial restraint and compelled to obey the processes of the courts, the administration of the duties of his high office might be interfered with.

Nevertheless, the Supreme Court does not hesitate to exercise control over the subordinates through whom the President acts in most cases, and it will refuse to sanction orders or regulations promulgated by him if they are unconstitutional. To this extent, his acts are subject to judicial control.

References.—ANDREWS, Manual of the Constitution, pp. 180-201. BEARD, American Government and Politics, ch. x. BRYCE, The American Commonwealth (abridged edition), ch. v. FAIRLIE, National Administration, chs. i-ii. HARRISON, This Country of Ours, ch. vi. HINSDALE, American Government, ch. xxxii.

Documentary and Illustrative Material.—1. Copy of an inaugural address of the President. 2. Copy of an annual message of the President. 3. Copies of executive orders and proclamations. 4. Copies of veto messages.

1. What is your opinion of Sir Henry Maine's saying that the President of the United States is but a revised edition of the English King?

2. How do the powers of the President compare in importance and scope with those of the King of England?

3. Have the President's powers increased or decreased since 1789? Give your reasons.

4. Name some of the Presidents who were notable for the vigorous exercise of executive power.

5. What is your opinion of the position taken by President Roosevelt that the power of the President should be increased by executive interpretation and judicial construction?

6. Is the President the judge of the extent and limits of his own powers? If not, what authority is?

7. Do you think the President ought to be prohibited from removing officers except for good cause? Ought the consent of the senate to be required in all cases of removal?

8. What is your opinion of the proposition that the members of the cabinet should be elected by the people?

9. Why are the powers of the President so much more extensive in time of war than in time of peace?

10. What were the principal recommendations made by the President in his last annual message?

11. Do you think he should be allowed to grant pardons *before* conviction? Would it not be well to have a federal board of pardons whose approval should be necessary to the validity of all pardons issued by the President?

12. In the exercise of his duty to enforce the laws, may the President interpret their meaning in case of doubt?

13. To what extent ought the President in making appointments to take into consideration the politics of the appointee? To what extent should he be governed by the recommendations of members of Congress?

14. Why should the executive power be vested in the hands of a single person while the judicial and legislative powers are vested in bodies or assemblies?

15. Do you think the present salary allowed the President adequate? How does it compare with the allowance made to the King of England? the

President of France?

CHAPTER XVII

THE CABINET AND THE EXECUTIVE DEPARTMENTS

The Cabinet.—The heads of the ten executive departments collectively constitute the President's cabinet. They are, in the order of rank, the secretary of state (first styled the secretary of foreign affairs), the secretary of the treasury, the secretary of war, the attorney-general, the postmaster-general, the secretary of the navy, the secretary of the interior, the secretary of agriculture, the secretary of commerce, and the secretary of labor. They are appointed by the President with the consent of the senate, which in practice is never refused; and they may be dismissed by him at any time. The salary of cabinet members is $12,000 a year.

Origin and Nature of the Cabinet.—There was no thought in the beginning that the heads of departments should constitute a cabinet or advisory council to the President, and during the first administration they were never, as a matter of fact, convened by him for collective consultation. When their opinions or advice were desired they were requested by written communication. During his second term, however, President Washington adopted the practice of assembling the heads of departments occasionally for consultation not only on matters pertaining to their particular departments but in regard to questions of general executive policy. Thus the cabinet meeting became a regular feature of executive procedure, and the cabinet a permanent institution. It is well to remember, however, that the cabinet as such is not mentioned in the Constitution, and the name "cabinet" never appeared in any law until the year 1907. No record is kept of its proceedings.

Cabinet Responsibility.—Unlike a European cabinet, the members of the President's cabinet are not, and cannot be, members of either house of Congress; they have no seats in Congress; they are not responsible to Congress for their policies, and they never think of resigning when Congress refuses to carry out their recommendations or to approve their official acts. They are responsible solely to the President for their official conduct, and are subject to his direction, except in so far as their duties are prescribed by law. They are, in short, the ministers of the President, not of Congress; administrative chiefs, not parliamentary leaders. It may happen, therefore, that members of the cabinet, like the President, may belong to the party which is in the minority in Congress.[86]

The Department of State.—At the head of the department of state is the secretary of state, who is the ranking member of the cabinet and the first in line for the presidency in case of the death or removal of both President and Vice President. He sits at the right hand of the President at cabinet meetings and is given precedence over his colleagues on occasions of ceremony. There are also three assistant secretaries in the department, and a counselor, who advises the President and Secretary of State in regard to questions of international law.

The duties of the secretary of state fall into three groups: first, he is the custodian of the great seal and of the archives of the United States. In this capacity he receives the acts and resolutions of Congress, publishes them in certain papers, and preserves the originals. Under this head also fall the duties of countersigning proclamations and important commissions of the President and of attaching thereto the great seal. In the second place, the secretary of state is the organ of communication between the national government and the state governments. Thus an application from the governor of a state for troops to suppress domestic violence, or a request for the extradition of a criminal who has taken refuge in a foreign country, is made through the secretary of state. In the third place, the secretary of state is the organ of communication between the United States and foreign powers, that is, he is the minister of foreign affairs. He carries on all correspondence with foreign governments, negotiates treaties, countersigns warrants for the extradition of fugitives from the justice of foreign countries, issues passports to American citizens wishing to travel abroad, and grants exequaturs to foreign consuls in the United States.

The Diplomatic Service.—For purposes of administration the department of state is organized into a number of bureaus and divisions. *The Diplomatic Bureau* prepares diplomatic correspondence with foreign governments, and has charge of the engrossing of treaties and other formal papers, the preparation of the credentials of diplomatic representatives, and of ceremonious letters. The United States government is now represented at the governments of nearly fifty different foreign countries by diplomatic representatives, and most of these governments maintain diplomatic representatives at Washington. Our representatives to Great Britain, France, Germany, Russia, Austria-Hungary, Italy, Japan, Mexico, Brazil, Turkey, Spain, Argentina, and Chile bear the rank of ambassador. The government is represented at most of the other countries by envoys extraordinary and ministers plenipotentiary; but to one country (Liberia) it sends a minister resident. The principal difference between the different classes of ministers is one of rank and precedence. At the more important foreign posts the ambassador or minister is provided with from one to three secretaries. There are also interpreters at the legations in Oriental countries, and at all the important foreign capitals military and naval attachés are attached to the legation.

Elimination of the Spoils System.—The efficiency of the diplomatic service has been much impaired by the existence of the spoils system, as a result of which diplomatic appointments are determined largely by political considerations, and changes are made by each new administration. In the administrations of Presidents Roosevelt and Taft, however, a beginning was made toward the introduction of the merit system into the diplomatic service.

Duties of Diplomatic Representatives.—The principal duties of diplomatic representatives are to watch over the interests of their country and its citizens in the country to which they are accredited and to see that they receive proper protection, to present and cause to be settled all claims against the foreign country in which they reside, to negotiate treaties, to settle disputes and adjust difficulties, to promote friendly relations, and, in general, to represent their government in its relations with the government to which they are accredited. It is also the duty of a diplomatic representative to keep his government fully informed on all matters in which it is likely to be interested. He is expected to transmit reports relating to political conditions, finance, commerce, agriculture, arts and science, systems of taxation, population, judicial statistics, new inventions, and other matters of possible interest to his government.

The procedure by which treaties are negotiated may take either of two courses: the secretary of state may conduct the negotiations with a foreign minister at Washington, or he may direct the American minister in the foreign country with which it is desired to treat to negotiate with the minister of foreign affairs of that government.[87]

The Consular Service.—*The Consular Bureau* in the department of state has charge of the correspondence with our consular officers in foreign countries. A consul differs from a diplomatic representative in being a commercial rather than a political representative. Consuls are stationed at all important commercial centers in foreign countries, to look after the commercial interests of their country, promote foreign trade, watch over shipping and navigation, administer the estates of American citizens dying abroad, assist in the administration of our customs, health, navigation, immigration, and naturalization laws, and to collect such information concerning the trade, industries, and markets of foreign countries as may be of value to the commercial interests of the United States.[88]

Recent Reforms.—In obedience to the widespread demands of the commercial interests of the country, notable improvements have recently been made in our consular service. Formerly political considerations largely determined appointments to the service, and at the beginning of each new administration a wholesale removal was made in order to find places for party workers. By acts of Congress passed in 1906 and 1909, however, the service was reorganized and attempts made to place it on a merit basis. The fee system was abolished, consuls were prohibited from practicing law or engaging in other businesses, provision was made for periodic inspection of consulates, and a system of examinations was inaugurated for determining the qualifications of appointees to the service. The adoption of these reforms has brought about a marked increase in the efficiency of the service and has tended to give to it the character of a permanent professional career such as it enjoys in Europe.

Other Bureaus of the State Department.—*The Bureau of Indexes and Archives* is charged with keeping the records and indexing the correspondence of the department of state. It also prepares the annual volumes of the foreign relations, containing portions of the diplomatic correspondence.

The Division of Passport Control is charged with the issue of passports to persons who desire to travel abroad. A passport is a paper signed by the secretary of state certifying that the bearer is a citizen of the United States or has declared his intention of becoming a citizen, and is entitled to the protection of the government when traveling abroad. They are granted not only to citizens but, by a recent law, to loyal residents of the insular possessions and to aliens who have declared their intention of becoming citizens and have resided in the United States for three years. A fee of one dollar is charged for each passport.

The other bureaus and divisions in the department of state are: accounts, rolls and library, appointments, information, Far Eastern affairs, Near Eastern affairs, Western European affairs, and Latin-American affairs.

The Department of the Treasury.—For the most part the department of the treasury is concerned with the management of the national finances, including (1) the administration of the revenue laws, (2) the custody of the national funds, (3) the preparation of the budget, (4) the administration of the currency and national banking laws, (5) miscellaneous functions such as those relating to the life-saving service, the public health and marine hospital service, engraving and printing, construction of public buildings, etc.

The custody of the government funds devolves upon the *Treasurer*, who is charged with receiving and disbursing upon proper warrant all public moneys that may be deposited in the treasury at Washington or in the subtreasuries at New York, Philadelphia, Baltimore, Cincinnati, Chicago, St. Louis, New Orleans, and San Francisco, as well as in national banks and federal reserve banks. He is also the custodian of miscellaneous trust funds, is the agent of the government for paying interest on the public debt and for issuing and redeeming government paper currency and national bank notes, and is the custodian of the bonds deposited to secure national bank circulation.

The Register of the Treasury issues and signs all bonds of the United States, registers bond transfers and redemption of bonds, and signs transfers of public funds from the treasury to the subtreasuries or depositories.

The Commissioner of Internal Revenue supervises the collection of the federal income tax and of the taxes on the manufacture of tobacco, etc., and supervises the enforcement of the prohibition law.

The Director of the Budget, provided for by the new budget act of 1921, prepares for the President the annual budget and all other estimates of revenues and expenditures, and with that end in view, has power to assemble, correlate, revise, reduce, or increase the estimates of the several departments or establishments. The President is, however, directly responsible for the budget, and transmits it to Congress. By the same act, the office of *Comptroller of the Treasury* was abolished, and the auditing and accounting functions were removed from the Treasury Department to an independent General Accounting Office, with the *Comptroller-General of the United States* at its head.

The principal officers who have to do with currency administration are the director of the mint and the comptroller of the currency. *The Director of the Mint* has general supervision of the administration of the coinage laws and the management of the coinage and assay offices.[89] *The Comptroller of the Currency* exercises supervision over the national banks. It is his duty to see that national banks are properly organized, that the capital stock is fully subscribed and paid in, that the necessary amount of United States bonds have been duly deposited with the government to secure the circulation of their notes, and that all national banks are properly examined from time to time. He also has important duties in connection with the management of the federal reserve banks. He has charge of the issue of national bank notes and (under the supervision the Federal Reserve Board) of Federal reserve notes.

Among the bureaus of the treasury department which have no direct relation to the public finances the most important is the *Public Health Service*, which is under the direction of a surgeon general who is charged with the supervision of the national quarantine stations and of hospitals for the relief of sick and disabled seamen, and discharged soldiers, sailors, and marines. He calls conferences of all state health boards. He is authorized to adopt regulations to prevent the introduction and spread of contagious diseases, and it is his duty to supervise the medical examination of immigrants seeking admission to the United States.

The Coast Guard, as organized in 1915, is charged with the duties of the former *life-saving service* and the *revenue cutter service*. It renders assistance to persons and vessels in distress, patrols the coast for the purpose of preventing violations of the customs laws, and enforces the laws relating to quarantine, navigation, protection of the game, fishery, and seal industries, etc. It constitutes a part of the military forces and is under the treasury department in time of peace and under the navy department in time of war.

The Supervising Architect is charged with the selection and purchase of sites for government buildings, such as federal courthouses, post-office buildings, customhouses, mints, etc.; with the preparation of plans and specifications and the awarding of contracts for such buildings.

The Bureau of Engraving and Printing is charged with the duty of engraving and printing all government securities, including United States notes, bonds, certificates, national bank notes, federal reserve notes, internal revenue, customs, and postage stamps, treasury drafts, etc.

The Secret Service Division is a body of detective agents employed to detect frauds and crimes against the government, such as counterfeiting or espionage. Some of the force are also employed in guarding the President.

The Bureau of War Risk Insurance (created in 1914) is charged with carrying out the laws relating to government insurance of American ships, soldiers, and sailors.

The Federal Reserve Board and the *Federal Farm Loan Board* (see p. 234) are also under the Treasury Department.

The War Department.—The secretary of war has charge of all matters relating to national defense and seacoast fortifications, river and harbor improvements, the prevention of obstructions to navigation, and the establishment of harbor lines; and all plans and locations, of bridges authorized by Congress to be constructed over navigable rivers require his approval.

The army is under the direction of the *General Staff* described on p. 263. Within the war department there are also a number of departments and bureaus, each under the direction of an army officer.

The Adjutant General has charge of the records and correspondence of the army and militia; of the recruiting service, including enlistments, appointments, promotions, resignations, etc. He communicates to subordinate officers the orders of the President and the secretary of war, and preserves reports of military movements and operations.

The Inspector General, with his assistants, visits and inspects military posts, depots, fortifications, armories and arsenals, and public works in charge of army officers, and makes reports on the conduct, efficiency, and discipline of officers and men, including their arms and equipment.

The Quartermaster General has supervision over the quartermaster corps which is the main supply service of the army (except for technical articles), and furnishes food, clothing, equipment, animals, and forage. It also has charge of building construction and transportation for the army.

The Chief of Finance has control over the finances of the army.

The Surgeon General has supervision over the medical service of the army; looks after the sick and wounded; provides medical and hospital supplies, and inquires into the sanitary conditions of the army. In addition to field hospitals permanent depots and hospitals are maintained at various points.

The Judge-Advocate General is the chief law officer of the army; he reviews records of the proceedings of courts-martial, courts of inquiry, and military commissions, and acts as legal adviser to the war department.

The Chief Signal Officer is charged with the supervision of military signal duties, the construction, repair, and operation of military telegraph lines and cables.

The Chief of the Air Service has supervision over aircraft production and the aviation service.

The Chief of Ordnance supervises the purchase, manufacture, and distribution of artillery, small arms, and ammunition for the army and the militia. For the manufacture of arms and ammunition there are arsenals at Springfield, Mass., Rock Island, Ill., Watervliet, N. Y., and elsewhere.

The Chief of Engineers is at the head of the engineering corps, a branch of the army which is charged with the construction of public works such as military roads, bridges, fortifications, river and harbor improvements, geographical explorations, and surveys. The construction of the Panama Canal is the most notable of the recent undertakings of the war department in this field.

The Chief of the Chemical Warfare Service has supervision over the production of chemical warfare materials as well as defensive appliances for protection against such warfare. He also supervises the training of the army in the use of both.

The Militia Bureau, created in 1916, has charge of all matters relating to the National Guard.

In addition to the purely military functions and construction of public works, the war department has certain duties in connection with the government of the insular possessions and the Panama Canal Zone. So far as these duties relate to Porto Rico and the Philippine Islands they are under the direction of the *Bureau of Insular Affairs*, at the head of which is an army officer with the title of chief of the bureau. This bureau also has charge of the collection of the revenues of Haiti and the Dominican Republic in accordance with treaties which practically establish an American receivership over those republics.

Finally, the war department has charge of the *United States Military Academy* at West Point, the various post-graduate schools of instruction for army officers located at different army posts, the national military parks at Chickamauga, Gettysburg, Shiloh, and Vicksburg, and the national cemeteries in various parts of the country. The military academy at West Point was founded in 1802. A certain number of cadets (the number—for a long time one only—has varied at different periods) are appointed from each congressional district and territory, upon the nomination of the representative in Congress from the district; also certain numbers from each state at large, from the District of Columbia, and from the United States at large. All candidates are required to pass a physical and intellectual examination; the course of instruction lasts four years; and each cadet receives pay sufficient for his maintenance. Graduates receive appointments as second lieutenants in the army, those standing highest usually being appointed to the engineering corps if they prefer assignment to that branch of the service. The secretary of war exercises general supervision over the academy, and it is inspected at regular intervals by a board of visitors of whom seven are appointed by the President, two by the Vice President, and three by the speaker of the house of representatives.

WEST POINT CADETS

The Department of the Navy was created in 1798. At its head is a secretary, who, like the head of the war department, is usually taken from civil life. Like the war department, the navy department is organized into the *Office of Naval Operations* and a number of bureaus.

The Bureau of Navigation has charge of the recruiting service, the training of officers and men, the naval academy; schools for the technical education of enlisted men, apprentice schools, the naval home at Philadelphia, transportation of enlisted men, records of squadrons, ships, officers and men; the preparation of the naval register, preparation of drill regulations, signal codes, and cipher codes. Under this bureau falls the publication of the Nautical Almanac, charts and sailing directions, the naval observatory, and the hydrographic office.

The Bureau of Yards and Docks has general control of the navy yards and docks belonging to the government, including their construction and repair, and also of the construction of battleships whenever such construction is authorized by Congress. The navy yards are located at Washington, Brooklyn, Mare Island (California), Philadelphia (League Island), Norfolk, Pensacola, Cavite (in the Philippines), and various other places.

The Bureau of Ordnance has charge of the supply of armament and ammunition for the ships. It supervises the manufacture of guns and torpedoes, installs armament on the vessels, and has charge of the naval proving ground and magazines, the naval gun factory, and the torpedo station.

The Bureau of Construction and Repair has charge of the planning, building, and repairing of vessels, and of their equipment, excepting their armament and engines.

Other Bureaus of the Navy Department, whose general duties are indicated sufficiently by their titles, are: the bureau of engineering, the bureau of medicine and surgery, and the bureau of supplies and accounts.

The Judge-Advocate General is the law officer of the navy department and performs duties similar to those of the judge-advocate general of the war department.

The Major General Commandant of the Marine Corps issues orders for the movement of troops under the direction of the secretary of the navy.

The department of the navy also has general charge of the *United States Naval Academy* at Annapolis. The academy was founded in 1846, by George Bancroft, then secretary of the navy. A specified number of midshipmen are allowed for each member of Congress and each territorial delegate, and certain numbers from the District of Columbia, from Porto Rico, and from the United States at large.[90] Appointments are made by the President after a physical and intellectual examination by a board, and an allowance is made for maintaining each midshipman while in residence at the academy. The course lasts four years and includes instruction in gunnery, naval construction, steam engineering, navigation, mathematics, international law, modern languages, etc. After the completion of the course, midshipmen spend two years at sea, after which they receive subordinate appointments in the navy or marine corps.

The Department of Justice.—The office of attorney-general was created in 1789, and from the first the attorney-general was a member of the cabinet; but for a long time the duties of the office were not extensive, and it was not until 1870 that the office was made an executive department with its present title and organization.

The Attorney-General is the chief law officer of the national government and is the legal adviser of the President and the heads of departments. He represents the United States before the Supreme Court in cases in which it is a party, exercises a sort of administrative supervision over the United States district attorneys and marshals and over the federal penitentiaries, examines applications for pardons, and advises the President in the exercise of his pardoning power. The opinions which he renders on constitutional and legal questions referred to him are published by the government in a series of volumes, and altogether they constitute an important body of constitutional and administrative law. Under the direction of the President he institutes proceedings and prosecutes cases against corporations and persons for violations of the laws of the United States, or directs the district attorneys to do so.

The Post Office Department.—At the head of the post office department is the postmaster-general. He establishes and discontinues post offices, appoints all postmasters whose compensation does not exceed $1,000 a year, issues postal regulations, makes postal treaties with foreign governments, with the approval of the President, awards mail contracts, and has general supervision of the domestic and foreign postal service. There is an assistant attorney-general for the post office department, who advises the postmaster-general on questions of law, has charge of prosecutions arising under the postal laws, hears cases relating to the misuse of the mails, and drafts postal contracts. There are also four assistant postmasters-general, each of whom has supervision over a group of services within the department. The postal service has already been described in chapter xiv.

The Department of the Interior.—The interior department, established in 1849, is one of the largest and most important of the ten executive departments. Next to the post office department, the services which it performs reach more people than those performed by any other department. Its staff of employees at Washington ranks second in numbers only to that of the treasury department. It has charge of the public lands, Indian affairs, pensions, patents, the geological survey, and, to some extent, the government of the territories.

The Public Lands.—Perhaps the most important bureau in the interior department is the *General Land Office*, which has charge of the public lands, and the care and control of the forest reserves. Before the public lands are sold or otherwise disposed of they must be surveyed. For this purpose there are seventeen surveying districts, in each of which there is a surveyor general.

Disposal of the Public Lands.—The public lands have been disposed of with a somewhat lavish hand. In the early days liberal grants were made to the soldiers of the Revolutionary War. Immense quantities have also been sold at low rates—much of it at $1.25 per acre—in order to encourage settlers to establish homes thereon. Considerable quantities have also been granted to the states for educational purposes and the construction of internal improvements. Beginning with Ohio in 1802, each new state admitted to the Union was given one section in each township for the support of elementary schools, and those admitted after 1850 were given two sections in each township. Under the Morrill act of 1862, 10,000,000 acres were given to the states for the establishment of colleges of agriculture and the mechanic arts. Some of the more recently admitted states were given from one to four townships each for the establishment of universities.[91]

Before the Civil War, large quantities were given to the states for the construction of canals and railroads. Large tracts of the public lands have also been granted to private corporations as subsidies for the building of transcontinental railways. Finally, by an act of 1902, the proceeds from the sale of all public lands in seventeen Western states are set aside for constructing irrigation works in those states.

By the *preëmption act* of 1841, it was provided that 160 acres of land should be given to any family living thereon for a period of six months and paying $200 therefor. This act was repealed in 1891, but millions of acres were disposed of during the fifty years it was in force.

By the *homestead act* of 1863, still in force, any head of a family may acquire 160 acres by living on it for three years (it was five years before 1912), cultivating a certain part of it, and paying a small fee.

The Public Lands now Remaining aggregate about 665,000,000 acres, including those in Alaska. Of these lands a large part have been set aside for Indian reservations, national parks, military reservations, and national forests, [92] and is therefore not open to purchase or entry under the homestead act. Arid lands are sold in tracts not exceeding 640 acres at $1.25 per acre; mineral lands are sold at from $2.50 to $5 per acre; timber and stone lands at a minimum of $2.50 per acre; town site lands at a minimum of $10 per acre; and agricultural lands at $1.25 per acre.

Land Offices are established in all the states where there is any considerable amount of public land left. At each office there is a register and a receiver who examines applications for entries and issues certificates upon which patents or deeds are finally granted.

Indian Affairs.—Another important branch of the government service falling within the department of the interior is the management of Indian affairs. For a long time each tribe was treated to some extent as though it were an independent community, and was dealt with somewhat as foreign nations are dealt with. In 1871, however, it was enacted that henceforth no Indian tribe should be acknowledged or treated as an independent nation or power with which the United States may contract by treaty—an act which marks the beginning of the end of Indian tribal authority.

The policy of extending the jurisdiction of the government over the Indians was begun by an act of 1885 which gave the United States courts jurisdiction over seven leading crimes when committed by Indians on their reservations. Previous to that time, crimes committed by Indians against Indians within a reservation were left to be dealt with by the tribal authorities themselves.

The Allotment Act.—By the Dawes act of 1887 the new Indian policy begun in 1871 was still further extended. This act provided for the allotment of Indian lands to individual members of the tribe, and declared that Indians who accepted such allotments or who should leave their tribe and adopt the habits of civilized life, should be considered as citizens of the United States and entitled to all the rights and privileges of citizens. Previous to this time the lands occupied by the Indians were owned by the tribe as a whole and not by the individuals who occupied them. Under this act, individual allotments aggregating more than 30,000,000 acres have been made to 180,000 Indians. There remain about 120,000 Indians, to whom allotments are still to be made. The result of this policy will ultimately be to extinguish the Indian tribes and incorporate them into the American body politic.

Indian Agents.—The control of the national government over the Indian reservations is exercised largely through Indian agents appointed by the President. They are charged with the regulation of trade with the Indians, and have control of the distribution of rations. At each agency one or more schools are maintained, and in addition to the reservation schools there are schools for the higher education of Indians in various parts of the country, the most important being at Lawrence, Kansas, and Carlisle, Pennsylvania. The aggregate annual expenditures on account of the service are now about $15,000,000, more than half of which consists of payments due the Indians under treaty stipulations or of interest on trust funds held by the government for them. The total amount of these trust funds is about $50,000,000.[93]

The Pension Bureau has charge of the administration of the pension laws. The payments on account of pensions now constitute the largest item of expenditure by the national government. Before the outbreak of the Civil War, pension expenditures rarely exceeded two million dollars a year, and the total outlay for this purpose during the entire period of our national history aggregated less than half the amount now appropriated for a single year. According to the report of the commissioner of pensions for 1919 there were 624,427 names on the pension rolls, and the amount expended for pensions that year was over $220,000,000. More than $5,000,000,000 has been expended for pensions since the Civil War, a larger amount than the national debt incurred on account of the war itself.

The Patent Office includes a large number of officers, examiners, and employees, who are under the direction of the commissioner of patents. Their work is described on p. 260.

Minor Divisions of the Interior Department.—*The Bureau of Education* was established in 1867. At its head is a commissioner whose duty it is to collect and publish statistics and other information concerning the methods, conditions, and progress of education in the United States. Each year he publishes an elaborate report summarizing the educational progress of the country, together with monographs by experts on special topics of educational interest. The commissioner is also charged with the administration of the funds appropriated for the support of the colleges of agriculture and mechanic arts and with the supervision of education in Alaska and the reindeer industry in that country.

The Geological Survey was established as a bureau in the department of the interior in 1879. It is under the control of a director who is charged with the classification of the public lands and the examination of the geological structure, mineral resources, and mineral products of the public lands and the survey of the forest reserves. The bureau has undertaken the preparation of topographical and geological maps of the United States, a considerable portion of which has been completed, the collection of statistics of the mineral products, the investigation of mine accidents, the testing of mineral fuels and structural materials, and the investigation of surface and underground waters.

The Bureau of Mines, created in 1911, is charged with conducting investigations looking toward the prevention of mine accidents, the introduction of improvements in the general health and safety conditions, the conservation of mineral resources, etc. The bureau reported in 1913 that it had brought about a reduction in the number of fatalities due to explosions, from 30 to 13 per cent.

The Department of Agriculture.—A so-called "department" of agriculture was established in 1862, though its rank was only that of a bureau and its head bore the title of commissioner. From time to time, the scope and functions of the "department" were extended until 1889, when it was raised to the rank of a cabinet department with a secretary at its head. Like the other departments, it is organized into bureaus, offices, and divisions.

The Weather Bureau has charge of the preparation of weather forecasts and the display of storm, cold wave, frost, and flood warnings for the benefit of agriculture, commerce, and navigation.

The Bureau of Animal Industry conducts the inspection of animals, meats, and meat food products under the act of Congress of June 30, 1906, and has charge of the inspection of import and export animals, the inspection of vessels for the transportation of export animals, and the quarantine stations for imported live stock; supervises the interstate transportation of animals, and reports on the condition and means of improving the animal industries of the country.

The Bureau of Plant Industry studies plant life in its relations to agriculture. It investigates the diseases of plants and carries on field tests in the prevention of diseases. It studies the improvement of crops by breeding and selection, maintains demonstration farms, and carries on investigations with a view to introducing better methods of farm practice. It conducts agricultural explorations in foreign countries for the purpose of securing new plants and seeds for introduction into the United States. It studies fruits, their adaptability to various climates, and the methods of harvesting, handling, storing, and marketing them.

The Forest Service is charged with the administration of the National Forests. It also gives practical advice in the conservation and handling of national, state, and private forest lands, and in methods of utilizing forest products; investigates methods of forest planting, and gives practical advice to tree planters; studies commercially valuable trees to determine their best management and use; gathers statistics on forest products, in coöperation with the bureau of the census, and investigates the control and prevention of forest fires, and other forest problems.

The Bureau of Chemistry conducts investigations into the chemical composition of fertilizers, agricultural products, and food stuffs. In pursuance of the pure food law of 1906, it examines foods and drugs intended to be sent from one state to another, with a view to determining whether they are adulterated or misbranded. It also conducts investigations of food stuffs imported from abroad and denies entry to such as are found unwholesome, adulterated, or falsely labeled. It also inspects food products intended to be exported to foreign countries where standards of purity are required.

Other Bureaus, whose duties are indicated by their titles, are: the bureau of soils, the bureau of crop estimates, the bureau of entomology, the bureau of biological survey, the bureau of markets, and the bureau of public roads.

The Department of Commerce embraces what remains of the department of commerce and labor created in 1903, and divided in 1913 by the creation of the department of labor. It is charged with the promotion of the commerce of the United States and its mining, manufacturing, shipping, fishing, and transportation interests.

The Bureau of the Census is charged with the duty of taking the decennial census of the United States, including the collection of such special statistics as Congress may authorize. The first census, that of 1790, was taken under the direction of the United States marshals in their respective districts; the statistics collected related only to population, and the schedule embraced only six questions. In 1880 the use of the marshals was done away with and a corps of census supervisors provided. Until 1902 the machinery for taking the census was organized anew for each census, but in the latter year provision was made for a permanent census bureau. The schedule of inquiries has increased from decade to decade until it now embraces a wide range of questions relating not only to population, but also to vital statistics, agriculture, manufactures, defective and criminal classes, cotton production, statistics of cities, state and local finances, transportation, mining, and various other matters, the results of which are published in a series of large volumes and in special bulletins. At the head of the bureau is a director, who is aided by an assistant director, a number of statisticians and experts, and a corps of local supervisors and enumerators. The census work was in the charge of the department of state until 1850, when it was transferred to the department of the interior.

The Bureau of Navigation[94] is charged with the general superintendence of the merchant marine of the United States and of the enforcement of the navigation laws. It has charge of the registration of American vessels engaged in the foreign trade, and of the enrollment and licensing of vessels in the coasting trade. It supervises the execution of the tonnage laws and the collection of tonnage duties; prepares an annual list of vessels registered under the American flag; and supervises the work of the United States shipping commissioners, who administer the laws for the protection of seamen.

The Steamboat Inspection Service is charged with the administration of the laws providing for the inspection of steam and sailing vessels registered under the American flag; with the examination and licensing of officers of such vessels, and with the protection of life and property on water. At the head of the service is an inspector general, who is aided by ten supervising inspectors, each of the latter having under his supervision a number of local inspectors stationed at the important commercial ports. All vessels must be inspected once a year as to their safety, construction, and facilities for protection against fire.

The Bureau of Fisheries has control of fish hatcheries in many parts of the country, for the propagation of useful food fishes; studies fish culture and the causes of the decrease of food fishes; collects statistics in regard to the fishery industry; and in general promotes the fishery interests. It supervises the salmon fisheries of Alaska and the fur seal industry on the Pribilof Islands of the Bering Sea.

The Bureau of Lighthouses is charged with the construction and maintenance of lighthouses, light vessels, beacons, fog signals, buoys, and other aids to navigation. The seaboard is divided up into lighthouse districts, in each of which is a naval officer who serves as inspector and has immediate charge of the supply, maintenance, and administration of the lighthouses in his district. At each lighthouse there is a keeper and one or more assistant keepers. The establishment now consists of more than 1,500 lighthouses and beacons, a fleet of light-ships, and more than 6,000 buoys. Since 1910 the service has been under the supervision of a commissioner.

The Bureau of Standards, established in 1901, is charged with the custody of the national standards, the testing of measuring apparatus, and the investigation of problems relating to standards of weighing and measuring.

The Coast and Geodetic Survey is charged with the survey of the coasts and of rivers to the head of tide water, and the publication of charts of the same; the investigation of questions relating to temperature, tides, currents, and the depths of navigable waters; the making of magnetic observations; the determination of geographic positions, and the like. The results are published in annual reports and special publications. It prepares tables, sailing directions, charts of the coasts, harbor charts, notices to mariners, and other publications for the use of mariners.

The Bureau of Foreign and Domestic Commerce is charged with fostering and developing the various manufacturing interests of the United States and extending the markets for manufactured articles abroad, by collecting and publishing all available and useful information concerning such markets and industries. It publishes statistics of commerce, finance, etc., consular and trade reports, and an annual volume known as the "Commercial Relations of the United States."

> *The Bureau of Corporations*, created in 1903, was intended mainly to furnish an agency for the investigation of corporations suspected of violating the anti-"trust" laws of the United States. It was authorized to investigate the organization and methods of any corporation or joint-stock company engaged in foreign or interstate commerce (except common carriers subject to the interstate commerce act) and to report to the President such information as might be of value in enabling him to enforce the anti-"trust" laws. It was abolished in 1914 and its duties were devolved upon the newly created Federal Trade Commission, which has already been described (see p. 245).

The Department of Labor was created in 1913, and is charged with fostering, promoting, and developing the welfare of the wage earners of the United States, especially the improvement of the conditions under which they work and the advancement of their opportunities for profitable employment.

The Bureaus of Immigration and Naturalization, formerly consolidated in the department of commerce and labor, were divided in 1913 and transferred to the new department of labor. They are charged respectively with the administration of the immigration laws and the administration of the naturalization laws of the United States.[95]

The Bureau of Labor Statistics, formerly known as the bureau of labor, was transferred from the former department of commerce and labor in 1913. It is charged with collecting and diffusing among the people of the United States useful information on subjects connected with labor in the most general and comprehensive sense of that word, and especially upon its relations to capital, the hours of labor, the earnings of laboring men and women, and the means of promoting their material, social, intellectual, and moral prosperity.

It is especially charged with investigating the causes of and facts relating to all controversies and disputes between employers and employees. It publishes from time to time the results of elaborate investigations on various subjects relating to labor and industry, and also issues a bimonthly bulletin on special topics within the same field.

The Children's Bureau, established in 1912, is charged with the investigation of problems relating to the welfare of children, such as the conditions of the employment of children, the causes of infant mortality, etc.

In 1920 the *Women's Bureau* was established to promote the welfare of wage-earning women.

References.—Andrews, Manual of the Constitution, pp. 327-352. Beard, American Government and Politics, ch. xi. Bryce, The American Commonwealth (abridged edition), ch. viii. Fairlie, National Administration of the U. S., ch. iv. Harrison, This Country of Ours, chs. xi-xviii.

Documentary and Illustrative Material.—1. The Congressional Directory. 2. Annual reports of the heads of department and other officials, such as the commissioner of pensions, the commissioner of the general land office, the commissioner general of immigration, the civil service commission, the interstate commerce commission, etc.

RESEARCH QUESTIONS

1. What is the origin of the term "cabinet"? On what days are cabinet meetings now held?

2. What are the principal differences between the American cabinet and the British cabinet?

3. Do you think the members of the cabinet should be members of Congress? If not, ought they to be allowed seats in Congress without the right to vote?

4. Do you think the President ought ever to disregard the advice of his cabinet?

5. Give the names of five distinguished secretaries of state since 1789.

6. Washington's first cabinet was composed of an equal number of members from both political parties. Would it be wise to follow that practice?

7. Why is the secretary of the treasury required to make his annual reports to Congress while the other heads of departments make theirs to the President?

8. Would it be wise to elect the heads of departments of the federal government by popular vote as those of the state governments usually are?

9. Do you think the secretary of war ought to be an army officer as is the usual practice in Europe?

10. Why is the postmaster-generalship usually given to an active party manager?

11. Why is an importer ineligible under the law to appointment as secretary of the treasury?

12. Why is the department of state really misnamed? Would the title "department of foreign affairs" indicate more precisely the duties of the department?

13. What is your opinion of the movement to establish a department of public health?

14. Do you think the bureau of education should be raised to the rank of a department?

THE UNITED STATES SUPREME COURT

THE SUPREME COURT ROOM

CHAPTER XVIII

THE FEDERAL JUDICIARY

Establishment of the federal Judiciary.—The Articles of Confederation, as we have seen, made no provision for a national judiciary. Hamilton declared this to be the crowning defect of the old government, for laws, he very properly added, are a dead letter without courts to expound their true meaning and define their operations. During the period of the Confederation, the national government was dependent for the most part, as has been said, on the states for the enforcement of its will. Thus if some one counterfeited the national currency, robbed the mails, or assaulted a foreign ambassador, there was no national court to take jurisdiction of the case and punish the offender. The only way by which he could be brought to justice and the authority of the national government upheld was through the kindly assistance of some state court, and this assistance was not always cheerfully lent nor was it always effective when tendered. Congress to be sure acted as a court for the settlement of disputes between the states themselves, but a legislative assembly is never well fitted for exercising judicial functions. In the absence of a national judiciary it proved impossible to enforce solemn treaty stipulations to which the United States was a party, a fact which led Great Britain to refuse to carry out certain of her treaty engagements with the United States.

The Judicial Power of the United States.—The framers of the Constitution decided that the jurisdiction of the national courts should be restricted to questions of national interest and to those involving the peace and tranquillity of the Union, such as disputes between the states themselves and between citizens of different states, and that the jurisdiction of all other controversies should be left to the determination of the courts of the several states. The jurisdiction of the federal courts, therefore, was made to include all cases whether of law or equity arising under the national Constitution, the laws of the United States, and all treaties made under their authority; all cases affecting ambassadors, other public ministers, and consuls; all cases of admiralty and maritime jurisdiction; all controversies to which the United States is a party; all controversies between two or more states; and between a state, or the citizens thereof, and foreign states or citizens or subjects thereof.
[96]

The wisdom and propriety of giving the federal courts jurisdiction over all such cases are obvious, since they involve either national, interstate, or international questions. Manifestly, the state courts could not properly be left to determine finally controversies involving the meaning or the application of provisions of the federal Constitution, laws, or treaties, since in that case they would not be what they are declared to be, namely, the supreme law of the land. Conflicting decisions would be rendered by the courts of different states, and in case of inconsistency between state constitutions and laws on the one hand and the federal Constitution, laws, and treaties on the other, the state courts would be under the temptation to uphold the validity of the former.

The Eleventh Amendment.—As originally adopted, the Constitution permitted suits to be brought in the federal courts against a state by citizens of another state or by citizens of foreign countries, and when a suit brought against the state of Georgia in 1793 by a citizen of South Carolina named Chisholm for the recovery of a debt was actually entertained by the Supreme Court, widespread popular indignation followed the decision. The authorities of Georgia felt that it was derogatory to the dignity of a sovereign state that it should be made the defendant in a suit brought by a private individual, and a demand was made that the Constitution be amended so as to prevent such "suits" in the future. As a result of this demand, the Eleventh Amendment was adopted in 1798 which declared that the judicial power of the United States should not be construed to extend to suits brought against a state by citizens of another state or of a foreign country. Nevertheless while a state cannot be made a defendant in a federal court at the instance of a private individual of another state, the federal courts may entertain jurisdiction of suits between a state and a citizen of another state provided the state is the plaintiff.

How Cases "Arise."—A case "arises" under the Constitution, laws, or treaties whenever a suit is filed involving a right or privilege thereunder. Until a case "arises," that is, until it comes before the courts in due form, they will take no notice of it. When President Washington in 1793 sought the opinion of the Supreme Court on certain points involving our obligations to France under the treaty of alliance of 1778 it declined to answer his question, holding that it could give opinions only in cases properly brought before it.

The Regular Federal Courts.—The Constitution declares that the judicial power of the United States shall be vested in one Supreme Court and in such inferior courts as Congress may from time to time ordain and establish. The Supreme Court, therefore, is the only federal tribunal which owes its existence to the Constitution, the others being created by statute. Even as to the Supreme Court Congress has considerable power of control, since it determines the number of judges of which it shall be composed, and the amount of their compensation. But it cannot remove any judge except upon impeachment, or reduce his compensation after he has once been appointed.

The Supreme Court is at present composed of one Chief Justice and eight associate justices. It holds its sessions in the city of Washington from October to May of each year. Practically all the cases which it hears are those appealed from the lower courts. When a case has been argued, the court holds a consultation at which the points involved are considered and a decision is reached. The Chief Justice then requests one of his associates to prepare the opinion of the court, or he may prepare it himself, after which it is scrutinized by the court at a second conference and approved. Any member of the court who disagrees with the majority may file a dissenting opinion, a right frequently taken advantage of. The concurrence of at least five of the nine judges is necessary to the validity of a decision, and as a matter of fact, many important decisions have been rendered in recent years by a bare majority of the court. The opinions rendered are published as the *United States Reports*, of which there are now more than 200 volumes. They constitute the great authoritative source of the constitutional law of the United States, are studied by lawyers and judges, and are relied upon by the courts as precedents for the decisions of future cases involving similar points of law.[97] There is a reporter who arranges and publishes the opinions, a clerk who keeps the records, and a marshal who attends the court, preserves decorum, and enforces its orders.

The Circuit Courts of Appeals.—Next below the Supreme Court are the circuit courts of appeals, nine in all—one for each of the judicial circuits into which the country is divided.[98] These courts were created by act of Congress in 1891 to relieve the Supreme Court from an accumulation of business that rendered the prompt decisions of cases impossible, the docket of the court having become so overcrowded that it was about three years behind with its business. The act creating the circuit courts of appeals, however, did not provide an additional class of judges to hold these courts, but enacted that each of them should be held by three judges assigned for the purpose from among the judges of the circuit. The judges of each circuit include one justice of the Supreme Court assigned to the circuit, two or more circuit judges appointed for the circuit, and a considerable number of district judges, each appointed for a district in the circuit. Most circuit courts of appeals are held by three circuit judges; but occasionally by two circuit judges together with a district judge or the Supreme Court justice. The circuit courts of appeals have only appellate jurisdiction, that is, they hear and determine only cases appealed from the lower courts, and their decisions are final in most cases. This relieves the Supreme Court of all but the most important cases, and enables it to give more attention to the cases before it and to dispatch its business more promptly.

Former Circuit Courts.—Prior to 1911 next below the circuit courts of appeals were the circuit courts, which were held in the different districts within the circuit, either by a circuit judge or by the justice of the Supreme Court assigned to the circuit, or by a district judge, or by the three, or any two of them, sitting together. In 1911 the circuit courts were abolished and their jurisdiction conferred on the district courts. The circuit judges, however, were retained and will henceforth sit in the circuit courts of appeal.

The District Courts.—The lowest grade of federal court is the district court, held in each of the districts (about eighty) into which the country is divided. In some cases a state constitutes one district; in other cases a state is divided into two, three, four, or five districts. Usually there is one judge for each district, though in a few cases there are several judges for a single district, each holding court separately.

The jurisdiction of the district court embraces civil and criminal cases under the laws of the United States—such as suits for the infringement of patents and copyrights, admiralty cases, bankruptcy proceedings, revenue cases; and offenses against the United States revenue laws, laws against counterfeiting, the public land laws, the pure food laws, the postal laws, and the interstate commerce laws. Controversies between citizens of different states may also be brought to this court.[99]

In most cases appeals may be taken from the decisions of the district courts to the circuit courts of appeals or to the Supreme Court.

Federal Attorneys, Marshals, and Clerks.—In each of the federal judicial districts, there is a United States attorney who prosecutes violations of the federal laws in his district. There is also in each district a United States marshal who bears somewhat the same relation to the federal court that a sheriff does to a state court. He executes the processes of the court, arrests offenders, and performs other ministerial functions for the court. In each district there is a clerk who has custody of the seal of the court and keeps a record of its proceedings, orders, judgments, etc. The marshal and attorney are appointed by the President, but the clerk is chosen by the court itself.

In each district, also, the court appoints a number of United States commissioners who are empowered to issue warrants for arrest, take bail, determine whether accused persons shall be held for trial, and perform other duties somewhat similar to those discharged by justices of the peace under the judicial system of the state.

The Regular Federal Judges.—*Appointment.*—All federal judges are appointed by the President, by and with the advice and consent of the Senate. The judges of most of the states, as we have seen, are now chosen by popular election, but that method did not commend itself to the framers of the federal

Constitution. The existing method of appointing federal judges has given general satisfaction, and with remarkably few exceptions, the persons appointed to the federal bench have been men of integrity and fitness.[100]

The *term* for which all the regular federal judges are appointed is good behavior. This is virtually for life, since they cannot be removed except by impeachment.[101] All other officers of the United States are appointed for definite terms, usually for four years. Except in a few states, the state judges are elected for definite terms ranging from two years to twenty-one years (p. 113). The framers of the federal Constitution, however, were deeply impressed with the advantages of a judiciary possessing the qualities of permanency and independence, and they wisely provided that the judges should hold their offices so long as their official conduct was above reproach.

Compensation.—The Constitution declares that the judges shall receive at stated times a compensation for their services which shall not be diminished during their continuance in office. As we have seen, the compensation of the President can neither be increased nor diminished during the time for which he is elected, but the prohibition in the case of the judges applies only to a reduction of their salaries. Increases are permitted to be made at any time. The compensation now allowed the chief justice of the Supreme Court is $15,000 a year, and the associate justices $14,500, amounts which are low in comparison with the salaries of the highest English judges, who receive $25,000 a year. The circuit judges receive $8,500 a year, and the district judges $7,500.

Any judge of a United States court having held his commission ten years and having attained the age of seventy years, may retire from the bench and receive the same salary during the rest of his life that was payable to him at the time of his resignation. Few judges do retire, however.

Power of the Supreme Court to Declare Laws Unconstitutional.—An important power of the Supreme Court for which there is no direct authority in the Constitution, is that of declaring acts of Congress which are in conflict with the Constitution, null and void and of no effect. This power was first exercised by the Supreme Court in 1801 in the famous case of Marbury v. Madison. Congress had passed an act giving the Supreme Court original jurisdiction in certain cases where the Constitution says it should have appellate jurisdiction, and when the act came before the court for enforcement it declined to be bound by it. The great chief justice, John Marshall, wrote the opinion of the court which held the act of Congress null and void. His argument, in brief, was that the Constitution is the supreme law of the land and the judges are bound to give effect to it. When, therefore, the court is called upon to give effect to a law of Congress which is clearly in conflict with the higher law of the Constitution, it must give the preference to the latter, otherwise the declaration in favor of the supremacy of the Constitution would have no meaning. Down to 1913 the Supreme Court had declared thirty-three acts of Congress, or parts of such acts, unconstitutional.

Power to Declare State Laws Unconstitutional.—Laws passed by the state legislatures, ordinances of municipal councils, and even the provisions of state constitutions themselves may be declared null and void by the Supreme Court in case they are in conflict with the national Constitution or the laws and treaties made in pursuance thereof. It has already been pointed out that appeals may be taken to the federal Supreme Court from the highest courts of a state whenever a right, title, or privilege under the federal Constitution is involved and the state court has decided against the right or privilege claimed. Thus where one is prosecuted and convicted under a state law or provision of a state Constitution which he claims is contrary to some provision in the federal Constitution or laws, he has a right to appeal to the United States Supreme Court and have the question of the constitutionality of the state law finally determined there. This is a necessary consequence of the supremacy of the federal Constitution and laws over those of the states. More than 200 acts of state legislatures have been pronounced null and void by the United States Supreme Court.[102]

Sometimes inferior federal courts declare acts of Congress and of the state legislatures to be unconstitutional, but in all such cases an appeal may be taken to the Supreme Court for final review.

Special Courts of the United States.—In addition to the three classes of United States courts, already described, several tribunals of a special or temporary character have been created to hear and determine particular classes of controversies. Some of these courts are held by judges who are appointed for definite terms.

The Court of Claims was created in 1855 to pass upon claims against the government. It consists of a chief justice and four associate justices who serve during good behavior. It is a well-established principle of public law that a sovereign state cannot be sued against its will. Before the creation of this court claims against the government had to be considered by Congress, a body which aside from being ill fitted for the hearing of such cases, was overburdened by the necessity of considering the large number of claims annually laid before it. The government now allows itself to be sued in this court on most claims of a contractual nature, but the judgments of the court cannot be paid until Congress appropriates the money for their payment, and hence the court cannot issue an execution to enforce its findings. At each session of Congress, an appropriation is made to satisfy any judgments made or which may be made by the court. Appeals are allowed to be taken from the court of claims to the Supreme Court on questions of law. Among the more important classes of claims that have been adjudicated by this court were the French Spoliation claims, and Indian depredation claims, both involving numerous claims and very large amounts in the aggregate.

In 1906 a United States court was established in China to exercise jurisdiction in certain cases previously exercised by the consuls. It is held by a single judge appointed by the President for a term of four years.

The tariff law of 1909 created a *United States Court of Customs Appeals*, consisting of a presiding judge and four associates, to hear appeals from the board of general appraisers in cases involving the construction of the law and facts respecting the classification of imported articles and the rate of duty imposed thereon.

In 1910 a *Commerce Court* was created, to decide appeals from the orders of the Interstate Commerce Commission; but in 1913 this court was abolished.

In the *District of Columbia* Congress has created two courts, with judges appointed to hold office during good behavior: the supreme court of the district, consisting of a chief justice and five associate justices; and the court of appeals, consisting of a chief justice and two associate justices. Appeals may be taken from the former to the latter, whose decisions in some cases are reversible by the Supreme Court of the United States. Appeals may also be taken from the decisions of the commissioner of patents to the court of appeals of the District of Columbia.

In each of the *territories* there are supreme and district courts established by Congress in pursuance of its power to provide for the government of the territories, but they are not considered as a part of the judicial system of the United States, although the judges are appointed by the President.[103]

Constitutional Protections in the Federal Courts.—The Constitution contains a number of provisions intended to protect accused persons against unauthorized prosecutions in the federal courts, as well as against arbitrary procedure in the course of the trial. As the Constitution originally stood, it contained few provisions of this kind; and this fact constituted one of the most serious objections urged against the ratification of that instrument. In consequence of this the first ten Amendments were adopted in 1790, and of these no less than five relate to the rights of accused persons on trial in the federal courts.

Most important of all, perhaps, the *Sixth Amendment* declares that in criminal prosecutions (in the federal courts) the accused shall enjoy the right to a speedy and public trial, by an impartial jury of the state and district wherein the crime shall have been committed; that he shall be informed of the nature and cause of the accusation; that he shall have the right to be confronted by the witnesses against him; that he shall have compulsory process for obtaining witnesses in his favor; and that he shall have the assistance of counsel for his defense.[104]

The *Fifth Amendment* protects the accused from prosecution in capital cases or cases involving infamous crime except upon indictment by a grand jury. Some of the states, as we have seen, have abolished the grand jury, and provided for prosecutions in their courts without the intervention of such an agency, but no person may be prosecuted in a federal court for a serious crime until he has been held for trial by a grand jury. The same amendment also forbids the trial of a person a second time for the same offense, if he was acquitted on the first trial; declares that he shall not be compelled to testify against himself; that he shall not be deprived of life, liberty, or property without due process of law; and that private property shall not be taken for public use without just compensation.

The Fourth Amendment declares among other things that no warrant for arrest (by the federal authorities) shall be issued except upon probable cause, supported by oath or affirmation and particularly describing the person to be seized. This provision is designed to prevent arbitrary arrests of persons on mere suspicion. It prohibits general search warrants such as were commonly used by the British authorities in the colonies prior to the outbreak of the Revolution and which were popularly known as "writs of assistance." Such warrants did not mention the name of the person to be arrested but permitted the officer to insert any name in the warrant and arrest whomsoever he might choose.

The Eighth Amendment declares that excessive bail shall not be required, nor excessive fines imposed, nor cruel and unusual punishment inflicted. The purpose of the first provision is discussed on p. 119. The purpose of the other two prohibitions is to prevent the old severities of the penal code that were common two hundred years ago.

Treason.—Among the crimes in the prosecution of which judges were frequently arbitrary and which were punished with undue severity, was that of treason. Treason has always been regarded as the highest crime known to society, because it seeks the overthrow or destruction of the government itself. In earlier times, judges frequently construed offenses to be treasonable which were not declared so by the laws. This was known as *constructive* treason. To prevent them from construing the existence of treason where it really did not exist, parliament therefore passed a statute during the reign of Edward III defining the offense with more or less precision, and this definition in substance was incorporated in the Constitution of the United States, This provision declares that treason against the United States shall consist only in levying war against them or in adhering to their enemies, giving them aid and comfort. The Supreme Court in interpreting this provision has ruled that in order to constitute treason there must be an actual levying of war or an assembling of persons for the purpose of making war; that a mere conspiracy to subvert the government by force is not treason, but after the war has once begun, all those who perform any part, however minute or remote, or who give aid and comfort to the enemy, are traitors and as such are liable to the penalties of treason. To protect persons accused of treason against conviction upon the testimony of a single witness, the Constitution requires the testimony of two witnesses to the act, or confession in open court, to convict. Congress is authorized to prescribe the punishment of treason, but the Constitution declares that no attainder of treason shall work corruption of blood or forfeiture except during the life of the person attainted. Under the old law, a person convicted of treason was not only put to death in a barbarous manner, but his blood, was considered as "corrupted" or "attainted," so that as a matter of course, without any decree of the court to that effect, his children could not inherit property or titles through him. Thus the innocent offspring of the traitor were punished for the offense of the parent. The provision of our Constitution places the punishment on the offender alone.

References.—ANDREWS, Manual of the Constitution, pp. 201-223. BALDWIN, The American Judiciary, ch. ix. BEARD, American Government and Politics, ch. xv. BRYCE, The American Commonwealth (abridged edition), chs. xxi-xxii. HARRISON, This Country of Ours, chs. xx-xxi. HART, Actual Government, ch. xvii.

Documentary and Illustrative Material.—1. The Congressional Directory, which contains a list of the higher judges and the judicial districts. 2. Specimen copies of decisions of the Supreme Court. These may be obtained from the clerk of the Supreme Court at Washington.

RESEARCH QUESTIONS

1. Name the Chief Justices of the United States Supreme Court from 1789 to the present time.

2. Name the present members of the Supreme Court and give the date of the appointment of each. (See Congressional Directory).

3. In which one of the nine judicial circuits of the United States do you live? Who is the Supreme Court justice assigned to the circuit? Who are the circuit judges of the circuit?

4. Who is the United States district judge for your district? At what places in your state are United States district courts held?

5. Who is the United States attorney for your district? The United States marshal?

6. What is meant by the terms "constitutional" and "unconstitutional" as applied to an act of Congress? Do you think the courts should be allowed to declare a law unconstitutional?

7. Do you think it is a wise provision which allows federal judges to serve during good behavior?

8. It has been proposed by a well-known public man that federal judges should be elected by the people. What is your opinion of the proposition?

9. Do you think the present salary allowed justices of the Supreme Court large enough to attract the best judicial talent?

10. Do you think the Supreme Court is ever justified in reversing its own decisions, or should it stand by the precedents?

11. What is the meaning of the term obiter dicta as applied to a judicial opinion?

12. Do you think it is a wise practice for judges who disagree with the majority of the court to file dissenting opinions?

13. A recent President took occasion to criticize publicly a federal judge for a decision which he rendered in a "trust" case. Do you think judges should be criticized for their decisions?

14. Are juries ever made use of in federal courts? If so, when?

15. Why have federal judges been criticized for issuing injunctions?

16. When may an appeal be taken from a state court to a federal court?

17. The Supreme Court has always refused to decide "political" controversies. What is a "political" as opposed to a "legal" controversy? Give examples.

CHAPTER XIX

GOVERNMENT OF THE TERRITORIES AND DEPENDENCIES

Power of Congress over the Territories.—The Constitution expressly confers upon Congress the power to dispose of and make all needful rules and regulations respecting the territory or other property belonging to the United States. In dealing with the territories the powers of Congress are general or residuary in character, whereas when it legislates for that part of the country which has been erected into states, its powers are specifically enumerated. Congress, therefore, may establish practically any form of government in the territories that it chooses. It may, if it wishes, set up therein a military government or it may establish civil government with such limitations and exceptions as it may wish. In the latter case it may allow the inhabitants a legislative assembly for purposes of local legislation, or Congress may legislate directly for them itself. And in case it permits the inhabitants to have a legislative assembly of their own and to enact their own laws, Congress may veto or modify any law passed by such legislature. Indeed, says the Supreme Court, Congress may make valid an invalid act passed by a territorial legislature as well as declare invalid a valid act passed by it.

Does the Constitution Extend to the Territories?—A subject much discussed, especially at the time of the acquisition of Porto Rico and the Philippines, was whether such provisions of the Constitution as were applicable extended of their own force to new territories immediately upon the establishment of American sovereignty over them; that is, whether the Constitution "follows the flag" or whether its provisions apply only when extended by act of Congress. One party asserted that such provisions go wherever the sovereignty of the United States goes, that the government cannot be carried to any new territory unless accompanied by the Constitution from which it derives its authority, and that Congress has no power to withhold such provisions as are applicable. The other party maintained that the Constitution was established only for the people of the United States; that whenever new territories have been acquired, Congress has extended such provisions as it saw fit; and that Congress is unlimited as to its power in dealing with the inhabitants of such territories. The Supreme Court in the famous Insular Cases, decided in 1900 and 1901, upheld the latter view and ruled that for all practical purposes the territories of the United States are completely subject to the legislative authority of Congress, and that it is not even restricted by those provisions of the Constitution which were adopted for the protection of individual liberty. In practice Congress has always extended to the domestic territories such provisions of the Constitution as were applicable, thus putting the inhabitants upon the same footing as those of the states so far as the enjoyment of *civil* rights are concerned, but not as to *political* rights. So far as the insular territories are concerned, it has also extended most of the provisions relating to civil rights, though in the case of the Philippines a few safeguards such as the right of indictment by grand jury, trial by jury, and the right to bear arms have been withheld.

The Origin of the Territorial System.—Before the Constitution was adopted, Congress had acquired by cession from certain of the original states a vast domain of territory north of the Ohio River, and later it acquired a considerable domain lying south of the Ohio (p. 159). One of the conditions upon which the territory north of the Ohio was ceded, was that Congress should form the territory into distinct republican states which should be admitted to the Union on an equal footing with the old states. It was felt, however, that the territory in question should be put through a sort of preparatory stage before being erected into states; that is, it should be held in a state of dependency until the population was sufficiently numerous to maintain a state government and the inhabitants had acquired sufficient political capacity to manage their own public affairs.

The Northwest Territory.—By the famous Ordinance of 1787, as reënacted and slightly modified two years later (after the adoption of the Federal Constitution), Congress provided a scheme of government for the northwest territory which was in force for many years. The Ordinance provided for two grades of government: one for the territory before its population should amount to 5,000 inhabitants; the other for the territory thereafter. The principal difference was that in the former case the territory was to have no local legislature of its own, while in the latter it was to have a legislative assembly. The scheme of government provided in the beginning consisted of a governor, a secretary, and three judges, appointed by the President. Although no legislature was provided, the governor, secretary, and judges were empowered, not to make new laws, but to select such laws from the statutes of the old states as were suitable.

When the population had reached 5,000 inhabitants, the territory was given the second grade form of government, that is, it was allowed a local legislature, the lower house of which was elected by the inhabitants on the basis of a restricted suffrage, the upper house or council to be appointed by the President from a list nominated by the lower house. The territory was now allowed to send a delegate to Congress with a right to a seat in that body, but no right to vote.

The scheme of government thus provided for the northwest territory became the model for the later territorial governments. It was introduced into the southwest territory and later to the territory acquired west of the Mississippi River.

The Organized Territories: Hawaii and Alaska.—The territories and dependencies of the United States may be grouped into two classes: the organized and the unorganized. A territory of the first class is said to be "organized" because it has its own local legislature, both houses of which are elected. At present the only territories of this class fully included as parts of the United States are Hawaii[105] and Alaska,[106] but since most of the states were organized territories before being admitted to the Union, this kind of government is of more than ordinary interest to the student of civics.

Executive.—In a fully organized territory there is a governor who is appointed by the President with the consent of the senate for a term of four years, and who enjoys the usual powers of a state executive. The appointment is usually made from the residents of the territory, though in a few cases outsiders have been appointed. There is also a secretary who keeps the records of the territory, compiles and publishes the acts of the legislature, and serves as governor during the absence or disability of the latter official. Other administrative officers of the territory are the attorney-general, treasurer, commissioner of public lands, superintendent of public education, surveyor, and auditor.

The Legislature is composed of two houses, both of which are popularly elected. Regular sessions of the legislature are held every two years and are limited to sixty days, though the governor may call extraordinary sessions with the approval of the President of the United States.

The territorial legislature is empowered to enact laws in respect to all rightful subjects of legislation not inconsistent with the laws and Constitution of the United States. Congress, however, has from time to time imposed various limitations upon the power of the territorial legislatures, and has shown a tendency to increase the restrictions, especially in regard to financial matters. Congress may veto any act of a territorial legislature.

Judiciary.—For the administration of justice, a fully organized territory has a supreme court, a number of district courts, and such inferior courts as the legislature may create. The judges of the higher court are all appointed by the President of the United States for a term of four years. The territory also has a United States district court, a district attorney, and a marshal.

Finally, a fully organized territory is given a limited representation, in the

Congress of the United States through a delegate, elected by the people of the territory every two years, who is allowed a seat in the house of representatives with a right to serve on committees and take part in debate, but not to vote.

Alaska, acquired by purchase from Russia in 1867, was for seventeen years after its acquisition administered directly by the President without any express authority from Congress. In 1884, however, an act was passed providing a system of civil government for the territory, to be administered by a governor appointed by the President for a term of four years. The general laws of the state of Oregon, so far as applicable, were extended to the territory. In 1898 a criminal code was provided for the territory, and in 1900 a complete civil code and a code of civil procedure were enacted. Finally, in 1912 Alaska was made a fully organized territory, with a legislative assembly consisting of a senate of eight members and a house of representatives of sixteen members. Acts can be passed over the governor's veto by vote of two-thirds of the members of each house of the legislative assembly.

The Organized Dependencies.—Porto Rico and the Philippines, acquired from Spain in 1898, were formerly, and are now to a certain extent, regarded more as colonies than as territories, although they are governed much like a territory. For many years they were classed as "partly organized" because in their legislatures only one house was elective. They now have legislatures in which both houses are elective; but unlike the territories they are inhabited by a foreign race, and had been at the time of their cession to the United States for centuries governed by an entirely different system of laws and administration from that to which the people of the United States were accustomed.

Porto Rico.—By an act of Congress in 1917, the supreme executive power of the island is vested in a governor appointed by the President, for an indefinite term. He has the usual powers of a territorial governor. There are six executive departments, namely, justice, finance, interior, education, agriculture, and health. The attorney-general and the commissioner of education are appointed by the President for a term of four years; the heads of the other four departments are appointed by the governor for the same term. The department heads collectively form an executive council charged with the performance of such duties as the governor may prescribe.

The Legislature.—Formerly the legislature was composed of an upper house, known as the council, the members of which were appointed by the President, and a house of delegates, popularly elected. The act of 1917, however, provided for a legislature, both houses of which are elected by the voters. The upper house is called the senate and is composed of nineteen members, elected for a term of four years. The lower chamber, called the House of

Representatives, consists of thirty-nine members, elected for a term of four years. The legislature is required to meet biennially and the governor may call extraordinary sessions. Laws vetoed by the governor and passed over his veto by the legislature must be transmitted to the President for his approval or disapproval. All acts of the legislature are required to be laid before Congress which may annul the same. To prevent deadlocks in the administration of the government, as several times happened in former years, the law provides that whenever the appropriation bills for the support of the government fail of passage the amount appropriated for the past year shall be considered to have been appropriated for the ensuing fiscal year.

Suffrage and Citizenship.—Practically all citizens over twenty-one years of age who can read and write are qualified voters. Formerly a source of complaint among the inhabitants was that they were denied the status of United States citizenship. They were designated as citizens of Porto Rico and were entitled to be protected by the United States and were eligible to receive passports for travel abroad, but they were not citizens of the United States. The law of 1917, however, removed this grievance by providing that all citizens of Porto Rico should be deemed to be citizens of the United States. The act also contains an elaborate bill of rights similar to those in the state constitutions.

Judiciary.—The elaborate system of Spanish courts and the Spanish legal system generally have been done away with, and in their place a system of law and procedure and a judicial system modeled upon those of the American states have been substituted. There is a supreme court consisting of five judges appointed for life by the President, and of these, three are Porto Ricans and two Americans. Below this court are a number of district courts each of which is presided over by one judge appointed by the governor with the consent of the council for a term of four years. There are also twenty-four municipal courts, and in the several towns there are courts held by the justices of the peace. The act of 1917 provided for the establishment of a District Court of the United States for the island.

Resident Commissioner at Washington.—The interests of the island are looked after at Washington by a resident commissioner who is elected by the qualified voters for a term of four years. Unlike the delegate from an organized territory he has no right to a seat in the house of representatives, but the house has granted him the courtesy of this privilege. He is, however, entitled to official recognition by all the executive departments whenever he wishes to discuss with them matters of business affecting PortoRico.

The island has its own internal revenue system for raising taxes, and the receipts from all customs duties on goods imported into the island are turned into the insular treasury. Unlike the Philippines, however, the island does not have its own monetary system, but uses that of the United States.

The Philippines.—The problem of governing the Philippines has proved much more difficult than that of governing Porto Rico. Instead of a single island inhabited by a fairly homogeneous population, the Philippine archipelago consists of several hundred islands inhabited by various races and peoples representing almost every stage of development from savagery to fairly complete civilization. It has been a difficult problem to develop a system of government adapted to the needs and capacities of so many different elements. In addition to the difficulties presented by these conditions, the Filipinos in various parts of the archipelago have resisted American rule, and no small amount of effort and expenditure of money has been directed toward the suppression of outbreaks and the maintenance of order.

Organic Act of 1902.—In 1902 Congress passed an organic act for the government of the islands, and shortly thereafter William H. Taft was inaugurated civil governor. This act continued for the most part the form of government that had been created by the Philippine Commission. The organic act provided, however, that as soon as the insurrection then existing was suppressed, a census of the inhabitants should be taken and if the islands were in a state of peace, steps should be taken toward the establishment of a legislative assembly, the lower house of which should be popularly elected. This provision was duly carried out, and in 1907 the assembly was chosen. The upper house was a commission of nine members, including the governor, appointed by the President; and members of the commission also served as heads of executive departments.

In 1916 the government was altered by abolishing the commission and creating a legislature in which both houses are elective. The governor general, at the head of the executive department, is appointed by the President, as are also the vice governor and the auditor. Acts of the Philippine legislature may be vetoed by the governor general (or finally by the President if passed over the governor general's veto), or may be annulled by Congress. The act of 1916 declared it to be the purpose of the United States to grant the Philippines independence as soon as a stable government can be established therein.

Resident Commissioners.—The legislature is allowed to choose two resident commissioners to represent the islands at Washington. Like territorial delegates, they have seats, but no vote, in the house of representatives.

The Judicial System of the islands consists of a supreme court of seven judges who are appointed by the President, a court of first instance in each province, the judges of which are appointed by the governor general, and various municipal courts. Unlike Porto Rico and Hawaii, no United States district court has been established in the islands. Appeals lie from the supreme court of the islands directly to the United States Supreme Court in all cases in which the Constitution or any statute or treaty is involved or in which the amount in controversy exceeds $25,000.

Local Government.—Each province is governed in local matters by a board consisting of a governor and other officers elected by the voters. The organized municipalities are governed by elective councils. Special provision has been made for the government of districts inhabited by certain non-Christian peoples by the creation of a Bureau of Non-Christian Tribes.

The Unorganized Territories and Dependencies.—The third group of territories or dependencies embrace those which have no legislative assembly whatever. These include Samoan Islands, Virgin Islands, Guam, the Panama Canal Zone, and the District of Columbia.

The American *Samoan Islands*, the chief of which is Tutuila with its valuable harbor of Pagopago, are governed by a naval officer—the commandant of the naval station at Tutuila. He makes the laws and regulations, and sees that they are enforced, but so far as possible the inhabitants are allowed to govern themselves.

By treaty of 1916, three of the *Virgin Islands* were purchased from Denmark for $25,000,000. They were placed under the jurisdiction of a governor appointed by the President, but the local laws were kept in force.

Guam was seized by the United States during the war with Spain, and was retained by the treaty of peace. It is governed by the commandant of the naval station.[107]

The Panama Canal Zone is a strip of land ten miles wide extending from the Atlantic to the Pacific Ocean across the Isthmus of Panama, and was acquired by treaty from the Republic of Panama in 1904, upon the payment of $10,000,000. Soon after the conclusion of the treaty, Congress passed an act placing the entire government of the Canal Zone in the hands of the President. The powers of the President prior to 1914 were exercised through the Isthmian Canal Commission consisting of seven members, with authority to make and enforce all needful rules and regulations for the government of the Zone and to enact such local legislation as might be needed, subject to the condition that it must not be inconsistent with the Constitution, laws, or treaties of the United States. In January, 1914, President Wilson, in pursuance of an act of Congress passed in 1912, issued an order abolishing the commission and organizing a system of civil government for the Canal Zone. Colonel George W. Goethals was appointed the first civil governor.

The District of Columbia is a territory with an area of seventy square miles, and was ceded to the United States in 1790 for the site of the national capital. The district was administered from 1801 to 1871 under the forms of municipal government, that is, by a mayor and council, but in the latter year Congress vested the government in a governor, a secretary, a board of public works, a board of health, and a legislative assembly. At the same time the district was allowed to send a delegate to Congress. Largely on account of the extravagance of this government in under-taking expensive public improvements, Congress in 1874 abolished the whole scheme and established the present system, which vests practically all governmental powers in the hands of a commission of three persons appointed by the President. Two of these must be appointed from civil life and the other must be an officer belonging to the engineering corps of the army. This commission has the general direction of administrative affairs and the appointment of employees, and exercises wide powers of a quasi legislative character, such as the issuing of health and police regulations. The legislature of the district, however, is the Congress of the United States. In each house there is a committee on the District of Columbia to which all bills relating to the district are referred, and on one day of each week an hour is set apart in the house of representatives for the consideration of such bills. No provision is made for the representation of the district in Congress, and the inhabitants take no part in presidential elections.[108] One half the expense of conducting the government of the district is defrayed out of the national treasury, and the other half is raised from taxation on private property in the district.

The judicial establishment of the district consists of a court of appeals of three judges, a supreme court of six judges, and the usual police courts and courts of justices of the peace. (See page 364.)

American Protection over Spanish American States.—In addition to the ownership of the various insular dependencies mentioned above, the United States, in pursuance of a long established policy known as the "Monroe Doctrine," exercises a certain degree of protection over Latin American states. As this policy is now interpreted it forbids the further acquisition by European powers of territorial possessions in the western hemisphere, or the extension by such powers of political influence on this continent. By virtue of special treaty arrangements the United States exercises a virtual protectorate over certain of the smaller Latin American republics. Thus under the "Platt Amendment," to the constitution of Cuba (also embodied in a treaty between the United States and Cuba) the United States has the right to intervene in Cuba for the maintenance of a stable government and for the protection of public order and security; and this power was exercised in 1906. Naturally it exercises the power of protection over the republic of Panama through whose territory the Panama Canal runs, and recently (1915) it has established a sort of financial protectorate over Haiti and the Dominican Republic. In pursuance of treaty arrangements it collects the customs revenues in those republics, applies them to the payment of their foreign debts, and has the right to intervene for the maintenance of order.

References.—BEARD, American Government and Politics, ch. xxi. BRYCE, The American Commonwealth (abridged edition), ch. xlvi. HART, Actual Government, ch. xx. WILLOUGHBY, Territories and Dependencies of the United States, chs. iii, iv, vi.

RESEARCH QUESTIONS

1. From what clause or clauses in the Constitution is the power to acquire foreign territory derived?

2. By what different methods has foreign territory been added to the United States?

3. Are there any limitations on the powers of Congress in legislating for the territories?

CHAPTER XX

CITIZENSHIP

Who are Citizens.—The population of every country is composed of two classes of persons: citizens and aliens. The larger portion of the inhabitants are citizens, but the alien class is considerable in some states of the Union, much more so than formerly, owing to the large influx of immigrants from Europe in recent years.[109] A citizen is one who has been admitted to full membership in the state, though he may not have been given full political privileges, such as the privileges of voting and holding public office. There is a large class of citizens in every state who can neither vote nor hold public office, such, for example, as minors, sometimes illiterate persons, those who have not paid their taxes, those who have been convicted of serious crimes, and others. On the other hand, aliens in some states are allowed to vote and hold office, especially if they have formally declared their intention of becoming citizens. The terms "citizen" and "voter," therefore, are not identical, since there are some citizens who cannot vote and some voters who are not citizens. (See page 125.)

How Citizenship is Acquired.—Under the Fourteenth Amendment to the federal Constitution, all persons born in the United States[110] are citizens of the United States, and also of the states in which they reside. Persons who come here from abroad may become citizens only by being naturalized.

Naturalization Law.—To acquire citizenship in this way, they must reside here for a period of five years, they must also be persons of good moral character, attached to the principles of the Constitution and well disposed to the good order and happiness of the same. Under the law of 1906 they must also be able to write their own language and be able to read and speak English. Two steps are necessary in the procedure of naturalization: first the applicant must go before a federal court or a court of record in some state and make oath that he is at least eighteen years of age, and that it is his intention to become a citizen of the United States. At the same time he must renounce all allegiance to the foreign state of which he is a citizen or subject and must furnish the court with a variety of information concerning his past life, including the date of his arrival in the United States and the name of the ship on which he arrived. He is then furnished with a certificate which is popularly known as his "first papers." When he has resided in the United States at least five years and possesses all the necessary qualifications the court will issue him a certificate of naturalization which makes him a citizen. Fees amounting to five dollars are now charged for filing the petition and issuing the final certificate. In order to prevent the wholesale naturalization of aliens in the large cities for election purposes, the law provides that no certificate of naturalization shall be granted within thirty days prior to any general election. Any honorably discharged alien from the United States army may be admitted to citizenship after a residence of one year, and the preliminary declaration of intention is not required of aliens who have served five years in the navy.

Disqualifications.—In addition to the qualifications mentioned above, there are certain disqualifications which serve to debar many foreigners from acquiring American citizenship. Thus only white persons and persons of African nativity are capable of being naturalized under our laws, so that those belonging to the Mongolian or other races, such as Chinese, Japanese, Burmese, and East Indians, cannot become citizens of the United States unless born here. Other persons excluded for different reasons are polygamists, anarchists, and certain other classes of criminals who are not considered worthy to enjoy the high privileges of citizenship.

The naturalization of a husband makes the wife and minor children citizens, so that they do not have to go through the process of taking out their "papers."

Other Methods of Acquiring Citizenship.—Citizenship may be acquired sometimes in other ways than the method described above. Thus a foreign woman becomes a citizen by marriage to an American citizen, and the inhabitants of foreign territory annexed to the United States become citizens by virtue of their incorporation into the body politic. In this way the inhabitants of the Louisiana territory, acquired from France, became citizens. In the same way those of Florida, Texas, California, Alaska, and Hawaii became citizens, but not those of Porto Rico and the Philippines. Residents of Porto Rico, however, were made citizens of the United States by act of Congress in 1917.

How Citizenship may be Lost.—As citizenship may be acquired in various ways so it may be lost by different acts. An American woman loses her citizenship by marriage to an alien. Acceptance of a commission in the service of a foreign country; if it involves the taking of an oath of allegiance to a foreign government, operates to divest one of his American citizenship. The most common mode by which citizenship is lost, however, is through voluntary removal from the country and naturalization in a foreign state. The right of the citizen to withdraw from the United States, renounce his allegiance, and acquire the citizenship of a foreign state, is declared by our law to be an inalienable right. Mere removal from the United States and the establishment of a residence in a foreign country, however, does not of itself operate to divest one of his citizenship. An American citizen may reside abroad many years for the purposes of business, education, or pleasure, and so long as he preserves an intention of returning to the United States he is not held to have abandoned his American nationality.

In order to prevent foreigners from coming to the United States, acquiring our citizenship, and returning to their native country for the purpose of living there without being subject to the burdens and obligations of military service, the law declares that a naturalized American who returns to his native country and resides there for a period of two years will be presumed to have abandoned his American citizenship, and unless he can show an intention of returning to America he will be considered as no longer being a citizen.

Federal versus State Citizenship.—In a country having the federal form of government, the inhabitants have a dual citizenship, that is, they are citizens of the country as a whole and of the particular state in which they are residents. Thus our federal Constitution declares that all persons born or naturalized in the United States and subject to the jurisdiction thereof are citizens of the United States and of the state in which they reside. A person, however, may be a citizen of the United States without at the same time being a citizen of any state, as is the case with those inhabiting the territories, the District of Columbia, and other places not forming a part of any state. On the contrary, it seems to be generally admitted that one may be a citizen of a state without necessarily being a citizen of the United States. Thus a state may give an alien full political and civil rights and declare him to be a citizen of the state before he has become a citizen of the United States. Some states have in effect done this. It follows, therefore, that federal and state citizenship are not necessarily identical and coexistent, since there may be a class of state citizens upon whom the United States has not conferred its own citizenship, and a class of United States citizens who are not citizens of any state. The citizenship of a particular state may be relinquished for that of another by removal from the former state and the establishment of a residence in the latter. No legal formality whatever is required to put off the one and take on the other.

Interstate Rights of Citizens.—There is a provision in the Constitution of the United States which declares that the citizens of each state shall enjoy all the privileges and immunities of the citizens of the several states. The purpose of this provision is to prevent one state from discriminating against the citizens of other states in favor of its own citizens. Whatever rights and privileges it accords to its own citizens must be accorded equally to citizens of other states who may be within its borders or who may wish to carry on business therein. The states are also forbidden by the federal Constitution to abridge the privileges and immunities of citizens of the United States, though the

Constitution does not specify or indicate what these privileges and immunities are. They include, however, such privileges as the making and enforcing of contracts, of suing in the courts, of inheriting, holding, and conveying property, of receiving equal protection of the laws, and, in general, of enjoying every right or privilege to which the citizen is entitled under the Constitution and laws of the United States.

Rights and Duties of Aliens.—Aliens, though in a political sense members of foreign states, are, nevertheless, fully subject to the jurisdiction of the state in which they are domiciled, and owe it a temporary allegiance. They are bound to obey the laws equally with citizens, and may be punished for violations of them equally with citizens. They must also share, to a certain extent, the public burdens, and may be required to serve in the militia or police (though not in the regular army) if the common defense and domestic safety require their services.

Right of Protection.—It is now universally admitted that they are entitled to the protection of the government under which they are living so long as they are within its jurisdiction, but not when they go abroad. So far as the enjoyment of civil rights is concerned, the tendency is to treat them on a footing of equality with citizens. Both the federal and the state courts are open to them on the same terms as to citizens, and if they suffer injuries in the course of riots and other disturbances, because of their foreign nationality, especially if the public authorities fail to use due diligence to prevent or punish attacks upon them, the United States government will indemnify them or their heirs for the injuries sustained.[111]

Disabilities of Aliens.—Formerly aliens were subject to disabilities much more commonly than now. Under the common law, for example, they could not inherit land, but this disability has been abolished in most of the states, though some still make a distinction between resident and nonresident aliens in this respect, allowing the former class to take land by inheritance as well as by purchase but excluding the latter class. Some states do not allow them to be employed on the public works, and a few subject them to other disabilities, but they are not important or numerous.[112] With regard to political privileges, however, the disabilities of aliens are still generally maintained.

Rights and Obligations of Citizens. —The chief privilege of citizenship is that of protection by the government in all personal and property rights. If the citizen goes abroad for the purpose of business or pleasure, the government will protect him from wrongful treatment so long as he obeys the law of the country to which he is, for the time being, subject, and demeans himself peaceably. If he is injured or discriminated against because of his foreign nationality, the government which fails to protect him will be required to make a suitable indemnity for the injury.

Equality of Native and Naturalized Citizens.—When it comes to protecting its citizens abroad, the United States government makes no distinction between naturalized and native-born citizens. In the case of a Russian, for example, who comes to America and is naturalized and goes back to Russia for business or pleasure, our government will insist that he be treated by the Russian authorities as if he were a native-born American citizen. At home a naturalized citizen enjoys the same privileges as a native-born except that he is not eligible to the office of President or Vice President of the United States.

Duties and Obligations of Citizens.—Rights and privileges seldom exist without corresponding duties and obligations, and so citizenship has its duties. One of these is to contribute to the bearing of the burdens of the state. This includes the payment of taxes, service in the militia or army for purposes of defense, and the discharge of such public trusts as may be imposed. It is, of course, the duty of the citizen, as it is of every one who lives in the state, to obey the laws and do what he can to secure their enforcement. Finally, if the citizen possesses political privileges, it is his duty to take an active part in securing the election of competent and honest officials to the end that the government which protects him may be efficient and well administered.

Obligations and Duties of Nations: International Law.—Nations, like individuals, are bound by rules of conduct in their relations with one another. The rules governing nations constitute what is known as international law, a subject of which we have heard much since the outbreak of the great world war in 1914. The rules of international law, unlike those of national or municipal law, are not enacted by a legislative body, for as yet, unfortunately, there is no world legislature. They consist partly of customary rules and usages, and partly of international treaties. The most important of these treaties are those negotiated to end the World War, and also the so-called conventions, sixteen in number, recommended by the Peace Conferences at the Hague in 1899 and 1907, and adopted, for the most part, by nearly all the civilized nations of the world. These conventions contain a large number of important rules prescribing the conduct to be observed by nations both in time of war and in time of peace.

Unfortunately, however, international law has one great weakness which national law does not have. National law has what the lawyers call a sanction; that is to say, a penalty is prescribed for its violation, and courts are established for punishing those who violate its rules. But in the case of international law there is as yet no machinery for bringing to the bar of justice and inflicting punishment upon a nation which violates its international duties and obligations, except as the League of Nations may succeed in performing this function. The only punishment which has often followed such an act is the reprobation of public opinion, which unhappily, as the World War has demonstrated, is not a sufficient deterrent in the case of nations which regard lightly their obligations of honor and good faith. Thinking men the world over realize how important it is to make international law more effective, to compel nations by force or otherwise to observe their international obligations, and to prevent war, the world's greatest curse.

References.—ASHLEY, The American Federal State, ch. xxix; also pp. 212-217. BEARD, American Government and Politics, pp. 160-163. FULLER, Government by the People, ch. ii. GARNER, Introduction to Political Science, ch. xi. HART, Actual Government, chs. ii-iv. HINSDALE, The American Government, ch. liv.

Documentary and Illustrative Material.—1. Copy of the federal citizenship law of 1907. 2. Copy of the naturalization act of 1906. 3. Copies of naturalization blanks and of naturalization regulations (these may be secured from the bureau of immigration and naturalization). 4. Copy of an application for a passport (this may be secured from the department of state). 5. Copy of a passport.

RESEARCH QUESTIONS

1. What is a citizen? Distinguish between native-born and naturalized citizens; between citizens and electors.

2. Is the citizenship of a child determined by the law of the place where it is born or by the law of the place of which the parents are citizens? Distinguish between the English and American practice in this respect, on the one hand, and the continental European practice on the other.

3. What would be the citizenship of a child born in the United States if the father were the ambassador of a foreign country, temporarily residing here? What would be the citizenship of a child born of American parents on the high seas? of a child born abroad of American parents? of a child born in the United States if the father were a foreign consul here?

4. A child born in the United States of French parents would be a citizen of the United States under our law; it would also be a citizen of France, according to French law. Which citizenship would prevail?

5. Do you think our law should admit persons of African descent to become citizens and yet deny the right to Japanese, Chinese, and natives of India?

6. May one be a citizen of two different countries at the same time?

7. What would be the status of an American woman who lost her American

citizenship by marrying a foreigner, in case of the death of her husband? How could she reacquire her original citizenship?

8. How long may an American reside abroad without losing his citizenship?

9. Many Europeans, in order to escape military service in their country, have emigrated to America, acquired our citizenship and returned to their native country. Will the United States government protect such persons against impressment into the military service?

10. Suppose a citizen of New York moves to Pennsylvania and establishes a residence there. Does that act without any legal formality make him a citizen of Pennsylvania?

ARTICLES OF CONFEDERATION

ARTICLES OF CONFEDERATION AND PERPETUAL UNION BETWEEN THE STATES OF NEW HAMPSHIRE, MASSACHUSETTS BAY, RHODE ISLAND AND PROVIDENCE PLANTATIONS, CONNECTICUT, NEW YORK, NEW JERSEY, PENNSYLVANIA, DELAWARE, MARYLAND, VIRGINIA, NORTH CAROLINA, SOUTH CAROLINA, AND GEORGIA

ARTICLE I.—The style of this confederacy shall be, "The United States of America."

ART. II.—Each State retains its sovereignty, freedom, and independence, and every power, jurisdiction, and right which is not by this confederation expressly delegated to the United States in Congress assembled.

ART. III.—The said States hereby severally enter into a firm league of friendship with each other, for their common defense, the security of their liberties, and their mutual and general welfare, binding themselves to assist each other against all force offered to, or attacks made upon them, or any of them, on account of religion, sovereignty, trade, or any other pretense whatever.

ART. IV.—The better to secure and perpetuate mutual friendship and intercourse among the people of the different States in this Union, the free inhabitants of each of these States, paupers, vagabonds, and fugitives from justice excepted, shall be entitled to all privileges and immunities of free citizens in the several States; and the people of each State shall have free ingress and regress to and from any other State, and shall enjoy therein all the privileges of trade and commerce, subject to the same duties, impositions, and restrictions, as the inhabitants thereof respectively; provided that such restrictions shall not extend so far as to prevent the removal of property imported into any State, to any other State of which the owner is an inhabitant; provided, also, that no imposition, duties, or restriction, shall be laid by any State on the property of the United States or either of them.

If any person guilty of, or charged with, treason, felony, or other high misdemeanor in any State, shall flee from justice, and be found in any of the United States, he shall, upon demand of the governor or executive power of the State from which he fled, be delivered up, and removed to the State having jurisdiction of his offense.

Full faith and credit shall be given, in each of these States, to the records, acts, and judicial proceedings of the courts and magistrates of every other State.

ART. V.—For the more convenient management of the general interests of the United States, delegates shall be annually appointed in such manner as the legislature of each State shall direct, to meet in Congress on the first Monday in November, in every year, with a power reserved to each State to recall its delegates, or any of them, at any time within the year, and to send others in their stead for the remainder of the year.

No State shall be represented in Congress by less than two, nor by more than seven members; and no person shall be capable of being a delegate for more than three years, in any term of six years; nor shall any person, being a delegate, be capable of holding any office under the United States, for which he, or another for his benefit, receives any salary, fees, or emolument of any kind.

Each State shall maintain its own delegates in any meeting of the States and while they act as members of the committee of the States.

In determining questions in the United States in Congress assembled, each State shall have one vote.

Freedom of speech and debate in Congress shall not be impeached or questioned in any court or place out of Congress; and the members of Congress shall be protected in their persons from arrests and imprisonments during the time of their going to and from, and attendance on Congress, except for treason, felony, or breach of the peace.

ART. VI.—No State, without the consent of the United States, in Congress assembled, shall send any embassy to, or receive any embassy from, or enter into any conference, agreement, alliance, or treaty, with any king, prince, or state; nor shall any person holding any office of profit or trust under the United States, or any of them, accept of any present, emolument, office, or title of any kind whatever, from any king, prince, or foreign state; nor shall the United States, in Congress assembled, or any of them, grant any title of nobility.

No two or more States shall enter into any treaty, confederation, or alliance whatever between them, without the consent of the United States, in Congress assembled, specifying accurately the purposes for which the same is to be entered into, and how long it shall continue.

No States shall lay any imposts or duties which may interfere with any stipulations in treaties entered into by the United States, in Congress assembled, with any king, prince, or state, in pursuance of any treaties already proposed by Congress to the courts of France and Spain.

No vessels of war shall be kept up in time of peace, by any State, except such number only as shall be deemed necessary, by the United States in Congress assembled, for the defense of such State or its trade; nor shall any body of forces be kept up, by any State, in time of peace, except such number only as, in the judgment of the United States, in Congress assembled, shall be deemed requisite to garrison the forts necessary for the defense of such State; but every State shall always keep up a well regulated and disciplined militia, sufficiently armed and accoutred, and shall provide and constantly have ready for use, in public stores, a due number of field-pieces and tents, and a proper quantity of arms, ammunition, and camp equipage.

No State shall engage in any war without the consent of the United States, in Congress assembled, unless such State be actually invaded by enemies, or shall have received certain advice of a resolution being formed by some nation of Indians to invade such State, and the danger is so imminent as not to admit of a delay till the United States, in Congress assembled, can be consulted; nor shall any State grant commissions to any ships or vessels of war, nor letters of marque or reprisal, except it be after a declaration of war by the United States, in Congress assembled, and then only against the kingdom or state, and the subjects thereof against which war has been so declared, and under such regulations as shall be established by the United States, in Congress assembled, unless such State be infested by pirates, in which case vessels of war may be fitted out for that occasion, and kept so long as the danger shall continue, or until the United States, in Congress assembled, shall determine otherwise.

ART. VII.—When land forces are raised by any State for the common defense, all officers of or under the rank of colonel, shall be appointed by the legislature of each State respectively by whom such forces shall be raised, or in such manner as such State shall direct, and all vacancies shall be filled up by the State which first made the appointment.

ART. VIII.—All charges of war, and all other expenses that shall be incurred for the common defense or general welfare, and allowed by the United States in Congress assembled, shall be defrayed out of a common treasury, which shall be supplied by the several States, in proportion to the value of all land within each State, granted to, or surveyed for, any person, as such land and the buildings and improvements thereon shall be estimated according to such mode as the United States, in Congress assembled, shall, from time to time, direct and appoint. The taxes for paying that proportion shall be laid and levied by the authority and direction of the legislatures of the several States, within the time agreed upon by the United States, in Congress assembled.

ART. IX.—The United States, in Congress assembled, shall have the sole and exclusive right and power of determining on peace and war, except in the cases mentioned in the sixth Article; of sending and receiving ambassadors; entering into treaties and alliances, provided that no treaty of commerce shall be made whereby the legislative power of the respective States shall be restrained from imposing such imposts and duties on foreigners, as their own people are subjected to, or from prohibiting the exportation or importation of any species of goods or commodities whatsoever; of establishing rules for deciding, in all cases, what captures on land or water shall be legal, and in what manner prizes taken by land or naval forces in the service of the United States, shall be divided or appropriated; of granting letters of marque and reprisal in times of peace; appointing courts for the trial of piracies and felonies committed on the high seas; and establishing courts for receiving and determining finally appeals in all cases of captures; provided that no member of Congress shall be appointed a judge of any of the said courts.

The United States, in Congress assembled, shall also be the last resort on appeal, in all disputes and differences now subsisting, or that hereafter may arise between two or more States concerning boundary, jurisdiction, or any other cause whatever; which authority shall always be exercised in the manner following: Whenever the legislative or executive authority, or lawful agent of any State in controversy with another, shall present a petition to Congress, stating the matter in question, and praying for a hearing, notice thereof shall be given by order of Congress, to the legislative or executive authority of the other State in controversy, and a day assigned for the appearance of the parties by their lawful agents, who shall then be directed to appoint, by joint consent, commissioners or judges to constitute a court for hearing and determining the matter in question; but if they can not agree, Congress shall name three persons out of each of the United States, and from the list of such persons each party shall alternately strike out one, the petitioners beginning, until the number shall be reduced to thirteen; and from that number not less than seven nor more than nine names, as Congress shall direct, shall, in the presence of Congress, be drawn out by lot; and the persons whose names shall be so drawn, or any five of them, shall be commissioners or judges, to hear and finally determine the controversy, so always as a major part of the judges, who shall hear the cause, shall agree in the determination; and if either party shall neglect to attend at the day appointed, without showing reasons which Congress shall judge sufficient, or being present, shall refuse to strike, the Congress shall proceed to nominate three persons out of each State, and the secretary of Congress shall strike in behalf of such party absent or refusing; and the judgment and sentence of the court, to be appointed in the manner before prescribed, shall be final and conclusive; and if any of the parties shall refuse to submit to the authority of such court, or to appear or defend their claim or cause, the court shall nevertheless proceed to pronounce sentence or judgment, which shall in like manner be final and decisive; the judgment or sentence and other proceedings being in either case transmitted to Congress, and lodged among the acts of Congress for the security of the parties concerned; provided, that every commissioner, before he sits in judgment, shall take an oath, to be administered by one of the judges of the supreme or superior court of the State where the cause shall be tried, "well and truly to hear and determine the matter in question, according to the best of his judgment, without favor, affection, or hope of reward." Provided, also, that no State shall be deprived of territory for the benefit of the United States.

All controversies concerning the private right of soil claimed under different grants of two or more States, whose jurisdictions, as they may respect such lands, and the States which passed such grants are adjusted, the said grants or either of them being at the same time claimed to have originated antecedent to such settlement of jurisdiction, shall, on the petition of either party to the Congress of the United States, be finally determined, as near as may be, in the same manner as is before prescribed for deciding disputes respecting territorial jurisdiction between different States.

The United States, in Congress assembled, shall also have the sole and exclusive right and power of regulating the alloy and value of coin struck by their own authority, or by that of the respective States; fixing the standard of weights and measures throughout the United States; regulating the trade and managing all affairs with the Indians not members of any of the States; provided that the legislative right of any State, within its own limits, be not infringed or violated; establishing and regulating post offices from one State to another throughout all the United States, and exacting such postage on the papers passing through the same, as may be requisite to defray the expenses of the said office; appointing all officers of the land forces in the service of the United States, excepting regimental officers; appointing all the officers of the naval forces, and commissioning all officers whatever in the service of the United States; making rules for the government and regulation of the said land and naval forces, and directing their operations.

The United States, in Congress assembled, shall have authority to appoint a committee, to sit in the recess of Congress, to be denominated "A Committee of the States," and to consist of one delegate from each State; and to appoint such other committees and civil officers as may be necessary for managing the general affairs of the United States under their direction; to appoint one of their number to preside, provided that no person be allowed to serve in the office of president more than one year in any term of three years; to ascertain the necessary sums of money to be raised for the service of the United States, and to appropriate and apply the same for defraying the public expenses; to borrow money or emit bills on the credit of the United States, transmitting every half year to the respective States an account of the sums of money so borrowed or emitted; to build and equip a navy; to agree upon the number of land forces, and to make requisitions from each State for its quota, in proportion to the number of white inhabitants in such State, which requisition shall be binding; and thereupon the Legislature of each State shall appoint the regimental officers, raise the men, and clothe, arm, and equip them in a soldier-like manner at the expense of the United States; and the officers and men so clothed, armed, and equipped shall march to the place appointed, and within the time agreed on by the United States, in Congress assembled; but if the United States, in Congress assembled, shall, on consideration of circumstances, judge proper that any State should not raise men, or should raise a smaller number than its quota, and that any other State should raise a greater number of men than the quota thereof, such extra number shall be raised, officered, clothed, armed, and equipped in the same manner as the quota of such State, unless the Legislature of such State shall judge that such extra number can not be safely spared out of the same, in which case they shall raise, officer, clothe, arm, and equip as many of such extra number as they judge can be safely spared, and the officers and men so clothed, armed, and equipped shall march to the place appointed, and within the time agreed on by the United States, in Congress assembled.

The United States, in Congress assembled, shall never engage in a war, nor grant letters of marque and reprisal in time of peace, nor enter into any treatise or alliances; nor coin money, nor regulate the value thereof, nor ascertain the sums and expenses necessary for the defense and welfare of the United States, or any of them, nor emit bills, nor borrow money on the credit of the United States, nor appropriate money, nor agree upon the number of vessels of war to be built or purchased, or the number of land or sea forces to be raised, nor appoint a commander-in-chief of the army or navy, unless nine States assent to the same, nor shall a question on any other point, except for adjourning from day to-day, be determined, unless by the votes of a majority of the United States, in Congress assembled.

The Congress of the United States shall have power to adjourn to any time within the year, and to any place within the United States, so that no period of adjournment be for a longer duration than the space of six months, and shall publish the journal of their proceedings monthly, except such parts thereof relating to treaties, alliances, or military operations as in their judgment require secrecy; and the yeas and nays of the delegates of each State, on any question, shall be entered on the journal when it is desired by any delegate; and the delegates of a State, or any of them, at his or their request, shall be furnished with a transcript of the said journal, except such parts as are above excepted, to lay before the legislatures of the several States.

Art. X.—The committee of the States, or any nine of them, shall be authorized to execute, in the recess of Congress, such of the powers of Congress as the United States, in Congress assembled, by the consent of nine States, shall, from time to time, think expedient to vest them with; provided that no power be delegated to the said committee, for the exercise of which, by the articles of confederation, the voice of nine States, in the Congress of the United States assembled, is requisite.

Art. XI.—Canada, acceding to this confederation, and joining in the measures of the United States, shall be admitted into, and entitled to all the advantages of this Union; but no other colony shall be admitted into the same unless such admission be agreed to by nine States.

Art. XII.—All bills of credit emitted, moneys borrowed, and debts contracted by or under the authority of Congress, before the assembling of the United States, in pursuance of the present confederation, shall be deemed and considered as a charge against the United States, for payment and satisfaction whereof the said United States and the public faith are hereby solemnly pledged.

Art. XIII.—Every State shall abide by the determinations of the United States, in Congress assembled, on all questions which by this Confederation are submitted to them. And the Articles of this Confederation shall be inviolably observed by every State, and the Union shall be perpetual; nor shall any alteration at any time hereafter be made in any of them, unless such alteration be agreed to in a Congress of the United States; and be afterward confirmed by the legislatures of every State.

And whereas it hath pleased the great Governor of the world to incline the hearts of the legislatures we respectively represent in Congress, to approve of, and to authorize us to ratify the said Articles of Confederation and perpetual Union, Know ye, that we, the undersigned delegates, by virtue of the power and authority to us given for that purpose, do, by these presents, in the name and in behalf of our respective constituents, fully and entirely ratify and confirm each and every of the said Articles of Confederation and perpetual Union, and all and singular the matters and things therein contained. And we do further solemnly plight and engage the faith of our respective constituents, that they shall abide by the determinations of the United States, in Congress assembled, on all questions which by the said Confederation are submitted to them; and that the Articles thereof shall be inviolably observed by the States we respectively represent, and that the Union shall be perpetual. In witness whereof, we have hereunto set our hands in Congress. Done at Philadelphia, in the State of Pennsylvania, the ninth day of July, in the year of our Lord 1778,[113] and in the third year of the Independence of America.

CONSTITUTION OF THE UNITED STATES— 1787[114]

We the people of the United States, in order to form a more perfect union, establish justice, insure domestic tranquillity, provide for the common defense, promote the general welfare, and secure the blessings of liberty to ourselves and our posterity, do ordain and establish this Constitution for the United States of America.

ARTICLE I

SECTION 1. All legislative powers herein granted shall be vested in a Congress of the United States, which shall consist of a Senate and House of Representatives.

SECTION 2. 1 The House of Representatives shall be composed of members chosen every second year by the people of the several States, and the electors in each State shall have the qualifications requisite for electors of the most numerous branch of the State legislature.

2 No person shall be a representative who shall not have attained to the age of twenty-five years, and been seven years a citizen of the United States, and who shall not, when elected, be an inhabitant of that State in which he shall be chosen.

3 Representatives and direct taxes shall be apportioned among the several States which may be included within this Union, according to their respective numbers, which shall be determined by adding to the whole number of free persons, including those bound to service for a term of years, and excluding Indians not taxed, three fifths of all other persons.[115] The actual enumeration shall be made within three years after the first meeting of the Congress of the United States, and within every subsequent term of ten years, in such manner as they shall by law direct. The number of representatives shall not exceed one for every thirty thousand, but each State shall have at least one representative; and until such enumeration shall be made, the State of New Hampshire shall be entitled to choose three, Massachusetts eight, Rhode Island and Providence Plantations one, Connecticut five, New York six, New Jersey four, Pennsylvania eight, Delaware one, Maryland six, Virginia ten, North Carolina five, South Carolina five, and Georgia three.

4 When vacancies happen in the representation from any State, the executive

authority thereof shall issue writs of election to fill such vacancies.

5 The House of Representatives shall choose their speaker and other officers, and shall have the sole power of impeachment.

SECTION 3. 1 The Senate of the United States shall be composed of two senators from each State, chosen by the legislature thereof for six years; and each senator shall have one vote.[116]

2 Immediately after they shall be assembled in consequence of the first election, they shall be divided as equally as may be into three classes. The seats of the senators of the first class shall be vacated at the expiration of the second year, of the second class at the expiration of the fourth year, and of the third class at the expiration of the sixth year, so that one third may be chosen every second year; and if vacancies happen by resignation, or otherwise, during the recess of the legislature of any State, the executive thereof, may make temporary appointments until the next meeting of the legislature, which shall then fill such vacancies.[117]

3 No person shall be a senator who shall not have attained to the age of thirty years, and been nine years a citizen of the United States, and who shall not, when elected, be an inhabitant of that State for which be shall be chosen.

4 The Vice President of the United States shall be President of the Senate, but shall have no vote, unless they be equally divided.

5 The Senate shall choose their other officers, and also a president *pro tempore*, in the absence of the Vice President, or when he shall exercise the office of President of the United States.

6 The Senate shall have the sole power to try all impeachments. When sitting for that purpose, they shall be on oath or affirmation. When the President of the United States is tried, the chief justice shall preside: and no person shall be convicted without the concurrence of two thirds of the members present.

7 Judgment in cases of impeachment shall not extend further than to removal from office, and disqualification to hold and enjoy any office of honor, trust or profit under the United States: but the party convicted shall nevertheless be liable and subject to indictment, trial, judgment and punishment, according to law.

SECTION 4. 1 The times, places, and manner of holding elections for senators and representatives, shall be prescribed in each State by the legislature thereof; but the Congress may at any time by law make or alter such regulations, except as to the places of choosing senators.

2 The Congress shall assemble at least once in every year, and such meeting

shall be on the first Monday in December, unless they shall by law appoint a different day.

SECTION 5. 1 Each House shall be the judge of the elections, returns and qualifications of its own members, and a majority of each shall constitute a quorum to do business; but a smaller number may adjourn from day to day, and may be authorized to compel the attendance of absent members, in such manner, and under such penalties as each House may provide.

2 Each House may determine the rules of its proceedings, punish its members for disorderly behavior, and, with the concurrence of two thirds, expel a member.

3 Each House shall keep a journal of its proceedings, and from time to time publish the same, excepting such parts as may in their judgment require secrecy; and the yeas and nays of the members of either House on any question shall, at the desire of one fifth of those present, be entered on the journal.

4 Neither House, during the session of Congress, shall, without the consent of the other, adjourn for more than three days, nor to any other place than that in which the two Houses shall be sitting.

SECTION 6. 1 The senators and representatives shall receive a compensation for their services, to be ascertained by law, and paid out of the Treasury of the United States. They shall in all cases, except treason, felony and breach of the peace, be privileged from arrest during their attendance at the session of their respective Houses, and in going to and returning from the same; and for any speech or debate in either House, they shall not be questioned in any other place.

2 No senator or representative shall, during the time for which he was elected, be appointed to any civil office under the authority of the United States, which shall have been created, or the emoluments whereof shall have been increased during such time; and no person holding any office under the United States shall be a member of either House during his continuance in office.

SECTION 7. 1 All bills for raising revenue shall originate in the House of Representatives; but the Senate may propose or concur with amendments as on other bills.

2 Every bill which shall have passed the House of Representatives and the Senate, shall, before it become a law, be presented to the President of the United States; if he approve he shall sign it, but if not he shall return it, with his objections to that House in which it shall have originated, who shall enter

the objections at large on their journal, and proceed to reconsider it. If after such reconsideration two thirds of that House shall agree to pass the bill, it shall be sent, together with the objections, to the other House, by which it shall likewise be reconsidered, and if approved by two thirds of that House, it shall become a law. But in all such cases the votes of both Houses shall be determined by yeas and nays, and the names of the persons voting for and against the bill shall be entered on the journal of each House respectively. If any bill shall not be returned by the President within ten days (Sundays excepted) after it shall have been presented to him, the same shall be a law, in like manner as if he had signed it, unless the Congress by their adjournment prevent its return, in which case it shall not be a law.

3 Every order, resolution, or vote to which the concurrence of the Senate and House of Representatives may be necessary (except on a question of adjournment) shall be presented to the President of the United States; and before the same shall take effect, shall be approved by him, or being disapproved by him, shall be repassed by two thirds of the Senate and House of Representatives, according to the rules and limitations prescribed in the case of a bill.

SECTION 8. 1 The Congress shall have power to lay and collect taxes, duties, imposts and excises, to pay the debts and provide for the common defense and general welfare of the United States; but all duties, imposts and excises shall be uniform throughout the United States;

2 To borrow money on the credit of the United States;

3 To regulate commerce with foreign nations, and among the several States, and with the Indian tribes;

4 To establish an uniform rule of naturalization, and uniform laws on the subject of bankruptcies throughout the United States;

5 To coin money, regulate the value thereof, and of foreign coin, and fix the standard of weights and measures;

6 To provide for the punishment of counterfeiting the securities and current coin of the United States;

7 To establish post offices and post roads;

8 To promote the progress of science and useful arts by securing for limited times to authors and inventors the exclusive right to their respective writings and discoveries;

9 To constitute tribunals inferior to the Supreme Court;

10 To define and punish piracies and felonies committed on the high seas, and

offenses against the law of nations;

11 To declare war, grant letters of marque and reprisal, and make rules concerning captures on land and water;

12 To raise and support armies, but no appropriation of money to that use shall be for a longer term than two years;

13 To provide and maintain a navy;

14 To make rules for the government and regulation of the land and naval forces;

15 To provide for calling forth the militia to execute the laws of the Union, suppress insurrections and repel invasions;

16 To provide for organizing, arming, and disciplining the militia, and for governing such part of them as may be employed in the service of the United States, reserving to the States respectively the appointment of the officers, and the authority of training the militia according to the discipline prescribed by Congress;

17 To exercise exclusive legislation in all cases whatsoever, over such district (not exceeding ten miles square) as may, by cession of particular States and the acceptance of Congress, become the seat of the government of the United States,[118] and to exercise like authority over all places purchased by the consent of the legislature of the State in which the same shall be, for the erection of forts, magazines, arsenals, dockyards, and other needful buildings; and

18 To make all laws which shall be necessary and proper for carrying into execution the foregoing powers, and all other powers vested by this Constitution in the government of the United States, or in any department or officer thereof.

SECTION 9. 1 The migration or importation of such persons as any of the States now existing shall think proper to admit, shall not be prohibited by the Congress prior to the year one thousand eight hundred and eight, but a tax or duty may be imposed on such importation, not exceeding ten dollars for each person.[119]

2 The privilege of the writ of *habeas corpus* shall not be suspended, unless when in cases of rebellion or invasion the public safety may require it.

3 No bill of attainder or *ex post facto* law shall be passed.

4 No capitation, or other direct, tax shall be laid, unless in proportion to the census or enumeration hereinbefore directed to be taken.

5 No tax or duty shall be laid on articles exported from any State.

6 No preference shall be given by any regulation of commerce or revenue to the ports of one State over those of another: nor shall vessels bound to, or from, one State be obliged to enter, clear, or pay duties in another.

7 No money shall be drawn from the treasury, but in consequence of appropriations made by law; and a regular statement and account of the receipts and expenditures of all public money shall be published from time to time.

8 No title of nobility shall be granted by the United States: and no person holding any office of profit or trust under them, shall, without the consent of the Congress, accept of any present, emolument, office, or title, of any kind whatever, from any king, prince, or foreign State.

SECTION 10.[120] 1 No State shall enter into any treaty, alliance, or confederation; grant letters of marque and reprisal; coin money; emit bills of credit; make anything but gold and silver coin a tender in payment of debts; pass any bill of attainder, *ex post facto* law, or law impairing the obligation of contracts, or grant any title of nobility.

2 No State shall, without the consent of the Congress, lay any imposts or duties on imports or exports, except what may be absolutely necessary for executing its inspection laws: and the net produce of all duties and imposts laid by any State on imports or exports, shall be for the use of the treasury of the United States; and all such laws shall be subject to the revision and control of the Congress.

3 No State shall, without the consent of Congress, lay any duty of tonnage, keep troops, or ships of war in time of peace, enter into any agreement or compact with another State, or with a foreign power, or engage in war, unless actually invaded, or in such imminent danger as will not admit of delay.

ARTICLE II

SECTION 1. 1 The executive power shall be vested in a President of the United States of America. He shall hold his office during the term of four years, and, together with the Vice President, chosen for the same term, be elected, as follows

2 Each State shall appoint, in such manner as the legislature thereof may direct, a number of electors, equal to the whole number of senators and representatives to which the State may be entitled in the Congress: but no senator or representative, or person holding an office of trust or profit under

the United States, shall be appointed an elector.

The electors shall meet in their respective States, and vote by ballot for two persons, of whom one at least shall not be an inhabitant of the same State with themselves. And they shall make a list of all the persons voted for, and of the number of votes for each; which list they shall sign and certify, and transmit sealed to the seat of the government of the United States, directed to the president of the Senate. The president of the Senate, shall, in the presence of the Senate and House of Representatives, open all the certificates, and the votes shall then be counted. The person having the greatest number of votes shall be the President, if such number be a majority of the whole number of electors appointed; and if there be more than one who have such majority, and have an equal number of votes, then the House of Representatives shall immediately choose by ballot one of them for President; and if no person have a majority, then from the five highest on the list the said house shall in like manner choose the President. But in choosing the President, the votes shall be taken by States, the representation from each State having one vote; a quorum for this purpose shall consist of a member or members from two thirds of the States, and a majority of all the States shall be necessary to a choice. In every case, after the choice of the President, the person having the greatest number of votes of the electors shall be the Vice President. But if there should remain two or more who have equal votes, the Senate shall choose from them by ballot the Vice President.[121]

3 The Congress may determine the time of choosing the electors, and the day on which they shall give their votes; which day shall be the same throughout the United States.

4 No person except a natural born citizen, or a citizen of the United States, at the time of the adoption of this Constitution, shall be eligible to the office of President; neither shall any person be eligible to that office who shall not have attained to the age of thirty-five years, and been fourteen years a resident within the United States.

5 In case of the removal of the President from office, or of his death, resignation, or inability to discharge the powers and duties of the said office, the same shall devolve on the Vice President, and the Congress may by law provide for the case of removal, death, resignation, or inability, both of the President and Vice President, declaring what officer shall then act as President, and such officer shall act accordingly, until the disability be removed, or a President shall be elected.

6 The President shall, at stated times, receive for his services a compensation, which shall neither be increased nor diminished during the period for which

he shall have been elected, and he shall not receive within that period any other emolument from the United States, or any of them.

7 Before he enter on the execution of his office, he shall take the following oath or affirmation:—"I do solemnly swear (or affirm) that I will faithfully execute the office of President of the United States, and will to the best of my ability, preserve, protect and defend the Constitution of the United States."

SECTION 2. 1 The President shall be commander in chief of the army and navy of the United States, and of the militia of the several States, when called into the actual service of the United States; he may require the opinion, in writing, of the principal officer in each of the executive departments, upon any subject relating to the duties of their respective offices, and he shall have power to grant reprieves and pardons for offenses against the United States, except in cases of impeachment.

2 He shall have power, by and with the advice and consent of the Senate, to make treaties, provided two thirds of the senators present concur; and he shall nominate, and by and with the advice and consent of the Senate, shall appoint ambassadors, other public ministers and consuls, judges of the Supreme Court, and all other officers of the United States, whose appointments are not herein otherwise provided for, and which shall be established by law: but the Congress may by law vest the appointment of such inferior officers, as they think proper, in the President alone, in the courts of law, or in the heads of departments.

3 The President shall have power to fill up all vacancies that may happen during the recess of the Senate, by granting commissions which shall expire at the end of their next session.

SECTION 3. He shall from time to time give to the Congress information of the state of the Union, and recommend to their consideration such measures as he shall judge necessary and expedient; he may, on extraordinary occasions, convene both Houses, or either of them, and in case of disagreement between them with respect to the time of adjournment, he may adjourn them to such time as he shall think proper; he shall receive ambassadors and other public ministers; he shall take care that the laws be faithfully executed, and shall commission all the officers of the United States.

SECTION 4. The President, Vice President, and all civil officers of the United States, shall be removed from office on impeachment for, and conviction of, treason, bribery, or other high crimes and misdemeanors.

ARTICLE III

SECTION 1. The judicial power of the United States shall be vested in one Supreme Court, and in such inferior courts as the Congress may from time to time ordain and establish. The judges, both of the Supreme and inferior courts, shall hold their offices during good behavior, and shall, at stated times, receive for their services, a compensation which shall not be diminished during their continuance in office.

SECTION 2. 1 The judicial power shall extend to all cases, in law and equity, arising under this Constitution, the laws of the United States, and treaties made, or which shall be made, under their authority;—to all cases affecting ambassadors, other public ministers and consuls;—to all cases of admiralty and maritime jurisdiction;—to controversies to which the United States shall be a party;—to controversies between two or more States;—between a State and citizens of another State;[122]—between citizens of different States,—between citizens of the same State claiming lands under grants of different States, and between a State, or the citizens thereof, and foreign States, citizens or subjects.

2 In all cases affecting ambassadors, other public ministers and consuls, and those in which a State shall be party, the Supreme Court shall have original jurisdiction. In all the other cases before mentioned, the Supreme Court shall have appellate jurisdiction, both as to law and fact, with such exceptions, and under such regulations as the Congress shall make.

3 The trial of all crimes, except in cases of impeachment, shall be by jury; and such trial shall be held in the State where the said crimes shall have been committed; but when not committed within any State, the trial shall be at such place or places as the Congress may by law have directed.

SECTION 3. 1 Treason against the United States, shall consist only in levying war against them, or in adhering to their enemies, giving them aid and comfort. No person shall be convicted of treason unless on the testimony of two witnesses to the same overt act, or on confession in open court.

2 The Congress shall have power to declare the punishment of treason, but no attainder of treason shall work corruption of blood, or forfeiture except during the life of the person attainted.

ARTICLE IV

SECTION 1. Full faith and credit shall be given in each State to the public acts, records, and judicial proceedings of every other State. And the Congress may by general laws prescribe the manner in which such acts, records and proceedings shall be proved, and the effect thereof.

SECTION 2. 1 The citizens of each State shall be entitled to all privileges and immunities of citizens in the several States.

2 A person charged in any State with treason, felony, or other crime, who shall flee from justice, and be found in another State, shall on demand of the executive authority of the State from which he fled, be delivered up to be removed to the State having jurisdiction of the crime.

3 No person held to service or labor in one State, under the laws thereof, escaping into another, shall, in consequence of any law or regulation therein, be discharged from such service or labor, but shall be delivered up on claim of the party to whom such service or labor may be due.[123]

SECTION 3. 1 New States may be admitted by the Congress into this Union; but no new State shall be formed or erected within the jurisdiction of any other State; nor any State be formed by the junction of two or more States, or parts of States, without the consent of the legislatures of the States concerned as well as of the Congress.

2 The Congress shall have power to dispose of and make all needful rules and regulations respecting the territory or other property belonging to the United States; and nothing in this Constitution shall be so construed as to prejudice any claims of the United States, or of any particular State.

SECTION 4. The United States shall guarantee to every State in this Union a republican form of government, and shall protect each of them against invasion; and on application of the legislature, or of the executive (when the legislature cannot be convened) against domestic violence.

ARTICLE V

The Congress, whenever two thirds of both Houses shall deem it necessary, shall propose amendments to this Constitution, or, on the application of the legislatures of two thirds of the several States, shall call a convention for proposing amendments, which, in either case, shall be valid to all intents and purposes, as part of this Constitution, when ratified by the legislatures of three fourths of the several States, or by conventions in three fourths thereof, as the one or the other mode of ratification may be proposed by the Congress; Provided that no amendment which may be made prior to the year one thousand eight hundred and eight shall in any manner affect the first and fourth clauses in the ninth section of the first article; and that no State, without its consent, shall be deprived of its equal suffrage in the Senate.

ARTICLE VI

1 All debts contracted and engagements entered into, before the adoption of this Constitution, shall be as valid against the United States under this Constitution, as under the Confederation.

2 This Constitution, and the laws of the United States which shall be made in pursuance thereof; and all treaties made, or which shall be made, under the authority of the United States, shall be the supreme law of the land; and the judges in every State shall be bound thereby, anything in the Constitution or laws of any State to the contrary notwithstanding.

3 The senators and representatives before mentioned, and the members of the several State legislatures, and all executive and judicial officers, both of the United States, and of the several States, shall be bound by oath or affirmation to support this Constitution; but no religious test shall ever be required as a qualification to any office or public trust under the United States.

ARTICLE VII

The ratification of the conventions of nine States shall be sufficient for the establishment of this Constitution between the States so ratifying the same.

Done in Convention by the unanimous consent of the States present the seventeenth day of September in the year of our Lord one thousand seven hundred and eighty-seven, and of the independence of the United States of America the twelfth. In witness whereof we have hereunto subscribed our names,

Go: Washington—

Presidt. and Deputy from Virginia.

(Signed also by thirty-eight other delegates, from twelve states.)

Articles in addition to, and amendment of, the Constitution of the United States of America, proposed by Congress, and ratified by the legislatures of the several States pursuant to the fifth article of the original Constitution.

ARTICLES I-X[124]

Article I. Congress shall make no law respecting an establishment of religion, or prohibiting the free exercise thereof; or abridging the freedom of speech, or of the press; or the right of the people peaceably to assemble, and to petition the government for a redress of grievances.

ARTICLE II. A well regulated militia, being necessary to the security of a free State, the right of the people to keep and bear arms, shall not be infringed.

ARTICLE III. No soldier shall, in time of peace be quartered in any house, without the consent of the owner, nor in time of war, but in a manner to be prescribed by law.

ARTICLE IV. The right of the people to be secure in their persons, houses, papers, and effects, against unreasonable searches and seizures, shall not be violated, and no warrants shall issue, but upon probable cause, supported by oath or affirmation, and particularly describing the place to be searched, and the persons or things to be seized.

ARTICLE V. No person shall be held to answer for a capital, or otherwise infamous crime, unless on a presentment or indictment of a grand jury, except in cases arising in the land or naval forces, or in the militia, when in actual service in time of war or public danger; nor shall any person be subject for the same offense to be twice put in jeopardy of life or limb; nor shall be compelled in any criminal case to be a witness against himself, nor be deprived of life, liberty, or property, without due process of law; nor shall private property be taken for public use without just compensation.

ARTICLE VI. In all criminal prosecutions, the accused shall enjoy the right to a speedy and public trial, by an impartial jury of the State and district wherein the crime shall have been committed, which district shall have been previously ascertained by law, and to be informed of the nature and cause of the accusation; to be confronted with the witnesses against him; to have compulsory process for obtaining witnesses in his favor, and to have the assistance of counsel for his defense.

ARTICLE VII. In suits at common law, where the value in controversy shall exceed twenty dollars, the right of trial by jury shall be preserved, and no fact tried by a jury shall be otherwise reëxamined in any court of the United States, than according to the rules of the common law.

ARTICLE VIII. Excessive bail shall not be required, nor excessive fines imposed, nor cruel and unusual punishments inflicted.

ARTICLE IX. The enumeration in the Constitution of certain rights shall not be construed to deny or disparage others retained by the people.

ARTICLE X. The powers not delegated to the United States by the Constitution, nor prohibited by it to the States, are reserved to the States respectively, or to the people.

ARTICLE XI[125]

The judicial power of the United States shall not be construed to extend to any suit in law or equity, commenced or prosecuted against one of the United States, by citizens of another State, or by citizens or subjects of any foreign State.

ARTICLE XII[126]

The electors shall meet in their respective States, and vote by ballot for President and Vice President, one of whom, at least, shall not be an inhabitant of the same State with themselves; they shall name in their ballots the person voted for as President, and in distinct ballots the person voted for as Vice President, and they shall make distinct lists of all persons voted for as President and of all persons voted for as Vice President, and of the number of votes for each, which lists they shall sign and certify, and transmit sealed to the seat of the government of the United States, directed to the president of the Senate;—The president of the Senate shall, in the presence of the Senate and House of Representatives, open all the certificates and the votes shall then be counted;—The person having the greatest number of votes for President shall be the President, if such number be a majority of the whole number of electors appointed; and if no person have such majority, then from the persons having the highest numbers not exceeding three on the list of those voted for as President, the House of Representatives shall choose immediately, by ballot, the President. But in choosing the President, the votes shall be taken by States, the representation from each State having one vote; a quorum for this purpose shall consist of a member or members from two thirds of the States, and a majority of all the States shall be necessary to a choice. And if the House of Representatives shall not choose a President whenever the right of choice shall devolve upon them, before the fourth day of March next following, then the Vice President shall act as President, as in the case of the death or other constitutional disability of the President. The person having the greatest number of votes as Vice President shall be the Vice President, if such number be a majority of the whole number of electors appointed, and if no person have a majority, then from the two highest numbers on the list, the Senate shall choose the Vice President; a quorum for the purpose shall consist of two thirds of the whole number of senators, and a majority of the whole number shall be necessary to a choice. But no person constitutionally ineligible to the office of President shall be eligible to that of Vice President of the United States.

ARTICLE XIII[127]

SECTION 1. Neither slavery nor involuntary servitude, except as a punishment for crime whereof the party shall have been duly convicted, shall exist within the United States, or any place subject to their jurisdiction.

SECTION 2. Congress shall have power to enforce this article by appropriate legislation.

ARTICLE XIV[128]

SECTION 1. All persons born or naturalized in the United States, and subject to the jurisdiction thereof, are citizens of the United States and of the State wherein they reside. No State shall make or enforce any law which shall abridge the privileges or immunities of citizens of the United States; nor shall any State deprive any person of life, liberty, or property, without due process of law; nor deny to any person within its jurisdiction the equal protection of the laws.

SECTION 2. Representatives shall be apportioned among the several States according to their respective numbers, counting the whole number of persons in each State, excluding Indians not taxed. But when the right to vote at any election for the choice of electors for President and Vice President of the United States, representatives in Congress, the executive and judicial officers of a State, or the members of the legislature thereof, is denied to any of the male inhabitants of such State, being twenty-one years of age, and citizens of the United States, or in any way abridged, except for participation in rebellion, or other crime, the basis of representation therein shall be reduced in the proportion which the number of such male citizens shall bear to the whole number of male citizens twenty-one years of age in such State.

SECTION 3. No person shall be a senator or representative in Congress, or elector of President and Vice President, or hold any office, civil or military, under the United States, or under any State, who, having previously taken an oath, as a member of Congress, or as an officer of the United States, or as a member of any State legislature, or as an executive or judicial officer of any State, to support the Constitution of the United States, shall have engaged in insurrection or rebellion against the same, or given aid or comfort to the enemies thereof. But Congress may by a vote of two thirds of each House, remove such disability.

SECTION 4. The validity of the public debt of the United States, authorized by law, including debts incurred for payment of pensions and bounties for services in suppressing insurrection or rebellion, shall not be questioned. But neither the United States nor any State shall assume or pay any debt or obligation incurred in aid of insurrection or rebellion against the United States, or any claim for the loss or emancipation of any slave; but all such debts, obligations and claims shall be held illegal and void.

SECTION 5. The Congress shall have power to enforce, by appropriate legislation, the provisions of this article.

ARTICLE XV[129]

SECTION 1. The right of citizens of the United States to vote shall not be denied or abridged by the United States or by any State on account of race, color, or previous condition of servitude.

SECTION 2. The Congress shall have power to enforce this article by appropriate legislation.

ARTICLE XVI[130]

The Congress shall have power to lay and collect taxes on incomes, from whatever source derived, without apportionment among the several States, and without regard to any census or enumeration.

ARTICLE XVII[131]

The Senate of the United States shall be composed of two senators from each State, elected by the people thereof, for six years; and each senator shall have one vote. The electors in each State shall have the qualifications requisite for electors of the most numerous branch of the State legislatures.

When vacancies happen in the representation of any State in the Senate, the executive authority of such State shall issue writs of election to fill such vacancies: *Provided*, That the legislature of any State may empower the executive thereof to make temporary appointments until the people fill the vacancies by election as the legislature may direct.

This amendment shall not be so construed as to affect the election or term of any senator chosen before it becomes valid as part of the Constitution.

ARTICLE XVIII[132]

Section 1. After one year from the ratification of this article the manufacture, sale, or transportation of intoxicating liquors within, the importation thereof into, or the exportation thereof from the United States and all territory subject to the jurisdiction thereof for beverage purposes is hereby prohibited.

Section 2. The Congress and the several states shall have concurrent power to enforce this article by appropriate legislation.

Section 3. This article shall be inoperative unless it shall have been ratified as an amendment to the Constitution by the Legislatures of the several States, as provided by the Constitution, within seven years from the date of the submission hereof to the States by the Congress.

ARTICLE XIX[133]

Section 1. The right of citizens of the United States to vote shall not be denied or abridged by the United States or by any State on account of sex.

Section 2. Congress shall have power, by appropriate legislation, to enforce the provisions of this article.